the
suburban
strange

the
suburban
strange

NATHAN KOTECKI

Houghton Mifflin

HOUGHTON MIFFLIN HARCOURT

BOSTON   NEW YORK   2012

For Amanda
(If you have a sister who you suspect has secret
supernatural powers, you understand.)

www.hmhbooks.com

The text of this book is set in Caslon Pro.
Music credits appear on page 357.

The Library of Congress Cataloging-in-Publication-Data control number 2011048209

ISBN: 978-0-547-72996-1

Manufactured in the United States
DOC 10 9 8 7 6 5 4 3 2 1
4500378693

◉

One night I shall be awakened
by the horn from the driver
and know before my eyes are fully opened
that the signal is for me.

Then I shall descend those stairs,
going out onto the avenue
to ride away in the passenger's seat
without so much as a glance at the driver.

◉

contents

through the looking glass

A T THE QUIET BEGINNING of a clear day, a black sedan rolled slowly down the empty street and came to a stop in front of Celia's house. She had known it would be coming, but it was a tiny shock to see it there, even so. She opened the front door and took long, slow strides down the walk to meet it.

The car's metal and glass glinted in the morning sun. In the passenger seat window Celia's reflection looked back at her: a tall, thin girl wearing a little black cardigan over a gray dress. Her skin was pale and her long, straight brown hair disappeared behind her shoulders. She looked past the glare on the glass and found a second girl sitting behind the steering wheel, who was not much older than she. The driver's razor-sharp black bob shifted and then fell back into place as her gloved hand lowered her sunglasses and she looked out at Celia. Around them the houses seemed to slumber on their lawns. The morning smelled of dew and grass. Soon it would be fall.

Celia opened the door and took her place in the passenger seat. The air in the car held traces of a perfume that reminded her of forests and spice cabinets and Christmas. "Are you ready?" the driver asked when Celia had closed the door.

"I think so."

The driver put the car in gear and eased away from the curb. They glided out of Celia's neighborhood at a stately pace, and in the amber light she felt as if they were driving through honey. A gloomy song played on the stereo, with ringing guitars and crashing drums, and a man singing:

> *One cold damp evening the world stood still*
> *I watched as I held my breath*
> *A silhouette I thought I knew came through*
> *And someone spoke to me*
> *Whispered in my ear*
> *This fantasy's for you*
> *Fantasies are in this year . . .*

"Who is this?"

"The Chameleons," the driver said. "You like it?"

"Yes."

The warm light flickered through the trees as they rode. Celia tried to imagine what she might have been doing, where she might have been instead, if she hadn't . . . She wondered which thing she might have done differently, which decision would have sent her in a different direction. It was hard to guess. At this moment she felt as though she had never had a choice, really. There were so many questions she couldn't answer, but it all seemed so inevitable, regardless. She turned around and looked at the back seat. A gray cashmere blanket lay there on the tan leather, neatly folded, waiting for the first cold snap of the fall.

They drove into a neighborhood Celia didn't know, where

the houses looked expensive and the lawns were wide. The car stopped in front of one of them, and soon the front door of the house released a handsome boy wearing a dark shirt and trousers and a brocade vest. His blond hair was short on the sides and swept into a fifties-inspired peak on top. "That's Brenden," the driver said. Brenden waved in their direction before he got into another expensive-looking black car parked in the driveway.

"He isn't riding with us?" Celia asked.

"That's not how it works. You'll see."

Brenden's car pulled out in front of them at the same slow pace, and they followed him into another neighborhood.

> *My whole life passed before my eyes*
> *I thought what they say is true*
> *I shed my skin and my disguise*
> *And cold, numb, and naked*
> *I emerged from my cocoon*
> *And a half-remembered tune played softly in my*
> *   head . . .*

They arrived at the curb in front of another house. Once again a boy emerged: olive-skinned with loose dark curls, he wore a slim gray suit jacket over a matching pair of knee-length shorts, and black loafers without socks. "That's Marco." The boy waved to them; then he climbed into the other car. Through its rear window Celia could see the two boys greet each other with a kiss.

"You're not dating anyone, are you?" the driver asked Celia.

"Me? No! I've never dated anyone."

"Why is that?" The driver sounded surprised, and Celia wished she had managed to sound nonchalant instead of alarmed.

She shrugged, trying to play it down. "I'm taller than everyone." She looked down at her long legs shrouded in dark tights, and her feet in buckled shoes with higher heels than she'd ever worn before, and she thought that now even fewer boys would be able to look her in the eye.

"You just need to date someone older," the driver answered simply as they followed the other black car down the street, sounding complimentary and slightly bitter at the same time. It was such an obvious solution, now Celia thought about it, but she never had tried to solve the problem. Telling herself she was too tall was one of the ways she made sense of not getting more attention from boys, but that couldn't obscure the deeper truth: Celia wouldn't have known what to do with a boy even if he had been delivered to her in a shipping crate with breathing holes cut into the top.

> *I realize a miracle is due*
> *I dedicate this melody to you*
> *But is this the stuff dreams are made of?*
> *No wonder I feel like I'm floating on air*
> *It feels like I'm everywhere . . .*

"Last stop. We're late. I hope they're ready." The two black cars pulled up in front of an imposing modern house with a huge bed of ivy in place of a lawn. This time two people emerged through the front door. "That's Liz," the driver said of a shorter girl with a wavy bob, black with deep blue highlights, wearing skinny black pants and a button-down shirt with long tails. A rosary hung from her neck. "And that's Ivo." Celia's guide's voice grew warmer as Ivo walked with Liz to yet another black car. He was tall and thin with his black hair severely parted and combed, wearing a black shirt and suit. "They're fraternal twins. They're the whole reason the Rosary exists."

"The Rosary?"

"I didn't tell you? That's the name of our group." The driver turned to look at Celia.

"Are you . . . religious?" Celia asked.

"No. We're a set of small black shiny beads who string around together, finding beauty the rest of the world has overlooked." Celia thought this was a description she should remember, but she couldn't make sense of it. The driver continued, "The Rosary is just the name we've given ourselves. But to describe us, I'd say we are the cognoscenti."

"I don't know what that means," Celia said.

"The cognoscenti are 'the ones who know.'" The girl behind the wheel gave her an appropriately knowing look, but Celia still had no idea how to respond.

Ivo and Liz were pulling out of their driveway in a third black car, and suddenly the image of shiny black things strung together wasn't just a metaphor. Celia felt as if she were riding in a funeral procession, and a familiar pain flared up in her. Only recently had her heart grown closed around what felt like the shards of a bullet that had lodged there when her father died. The pain wasn't sharp every day now, but the shards were always there. They would always be there.

*Like when you fail to make the connection you
know how vital it is*

When something slips through your fingers you
know how precious it is
And you reach the point where you know it's only
your second skin
Someone's banging on my door . . .

"What are you thinking?" the driver asked.

"I . . . well, it feels like we're going to a funeral."

"Good," her guide said. "I suppose we're a little melodramatic. You know, *In the midst of life we are in death,* and all that. But that's what makes it interesting—most people only think about dark things when they're forced to, even though dark things can be very beautiful. You understand?"

"I think so." It all sounded rather deep to Celia. For the moment she was relieved that the pain that had flickered in her seemed to be passing. This ride and the memories it evoked weren't cutting into her the way she had feared. Today there would be no casket awaiting her when they reached their destination. Still, she hoped the time would come when she understood it all.

The procession crept along and turned onto a road that approached a sprawling building arching into the sky like the armor of a stegosaurus, halls and wings poking out in all directions. It stood by itself, with open fields on either side and across the street. But at its feet, cars of other colors and people in conventional clothes moved quickly in every direction, and the stark serenity of the drive began to evaporate. The Rosary's three black cars filed smoothly into the midst of it all and finally stopped side by side in the parking lot. Celia opened her door and the dreamlike feeling of the journey was gone instantly, like a hubcap clattering to the pavement. She put her feet back down on the ground and stood up, looking around, nervously waiting to be introduced to the others.

"Hello, Regine," Marco said to Celia's driver. "And finally we get to meet Celia." He looked at her with curious, kind eyes.

"Here she is." Regine presented Celia by touching her elbow, and Celia wondered if she should step forward. "Marco, Brenden, Liz, Ivo, this is Celia." They all nodded at her. She didn't know what she was supposed to do. But in the next moment they began to speak to each other, and she felt as if she had faded away like a ghost.

"You saw the new wing?" Ivo pointed along one side of the huge building. "As if this place weren't large enough already."

"You won't be swimming in the new pool, then?" Brenden said to him, and Ivo feigned horror.

Their conversation was dotted with names and topics that were foreign to Celia. She forced herself not to fidget.

"Do you have a mix for us?" Liz asked Brenden.

"Of course I do." Brenden opened his bag and pulled out a slim stack of jewel cases. "Everything is better with the right soundtrack."

"Even something as depressing as the first day of school?"

"Especially something as depressing as the first day of school." Brenden passed the CDs around.

"We have to make the most of it—it's our last year together," Ivo said, studying his copy. "You put 'The Headmaster Ritual' on here! That's perfect!"

Brenden turned to Celia, one CD left in his hand. "I thought you might like one, too," he said, smiling.

"Thank you!" Celia accepted it and studied the track list

along with the others. Few of the artists were familiar to her, and those only because Regine had begun her initiation into the group's musical tastes a few months earlier.

"I have a good feeling about this year," Marco said. "It's going to be great."

Celia looked around. Other kids who had parked nearby were staring curiously at her group. It was obvious, though, these five dark friends didn't care. When the Rosary started toward the building, they walked purposefully and slowly, just as they had driven, carrying themselves with a careful indifference. They didn't look at the other kids, and they spoke quietly so no one else could hear. Celia did her best to mimic them. She was surprised to note the intrigued, even mystified respect from the others for the Rosary. Before she had met Regine, whenever she was in public, Celia had wished to be invisible, but there was no point in holding on to that desire now. If this morning was any indication—the procession of cars, the austere clothes, the deliberate manner—the Rosary cultivated mystique deliberately. And if it weren't for a chain of unlikely events, Celia would have been on the other side, the outside, staring at this group, unsure and alone. By some strange chance, here she was in their midst, and she hoped she looked at least a little as if she belonged, even though she felt like an imposter. It was completely new, and a little thrilling, but she was scared she would drop something, or fall down and be exposed as a fake. Then they would just walk smoothly away from her . . .

Suddenly, ahead of them a girl broke away from her two friends, zigzagging across the pavement with her head ducked and her arms flailing around her face. "No, no, no!" she shrieked. Collectively the Rosary stopped walking, and Celia stopped with them.

"What are you doing?" the frantic girl's friends called, laughing and confused.

"Ai!" The tormented girl jumped, her whole frame tensing. Then she came down, knees bent, and turned around slowly to look at her friends with wide eyes. She had left them behind, and they stayed put, unsure whether they wanted to be associated with such spastic behavior on the first day of school.

The girl had stopped near a jock in an orange T-shirt. "Hey, Elsie, what's wrong?"

"A bee stung me!" Elsie held one hand to the side of her neck. "I'm allergic!"

"Whoa—we have to get you to the nurse!" The boy took her arm, but she sank to the asphalt. Her hand waved around her face again as she gasped for air.

Celia glanced at her group. Each of them stood calmly, unaffected by the girl's plight. Where she was sprawled, the stung girl blocked their path to the school, and the Rosary only seemed to be waiting for the way to be cleared before they continued. Even from twenty feet away, Celia could see that Elsie's face was swelling noticeably. The girl's two friends had rushed over, and the jock had dropped to his knees next to her, his hands hovering uselessly around her as he scanned the parking lot. He called out, "Help! Somebody get the nurse!" Several kids took off running into the school.

Still the Rosary didn't move. Celia couldn't fault them for not getting involved. There wasn't anything to do that wasn't already being done, and there was no point in crowding the poor girl. But Celia was bothered by her feeling of helplessness and her friends' seeming indifference to Elsie's plight. Everyone else in the parking lot had stopped in their tracks, too, but they screamed and pointed, telling each other what was in front of them.

"What's going on?" A young teacher came running toward the heaving girl.

"She's allergic to bee stings!" the boy in the orange shirt told him as the teacher crouched next to him. But the teacher didn't seem to know what to do, either. He stared at Elsie, and after another moment the jock urged him, "We have to get her that shot, what's it called?" He looked around again and shouted, "Does anyone have that shot for allergic reactions?"

"I have an EpiPen!" Another boy came running out from a row of cars, digging in his satchel. He pulled out a small plastic case and handed it to the teacher on the ground by Elsie.

But the teacher stared at him, saying, "I've never . . ." The boy took the case back, popped the cap and pushed Elsie's skirt up her leg, then jabbed the syringe into her thigh and held it there. He spoke in a low voice to the girl, who nodded and gasped. The boy tried to keep her hair out of her eyes.

The tension began to drain from the air. The spectators began to move again, and Elsie's body started to relax. The nurse lumbered into the parking lot and looked relieved to find that the critical help already had been administered. In another minute the nurse and the teacher helped Elsie to her feet, one on each side, and escorted her into the building. Her friends collected her things and trailed behind her.

The jock stood up, his bright orange T-shirt the last bit of crisis left in the parking lot. He said something to the boy who had provided the EpiPen, and they nodded seriously at each other. The boy went off toward school, but the jock looked over in the direction of the Rosary. "Hey, Liz," he said. "That was kind of intense."

Liz opened her mouth and spoke a few syllables that didn't add up to words. As if on cue, the Rosary began to walk again. Liz strugged to maintain their sedate pace as they stalked past the jock, who looked disappointed, but not surprised. Celia couldn't decide what was strangest: that such an alarming thing had happened right in front of her on the first day of school, that this gloomy clique had been so aloof throughout it, or that a jock would feel as though he could engage Liz in a conversation.

They reached the school lobby without further incident, and Celia listened for them to comment about what had happened outside. "What did you say about it being a good year?" Ivo said to Marco. "If that was any indication, this year is cursed already." They traded wry smiles, but in the next moment this group to which Celia was both a stranger and a ward had moved on to more unfamiliar names and things she didn't understand. She gave up trying to follow the conversation and looked around.

Suburban High School wasn't nearly as dark and glamorous as she suspected the Rosary would have preferred. The tile walls and textured plaster ceiling looked antiquated, and their colors were too drab to have names. When the group parted ways and Regine walked her upstairs, Celia found that the sophomore hall had all the sophistication of a strip mall or a jail. Against this backdrop Regine looked even more exotic than she had in the black sedan—even more exotic than she had in the summer drawing class where the two of them had met two short months ago. Celia glanced down and reminded herself she looked exotic now, too.

"So you see how we are, right?" Regine said to Celia. "Some kids might give you a hard time, and some kids are going to want to be friends with you just because you're friends with us, and all I'll say is you should use your best judgment. You decide if they're smart enough, and if they look good enough. You decide who is worth your time." Celia had never thought about it that way. She always had been on the receiving end of those evaluations. She had a hunch that if anyone else at Suburban met the standards Regine had laid out, the Rosary would have befriended them already.

"Do you know that girl?" she asked Regine, who looked at her uncomprehendingly. "The one who got stung?"

"Not really," Regine said.

Celia's concerns shifted away from sympathy and back toward herself. In a moment Regine was going to leave her, and the prospect of continuing alone floated up the same fears Celia had forced down several times already that morning.

She said goodbye to Regine and turned to her homeroom door. The room was full of kids in jeans and sneakers and brightly colored shirts who all fell silent when she walked in, looking her over. The air seemed to change, becoming drier and hotter. No longer could Celia pretend to be exotic — she was simply out of place. She considered running back out the door, but she was sure Regine would disapprove of such a display of weakness. This new moment had all the substance of a nightmare, and the next moment would be even worse. *What are they going to say?* she thought, realizing she had stopped cold a few feet into the room.

Celia knew her outfit was a little morose, and her dark eye shadow didn't help. She knew she wasn't making herself any more approachable than her sloppy jeans, faded T-shirts, and hunched shoulders had made her at her old school last year. She had spent all of ninth grade—all of middle school, even—trying to disappear but never quite succeeding, and that impulse still lurked just under the surface. During the summer, with no other kids around, Celia had been able to ignore the risk she was taking by making these bold changes to her appearance. Now she felt the risk like a blast from a hair dryer down her back. It was the same hot gust she had felt whenever more than one of her old classmates had looked at her at the same time. It was the precursor to something bad. If they were merciful, it was only ridicule: She was too tall. She wasn't savvy enough to conform. She wasn't strong-willed enough to defend herself. Her best friend was a sketchbook.

Celia had hoped a new high school would somehow be different, but now she thought of course it wasn't—at least, not in the ways she needed it to be. Had she made a fatal miscalculation with the new strategy she had chosen? These dark clothes? Her dark straight hair, carefully blown even straighter, which now reached midway down her back? The hours spent in front of the mirror learning to make her eyes look smoky instead of blackened? She might match the blackboard now, but she couldn't expect to fade into it.

The misgivings she had entertained at home less than an hour ago were nothing compared to the panic and despair she felt now. This was not at all like walking into the studio at the art institute. She was alone in a crowd of kids who looked exactly like the ones she had fled at the end of last year. *Stork,* she thought; *pencil-girl. Ghoul*—there would be new names for them to call her now: *goth freak, vampire.* The epithets careened around inside her head, and she waited to hear them.

No one said anything to her. She saw a seat off to the side and willed herself to walk as deliberately as possible over to it. Her ankle wobbled a little, but she pretended everything was fine. She sat down and heard the conversations around her start back up. Then she pulled her sketchbook out of her bag, opened it to the first blank page, and wrote, *What is going to happen?* She looked at the question for a moment, then crossed it out and wrote another.

What is happening to me?

Celia summoned back the confidence she was trying to learn from Regine, and memories of the recent times she'd succeeded in feeling mysterious and exotic, qualities she never had possessed before. She pushed her shoulders back a little farther, hearing Regine's voice in her head admonish her for slouching. She thought back to the summer drawing class where she had met Regine.

THE ART INSTITUTE HAD BEEN the first and was still the only foreign place Celia ever had walked into without desiring to disappear. She was one of the youngest students in the class, and while she wasn't about to go up to strangers and start talking, this was a place where a battered sketchbook was a badge of honor and her felicity with a pencil would work in her favor. The drawing class had been her mother's suggestion. Celia had understood it immediately as a transparent attempt to find something she would do that included other people in the room. She had agreed, in the way someone who is fluent in French condescends to take a conversation class. For once she believed she was on solid ground, and she entered that studio full of strangers knowing that some of them might draw as well as she did but that it was unlikely any of them drew better. On the first day of class Celia enjoyed a rare taste of confidence, like the spatter of carbonation on her tongue that went to her head and made her a little giddy, though no one would have been able to tell from looking at her.

The instructor had built a towering still life on a round table in the middle of the room, and after a cursory introduction he told the class to choose anything to sketch so he could assess their individual skill levels. Celia considered the depressing pile of props, but nothing inspired her. She always drew things that were alive, and the table had the look of a wake, somehow. Less than five minutes in and she panicked—was she going to fall flat in this place where she had dared to imagine she would fly? The others were starting to draw. She stared at them, and then at the still life, and then at her empty pad. She looked around again, and her attention was drawn to a striking girl on the far side of the circle who had pulled off a pair of dove gray driving gloves and was digging in her case for a pencil. Before Celia made a conscious decision, her hand captured on her pad the girl's shiny black hair, which hung in a severe bob, framing her Latin eyes and heart-shaped face. Celia used a few crisp lines to describe the girl's white collar, which lay atop her black cardigan, and a few more for the short-sleeved cuffs that peeked out from rolled sweater sleeves. She roughed in the plywood box on which the girl sat, and her black jeans, which tapered to oxblood penny loafers. Celia softened the girl's pose, removing the tension in her frame as she labored over her own drawing. And there she was, alive on the paper: the intriguing girl at work on a drawing, her face serious and somehow meditative, the studio light slanting across her body.

Celia was pleased with her work, but upon reflection she feared she had disobeyed the teacher's instructions, and her blood raced when it was time for the class to pin their drawings up on the wall for the critique. Would he reject her, no matter how good her drawing was, because she hadn't drawn the plastic fruit or the plaster column? Celia was tempted not to care, because she had found the joy drawing gave her — the joy of capturing a person on paper. But she couldn't be sure. What if the teacher had wanted something else? She tried to think of something she might stammer in her defense.

They spent a few minutes looking at each other's work before the teacher began the critique. Everyone else had drawn something from the still life. Most of the sketches were amateurish, including the one Celia's subject had pinned up, a timid cartoon of the vase draped with fabric. The girl with the black bob had noticed herself on the wall and was studying Celia's portrait. Then the teacher took over and worked his way down the wall. His notes were brief, but Celia could tell he was good at his job. He talked about using one line instead of many, and about when it was right to show something with space instead of lines. When he reached Celia's drawing, he said, "This is lovely. Someone is not going to learn very much from me. Whose is this?"

Celia felt the hair-dryer blast of panic when she half raised her hand and everyone focused on her. But the instructor gave her a kindly look. To Celia it was the same as if he had dumped ten pounds of confetti on her. Then he moved on. Her pulse slowly returned to normal. She had survived.

The subject of her drawing made a beeline for her after the class. "I'm Regine," she said. "You are really talented."

"Thank you! I'm Celia." Usually Celia did anything to avoid speaking with strangers, but this was the best possible scenario in which to attempt it. She felt herself in a position of strength, and she wanted to reassure this girl, Regine, the way Celia would have wanted to be reassured if the conversation had been about anything else. "You picked the hardest things to draw."

"You're just trying to make me feel better." Regine smiled. "I do not have the natural gift for this that you obviously do."

"I've been drawing for a long time," Celia offered.

"How old are you, sixteen?"

"Fifteen." Celia knew Regine was implying she was too young to have been doing anything for a long time, but in this case that was like doubting the sea legs of a child who had grown up on a boat. Every day of every summer Celia could remember, her mother had begged her to leave her sketchbook behind on the dining room table and go outside for just a little while, please. Once, years ago, Celia's father had cajoled her into a girls' camping group, but after a few drenched weekends he had admitted he was as miserable as she was, and her days at the dining room table were restored. She spent them copying the faces of models out of advertisements in her mother's magazines. For Celia drawing wasn't an escape. She didn't populate alternate universes with fanciful characters. Drawing was her way of knowing the world. She studied the people around her, imagined how they felt, what they thought, what they dreamt, and then she tried to capture these ephemeral things in a portrait. In a way, people weren't real for her until she had drawn them a few times, from different angles. They were safer on paper, too—no sudden movements, no betrayals.

Regine couldn't know it, but by rendering her on paper, Celia had welcomed Regine into her life in her own timid way that first day of drawing class.

"Where do you go to school?" Regine was composed and not intimidated even after she had conceded her lack of talent. Celia admired her for it.

"Suburban. I'll be a sophomore."

"I go to Suburban! Wait, were you there last year?"

"No, we moved across town a month ago."

"I'll be a junior. We are going to have to be friends in this class. I'll tell you all about Suburban, and you try to show me how to draw something—anything."

Celia had agreed, a little surprised by how easily it was happening. From the next class on she had sat with Regine. Regine's drawing skills would not improve much over the summer, but she didn't hold it against Celia.

"My first love is making collages," Regine explained as they settled in next to one another the following week. She reached for her bag and pulled out a little album designed to hold a single photograph in each of its page sleeves, with an oval window on the front to let the first image show through. Instead of photographs, Regine had filled the book with a series of twenty-four tiny collages that told a dark story of unrequited love, assembled from fragments of text and images clipped out of magazines. A beautiful woman sat next to a beautiful man with smooth white hands as he drove a luxurious car. She stood in the background, watching him drink from a fluted glass. She peered out from under a curved staircase while he looked up at a stained-glass skylight, a tear on his cheek. A cluster of mismatched words cut from different advertisements read, *He caught me staring but soon his eyes moved on.*

"It's beautiful," Celia said, turning back to study each page again.

"Thank you. But I couldn't have drawn any of it to save my soul. It's all other people's things that I've stolen."

"Still, it's so creative, so delicate. And collage—" Celia was going to say collage was difficult. She had tried it on a few occasions and always made a mess with the glue. But Regine cut her off.

"I know—Schwitters, Cornell, Picasso—everybody does it," Regine said dismissively. "I still wish I could draw."

Celia didn't recognize the first two names, and she had thought Picasso was a painter. She heard both pride and insecurity in Regine's voice, and she didn't know what to make of it. She let it go and admired Regine's latest outfit. This week it was a sleeveless black sweater and a pleated gray skirt. Regine had knotted a gray and cream silk scarf at her throat, tucking the ends into the neckline of the sweater, and Celia thought this girl had such a flair for wearing black and gray, she must have been dressing that way since she'd begun to walk. To Celia, Regine was a cross between a silent-movie star and a creature from a foreign fashion magazine. Regine brought a fan to class with her on hotter days, waving it in a short arc below her face during critiques, and Celia wondered how someone could do something like that and not be ridiculed. But Regine made it look so natural, so glamorous; no one possibly could mock her for it.

Celia felt like a different kind of foreigner in her own barely considered clothes—compared with Regine, she might as well have arrived on a boxcar of a freight train, using a flannel shirt interchangeably as a hobo's bindle. Celia glanced down at her loose T-shirt and cutoff jeans and hoped Regine was looking only at her drawings. In that moment Celia discovered a new desire to dress like Regine, but she had no idea how to go about it. Celia's frizzy hair escaped from behind her shoulder and she pushed it back, wondering if it could be as smooth as this cool girl's.

"Are you excited about a new school?" Regine asked her.

"Curious, I guess. I hope it's better than my last one," Celia said.

"It's all right. Some parts are better than others, but that's true of any place, isn't it? Having good friends can make any place bearable. What kinds of things do you like?"

"I don't know," Celia said, wondering how one was supposed to answer such a question.

"Well, what kind of music do you like?"

Celia never had considered her musical tastes. "I don't know . . . I just listen to whatever's on the radio."

Regine scoffed, "That's not good music. There is so much amazing music that isn't on the radio. None of my favorite bands get played on the radio."

"Then how do you know about them?"

"My friends told me about them, and gave me things to listen to," Regine said, and then she smiled conspiratorially. "Like I'm going to do for you."

It was a thrilling thing for Celia to hear, not so much because something hidden would be revealed to her, but because Regine had just implied she wanted to be Celia's friend.

That day after class Regine had retrieved a compact disc from the glove compartment of her sleek black car to lend to Celia. Celia's mother pulled up as the transaction was taking place, and when Celia got into the car she asked her who the girl was. "Regine. She's in my class," Celia said, unsure what more she could explain to her mother, since Regine still was a mystery to her, too. Celia turned her attention back to the CD and studied the old black-and-white photo of a tornado on the cover. She had no idea what to make of the title—*Tinderbox*—or the name of the band—Siouxsie and the Banshees. The tornado in the photo was not the theatrical type that carried Dorothy away and only killed witches. It writhed against the sky like a poisonous snake, and the weather-beaten barn in its path would not be going anywhere in pieces larger than splinters. In Celia's hands the CD seemed like an artifact from a country worlds away from Oz—ominous, yet oddly beautiful. It felt like a piece of Regine, which she had sent home with Celia.

Celia could remember as if it were yesterday the miraculous afternoon when she had lain on her bed and listened to *Tinderbox* for the first time. She wished to never forget that feeling. Hearing that music had been like seeing a color she never had seen before, or finding a new room in the house where she had lived for years. Celia hadn't realized pop music could sound like that: prickly and ominous but passionate and smart at the same time. She pored over the photograph of the band and wound up reproducing the image in her sketchbook while she pondered these severely beautiful people, who wrote songs about the temperature when the most murders are committed and the destruction of Pompeii by volcanic explosion. She listened to Siouxsie's throaty voice singing about fearing someone but calling his name, and she wondered what that felt like and how someone could find herself in that situation. These songs weren't something to distract her for three minutes, like the songs on the radio. This album challenged her. It made her think about things she hadn't considered before. And it was beautiful in ways Celia hadn't known things could be beautiful.

It upended her week. Time she would have spent laboring over a page in her sketchbook was spent sprawled across her bed, her ear close to the speakers of her CD player. By the time she returned *Tinderbox* to Regine the next week, Celia had made a copy for herself and nearly memorized all the songs. Regine was exuberant when she heard Celia's reaction.

"I knew you'd like it!" Regine clapped her gloved hands. "There are so many things I want to show you!"

Regine meant what she said. Each week she lent Celia a new CD and eagerly heard her reaction to the previous one. "You don't have to like it all. I'm just trying to figure out what your tastes are," she explained. Celia didn't understand quite what Regine meant by that, because every new song was a revelation to her. As her collection of dark musical treasures grew, so did her appetite for them. She played some of her new favorite songs for her mother and enjoyed her mystified response.

After a month, her mother said, "I've never heard you talk about anyone as much as you talk about Regine. Why don't you invite her over?" It took two more weeks for Celia to work up the nerve, and then she was mortified when Regine readily accepted. Celia felt as though she was going to receive a distinguished ambassador, and she judged her own house wanting. She had plenty of conflicted feelings about the house. Her family had started building it shortly before her father had died two springs ago, leaving Celia and her mother to move into it alone. If they had stayed in the old house, memories of her father would have crowded every room, but in the new house it felt sometimes as though she had left him behind. Either way, the white siding and green shutters and evergreen trees didn't

THE SUBURBAN STRANGE ❧

feel impressive enough for Regine. Worse, she thought Regine might actually get a rash if she entered Celia's pink bedroom, which was dominated by a ruffled pink queen-sized bed. But Regine had come, and if she passed judgment she was too gracious to let it show.

Perched on the edge of Celia's bed, seeming every bit the foreign dignitary in a vintage-looking dark plaid jumper, Regine said coyly, "I'll show you mine if you show me yours." She handed Celia the sketchbook she had brought. Celia reached for her own and turned it over to her. Before she even opened Regine's volume Celia could tell it was of a different species than hers. The outside was covered completely with all manner of stickers, most with names of bands or graphic designs. One sticker advertised a Hong Kong company that specialized in obscure rock T-shirts. Celia believed without a doubt Regine ordered T-shirts from Hong Kong, and she was sure T-shirts looked very different on Regine than they did on her.

On the inside of Regine's volume, page after page was covered with hundreds of things she had collaged intricately together, no space left blank. The battered binding had stretched almost double to accommodate all the paper. In one picture a rustic woman sat at a farmhouse table piled high with hundreds of crisply folded men's white dress shirts. There was a black-and-white image that looked like a film still of a wide-eyed Scandinavian woman in a drab room. Another picture showed a woman in profile, her blond hair cut in a severe bob halfway down the back of her head and shaved to the skin underneath. There were portraits of men named Olivier Theyskens and Hussein Chalayan, and photographs of dramatically lit rooms and foggy tree-lined courtyards. She saw a copy of a poem by

Emily Dickinson alongside a picture of a dancing woman with her wrist pressed to her forehead as she bent over, kicking her long white skirt up behind her. There was a page on which all the images contained spirals: conches and staircases and raked stone gardens. On another page everything was a shade of blue. Celia thought Regine must have spent years compiling this book. She wished she could look out her window and see the world Regine had pressed into these pages. "This is amazing."

"Peter Beard is my idol," Regine said proudly. "If you've seen his books, you'll know I'm an amateur compared with him." Meanwhile, she was paging through Celia's sketchbook as though it were an illuminated manuscript. Celia knew what Regine was seeing: portraits of Celia's mother and father, sketches of people she'd copied from photographs, a few attempts at landscapes and still lifes, and some self-portraits from the mirror. There were studies of hands, torsos, dancers in motion, but Celia spent most of her time drawing faces. Her greatest talent was in capturing the life in someone's eyes, the subtleties of a facial expression.

"These are brilliant." Regine looked up at her. She spoke carefully, as though she had rehearsed what she said next. "You know, when I look at these and then I look at you, it's hard to imagine them coming from you. You take such care with them, and your attention to detail is so perfect. Do you ever think of doing the same thing for yourself?"

That had been Regine's coded invitation to make Celia her project, and Celia had deciphered it easily and accepted it gratefully. She was completely enthralled with Regine, who offered answers to questions Celia hadn't been quite able to articulate. Regine made it clear she wasn't out to clone herself. She gave Celia all sorts of options and let Celia choose. Had Celia ever thought about bangs, or wearing a ribbon as a headband? Had she ever considered wearing deep colors against her fair skin? Had she ever worn jewelry? In the weeks before school started Celia found a new sense of herself by investing more in her appearance. She thought she was developing a new style, then admitted that perhaps she was developing *a style* for the first time. It was a dark style, probably inevitable with Regine as her mentor. It felt sophisticated. And, Celia realized with pleasant surprise, it was somewhat bold. Clothes stopped being something in which to hide. Now they were something in which to be seen.

"I told my friends about you," Regine said as she worked systematically through Celia's closet and drawers, rejecting almost all of Celia's clothes as too big, too worn, too bright, or too boring. "I think they'll like you, too, and maybe you can be a part of our group."

"What kind of group?" Celia watched her vagabond wardrobe pile up on the bed. She was not sorry to see any of it go and only wondered what she was going to wear once it was all gone. Already she was living almost exclusively in a black T-shirt and the one pair of jeans Regine had deemed acceptable. Celia felt practically naked in the little cap-sleeved tee she had worn only as an undershirt before then. But one of the first things Regine made clear was that no matter what Celia wore, it had to fit her properly, not envelop her like a cocoon. Slowly Celia was becoming more comfortable revealing the shape of her long, slender body.

"There are five of us who like a lot of the same music and the same style. During school we do almost everything together. This is nice." Regine examined a black pencil skirt she pulled from the closet. Celia didn't recognize it. She guessed it was her mother's, put there by accident. The moment Regine left, she would try it on. "And this"—Regine set aside an orange floral dress Celia had worn to a party under duress from her mother—"this we'll keep for a special occasion." Celia couldn't guess why such a garish dress had made it through Regine's harsh triage. "We are definitely going to have to go shopping, and I'll lend you some things until we get your wardrobe in order." Regine smiled at her. "We're all juniors or seniors, but I think we'll enjoy having a protégé."

Celia hadn't needed to hear any more. She just hoped Regine's friends would be as nice to her. It was a risk she was willing to take, regardless. No one ever had made such an offer to Celia, and for all she knew, such an offer might never come again. The summer class had ended, and Celia's steadfast drawing habit relaxed its grip on her life just a little as the school year approached. Her initiation into Regine's music and dark sense of style was the new focus of her days and her new dream at night.

THE HOMEROOM TEACHER ARRIVED, bells rang, and the room became a focused hive of activity. There was no more time for Celia to reminisce, avoiding the reality of the strangers around her. Then they were launched out into the morning, scrambling to navigate a rushing current of teachers and books and first assignments. She hunted her way through Suburban's tributaries to find each new destination. By lunchtime the top shelf in the locker that had been assigned to her was full of books.

Celia barely had spoken all morning. It still came naturally to her to be silent and unimposing—one of the things Regine hadn't asked her to change. It was easy to keep to herself when everyone else already knew each other, and her classmates seemed to expect it of her based on her somber outfit. Celia found herself on the receiving end of a few raised eyebrows, but that was all. She knew she could live with that. In fact, she had to admit it was kind of gratifying.

When it was time for lunch she was swept off to the cafeteria in a river of chattering students, but she stopped short at the sight of a sea of crowded tables. She faltered while students brushed by her, wondering where she could find a place to be invisible and eat, but then she saw Marco standing and waving at her from a table in the middle of the room. Brenden sat by his side. Marco no longer wore the suit jacket she had seen him in before school, and on the front of his T-shirt large embroidered letters spelled DRINK ME in elaborate type.

"Hi," he said when she made it to them. "You looked like a deer in headlights over there."

"I felt like one," Celia said. "How did you guys get a table to yourselves?"

Marco's expression suggested he hadn't ever considered the question. "Leave your stuff and go get lunch. We'll be here. I don't know if you like soup, but they make really good soup." He sat down and Celia gratefully went to get food.

"So, Regine told us you're a talented artist," Brenden said when she returned.

"I don't know . . . I like to draw." Celia wondered why she was being modest. Out of the corners of her eyes she felt nearby students looking at the three of them curiously, but Brenden and Marco were oblivious. There at the table with them she felt insulated from the rest of the students in their athletic clothes and cargo pants, and she enjoyed the feeling of being separate from those others. "What does your T-shirt mean?" she asked Marco.

"Well, *Eat me* would be vulgar," Marco said, laughing. "This is more mysterious."

"I'd love to see your drawings," Brenden said to Celia. "What style do you work in?"

"Realism, I guess? As realistic as I can get." Celia turned over her sketchbook and watched the two of them handle it delicately, just as Regine had.

"What artists do you like?"

"I — I don't really know that many," Celia said.

"It's good to have heroes," Brenden said. "Admiring someone makes you want to be better in your own way. You should check out da Vinci's drawings, or maybe Albrecht Dürer's engravings." Celia wished she had thought to say da Vinci. She took out her notebook and scribbled down the second name; she wasn't sure she was spelling it correctly, but she didn't want to ask.

"Regine's really happy she found you," Marco said.

"She is?"

"Sure — now she has someone to ride with her. And I know she wanted another girl in the group. She and Liz aren't all that close."

"That's not true," Brenden said to him. They exchanged a loaded glance and Marco kept silent. Celia wondered if she would come to understand the things they weren't saying out loud.

"Thank you again for the mix," Celia said.

"You're welcome! I hope you like it — did you know any of the songs?"

"No," Celia admitted. "Regine's given me a lot of music, but I really don't know very much. She says you write a blog."

"I do. You should check it out." Brenden scribbled a website address on a piece of paper and handed it to her. "Actually, before you got here Marco and I were having one of our ongoing discussions about music. You'll get to hear quite a bit of those if you hang out with us. Today's topic: best opening lines to songs."

"My vote is: *'Love is a stranger in an open car, to tempt you in and drive you far away,'*" Marco said.

"And mine is: *'Come closer and see, see into the trees; find the girl while you can,'*" Brenden said. "We must have been thinking about you," he added, smiling.

Celia blushed. "I don't know either of those."

"That's okay. What's yours?" Marco asked.

Celia thought for a moment, trying to come up with something impressive. She felt it was a test, whether they intended it as one or not. "How about: *'Every finger in the room is pointing at me'*?"

Marco nodded in admiration and Brenden said, "That is a good one. I wouldn't have thought of that." They ate in silence for a moment and Celia breathed an inward sigh of relief.

"So, what do you think of Suburban so far?" Marco asked.

"It's a lot bigger than my old school. And the teachers are going really fast. But I think I like it."

"We all take school very seriously, and we get good grades," Brenden said. "You should get involved in a lot of things, but classes always are the most important."

"We all do other things, too, of course," Marco added. "Brenden's on the student council, and I would spend all my time making clothes if I could. But school always comes first."

"If you're having trouble with any subject, we can help you."

"A lot of kids come down here on their free periods and waste time. We go to the library and get our homework done," Marco said. "Let me see your schedule." Celia turned it over to him and Marco studied it. "We have some free periods together." He drew a little star in some of the boxes on her schedule. "Look for us in the library."

Celia noticed a group of black-clad students off at a corner table. Most of them had hair of multiple colors and lengths, and so many metal accessories; though the kids were sitting still, Celia thought she could hear them clanking. Even at a table in a school cafeteria they looked like they were loitering. But the darkness and the severity of their style made Celia wonder if they might share some interests with the Rosary. "Do you know them?" she asked Brenden and Marco.

"Not really," Brenden said. "We don't have that much in common."

"Every day is not Halloween," Marco said. "But they show up in their costumes nonetheless."

"More than that, they don't take school very seriously, and they seem a little lost," Brenden said. "Besides, if all your strangeness is on the outside, doesn't that make you kind of dull on the inside? What's that quote Liz says all the time?" he asked Marco.

"The one by René Char? *A new mystery sings in your bones. Develop your legitimate strangeness.*'"

Celia repeated it to herself, trying to tease out the meaning. She could tell Brenden and Marco subscribed to it, but she wondered how one went about doing such a thing. "I see what you mean," she said, because she could understand at least how those other kids weren't polished or ambitious enough to have a place in the Rosary.

"What's your last name?" Brenden asked. "Regine told me and I thought it was beautiful, but I can't remember."

"Balaustine," Celia said. "It means 'flower of the pomegranate.'"

"Really? That's fantastic. It reminds me of my favorite song, 'The Spangle Maker' by the Cocteau Twins. Do you know them?"

"No," Celia admitted.

"I wrote a blog post about the song. You can read it if you like." Brenden pointed at the piece of paper he had given her with the website address. "It's kind of impossible to understand her lyrics, and in the chorus I'm pretty sure she sings, 'It's pomegranate,' but who knows what she's really saying."

"I'll definitely check it out." Celia tucked the paper inside her sketchbook. "How long have you guys been together?"

"The five of us, or the two of us?" Brenden smiled. "Ivo and Liz and Regine and I have been friends since we were sophomores and Regine was a first year. Marco transferred here last year, and we've been dating since last fall. It'll be a year in October." He grinned at Marco, who winked at him.

"Do you not say freshman?" Celia said.

"Were you a man last year?" Marco asked.

"No, of course not," Celia said.

"There wasn't any doubt in my mind," Marco said. "You're gorgeous. You have such an elegant neck."

"Thank you," Celia said, blushing again. She couldn't remember a boy saying anything like that to her before. It didn't even matter that this one was gay. She pushed her hair back on her shoulder, relieved it was smooth and shiny now that Regine had steered her to some products and a good brush.

"Regine's going to be really protective of you. Just make sure she's not doing it because you're getting more attention than she is," Marco said.

"Hey!" Brenden said. "What's with the snide comments about Regine?" He turned back to Celia. "I don't think she cares how much attention you get."

"But she's dating Ivo, right?" Celia asked. "She told me almost nothing about all of you, but she must have told me she was going to homecoming with Ivo a dozen times."

"They *are* going to homecoming," Marco said carefully, "and Brenden and I are going with them, but I think it means something very different to Regine than it does to Ivo."

"Oh," Celia said. She wanted to know more, but she didn't feel comfortable asking.

LATER CELIA SEARCHED OUT the chemistry lab and discovered that the man who had tried to help Elsie in the parking lot that morning would be her chemistry teacher. He wasted no time distributing books and a permission slip for a field trip to the water purification plant. Then he asked them to choose lab partners. There was a flurry of movement, and as the class sorted itself from oxygen atoms into oxygen molecules Celia's timidity reared up, and she was rooted in place. Across from her a girl was looking at her with an expression she couldn't interpret. She didn't think anyone ever had looked at her this way before—as though Celia might be the answer to someone else's question. The other girl had made no attempt to find a partner, either, and by then they were the only two left. Celia crossed her fingers and went over to her.

"Hi! You're new, right? I'm Mariette!" the girl said brightly. "Mariette Ann, but I just go by Mariette. Lots of people think my name's Mary Ann, but it's Mariette."

Celia introduced herself and they looked each other over. Mariette was the kind of girl Celia would have been if Regine hadn't intervened. She had on nondescript clothes that didn't quite go together. Her curly strawberry blond hair made an unruly halo around her face. Celia thought with a little attention it might be very pretty; then she smiled for a moment, amused to note she barely had emerged from her own makeover and already she had ideas to make over someone else. Socially, however, Mariette was her opposite. Rather than being intimidated by Celia, who was nearly a foot taller than she, Mariette chatted easily as they went over to an open lab table, and Celia wondered if she was like that all the time or if it was just nerves.

"What school did you go to last year? Suburban's pretty cool. I went to Mount Rose for middle school, but not a lot of kids from there come here. The teacher looks so young! He probably just got out of college. He's supposed to be really tough, though. Is he serious with those crocodile loafers?" The teacher's shiny, wavy hair lay close to his head, reminding Celia of tortoiseshell. He had written *Mr. Sumeletso* on the board, and she wondered what country the name came from. His chinos were a little too big, and his knit tie looked like he had been wearing it since his own high school days. He smiled a little timidly as he mingled with the students.

Celia tried her hand at making conversation. "Some girl

got stung by a bee in the parking lot before school and had an allergic reaction. Someone had an EpiPen for her, though. Mr. Sumeletso was there, and he helped her into the building when it was over." That sparked Mariette's interest, and they studied the teacher for another moment.

"I guess he looks nice enough." Then Mariette moved on. "Have you ever gone rock climbing? I want to learn. Look—there's a hummingbird!" Celia followed Mariette's finger and saw the blur of a bird just outside the nearest window. They watched it for a few seconds before Mariette's attention flitted away again. "What bus do you take?"

"I get a ride with a friend," Celia said, but she realized that much of what Mariette said didn't require a response, largely because she didn't pause long enough to receive one. *At least there won't be any awkward silences,* Celia thought. Nor did the commentary stop when Mr. Sumeletso began talking. Mariette scribbled things in the margin of her notebook for Celia to see. *He can't be more than 24—he looks like he's 17!* Celia tried to concentrate. Toward the end of the class Mr. Sumeletso announced he would be coaching the new swim teams, now that Suburban had a swimming pool, and he hoped they would consider trying out. Mariette scribbled *I can't swim!* with a scaredy face, and Celia wrote *Me neither* next to it. They grinned at each other. Celia wondered if Regine would have wanted her to remain aloof, but she didn't dwell on it.

AT THE END OF THE day, trying to put her locker in some kind of order before she left, Celia thought she had done pretty well. The only life-threatening thing that had happened had been to someone else. She had made it through unscathed, and a few moments even had been pleasant. She wasn't completely sure how she would fit into the Suburban cosmos, but she had an idea. It came largely under the auspices of the Rosary, who had cornered the market on mysterious and sophisticated at Suburban. Throughout the day Celia had watched the first year students, as new to Suburban as she was. They faltered and shrank back, still looking for their allies. Surely she would have resembled them if it weren't for Regine and the Rosary.

Mariette was the only one so far who challenged Celia's belief that everyone needed allies. This girl clearly navigated her day with a force of will that required no assistance. Mariette didn't seem to need a team, and she didn't care to wear the uniform of one, either. That made her fascinating to Celia. She remembered her panic in homeroom that morning, and knew she possessed nowhere near Mariette's level of confidence. Celia wondered if she might learn things from Mariette, different things than she expected to learn from the Rosary.

Burdened with her bag of books, Celia went down to the lobby to meet Regine, but when she got there she saw only Liz by herself on the far wall. From across the lobby, Celia followed Liz's gaze to an athletic guy in an orange T-shirt, and Celia recognized him as the jock who had flustered Liz in the parking lot that morning. He had no idea he was being watched. Then Regine arrived and Celia walked with her to meet Liz and wait for the others.

"I feel like I've been here a week already," Liz said wearily.

"I'm freaking out—I got Mr. Sumeletso for Chem Two." Regine turned to Celia to explain. "He just got here last year, and I had Mrs. Merino for Chem One, but everyone who had Mr. Sumeletso last year practically failed his class. I aced Chem One last year, but in Mr. Sumeletso's first class today I felt like I had forgotten *all* of it."

"I have him, too, for chemistry," Celia said, watching Regine's concern expand to include her. "He seemed nice."

"Get ready. It's going to be hard," Regine warned.

"I'm glad I got through chemistry before he showed up," Liz said. "How was the rest of your day?" she asked Celia.

"Good. Definitely a lot of homework."

"When you get home, force yourself to start right away. Don't wait until after dinner. It's the best habit you can form," Regine advised her. Liz nodded absently, but her eyes were across the lobby again.

When the boys arrived, they all repeated their smooth, purposeful walk out to the cars, and the group chatted for a moment before splitting up into vehicles. Brenden and Marco asked Celia about her day, but Ivo looked around idly, and Celia thought again he didn't seem very interested in knowing her. After only one day she desperately wanted approval from all of them, but she told herself not to ask for too much too soon.

"You know, we have to get you a job," Regine said as she pulled slowly out of the parking lot, in line behind the other two cars.

"A job?"

"Sure. We all have jobs. I work at a frame store. Marco helps with his mom's tailoring business. Brenden works at a music store. Liz works at the library, and Ivo works at an interior design firm. You need to start earning money for college. And to pay for clothes and music, and Diaboliques."

"Diaboliques?"

"It's the club we go to on Fridays. You'll love it."

"Are your parents going to help you pay for college?"

"Sure, but it's going to be expensive," Regine explained. "If you want something you have to do the work to get it, right? I've saved five thousand dollars over the last two years for school."

"Wow." Celia was impressed. "I wonder where I can find a job."

"We can go look this weekend. No tacky clothing stores, and no food service," Regine said firmly. "Maybe you could work at an art supply store?"

Celia arrived home feeling as if she were back from a long-distance trip. She wondered if the others truly were getting straight to work on their assignments before dinner, but she decided to follow Regine's instructions, because it didn't seem like a bad idea. As she dug into her pile of books, her thoughts were never far from the Rosary and how they had transformed her high school experience in a single day.

When she went downstairs for dinner, Celia again saw the look that had been in her mother's eyes ever since she had started her transformation. It was a look that said, *I'm glad you've finally started to pay attention to your appearance, and maybe what you've chosen isn't terrible, but it isn't what I had in mind, either.* But it wasn't lost on Celia that her mother never had asked her to justify her decisions.

"How was your first day?" her mother asked. "Tell me all about it."

"I don't even know where to begin." Celia exhaled. "One thing I know for sure: I was a different person yesterday."

2

songs to learn and sing

ELIA QUICKLY CAME TO enjoy the morning and afternoon rituals of the Rosary's funereal procession. "What's this?" she asked each morning. *"Some Great Reward,"* Regine would answer, or "Clan of Xymox." Celia's love affair continued to grow with this new musical landscape that had been seemingly just beyond her awareness. Every song was another dot on the map. Sometimes during the first week she looked around at her classmates, thinking they didn't know such darkly beautiful things, and they probably wouldn't appreciate them if they did.

She got along well enough with her classmates, but for the most part they left her alone. At school personas and reputations solidified very quickly, and Celia was gratified to be identified as the newest member of the exotic upper-class clique. Her real joy came from the Rosary and from knowing that throughout the day she would come in contact with one or more of these people with whom she dared to hope she was becoming friends. They would wave to her when they crossed paths in the hall, which felt like a sunbeam to Celia. She would join them in the library to study, finally understanding what it was like to be on the inside of a circle. And she would sit among them at lunch, drinking in their conversations and laughing at their jokes. Half an hour later, in her next class, the buzz still would be there. Celia didn't care if she didn't make a single other friend at Suburban, and she didn't try.

The only exception was Mariette, who was almost relentlessly friendly, and whom it was impossible for her to dislike. Celia marveled that Mariette didn't get in trouble with Mr. Sumeletso, as often as she whispered and jotted random notes during class. *Have you ever had fondue?* And there were times Mariette just flat out ignored the lesson. On the second day Celia had noticed her drawing an elaborate diagram of the sophomore hallway and listing students' names next to their lockers from memory. Celia was concerned Mariette was a little crazy, but over and above that, she was concerned Mariette wouldn't be a good lab partner because she didn't pay enough attention.

Friday was their first experiment, and Celia was nervous as she walked through the science wing. She fully expected to have to keep Mariette focused and to ensure the accuracy of their experiment. Lost in her thoughts, Celia didn't notice right away that a tiny girl had stopped by a window ahead of her. At first Celia thought the girl was looking outside, but her head was down and she supported herself with her hand on the sill.

On the other side of the hall a boy had noticed the girl, too, and changed course to approach her. "Hey, Lacie, are you okay?" Lacie shook her head and promptly fainted. Her books slid across the floor, and passing students started and yelped. The boy dropped to his knees and hunched over Lacie, taking her wrist.

Celia kept walking toward the scene. She guessed the

Rosary would have stopped and waited as though the girl were another obstruction to be cleared, like Elsie in the parking lot on the first day of school. But Celia wanted to try to help. As she neared Lacie on the floor, Celia recognized the boy who knelt next to her. She should have sooner, since he was wearing an orange hoodie. It was the jock she had seen in the parking lot — the same jock who had helped Elsie and confounded Liz. His backpack lay on the floor next to him, with a row of patches with different symbols of swimmers sewn onto the canvas, and Celia guessed he was a lifeguard. He had bent his ear close to Lacie's mouth, and now he pinched her nose carefully between his thumb and forefinger with one hand and pulled her mouth open with the other.

The commotion in the hall had brought Mr. Sumeletso out of his classroom. He saw Lacie in a heap and ran over. "What happened?"

"She just fainted." The jock looked up at him. "I don't know what happened."

"Is she breathing?"

"I think so."

"Then you don't need to give her mouth-to-mouth." Mr. Sumeletso stared at Lacie for a moment, then turned to the students who lingered around them. "Go to class!" He saw Celia and said, "Tell everyone I'll be back in a few minutes. Set up for the experiment."

Celia nodded and continued to the classroom door. Before she went in she looked back and saw that Lacie had regained consciousness. The jock helped her up, and Mr. Sumeletso gathered her books and accompanied them down the hall.

What is going on around here? Celia thought. She went into the lab, but she didn't have the nerve to raise her voice and give everyone Mr. Sumeletso's instructions. Celia told Mariette, then stood back as her lab partner took charge and spread the information around the room.

"Where did Mr. S. go?" Mariette asked her.

"Some girl passed out, just down the hall," Celia told her. "That's the second time something completely random has happened, and we've only been here four days. Is this place cursed?"

Mariette had been grabbing graduated cylinders and clamps off shelves, but she turned sharply. "What did you say?"

"I mean, for two girls to get hurt—to be injured some-how—within four days, that's strange, isn't it?"

"I guess it is," Mariette said slowly. It was the first time Celia had seen her come to a complete stop since they had met. But in a matter of seconds, the familiar, bubbly Mariette returned. "C'mon, we have to get started." And just as Celia had feared, Mariette acted as though they were baking a cake, the way she casually rattled off the substances they would need and fired up a Bunsen burner. Celia watched her closely, but for all her apparent carelessness, Mariette wasn't making any mistakes. In fact, it was Mariette who noticed the smaller details and even Celia's minor errors. As Mariette was elaborating about her attempts to cultivate a bonsai tree, she broke off midsentence to ask, "Is that too full?" And when Celia double-checked, it was, if only slightly. "I don't think that's quite hot enough," Mariette suggested another time, and the thermometer bore her out before she resumed a monologue about riding the bus.

By the time Mr. Sumeletso returned, they were well along. When it came time to measure the next substance, Mariette poured it quickly and judged the amount with a quick glance. "Just a little more," she murmured, and tapped a small amount in. When Mariette went to put the jar away, Celia quickly checked the quantity in the vial but found it to be exactly right.

"Have you done chemistry before?" she asked when Mariette returned.

"Not like this," Mariette said guilelessly. "I made a volcano out of vinegar and baking soda for a science fair once. Does that count?"

They finished their lab early and Mr. Sumeletso complimented them on the precision of their results. Celia was thrilled. Apparently her lab partner was a natural, and that was enough to remove any doubts she'd had before the experiment.

They chatted quietly while the rest of the class finished up. "How do you like school so far?" Mariette asked her.

"It's good. I was really unhappy at my old high school."

"Why?"

"You should have seen me last year. I wore sweatshirts and jeans, didn't know how to do my hair. I didn't have any friends. I'm not really good at making friends."

"It's hard to imagine you like that," Mariette said. "No one is going to tease you for the way you dress now. And you're friends with those juniors and seniors, aren't you? The ones in the black cars."

"I am." Celia smiled at the thought.

"But I know what you mean. People will use anything they can to hurt you sometimes." Mariette glanced around at their classmates.

"It doesn't seem to bother you, though," Celia said. "I heard those girls calling you names the other day, and you just shrugged it off."

"Sideshow Mariette?" She plucked at her unruly golden red hair. "That's been my nickname since the beginning of last year. There are two kinds of days, you know? There are the days when you manage to stay under the radar, and no one really takes aim at you. And then there are days when you just have a bull's-eye painted on your back, and every time you turn around someone is doing something cruel."

"I know *exactly* what you mean," Celia said.

"But I don't let it get to me," Mariette said with clear resolve.

As confident as Mariette sounded, Celia knew from personal experience it was impossible for Mariette to inure herself completely from all the teasing. Celia wondered if she should make overtures to Mariette outside school, but she couldn't decide how. Perhaps it was selfish, but Celia wanted to keep her time for Regine and the Rosary, and apparently she was supposed to be looking for a job. And after all, Mariette hadn't asked her for anything.

3

night time

O N FRIDAY NIGHT CELIA prepared as best she could for her first visit to Diaboliques. She didn't have a clear idea what she should do. Her only frame of reference was the couple of school dances she had attended last year. Celia hoped fervently this new experience would be nothing like those extended bouts of anxiety and self-consciousness, when she'd been trapped in a darkened gymnasium, conspicuously alone in a crowd. She put on the black dress Regine had picked out for her, carefully applied her smoky eye shadow, and brushed her hair over and over until it shone. She stood in her front hallway as Regine patiently fielded her mother's questions. "No alcohol. It's just a little all-ages club. I've never seen a fight there. We'll be home before one."

"Well, I've never let her do anything like this before," Mrs. Balaustine said, her smile a little tight as she glanced from Regine to Celia. "But you ask to go out so seldom." (*Never,* thought Celia.) "I really want to give it a try." She focused on her daughter. "Have fun, but be safe, okay? Stay with your friends."

"I will," Celia promised. She planned to stay as close as a shadow to Regine.

"And don't think I'm going to start letting you stay out past midnight every night of the week."

"No, Mom."

In the car Regine said, "I have seen fights at Diaboliques. But both times it was one person being stupid and getting thrown out by the bouncers. I don't think your mother needs to know about that."

"Probably not," Celia agreed.

"Plus, they do serve alcohol, but they put wristbands on the people who are over twenty-one. The bartenders won't serve anyone without a wristband, but we don't drink anyway. There's plenty of time for that when we're older. And they're open until three, but we can cross that bridge later."

"Oh, okay . . ." Celia was surprised by how deliberately Regine had misled her mother. Before now Regine had seemed so principled—everyone in the Rosary seemed to be. Celia supposed attending Diaboliques must be an opportunity they all treasured, and it must not pose a serious risk, or else they wouldn't go. But the truth—the parts Regine had concealed from Celia's mother, which Celia prayed she wouldn't discover by phoning the club to verify Regine's account—now made Diaboliques feel a little dangerous, both scarier and more alluring than it already had been.

"This is the brand-new driving-to-Diaboliques mix Brenden made," Regine said, handing her a CD. "Except he likes to title the Diaboliques mixes in hyperbolic French, so it's *Voyage aux Diaboliques Neuf.* Yes, there have been eight mixes before this one." Celia studied the track list and surmised "Nightclubbing" must be the song playing on the car stereo.

They followed the same route as in the mornings before school to assemble the chain of black cars, and the procession felt even more glamorous to Celia in the nighttime than during the day. She had a momentary desire for sunglasses, which made her smile. From Ivo and Liz's house the Rosary drove downtown to a warehouse neighborhood that was unfamiliar to Celia. But the street where they parked was clean, and she saw an all-night diner on the next block down.

Everyone wore a dressier version of their daytime style, and Celia thought they were a remarkable sight. As they got out of their cars, she looked around at this group of people who barely had stopped being strangers to her and in whose presence she still felt like a guest.

Ivo had on a morning-length suit coat over a shirt collar that spread out on either side of his polka-dotted black tie. It was clear to Celia he was the leader of this tribe, though she hadn't learned why. Perhaps no one wanted to challenge him for the position. He was confident but quiet. She still hadn't seen him look directly at her, but she was sure he had passed judgment on her somehow. Among the Rosary, Ivo remained the biggest mystery.

Liz wore a charcoal strapless dress over a fitted white blouse, a combination that never would have occurred to Celia. Liz had shown flickers of interest in her, and she had smiled at her on a few occasions, so Celia felt a little more comfortable with her. At school Liz carried a notebook in which she scribbled constantly, and even if the scribbles were words instead of drawings, Celia felt a kinship with her because of it.

Brenden wore a velvet suit of such dark midnight blue, it might as well have been black. With his hair swept up to its usual height he reminded Celia of a matinee idol, but the henna patterns on his palms made it harder to pigeonhole him. Brenden's encyclopedic knowledge of the music Celia was just discovering made him the most impressive to her, and she longed to see his music collection. In the meantime she hung on his words whenever he told her the name of an artist or a song. She didn't feel as though she was imposing because Brenden always was so pleased to share what he knew.

Marco sported a mandarin-collared jacket buttoned up to his neck and a piece of embroidered fabric wrapped like a long skirt over his dark pants. Celia thought he was adorable, but to her he also was fearless. She was amazed by his ability to push the boundaries of men's fashion the way he did and somehow walk through high school unscathed. She knew it helped that he was so handsome. Nearly every day at school she heard girls talk about him with regretful longing.

Regine wore a corset over her black blouse and long skirt. The corset had a pocket on the side seam that held a watch with a silver chain that draped across her waist and clipped on the other side. Marco seemed to be correct that one of the reasons Regine had embraced Celia was in order to rise slightly in the hierarchy of the Rosary, if only by bringing in someone younger. Celia didn't care. She was grateful to be there.

On a strange dark street, assembled with these alluring people, Celia felt a little plain in her comparatively simple black dress and black heels, but Marco whispered to her, "You look great. Regine wouldn't have let you out of the house if you didn't." Still, Celia was nervous. This was a different kind of unease than she had felt on Monday at Suburban. That first day she had been scared of asking for attention she didn't really want. Tonight she was scared of not being interesting enough. They walked down the block, a series of uninviting buildings that might have housed heavy manufacturing in earlier decades. The muted bass thud of dance music signaled that the club must be close, but from the outside Diaboliques offered few clues about its contents. A single red light bulb glowed in a bare socket above an unmarked door in a brick wall, guarded by a brutish-looking guy dressed in black jeans, boots, and a black leather jacket, smoking a clove cigarette. The spicy smoke was foreign, making Celia nervous and reminding her she had allowed herself to be taken someplace about which she knew practically nothing. When they approached, the bouncer broke character and greeted them familiarly.

"Hello, folks! Good to see you all! Who's this?"

"Hey, Rufus. This is Celia," Liz introduced her, and Celia's hand felt tiny in Rufus's broad grip. He grinned at her, and she wondered what it was like to stand outside a club all night while everything went on inside.

"It's very nice to meet you, Paperwhite. Have a good time." Grasping the door handle, he cleared his throat and said in a dramatic voice, "Twinkle, twinkle . . ." Celia was surprised to hear the Rosary chime in, adding "Release the bats!" in unison.

"What does that mean?" she whispered to Marco.

"It's one part Alice in Wonderland, one part of the song by the Birthday Party," Marco whispered back. "It just amuses us."

Meanwhile, Rufus had opened the door for them. Instead of a room full of people, though, a dark flight of stairs awaited them. Celia followed the Rosary inside and up, then along a hall with no doors and plain black walls. The corridor turned left and right and then they arrived at a vestibule with a podium. A plump girl in a Victorian gown put down her nursing textbook. She took their money and marked their hands with a hint of contempt. After they passed, Marco whispered to Celia, "She's always sour. I gave up trying to win her over a long time ago. Plus, I've only ever seen her in three different dresses all the time we've been coming here, so how interesting can she be?"

After another stretch of hallway, at which point Celia thought they surely must have reached the back side of the building, they emerged through a doorway onto a mezzanine that was dark except for a few candles on low tables and the occasional sweep and flash of lights from the dance floor below. In those flashes Celia could make out couches on which a few darkly clad people practically disappeared into the shadows; all she could glimpse were some pale faces and a plume of fiery red hair.

"Come take a look. We never go down there," Regine said, and Celia walked with her to the mezzanine railing next to the stairs leading down. Below her lay a dance floor the size of a basketball court, filled with people dancing like frenetic circus performers.

She looked over the railing for another moment, but she sensed the others were waiting for her, so she turned back to them and they moved to the far side of the room. The perimeter of the mezzanine was so dark Celia hadn't noticed another flight of stairs, but there it was, and the Rosary climbed higher. At the next landing there was an awkward little antechamber with several doors and people passing through in all directions. A man with metal spikes protruding from his ears and his chin walked by them. Celia wasn't sure whether the others had surrounded her intentionally, but she was glad to have them as a buffer. They went through the door on the left and Celia saw another bar tended by a man and a woman clad head to toe in vinyl. Beyond the bar lay an even larger dance floor with a crowd that heaved and spun, this time to music that sounded more like rock. She saw people who looked like characters from

Tim Burton films and was as entranced as she might have been at the theater. She would have been happy to stand there and watch for quite some time; she wished she had her sketchbook with her.

"It's a little of everything out here," Marco said. "We check it out every once in a while, but the music is all over the place. Patrick plays a more consistent set."

"Who is Patrick?"

"You'll meet him. He's the main reason we're here."

Celia gathered that there was even more to come, and sure enough, the Rosary moved again, back through the crowded landing and across to a door on the opposite side. As they passed into another hallway the energy seemed to focus a little. Not as many people came in this direction.

The next room they entered was closer in size to a living room, with crushed velvet upholstered banquettes around the perimeter and a smaller bar on one side, where a beautiful, slender but strong-looking man with black hair down to his waist held court.

"I know this song," Celia said excitedly to Marco. " 'Alice' by the Sisters of Mercy."

Marco looked impressed. "Regine really is taking your musical education seriously, isn't she? This is where we spend all our time. The music is a little older, more obscure, and the people are a little more mature. It's more sophisticated than the other two rooms."

She could see the difference as she looked around. The people in this room wore beautiful dresses and sharp suits, as well as items of clothing Celia would have been hard-pressed to name. Marco rattled off the names of fashion designers Celia barely recognized: Alexander McQueen, John Galliano,

Thierry Mugler. Some ensembles looked custom-made. There were people whose gender was difficult to discern. Celia felt plain again, even in her black dress, which was by far the most formal thing she had ever worn—the same black dress that an hour ago had made her wonder where she could go and not feel overdressed. The elegant clothes her friends wore made complete sense to her, now that she saw them in this context.

"Come with me. Let me introduce you to Patrick," Brenden said, taking Celia's hand. The contact made her flash back to when she was younger, holding hands with her father. But Brenden's hand around hers also quickened her heartbeat. She understood the act for exactly what it was—a protective older friend trying to make her feel comfortable—but she couldn't remember ever holding hands with a guy before for any reason, and Celia thought she must be smiling idiotically. Brenden led her over to the DJ booth, where a wiry man with carefully messy hair turned away from his music to greet them.

"Brenden!" Patrick kissed him on both cheeks and then looked curiously at Celia.

"Patrick, I'd like you to meet Celia. This is her first time here."

"Hi, Celia, thanks for coming!" Patrick took her hand and kissed her cheeks, too. She felt like a celebrity, looking out over the room from the booth while Patrick and Brenden talked. This place was the opposite in every way of what Celia had been tempted to imagine based on the miserable school dances she'd endured. There was no jumping or running around, no yelling. The people in this room behaved as though they were part of a stylized performance. Whether they stood or sat, it was as if they expected to be photographed. When they talked, they looked almost formal, bending their heads together and speaking carefully. When they danced, it was minimal but expressive, with deliberate steps and gestures. Many of them moved their lips along with the lyrics of the songs, making it clear they knew the music intimately. When Brenden was done chatting with Patrick, Celia returned with him to the others, who had taken their places at one side of the room.

A new song began and Brenden started as though he'd been pinched. "'Whispered in Your Ear,'" he told her in haste on his way out to the dance floor. "Patrick knows I love this song!" The other four moved just as quickly to join him. Celia hadn't contemplated dancing, and she stayed behind, unable to summon the confidence to join them. She desperately wanted to avoid making a fool of herself in this place, so she watched them, hoping to learn some sort of proper dance technique by observation. Ivo's dancing was restricted almost completely to a stately step-touch back and forth, his eyes often closed. Liz tended to work in a small circle, hands clasped behind her back, looking down as though she had lost something. Brenden occasionally made small gestures that illustrated the lyrics. Marco was the loosest of them, moving his hips and raising his arms. And Regine had the most elaborate style, windmilling her arms around her in an exotic manner, pushing and pulling the air with her hands as though she were performing an incantation. Other people watched her admiringly. Celia badly wanted to dance, but she had no intention of attempting it and being exposed as an amateur.

The inner sanctum of Diaboliques was so much better than she could have imagined, even if she had let her fantasy run wild. Instead of looking the same and doing the same things, as people often did in the outside world, in here everyone clearly valued individuality as long as it was executed well. They seemed to have noticed Celia, but to her relief, no one scrutinized her as if she might do something wrong. The ones who came over to greet members of the Rosary nodded in her direction, and she assumed she was being introduced in absentia. The room, the people, the night—everything was beautifully theatrical, and now Celia understood: the Rosary attempted to reproduce this feeling, this experience of Diaboliques, elsewhere in their lives. Being here helped her to understand the choices they made and the way they lived during the rest of the week. The next time she was in the middle of the chaotic school cafeteria Celia was going to find it that much easier to ignore everyone around her, as her friends did. Spending Friday nights here in this beautiful room, where everyone else from school would have been so obviously out of place, was the prize for enduring everyday life for the rest of the week. Celia realized she only had been on the outside, fearful of the eyes that dismissed her, thinking it was easiest just to disappear, because she hadn't figured out where the inside was. It wasn't with those kids at school any longer. It was here at Diaboliques. It was with the Rosary.

"How do you like it?" Liz asked her at one point when they were standing off to the side again.

"It's beautiful. I didn't know anything like this existed," Celia replied. "If you had described it to me I wouldn't have believed you, and now here I am, in the middle of it!" Every song was strange and amazing. Every time she looked around she found something or someone new to admire. There were elaborate wall sconces that dripped cut glass like chandeliers. A woman in a fitted smoking jacket and floor-length gown used the mirror in her compact to check the flat, shiny waves of hair on her temples. A man arrived dressed completely in ivory. A sort of shawl-collared knee-length coat over a cream ribbed sweater and wide-legged canvas pants made him look like some kind of heavenly longshoreman. Celia studied everyone at Diaboliques, wanting to take as much of it home with her as she could. She felt the familiar impulse to re-create all of it in her sketchbook, knowing she could spend the rest of the weekend capturing all these stunning people. But for the first time, underneath that impulse was a new one: Celia wouldn't be content to know this world from behind a sketchbook—she wanted to take her place in it.

In the midst of this sensory overload Celia noticed a tall boy with closely cropped black hair on the other side of the room. His broad shoulders and thick forearms made him look powerful even standing still. He wore a black shirt and pants that were plain by Diaboliques standards, but Celia was more taken with the silvery sparks in his gray eyes, which she could see from twenty feet away—because he was staring at her. She looked away and then looked back, and still he stared. Celia felt a strange current flow through her, a mix of anxiety and pleasure. She wanted to decode the boy's gaze, but she wasn't sure she dared.

"Who is that?" Regine asked, easily locating the source of Celia's distraction. Regine turned to Liz and pointed at the boy without even attempting to be subtle about it. Liz looked and then shrugged at Regine. Celia was embarrassed, but the boy across the floor didn't seem to care. He continued to stare at Celia, keeping his hands deep in his pockets. "I don't know about him," Regine said. "Maybe I'm being overprotective, but I've never seen him before. We know all the regulars in this room."

As it turned out, no action was required. The boy never

came over, nor did he try to speak with any of them. A few times Celia saw him dance to the most abrasive songs Patrick played that night, and Brenden told her the names of the bands: Fields of the Nephilim, Christian Death, and Virgin Prunes. The boy had a leonine grace, gliding surely from foot to foot, but he kept his eyes down, and to Celia he looked as though he were hearing the music through headphones rather than loudspeakers. He didn't seem to notice anyone around him until he finished, returned to his place across the room, and raised his silver eyes to find her again.

"If you keep watching him, he might think you're interested," Regine said.

"He's the one watching me!" Celia protested. "I don't know if I'm interested, but he *is*, well . . ." She studied the boy the way one searches for lightning in the night sky or peers down over mountain cliffs from an airplane window. The danger was beautiful as long as it stayed at a distance. As unexpected, as unprecedented as it was to be stared at this way by a boy, Celia wasn't disconcerted by it. She had been transported to an alternate universe where everyone was brilliant and stunning, and everything was perfectly appointed, and all the new secrets she cherished were brought out into the open; why wouldn't there be a brooding, handsome boy waiting there for her to arrive? Celia wasn't about to question the rules of this new world, whom it would contain or what role he might play. And she wasn't about to exert her own will, either. She had gotten this far with barely a single decision of her own. Celia was keenly aware that she wouldn't be here at all if it weren't for the Rosary, so if Regine and Liz told her to be wary, she would play by their rules.

Throughout the night Brenden gave her background details about the music she heard. "Ah, this is a classic! Killing Joke, 'Love Like Blood.' I'll make a copy of it for you. The lead singer decided the world was going to end, and he moved somewhere like Iceland to prepare for it, and then it didn't happen, at least not yet. The words are really intense." Celia made another mental note to look up Brenden's blog the next day.

"How did you find this place?" she asked Liz.

"Ivo found out about it. But if you start looking around for places to hear this kind of music, there really isn't anywhere else. When Ivo and I started coming here, it was like we had found Wonderland. We never expected to hear these songs anywhere outside our own houses, and we definitely didn't think there were all these other people who loved it, too! We were so reverential about it, we didn't talk to anyone here for six months," Liz said. "Brenden was the first to crack. He was hearing songs and having no idea who they were by, and it drove him crazy, so he started asking Patrick. And then we gradually met the rest of Patrick's regulars."

Too soon it was midnight and Ivo rounded them up to make their departure. Celia stole a final glance at the silver-eyed boy as they started off. She had a twinge, wondering if he would be there next Friday, if she would feel the strange current flow through her again. When she looked over at him she thought he could tell she was leaving, and he almost seemed to be fighting the impulse to approach her, but that could have been wishful thinking on her part. She processed with the group to the booth, where Patrick kissed them all again. "Leaving so early?" he asked.

"We're still earning Celia's mother's trust," Ivo told him. "So it'll be early for a little while."

"You could stay," Celia said to the other four, hoping Regine wouldn't resent her for having to take her home.

"No, we're a group. We arrive together, and we leave together," Ivo said firmly. Celia was touched. It was the clearest demonstration the Rosary had made that they considered her one of them. She wished they could have stayed until Diaboliques closed.

They made their way through the other rooms, down and out to the cars. The aura of Diaboliques gradually lifted as Celia traveled farther from the inner sanctum where Patrick was king and mysterious tall boys waited. Rufus called her Paperwhite again and wished them good night.

"Did you have a good time?" Marco asked as the other four walked ahead.

"I loved it! Thank you so much for bringing me," Celia said.

"Well, we do it every Friday. It's like church," Marco joked. "Were Regine and Liz keeping you from talking to that guy?"

"I wouldn't have talked to him anyway. They're just being protective."

"Sure." Marco's tone was a little sarcastic. "And the two of them manage their own love lives so well. Someday I'll have to tell you about Regine's unrequited love for Ivo and Liz's unrequited love for one of the football players, of all people."

"The guy in the parking lot on the first day of school, right? Who is he?"

"His name is Skip—I know, Skip, right? His favorite color is *orange*. What more do you need to know? Liz refuses to talk about him, so don't bring it up or I'll just get in trouble for gossiping again," Marco said.

They said good night by the cars. As she put the key in the ignition, Regine told Celia, "When you're allowed to stay out later, we can stop at the all-night diner and get food before we head home. On a good night we don't get back until three or four."

Celia sank back in the passenger seat, enveloped by the sumptuous music on the second half of Brenden's mix. She thought life really was better with the right soundtrack. Out the window she could see the stars, and she felt as though all of it had been made for her. After she slipped in her front door and crept up her stairs, the thing that kept Celia from falling asleep was her happiness. The beginning of school had been a lovely adventure, but now another adventure had overshadowed it, one that felt even more vivid, more life-changing. Celia wondered if moments like these would happen all her life, or if they were a special kind of alchemy that was only possible for teenagers. She took out her sketchbook and made a quick drawing of Regine at Diaboliques, her arms unfurled, one foot touching lightly in front of the other, her head tilted to the side. She was tempted to draw the silver-eyed boy, but she resisted. It felt like a girlish, lovesick thing to do, and not at all behavior of which the Rosary would approve. She wanted to be cool and unaffected like her friends. Celia looked around her bedroom, full of pastel colors and frills, and thought, *I need to redecorate.*

THE NEXT DAY CELIA SAT in front of her computer and typed in the website address Brenden had given her for his blog. The dark and lush graphic design reminded her of the décor at Diaboliques. There were categories of posts from which to choose, and she clicked on "Strangers in Open Cars—Songs

You Should Know." The first entry on the list was Cocteau Twins— "The Spangle Maker." In the margin she clicked on an audio player to hear the song while she was reading Brenden's essay-length post.

"The Spangle Maker" was unlike anything Celia had ever heard, even including all the new music she'd encountered in the previous months. It was a song that would have mystified her just a few months ago, but now it seemed to unfold like a treasure map, revealing details and ideas as Brenden pointed them out to her. When the song ended, she clicked the player link to start it again. As it began a second time, she felt that already she was hearing it differently. The song's strangeness was wrapping around her like a shawl.

Brenden had been right about the lyrics. Celia barely could make out more than a word or two, and those didn't really add up to anything. In the chorus she heard what sounded like "It's pomegranate" and smiled. It felt as if the song was about her, just a little. Celia played the song yet again, and she re-read Brenden's post. Then she kept clicking the link, until she had heard "The Spangle Maker" a dozen times. It was just as strange and wonderful as Brenden had described it, and his writing was the perfect tour guide to embrace the strangeness, wade into it, accept it on its own terms. Celia remembered what Brenden had said about having heroes to inspire her, and she wondered if she should tell him he, and the rest of the Rosary, had attained that status for her.

The aroma of Diaboliques lingered in her memory—a mixture of industrial space, exotic perfumes, and alcohol. The people posed and danced in her mind. Celia's first impulse was to open her sketchbook again and see how well she could re-create it all. But her hand stopped on the cover. *I have to learn to dance,* she thought. *And not just dancing acceptable in a high school gymnasium. I have to learn to dance well enough for Diaboliques.*

Celia went to her bureau, where her treasured stack of discs from Regine and Brenden sat next to her CD player. She chose one and put it on. In a moment Gene Loves Jezebel's "Desire" began to play, and Celia looked at herself in the mirror.

What do I do? She moved her feet back and forth and felt awkward. She waved her arms around but felt foolish. *This is not going to be easy.*

Celia closed her eyes and tried to imagine a time when she would feel completely at home at Diaboliques. When she, too, would stand and speak with the Rosary as though posing for a portrait. She would hear a song she liked and step out onto the dance floor. Celia felt her hips moving smoothly from side to side, and her hand rose, sweeping back and forth in front of her.

She opened her eyes and found herself in the mirror, looking like a flamingo caught in a bog. She laughed in horror and returned to her desk to open her sketchbook and draw.

4

some girls wander
by mistake

THAT WEEKEND CELIA FOUND a job at a small bookstore in a cluster of shops on a charming street about a mile from her house. She could walk there when the weather was nice. She wasn't sure why the owner hired her, though. Celia had confessed she wasn't very well read, but the woman had laughed and said she couldn't imagine how Celia would be, at her age. "I have the opposite problem." She smiled. "I've read everything, and now I'm down to the dregs." She held up a book. "*The Correspondence of Edwin and Morcar, Earls of Mercia and Northumbria*. It's the driest thing I've ever read. What I wouldn't give to be blown away by Faulkner for the first time, all over again." Celia nodded, wishing she knew who Faulkner was.

Regine had advised Celia to say she was available on Saturdays only after one o'clock so she wouldn't have to get up too early after Diaboliques. When Celia's mother learned Regine was the impetus behind her employment, Mrs. Balaustine admitted Regine permanently into her good graces and extended Celia's Friday curfew to two a.m. "I'm probably crazy, but I'm glad you're making friends," her mother told her.

"Me too," Celia said. "I think I'd like to paint my bedroom."

"We just painted it last year!"

"I know, but I didn't pick the color! You did!"

"I just thought you liked your old room, and it matches your comforter! I suppose it's all not dark enough for you, now?" her mother teased. "All right, we'll do it again. How about this weekend?"

On a whim, Celia dug out their Polaroid camera and took a picture of her room before the transformation began. Changing her clothes, making friends at Suburban, and now redecorating her room, Celia had a profound sense of leaving a part of her life behind—not by chance, but deliberately. It was a new feeling, like shedding her skin, revealing a new self. She wasn't entirely sure who her new self was yet. She wondered if that was something she would create, or discover, or maybe a little of both.

Changing her room was a daunting prospect because Celia had a better sense of what she didn't want it to be—pink, ruffled, childish—than what she did. But she felt strongly she must figure it out herself, rather than ask for suggestions from Regine or any of the others. She wanted her room to be a reflection of herself, not of how they saw her or how they might want her to be.

Her closet was quite sparse already—Regine had seen to that. Celia filled a few boxes with the trinkets and toys that cluttered her shelves and banished them to the attic. Only her sketchbooks were allowed to stay, lined up on one shelf. She evicted the overstuffed chair in which she never sat and a rag rug whose best years had passed. Her mother helped her paint the walls a warm gray color, not too light and not too dark. They went out and found a set of charcoal bedding, and when she had remade the bed, Celia looked around, a little shocked. She was pleased because the room felt chic, in part just because it looked new and different. It also looked like a place in which the new person she thought she was becoming would feel at home. At the same time, the smell of paint lingered. Every sound seemed to echo now, and the empty walls stared back at her expectantly, as if to ask, *Who are you?* That night she sat looking around her Spartan new room, wondering what to put in it. She vowed she would choose carefully; anything that came in really had to deserve to be there. She compared her surroundings to the photograph of her room in its prior incarnation, tucked into the frame of the mirror over her dresser. Outside her window the moon was about half full. Celia thought that was appropriate.

BY THE SECOND WEEK OF SCHOOL Celia had settled into the rhythms of Suburban. Her classes were challenging but manageable, and she went into each day anticipating the times she would spend with various members of the Rosary. Now and then something would pull her anxiety back up — being called on to speak in class, finding herself in the midst of a group of cheerleaders in the hall — but there was no doubt things were going much better than they had last year.

At lunchtime that Wednesday, Celia rounded the corner into the short hallway that led past the teachers' lounge and into one end of the cafeteria, on her way to meet the Rosary. Her path was blocked by a group of students in a huddle, studying something on the floor by the wall. A pair of legs extended into the middle of the hall, and as Celia drew near she glimpsed a girl lying there, her head and shoulders slumped against the base of the wall. She looked exhausted.

Another girl stood up from where she had been squatting next to the victim. "She said it's never happened before," this girl told the others.

"That doesn't mean she's not epileptic," another girl chimed in. "My dad's a doctor. Epilepsy can start at any time."

"It's such a shame. Tomorrow's her birthday."

Then the nurse arrived and shooed the onlookers away to get to the girl on the floor.

Celia wondered again if Suburban was cursed. None of these things by themselves—the bee sting, the girl passing out, the epileptic seizure—would be more than a tragic interruption to a day. But when she considered them together, it was hard not to connect them, even if there was no way the health problems of three different girls could be related.

Celia moved on. As she entered the cafeteria she crossed paths with Skip, the jock she seemed to see everywhere. Today he was wearing an orange and gray striped polo. Their eyes met for a moment, and Celia had to admit his face was kind. But she couldn't ignore a pattern: Skip had been close by each time these bad things had happened.

5

strangeways, here we come

SUBURBAN HIGH SCHOOL WAS surrounded by a grove of maples, and gingko trees flanked its walls. Celia began to track the leaves' progress from emerald to golden orange as the autumn unfolded. She had stopped at a favorite window in the front stairwell to look over a cluster of them on Friday morning when a bus pulled up on the other side of the golden trees. The kids streamed out, but several of them waited by the bus door. Then Mariette got off, and Celia was dismayed to witness the taunting the other kids heaped on her lab partner. Mariette hunched her shoulders over the books in her arms and hurried past them. In the slanted morning sun, her shadow lunged across the pavement, and it flickered like a weak candle flame, as though Mariette were turning invisible briefly. Celia blinked and Mariette passed into the building below her. When Celia looked up at the trees again, some of the lowest leaves had turned from gold to crimson, as though a droplet of blood were diffusing into a bowl of apricot juice.

AT LUNCH CELIA LOOKED AROUND at Regine, Liz, Ivo, and Brenden. Though she felt more comfortable with them, still she rarely initiated conversation, being content to be included whenever they saw fit. Now she summoned her courage and said, "Do you think there's anything strange going on at school?" They looked blankly at her, and she half wished she had kept quiet. But she had to try to explain herself now. "Girls are getting hurt—having accidents, or some kind of health problem."

"Like a curse?" The way Liz said it, it was clear she was not inclined to give the idea much credence. "I guess I'm not that superstitious."

"I'm not either," Celia quickly agreed. "Or I wouldn't be . . . but I think there's something strange about my chemistry lab partner, too."

Regine took over as the voice of skepticism. "Like what?"

"I don't know . . . She's really nice, but she does some things that are hard to explain. She doesn't measure anything when we do our experiments, but everything turns out perfectly. And this morning I saw her coming in from the bus, and I swear her shadow was flickering."

"You think she's what, a witch, and she's putting curses on other girls?" Ivo asked. Celia couldn't tell if he was mocking her, but she thought it was likely.

"A witch? Do people believe in witches anymore?" Brenden asked.

"Well, they still make movies about them," Liz replied. She turned back to Celia. "Seriously, you think she's a witch?"

"I don't know. Some boys were being mean to her, and the leaves on the tree above her changed color."

"Are you sure? I mean, that's wild," Liz said.

"I'm pretty sure."

"It would be pretty crazy to make that up," Ivo said. "So you're wondering if the injuries aren't accidents at all, but something more sinister. What does this girl look like?"

"She's kind of plain—actually, she's over there," Celia said, spotting Mariette across the cafeteria, "with the reddish blond hair and the pink sweater."

The four of them watched Mariette put her books down at a table, and her notebook fell to the floor. She gathered it up, and then sat down to tie the frayed lace on her weather-beaten Converse. Her frazzled hair went in every direction, including over her face, and she pushed out her lower lip to blow the curls away. Celia saw Mariette through her friends' eyes and knew they weren't going to be impressed with her.

"Well, if she's a—we're going with witch, are we?—then she doesn't seem to be doing anything to help herself," Brenden said. "I'm sorry, but wouldn't she use her powers to look a little more put-together? She just looks kind of a mess."

They turned back to the table. "Yeah, I'm crazy," Celia said, suddenly wishing she never had brought this scrutiny to Mariette.

"If she's a good chem partner, no problem there," Regine said. "Isn't Mr. Sumeletso insanely hard?"

"Not really. We got an A on our first experiment," Celia told her.

"See, Regine, it's just you," Ivo said.

"That's not true! I got the highest grade on *our* first lab, and it was a C-plus!"

"Hey, do you want to do an illustration for the school paper?" Liz asked Celia. "The next issue is in two weeks, and I was going to run a photo of the school that features the new wing, but a drawing might be a nice touch."

"Sure," Celia said, relieved that the subject of Mariette had been dropped.

"What are you doing this weekend?" Regine asked her.

"I don't know. I need to spend some time on my room. I painted it gray, and it looks so much better than when you saw it. But I cleared a lot of stuff out, and it's kind of empty."

"That's cool. What do you have in mind?"

"I'm taking my time with it. It just didn't feel like me, you know? I want to make sure it feels right when I'm finished with it."

"There's this great field in sociology called symbolic anthropology—it's the study of how the objects you select to surround yourself express who you are. Your room is like a self-portrait," Regine said.

"That's what I was thinking," Celia said.

"Did you ever watch those John Hughes films, like *Pretty in Pink* and *Some Kind of Wonderful*?" Regine continued. "I love them for so many reasons, but the characters' bedrooms are brilliant. You look at them and you just know so much about who these people are, before the story even starts. The guy who's the artist in *Some Kind of Wonderful*? I bet you'd love his room. We should watch those movies. I've seen them so many times. I'd bet Brenden and Marco would be up for it, too. We had a *Sixteen Candles* party once."

"What did you call it—symbolic anthropology? Is that taught in a high school class?"

"No. I strive to be a person 'on whom nothing is lost,'" Regine said proudly. "That's a Henry James quote. I think all of us try to live by those words. The world is so big, and the more I learn, the more I'm sure I don't know anything at all. Don't you want to know more?"

"Sure I do," Celia said. "I just feel like every conversation I have with any of you, I hear about something completely new."

"Well, I hope we never make you feel like we're talking

down to you," Regine said. "None of us is ever going to say to you, 'I am older than you and must know better.' You're smart, and you shouldn't be ashamed of being smart, or embarrassed to learn something new. We all do, all the time. A few years ago we were right where you are, or worse. And you know I've already learned things from you. I'm sure we all will."

"Don't hold your breath." Celia smiled.

"Maybe I will." Regine smiled back. "Are you ready for Diaboliques tonight?"

"I've been looking forward to it all week!"

That night Celia felt all the same things she had felt the week before, even though this time she knew what would happen: the cinematic drive, Rufus, the mazelike ascent past the grumpy girl, the walk through the darkened mezzanine and finally into Patrick's room.

"Are you going to dance?" Marco asked soon after they arrived.

"I need to practice more," Celia told him. She had attempted it several times over the course of the week, but earlier that evening, even wearing her mother's black skirt and a charcoal blouse Liz had lent her, none of the movements Celia tried in the mirror satisfied her. "Do you dance around in your bedroom? I mean, did you when you were starting out?"

Marco gave her a smile. "Everyone does. Anyone who tells you they don't practice their dancing when no one's looking is lying."

He left her to join the others on the dance floor, and Celia enjoyed watching them again. And again she sampled the strange feeling of being watched by a tall boy, dressed in black, whose gray eyes pierced her from the other side of the room. Just like the previous week, he stayed in place, watching her as though she were the most fascinating person there, and that made him the most fascinating person to her.

OVER HER FIRST SHIFTS at the bookstore Celia gradually had let go of her nervousness. Her recent experiments in ignoring her fear—with Regine, at Suburban, at Diaboliques—made it easier to do with her first job. Her boss was a charming petite woman who favored clothes with lush textures: velvet, bouclé, angora, and ultrasuede. Her black-rimmed glasses set off her pale skin and white pixie haircut. Her name was Lippa Doeter, and Celia guessed she was German or Austrian, though her accent seemed to thicken and thin without warning. Lippa constantly chewed gum, barely moving her jaw and making small clicking noises that Celia found oddly relaxing. Lippa made her feel at home but quickly left her alone and returned to the back office, instructing her to call if she had any questions. There weren't many customers, so Celia had time to wander around and familiarize herself with the place. The walls were the color of mushrooms, and accent lights washed the chestnut wood shelves but left the rest of the room dim and cozy. Plush chairs upholstered in taupe linen stood waiting in alcoves. Lippa liked to play minimal classical music, and Celia kept returning to the computer screen to find out what she was hearing: Bach's unaccompanied cello suites, Schubert's piano impromptus, and newer works by Steve Reich and Hauschka.

Celia came to understand the bookstore as an act of civilized defiance on Lippa's part. Space was begrudgingly given to the bestsellers and the mass-market successes, but that was not the customer she wanted to attract. Most of the store was devoted to enormous selections of literature, art, philosophy, and history, with subsections that were even more highbrow:

criticism, cultural studies, performance theory, and linguistics. Celia figured she might have won the job because even if she wasn't as refined as all these subjects, at least she didn't look mass-market herself. Realizing this, she took care to dress the part. A few times Lippa complimented Celia on her outfits, and on her fourth day of work Lippa presented her with an unconstructed cropped blazer made of moss-colored crushed velvet.

"It's by Romeo Gigli from back in the eighties. No one will design clothes like this ever again." Lippa sighed, holding it so Celia could slip her arms into the sleeves.

"It—it's gorgeous," Celia stammered, looking down at her arms. "Maybe I should just borrow it?"

"No, it's yours." Lippa admired it on her for a moment. "I haven't worn it in years. The sleeves are too long for me. It practically begged me to give it to you."

Lippa's attention shifted to the two women who were coming into the store. She left Celia to greet them, and Celia ran her hand over the soft fabric of the jacket, marveling at the gift. Lippa clustered together with the other two women. They looked like a trio of tiny birds as they linked arms and chatted. Celia gathered that the women were more than customers, and she smiled when they peeked over Lippa's shoulder at her. They retreated to the end of an aisle to continue their conversation.

Celia decided the jacket was Lippa's way of telling her she approved of Celia's style at the bookstore, and she thanked the stars to have found a job where her newfound style was encouraged.

The clientele at Lippa's was pleasant and Celia enjoyed helping them, but the evenings were a little slow, so she perused the shelves, finding treasure after treasure to explore. In the fine art section, she pulled down a volume of Mark Rothko's paintings and had a delicious moment of déjà vu. The paintings with yellow reminded her of the golden gingko trees outside Suburban. She spent a few shifts with it at the front counter, and when she received her first paycheck she purchased the book and brought it home, putting it up on the shelf in her room to keep her sketchbooks company.

Her mother noticed it. "You like Mark Rothko?"

"I do. I wish I could see his paintings in person."

"You did, when you were little. There was a retrospective at the National Gallery, and you saw the entire thing from a stroller. Most of them are really large. They take over your whole field of vision. It's interesting that you like him, since your art is so different from his."

"I know. It's pretty much the opposite. I think that's why I love it so much." Celia wondered if anyone in the Rosary liked Mark Rothko.

midnight to midnight

ON A BRIGHT SEPTEMBER afternoon, Celia thought if she could go back and meet up with the girl she had been in July, her two selves might not recognize each other. She spent her days differently. She thought about the world differently. She carried herself differently. She spoke to people differently. She wanted different things. At night Celia thumbed through the book of reproductions of Mark Rothko's paintings. She read the preface, about how each painting had an emotional resonance that verged on the spiritual, and remembered Marco's comment about Diaboliques being like church. He hadn't been serious, but she understood how it was true, in a way. Celia had seen a quote on Liz's notebook, from John Updike: *You must imagine your life, and then it happens*. She agreed. That was exactly what the Rosary did, and what she was trying to do, too, now. Liz used the cover of her notebook as a personal graffiti wall, and she had filled it with quotes from literary authors like Updike that Celia carefully transcribed into her own sketchbook.

"Have you read all these books?" she had asked Liz.

"Well, not all of them came from books—the Edith Wharton one is from one of her letters." Liz pointed it out:

The human heart is insatiable, and I didn't know, my own, I didn't know! "I've probably gotten half of these from books I've read. The others have come from other people, or from reading the quote somewhere. They make me want to be a better writer."

As each Friday approached, Celia felt the growing buzz of anticipation for Diaboliques. She spent the week working on the new person she was becoming—stylish, a little mysterious, refined in whatever way it was possible for a sophomore in high school to be refined—and then she returned with her friends to the ideal place, Diaboliques, to see how her new persona felt. The music, the beautiful people, the sense of exclusivity—she loved it all.

Her fascination with the Leopard, as she'd secretly nicknamed the brooding gray-eyed boy who stared at her each week at Diaboliques, continued unchanged. He wasn't spotted, of course, but he was lean and powerful, regal and untamed. Even though Regine had insisted the boy wasn't a regular, he seemed like a fixture on the far side of the dance floor, always keeping his distance. Celia would find him across the room and they would stare for a moment at each other, making no gesture, no expression. And she would leave it at that and turn back to her friends. Except her heart beat faster, and she had to work harder to keep her expression cool and impassive.

As they were ascending to the top floor on their way to Patrick's room on Celia's fourth visit, she began to think about seeing the boy again, in his usual place across the room. Celia was in the front of the group this time, having realized no one was going to threaten her at Diaboliques, no matter how intimidating they looked. She enjoyed feeling confident. It made her want to do other confident things.

When she reached the crowded landing she turned back to the others just as a tall figure passed between her and them. Celia stepped back to give him room and realized a moment too late it was the Leopard. It was the closest by far he had ever come to her, and she felt a strange charge like a cloud of static electricity brushing against her as he walked by. If he had seen her, he didn't stop. She turned to see his broad shoulders moving away from her as he made his way through the door into Patrick's room. The Rosary were watching her expectantly, and Celia felt her confidence sputter inside her like a balloon losing air.

"Are you going to pass out, like that girl at school?" Brenden asked, his eyes laughing.

"Are you ever going to talk to him?" Marco asked her when they were inside Patrick's room, safely across the dance floor from the Leopard. "Are you waiting for the clouds to part, for some kind of sign?"

Celia had regained her cool. "Maybe he's waiting for a change in the weather, too. I don't know what I would say."

"I have a feeling you've thought about what you would say to him."

"Maybe. But what happens? I find out he's a jerk? Or we talk, and it starts out nice, but something goes wrong and then I don't have this handsome fantasy guy staring at me anymore?"

"You sound like someone who has already crashed a handful of relationships, not someone who's never had one," Marco said. "Don't be so pessimistic."

"I don't mean to be pessimistic. But I'm okay with this. I *am*. In case you haven't noticed, I am not the fastest girl you've ever met. I don't think I'll ever be the kind of girl who plays with love."

"Who said anything about love? How about some old-fashioned flirting? I'd just hate for him to lose interest because you didn't give him any encouragement."

"Oh, I'm supposed to encourage him?"

"Just a little." Marco grinned, pinching his thumb and forefinger together. "Don't worry. I won't tell Regine and Liz," he said. "If you want, I'd be happy to distract them."

"I don't know. I kind of like it like this," Celia said. "Everything is mysterious here."

"Including you." Marco held up his thumbs and forefingers to make a frame and peered at her through them like a photographer setting up a shot. "Well, if you change your mind, let me know."

In the safety of real life, away from Diaboliques, Celia liked to daydream about the Leopard. She did think he admired her, even though she didn't have a clear idea what was supposed to happen next. She couldn't decide if she should be concerned. After all, the Leopard looked as though he easily could throw her over his shoulder and walk away with her, but she couldn't find anything threatening in his stare. Celia really liked that he was so tall. She loved the idea of actually looking up into his steely eyes, if she ever stood close to him. And she could make herself blush simply by thinking about the way his clothes fit his athletic body, something she never could have brought herself to say out loud, even to Marco.

What would happen if the Leopard ever spoke to her? She couldn't imagine his voice, but she could visualize him walking smoothly down the stairs from Diaboliques and out into the street and then climbing into some dark car, perhaps an old European model, forest green, which he drove to a secluded house, maybe sitting up until the late hours watching foreign films. Her fantasy went off the rails at some point, and she could no longer recognize the tall, quiet boy across the dance floor in it, but she kept trying, whenever she had a spare moment.

The Leopard took up a regular presence in Celia's thoughts during the week now, as well. The chemistry class took their field trip to the local water purification plant, and on the bus Mariette quickly noticed that Celia's thoughts were elsewhere.

"What did you say?" Celia asked her when Mariette's voice broke through her daydream.

"I *asked* you if you'd ever seen any of Pedro Almodóvar's movies. What are you thinking about? Or should I say, about *whom* are you thinking?" she asked.

"A guy I've seen at the club I go to on Fridays."

"Diaboliques?"

"How did you know?" Celia was startled.

"Just a guess, based on your friends. I've never gone," Mariette said. Celia was relieved, and then felt guilty for it. "What's his name?"

"I don't know. I haven't talked to him. We just stare at each other."

"That's cool." Mariette smiled and looked out the bus window. "Maybe you'll talk to him soon."

"Maybe." Celia looked up at Mr. Sumeletso as he came walking down the aisle of the bus. He smiled pleasantly at her, and she smiled back.

Confident she had Celia's attention, Mariette began to chatter. "So, I'm trying to memorize the periodic table, but I can't decide: does it make more sense to do them in order? One is hydrogen; two is helium; three is lithium; four is beryllium. Or if it's better to know them by columns because they share properties, like the halogens: nine is fluorine; seventeen is chlorine; thirty-five is bromine; fifty-three is iodine . . ."

Celia rolled her eyes and let her thoughts wander again. She liked the way the Leopard took the whole Diaboliques scene on his own terms, leaving the theatricality of it to the others, the Rosary included. She liked the way he kept his distance from her—except for that one intoxicating near miss—while always making it clear he was interested. Mariette had fallen silent again, and Celia glanced over at her. Her lab partner had raised her hand to the bus window and was touching it absentmindedly with her index finger. At each tap, ice crystals flared out across the glass, only to sublimate away a moment later. Celia didn't say anything.

scary monsters

As SEPTEMBER WORE ON, the first cold snap of the season brought out new elements of the Rosary's wardrobes for Celia to admire. "Best cover version." Liz looked around the lunch table, a large stone-encrusted cross hanging from a chain around her neck over a chunky black turtleneck sweater. "I say Echo and the Bunnymen's cover of 'People Are Strange' by the Doors."

"Too faithful. Martin Gore's version of 'Gone' by the Comsat Angels," Ivo suggested. His knit blazer had cables running down the sleeves.

"Siouxsie and the Banshees' cover of 'Trust in Me' from *Jungle Book*. Actually, that whole album of covers," Regine said. She wore a dark wool dress with a series of kilt pins closing it down the front.

"Cocteau Twins' version of 'Frosty the Snowman,'" Brenden said distractedly, paging through a catalog. The wide knot on his necktie filled the space between his collar and the V-neck of his marled sweater.

Ivo looked over Brenden's shoulder. "You're really going to get a class ring?"

"Yeah." Brenden smiled a little sheepishly. "I know it's kitsch, but I want one."

"So, that curse you thought was happening, on sophomore girls?" Liz turned to Celia. "It seems you're not the only one."

"Really?" Celia thought Liz was toying with her.

"What are you talking about?" Ivo asked.

Regine was happy to explain. "Remember when Elsie got stung in the parking lot on the first day of school? It was the day *before* her birthday. Then somebody noticed that the other four girls who've turned sixteen since school started have all had bad things happen on the days before *their* birthdays. Lacie passed out in the science wing on the day before her birthday, and they finally figured out she had mono. She'll be out for the rest of the semester. Tillie had an epileptic seizure, Louisa got glass in her eye and scratched her cornea really badly, and Carol got her hair caught in a fan in shop class—all on the days before their birthdays."

"Who is naming these girls?" Ivo said dismissively.

"Their parents, I would imagine," Liz offered, and exchanged smirks with her brother.

"It's probably just a coincidence," Celia said.

"Or your friend Mariette could be casting spells on people," Brenden said, making googly eyes at Celia and grinning.

"I never should have said anything about Mariette." Celia smiled helplessly. She was pretty sure her friends didn't think Mariette really was a witch. It was such a strange thing to think, anyway, but Mariette probably didn't interest the Rosary enough for them to give her that much thought. The conversation made Celia realize she was fiddling with the lock on Pandora's box. If anyone else witnessed the inexplicable things

Mariette did, it couldn't end well for Mariette. Celia hoped Mariette would drop back off the Rosary's radar.

The birthday curse, however, had become a popular topic of speculation around school. It was sensational and ominous, and since there weren't many facts, people felt free to embellish them as they saw fit. When another girl slipped and fell down the stairs on the day before her birthday, knocking out a tooth on the way, the curse was accepted as fact. Soon a list of girls with upcoming sixteenth birthdays was compiled and circulated, and it was taken for granted the girls on the list were at risk. The next girl who reached the eve of her sixteenth birthday spent the day under heavy scrutiny.

"The poor thing. I'd feel like I was living in an aquarium," Mariette said, glancing over at the girl in question that afternoon in chemistry lab.

"It's ridiculous," Celia said. "People are ridiculous." She was bored because they were going to finish their experiment early, as usual. Mr. Sumeletso was standing at the next table over, his hands on his hips as he advised their classmates. Celia picked up her pencil and idly began to sketch him from the back. She roughed in his shoulders and arms with a few lines and had started on the curl of his right hand when he flinched and pulled his hand up to his face as though he had been bitten. Celia didn't see an insect flying away from him, and she wondered what had happened.

Her thoughts were disrupted by an explosion. A beaker shattered on the birthday girl's burner two tables away, and the classroom erupted in shouts and screams. Mr. Sumeletso rushed to the girl and hauled her over to the big sink to rinse her eyes and skin. "Call nine-one-one! And someone go to the office!" he bellowed as the lacerations on the girl's arms began to bloom red. Mariette and Celia stood back with most of their classmates, stunned into silence. Mr. Sumeletso wrapped the crying girl's arms in towels and took her downstairs, and in a few minutes they heard the ambulance wailing toward the school.

"You know, I would be so on edge from being watched like that, I'd probably blow something up, too," Celia said as they returned to their experiment.

"I don't know. There could be something to the whole curse thing," Mariette said, her tone more serious than Celia was used to hearing it.

"You think there is?"

"Well, it's seven for seven now, which is a bit more than a coincidence, right?" Mariette brightened up. "At least my birthday isn't until May, and you're not until April. So I guess we don't have to be too concerned for a while, hm?"

Celia nodded, watching Mariette casually toss solutions together, marveling that even an accident two tables away wasn't enough to make her more cautious.

"Hey, do you want to hang out on Saturday? We could go get ice cream sundaes."

"Oh, I would, but I have to work at the bookstore." Celia thought it would have been nice. She hoped Mariette didn't feel like she was avoiding her.

CELIA WAS SURPRISED WHEN REGINE announced that the Rosary would be attending the first school dance of the year. "You guys go to school dances? Really?"

"We do. It's not nearly as much fun as Diaboliques, but I guess it is fun, in its own way," Regine replied. "The student council is expected to attend, so Brenden has to be there, and we go to keep him company."

"Most of the music is terrible, although sometimes Brenden convinces the DJ to play something cool, and then we all get to dance while everyone else looks confused," Liz said, smiling. Celia thought she could imagine it, and smiled along.

"We set ourselves apart from most people around here," Ivo said, "but we are part of the school, and I think some people almost expect us to show up. We are pretty well known, after all."

"I don't know about that," Brenden said. "It's a touch egocentric, isn't it?"

"We're in high school. Of course we're egocentric," Ivo replied matter-of-factly. "And there's no doubt in my mind everyone here knows who we are."

"I don't think that translates to people hoping we're going to show up at a dance," Brenden countered.

"Anyway, we'll leave as soon as Brenden can get away, and go straight to Diaboliques," Regine said. "No school function is worth missing Diaboliques."

The school dance matched up with Celia's memory of the ninth grade dances she'd fled—far more juvenile than Diaboliques, and in no way picturesque. The difference was that this time it didn't matter to her. She easily could remember the slow-motion panic she had felt before, lost in her own thicket of doubt in the darkened cafeteria of her old school, standing alone, then leaving alone, going home and crying and wanting to die . . . Now the kids flailing around, clothes askew, only made her long for the sophisticated darkness of Diaboliques. She held court with the Rosary on the first two bleachers off to one side in the darkened gym, and they watched the proceedings idly, rarely bothering to comment. Mr. Sumeletso stood in a cluster of bored teachers making small talk by the doors, and Celia thought of Mariette, who had told Celia she wasn't coming, mumbling something about starting a quilt. Mariette's list of interests grew constantly—unicycling, bonsai, meditation, sign language—but they all were things she did alone. Celia wondered if Mariette had any friends, and then it occurred to her that Mariette probably considered Celia a friend. She decided that was true.

Liz was staring across the gymnasium at Skip the football player, who was dancing with his date. Celia traded a knowing look with Marco. But in the next moment the dance came to an abrupt halt when a girl slipped and fell on her arm. Word spread that her wrist was broken, along with the news tomorrow was her sixteenth birthday. She'd been exuberantly celebrating having made it through her curse day unscathed.

"Still a coincidence?" Liz said to Ivo as they waited for the music to start again.

"It's freaky, but would she have been jumping around so much if she weren't relieved about dodging a curse?" Ivo said.

"That's eight for eight," Brenden said.

"Maybe we should ask Mariette," Ivo said.

"This has nothing to do with Mariette," Celia protested. They all looked at her and she weakly added, "She's not even here." She wasn't sure what to think about Mariette and the curse, but she didn't like to hear her friends impugn her other friend.

Marco didn't let it go. "If she's a witch, would she have to be here to curse someone? She could be at home putting pins in a doll or something."

"We should conduct an investigation of our own, to see if there's anything suspicious," Ivo suggested.

"Anything suspicious where?"

"In her locker."

Liz looked at him incredulously. "Are you kidding? Even if she *is* a witch, do you think she keeps her grimoire in her locker?"

"Well, this dance is particularly boring. What else are we going to do?"

"I could go request something," Brenden said.

Ivo looked around at them with an uncharacteristic gleam in his eye. "I'll get a bolt cutter from shop and meet you in the sophomore hall."

They got up, and Celia appealed to Marco, "We shouldn't do this. It's not right, and it doesn't make any sense anyway. You guys don't really think she's a witch, do you?"

"No, nobody really thinks Mariette is a witch." Marco sighed as the others walked out of the gym ahead of them. "This is a flimsy excuse to make a lame dance more interesting. I'll tell you what's going to happen. We're going to go up there, and Ivo's going to show up and say that the shop was locked, and that'll be the end of it. If he even goes to the shop in the first place. If he even knows where the shop *is*. We're going to walk around in the dark hallways and startle each other, and then it's going to be over, and we'll have wasted half an hour before we can leave. The thing with Mariette is just an excuse. It's an empty dare, like running up Boo Radley's front walk. I promise."

"Please tell me who Boo Radley is," Celia said.

"Junior lit. You'll read it." Marco smiled, linking arms with Celia. "C'mon."

They made their way up to the sophomore hall, which was darkened and still. Up ahead were the silhouettes of Regine,

Brenden, and Liz. Marco crept up and tickled Liz, who shrieked.

"Stop that! Where's her locker?" Liz asked.

"Over there." Celia reluctantly led them to it, but she was confused when she got there. "I thought it was this one."

"Without a lock? Are you sure?"

"It's fourth from the left—yeah, I'm sure this is hers. I don't know why there isn't a lock on it."

"Well, this will make our job easier," Liz said. "Who wants to open it?"

They stood there looking at each other in the darkness. The exit signs glowed like jack-o'-lanterns over the stairwell doors at either end of the hall. "You should do it, Celia. You can always tell her you needed to borrow her notes or something."

"I don't want to," Celia said. "She's done nothing wrong, and she's always been nice to me." Marco gave her a look that said, *Humor them.*

Ivo arrived. "The shop is locked. I guess the Bloodhound Gang is done for the night."

"Her locker is unlocked." Brenden pointed.

"So, did you open it?" Ivo asked.

"Not yet. Celia doesn't want to do it because she has a sense of integrity," Liz said, and her approving tone reassured Celia.

"Well, I can respect that. It was my idea, so I should do it," Ivo said. He went up to the locker and tried to lift the latch. "I think it's stuck." He jiggled the latch but couldn't get it to rise. "It's jammed."

"Maybe that's why it's not locked. She got a new locker," Liz said.

They stood there looking at the latch. Marco had failed to

predict this outcome. Celia knew she had seen Mariette open that locker earlier that same day, but she didn't want to prolong this excursion, so she wasn't about to share that information. Brenden took a turn at the latch, and then Marco, but no one could open the locker.

"Oh well, I guess we're done," Ivo said. "But you should keep an eye on her, Celia. If bad things are happening and you've seen her levitating, she has to be considered a suspect in our curse investigation."

"I haven't seen her levitating!" Celia laughed in spite of herself. She wasn't sure if she was more surprised that Ivo had made a joke or that he'd looked directly at her.

They took the long way back to the gymnasium, and then Brenden decided it was time to make his play with the DJ. "Okay, Book of Love, coming right up," he said. When the song started, Marco pulled Celia to her feet, saying, "Will you, won't you, will you, won't you, will you join the dance?" She knew he was trying to distract her after the strange excursion upstairs, but she shook her head, not ready to try it, even here. The rest of them went out to the floor, and Celia enjoyed the way the rest of the students looked on in uncertainty as the Rosary danced.

"It's amazing how none of these people will dance to a song unless they know it," Liz said, passing close by Celia. The whole scene was the exact opposite of Diaboliques. Here the Rosary were the exception, not the rule. They were rebels instead of compatriots. The five of them had their moment, and then the DJ returned to the familiar format and the Rosary evacuated the dance floor as it filled back up. *It's almost as though they gave a performance*, Celia thought.

8

unknown pleasures

ON MONDAY MORNING CELIA positioned herself in a doorway with a view of Mariette's locker, which was still missing the lock. October was a few days away, and on the classroom door across from Celia a cardboard witch with green skin and a mangy broom ogled her. Soon enough Mariette arrived. Celia watched her touch her finger to the front of the locker, quickly tracing a symbol before she easily lifted the latch and opened the door.

Celia felt tangled in a web of concerns. Even though she had done her best to suppress the idea with her friends, Celia wondered: Did Mariette really have supernatural powers? Was there really a curse? Did Mariette have anything to do with it? Should she confront Mariette? Or should she try to protect her if someone else became suspicious of her? Did Celia have any real ability to protect her, even if she wanted to?

That night at the front desk at the bookstore Celia half-heartedly thumbed through books on witchcraft, hoping to clarify anything at all. Lippa's two friends arrived, and as they passed the front desk the three of them noticed Celia's choice of reading material.

"Are you interested in the occult?" Lippa asked while her friends looked on.

Celia thought of a plausible answer. "Not really. I have a friend who is, and I was just curious. Are you?"

"In a roundabout way, we are. We are conspiracy theorists," Lippa said, sharing a smile with her friends. "We like to study all those stories about things that aren't easily explained: the occult, hermetism, alchemy. Fascinating, aren't they?"

Celia thought Lippa could join the Rosary, if she was going to rattle off mysterious lists like that. "I really don't know much about those things."

"You should join the Troika." Lippa gestured at herself and her two friends, who peered around her at Celia, their faces crinkling into curious smiles. "We like to read about them."

"The Troika?"

"Every group has to have a name, doesn't it? C'mon, ladies, I have the tea on in back. Let us know if you're interested, Celia." Lippa took her friends back to her office.

Celia opened an encyclopedia of Wicca, but she was distracted by what Lippa had said. The Troika studied things like witchcraft, but did that mean they believed it was real? Might Lippa be able to help her figure out Mariette? She heard the bookstore door open again, and Celia closed the book. A tall man dressed in black was entering, and her heart turned over in her chest. It was the Leopard. He noticed her immediately and came up to the counter.

"Hi," he said. In the dim store he looked exactly as he did at Diaboliques. It felt as if he carried some of the darkness of the club into the bookstore with him.

"Hi," she said, setting aside the book, feeling nervous, hoping she wouldn't sound nervous, trying to keep her thoughts from running off in all directions.

"I wondered if I'd ever get to speak to you." His voice was a little deeper than she'd expected, and he pronounced his words carefully, as though he didn't speak very often.

"Really?" Now that he was only a few feet from her, the counter separating them, he was bigger than she remembered. She looked up into his eyes and thought she saw sparks among the gray of his irises.

"Maybe not. I'm Tomasi." He offered his hand a little awkwardly.

"I'm Celia." His hand was smooth and warm around hers, and she felt herself blushing.

"So, you work here? This is a great store."

"It is. I've only been here for a month or so."

"You like to read?"

"I do, but I haven't really read anything."

"I know how you feel. The more I read, the more I realize I've barely scratched the surface." He looked around, and she was in agony about how stilted the conversation was.

"All my friends say that, too. They're all older, and they make references I don't get. They mentioned a book called *Boo Radley*, but I can't find it."

"He's a character in *To Kill a Mockingbird*," Tomasi said, and she was grateful he didn't care that she didn't know. "That's a great book."

"Now you're finding out just how much I haven't read," Celia said, reddening again.

"We're young. We've barely begun to read," he said, his voice warming. "We have our whole lives to read all this." Celia thought he seemed both at home and uneasy there in the store. She felt it too. This place suddenly felt unfamiliar with him in it.

"I guess. What do you like?"

"My problem is I like everything," Tomasi said. "I read something older, like Thomas Hardy, and I love it. I read something new, like Salman Rushdie, and I love it. I read someone like James Joyce, and I don't think I understand it completely, but I love it."

"I haven't read any of them," Celia said.

"They're all here." Tomasi lifted one arm toward the stacks, silent centurions standing guard over the conversation.

"Would you recommend a book for me to read?" Celia asked.

"Hm." Tomasi thought a moment. "*The Awakening*, by Kate Chopin. It's not too long, but it's brilliant. I remember I finished it on a bus, and I was so amazed, I almost turned to the stranger next to me and started telling her about it." Tomasi strode off toward the literature section, and to Celia he was still the Leopard. In his dark jeans and close-fitting black sweater, he looked like an off-duty soldier from a foreign army. She tried to imagine him riding a bus. Soon he returned with a copy of the book, which he handed to her.

"Thank you. I will definitely read this." On the cover a woman in white stared directly out of a painting at Celia. Celia wanted to study Tomasi's face, his eyes, but it was so much easier to look down at this woman's pensive expression or to examine the mottled surface of the counter.

There was a moment when she didn't know what to say, and it seemed as if he didn't, either. A Philip Glass piece roiled in the speakers overhead. "You like Diaboliques?" he finally asked.

She looked up and got to see the mercury in his eyes again. "I do, I love it. I just found out about it, about all of that, the music, everything, this fall."

"I just started going, too. I like it, but I don't know if I take it as seriously as the other people there."

"Maybe that's a good thing," Celia said, feeling a little guilty, as though she were betraying the Rosary somehow. "I mean, I like dressing up for it, and how it almost feels like a show, but sometimes at home I just jump around to the songs I like."

"I know! When he plays something like 'This Corrosion' by Sisters of Mercy, people should go nuts. You know, the one with the New York Choral Society at the beginning, all dramatic and religious, and then it just blows up."

"I love that song."

"It's kind of an overplayed classic, and I don't listen to it at home anymore, but in a club, when it's really loud and everyone's reaching up toward the lights like they're in some kind of ecstasy, it's pretty awesome."

"I'm still learning about all the music."

"It's what keeps me coming back. And I like seeing you." Tomasi looked uncomfortable the moment he said it. "Well, I'll see you Friday," he mumbled, and strode out the door. Celia said goodbye, but she wasn't sure if he heard her.

He'd gone like a wind. She caught his profile as it passed outside the shop window, and she was tempted to go to the door to try to glimpse him on his way down the street. Instead, she looked down at *The Awakening* on the counter in front of her, proof he really had been there. The woman on the cover stared back up at her. *Well*, Celia thought, *his name is Tomasi. I like his voice, and he doesn't waste words. He wears the same clothes during the day that he does at Diaboliques. I wouldn't have guessed he liked literature, but I like that he does. Did he come in here to buy something?* After this meeting, Tomasi was even more mysterious to Celia, and she didn't expect she would feel any different under his gaze come Friday. But she would speak with him this time, and that gave her an immediate thrill. *Just wait until Regine sees . . .*

The gentle clicking of Lippa's gum told Celia she had come up next to her. Lippa noticed the book on the counter. "He's not your boyfriend. You were too nervous. But you like him."

"I don't know him very well at all," Celia heard herself protest, and knew she only was proving Lippa right.

"You don't have to know someone to like him. Sometimes it's easier if you don't know him at all—at least, for a while. The two of you definitely look like you're going to the same party, though." The expression made Celia smile. "So, what do you think?"

"I think—I'd like to talk to him some more," Celia said. "We'd never spoken before."

"Very mysterious." Lippa raised an eyebrow. "I like that. I like mysterious things."

"I think you are mysterious," Celia said.

"Yes, but you have to be careful. When you are young and mysterious, men write songs about you. When you are old and mysterious, boys throw stones at you." Lippa tilted her head at Celia and then went back to the office.

READING *THE AWAKENING* WAS like hearing *Tinderbox*. Celia was absorbed into its world and held, transfixed. She finished the book in a few days, and she was so shocked by the ending, she started all over again, trying to make sense of it. If the books she'd read before then were the equivalent of those coarse high school dances, *The Awakening* was in league with Diaboliques. The primary reason Celia hadn't fallen in love with reading, she realized, was that she simply hadn't read the right books. Each new song, and now this new book, made her yearn to find more. At the bookstore Celia stood in the literature section as though it were a newly discovered shrine, wishing she could remember the other authors Tomasi had mentioned. Overwhelmed by the possibilities, she finally decided to pick a book by an author whose last name began with "A," and then "B," and read her way through the alphabet. It was arbitrary, but at least it helped her to narrow down her options. Jane Austen was the winner.

"Have you read *The Awakening*, by Kate Chopin?" she asked Regine in the car.

"No, is it new?"

"No, it was published in 1899. It's so good I read it twice."

"What's it about?"

"It's hard to explain without giving it away. A woman who won't accept the limitations of her life," Celia said.

"Will you lend it to me?" Regine said.

"Sure." Celia slipped it out of her bag and presented it.

"See, I didn't have to hold my breath very long before I learned something from you." Regine smiled at her. "I wonder if Liz has read this. How did you find out about it?"

"Someone at the bookstore recommended it," Celia said. She deliberated for a moment and then plunged in. "You know the guy at Diaboliques who stares at me?"

"Yeah?"

"He came into the bookstore last week. He loves to read."

"Wow! You talked to him? He recommended this? What's

his name?" Regine was genuinely curious, and Celia thought her tone was partly protective, partly alarmed that something interesting had happened to her when Regine hadn't been there to see it.

"Tomasi."

"Beautiful name. Where does he go to school?"

"We didn't talk about that. We didn't get to talk that long."

"Well, I guess we'll have to meet Tomasi on Friday," Regine said. "I just know there are some creepy guys at Diaboliques. You know that's why I was so cautious, right?"

"I understand," Celia said. "It's okay. I like that you guys look out for me."

9

the downward spiral

DURING THAT WEEK, AS October pinched off the last warm afternoons, everyone at Suburban buzzed about the upcoming eve of the next girl's sixteenth birthday. She was a bit dramatic about it, and spent her curse day shrieking at any sudden movement, but by the end of the day nothing had happened. Everyone waited for the next morning to find out if she had broken the curse. She arrived in splendor and paraded around, collecting accolades and trying to capitalize on having thwarted a superstition, even though she had no idea how she had done it.

"Leave it to the class slut to break the curse," Regine said archly.

"That's not nice!" Liz said.

Regine stood her ground. "Okay, leave it to the girl who *has a reputation* for being the class slut to break the curse."

"I'm sure that has nothing to do with it," Liz said.

"I've heard she *is* kind of a slut," Celia whispered to Marco.

"So is the curse broken, then?" Brenden asked.

"Sure, the curse is broken. The stupidest thing I've ever heard," Liz said. "Forget that. I want to know about—what's his name? Tomasi? I hear you've started a book club with your new friend from Diaboliques."

"No," Celia giggled. "He just recommended a book to me."

"I've only had it two days and I'm already halfway through it. You should borrow it when I'm done," Regine told Liz. "I don't think I've ever read anything like it."

"The end will blow your mind," Celia added.

"So does this mean the embargo is lifted and she can talk to the poor guy?" Marco asked.

"That's not what 'embargo' means," Regine said. "But yes, I'm looking forward to meeting him."

"Why should you meet him?" Brenden said. "He hasn't recommended a book for *you*."

"Hey, you know perfectly well why we were telling her to be careful. And it's not like we're just going to turn her loose now. I'd do the exact same thing again." Regine sniffed.

"Okay," Brenden said, winking at Celia.

She was tickled by how they all had taken such an interest in this development. It would have been enough to savor her experience with Tomasi on her own, but it was more delicious to share it with them. Celia thought about telling Mariette that she had been right when she had predicted Celia would speak with Tomasi soon.

But in chemistry Mariette surprised Celia by bringing up the curse before Celia had the chance to say anything. "So, that girl who turned sixteen without anything happening to her—she's, well, sexually active?" Mariette asked.

"Sexually active?" Celia tried to tease her for being so clinical, but Mariette didn't take the bait. "She has a reputation, but I don't really know. Why?"

"Just wondering."

"Do you think it has something to do with why nothing happened to her? The curse, I mean?"

"Maybe. Or maybe she figured out some way to avoid it."

"So, maybe it's over?"

"Maybe. Somehow I don't think so," Mariette said, and Celia was shocked to see her silent for a while, lost in thought. When Mariette spoke again, it was to change the subject. "Has anyone from the other chemistry class asked you to tutor them?"

"A couple people have asked me for help with homework problems. Why?"

"I heard the other class is not doing well—like, everyone. They're trying to say it's Mr. Sumeletso's fault, that he's too hard. But our class is doing fine, so that doesn't really make sense. I heard his Chem Two classes are struggling, too." They looked across the room at Mr. Sumeletso, who was setting up a demonstration of vapor pressure. He smiled amiably at the students as they gathered around him.

"My friend Regine is in his Chem Two class, and she's completely stressed out about it. It's weird. I mean, he expects a lot, but we're doing fine. I don't think anyone in our class is failing, are they?"

"Not that I know of. It is weird."

THAT FRIDAY THE ROSARY ARRIVED at Diaboliques, and Celia couldn't decide if she was more nervous to see Tomasi again or to see what would happen when he met her friends. She could imagine it only being awkward. The way their conversation had gone at the bookstore, she and Tomasi might as well have been on stilts, and it wouldn't be any easier with five people watching them. Once Celia told him all their names, the conversation probably would die a swift death. Then again, Regine probably would interrogate him, which would be mortifying, but at least that would prevent everyone from standing around staring into space. Celia resigned herself to all of it because she really wanted to see Tomasi, to attempt to talk more with him, maybe without blushing. Maybe she would touch him again. Not shaking hands this time. She might touch his shoulder or something . . .

But Tomasi wasn't there when they made it upstairs at the club. And as the night wore on and he didn't appear, Regine gave Celia a hard time about it. "Didn't he say he was going to be here?"

"No, he didn't. I just assumed because he's been here every week," Celia said.

"Ignore her," Marco said when Regine had gone to dance. "That girl has her own plan for the world, and she spends way too much time trying to get the world to conform to it." His voice turned conspiratorial. "You should have seen her at homecoming. It didn't matter what Ivo did, as long as he was standing next to her. She had the time of her life."

"I don't understand—are they dating or not?"

"The simplest way to put it is this: she's dating him, and he's not dating her back," Marco said. "Don't tell me you can't see it."

Celia knew what Marco meant, and she struggled to understand how a smart, confident girl like Regine could cultivate such a large emotional blind spot. She also wondered why Ivo would lead Regine on, and why the rest of them were content to ignore this large, dark elephant that crashed around the two of them every time they were together. Celia feared it was inevitable Regine would have her heart broken.

Soon, though, Celia's thoughts returned to her own disappointment. Fortunately the others had given up on Tomasi, and she could belabor it by herself. She wondered why he wasn't there. Perhaps he had just taken the night off. That excuse rang hollow, since he had been there consistently, every week before. It was the first time Celia had experienced Diaboliques without the Leopard watching her from the other side of the floor, and while it still was a magic place, it wasn't quite as miraculous without him.

CELIA HOPED TOMASI WOULD STOP in at the bookstore that week, but he didn't. And he wasn't at Diaboliques the next Friday, either. Celia regretted that she hadn't been forward enough to exchange phone numbers with him, but she knew it was foolish to reproach herself that way. It was a kind of courage she could muster only in hindsight. She reminded herself that she barely had carried on a somewhat intelligent conversation with him when they'd met, barely had managed to meet his gray stare when it was so close to her. She had taken for granted that she would see him at Diaboliques in a matter of days. And he had turned bashful and left so quickly . . .

Another week passed and Tomasi failed to return to Diaboliques. Though he had vanished, the curse reappeared just in time to catch the next girl on the birthday list completely off guard. The conventional wisdom at school had decreed confidently that the curse must have been broken by the girl who made it through unscathed—even though no one could explain why—and this next girl had expressed her relief to be safe from harm several times during the day before her birth-day. In seventh period, her appendix ruptured and she was carted off, and the school returned to a state of agitation. How had the other girl escaped the curse? Was there something girls could do to protect themselves? Instead of being exasper-ated by it all, this time Celia was a little more credulous, as though the exception had somehow proven the rule. In taking the curse seriously, Celia's interest in Mariette became more serious, too. All the unanswered questions Celia had pon-dered about her free-spirited friend returned to preoccupy her again.

In chemistry lab she watched Mariette, wishing she could read her mind. She couldn't think how to start a conversa-tion that would get Mariette to reveal the answers to her half-formed questions, and she didn't have the nerve to just come out with it and interrogate her, as she imagined Regine would. To make matters worse, Mariette was going on about her at-tempts to learn to play the dulcimer. When Mariette finally wound down, Celia asked, "What do you think of the curse?"

"I think there's definitely something going on, but I don't think it's a curse," Mariette said, not looking up as she shuffled chemicals around. Celia noticed how seriously Mariette an-swered the question, almost as if she had been expecting to be asked.

"What do you mean?"

"Well, a curse is just causing someone harm or misfortune. I can understand why people would call what's happening here a curse, because girls definitely are suffering harm or misfor-tune." Mariette filled a beaker with water and sloshed a little back into the sink before she was satisfied with the amount. "But I think there's more to it than that. I think there's someone who stands to *gain* something if something bad happens to a girl before she turns sixteen, and so that person keeps trying to make it happen."

"What do you mean, trying? It's happened every time except one," Celia said.

"Not if this isn't the intended result. I don't think the point is to hurt a girl," Mariette said.

"What is it, then?"

"I think the point is to kill her." Mariette looked Celia straight in the eye for a moment; then she turned back to the solution she was heating.

"Kill her?" Celia gasped. Mr. Sumeletso passed by and she dropped her voice, hoping he hadn't heard her. "You think someone is trying to kill girls at Suburban?"

"Not all of them, just one. And then that person will be rewarded when they succeed, though I don't know what the reward is."

"Who would reward someone for killing an innocent girl?" Celia stared at Mariette, who stared back, only shrugging. "Have you lost your mind?"

"You tell me," Mariette replied, partly amused and partly curt. "Clearly if you think there's a curse, you've considered the possibility something supernatural is happening. Well, I agree with you about that, but there's more to it than getting hurt before you turn sixteen. You asked me what I thought, and I told you."

Celia repeated Mariette's theory, in an attempt to consider it at face value. "So you think there is someone who believes killing a girl on the day before she turns sixteen will bring some kind of reward?" Around them their classmates labored at their experiments.

"Yes, some kind of power. The problem is, I don't think this person is very skilled at it, so the spells are harming girls, but they aren't strong enough to kill them."

"The person is casting spells?"

"Well, trying to. That's what I think."

"So this is, like, black magic or something? Do you believe in that?"

Mariette's curt amusement returned. "Doesn't a curse count as black magic? And weren't you prepared to believe there was a curse?"

"But people casting spells?"

"Someone casting spells in hopes of sacrificing a girl at a precise moment in her life, in order to gain some kind of supernatural reward. I'm just guessing," Mariette said. She blew her hair out of her eyes and picked up a pencil to make notes on the experiment, as though she had been humoring Celia with the entire conversation.

Celia kept staring at her, and eventually Mariette turned back to meet her gaze, daring her to pursue it further. But Celia lost her nerve. She couldn't bring herself to just come out and ask Mariette a question as insane as *Are you a witch?* She was disoriented by how serious Mariette was now, when usually she was so bubbly, so flighty. Celia wanted to believe that Mariette was a good, honest person, even if she suspected Mariette had secrets that were more significant than the type kept by most high school girls. But this conversation, almost completely made up of sentences Celia never would have expected to say or hear in real life, made her wonder things she never would have expected to wonder.

All afternoon she thought about it. As bizarre as her conversation with Mariette had been, Celia couldn't imagine that she was responsible for the bad things that were happening to their classmates. Maybe it was taking the path of least resistance, but Celia decided that for the moment, as strange and scary as things were, she had faith in Mariette. She didn't think she had much of a choice. And she knew for sure she couldn't speak of her suspicions to anyone, not even to anyone in the Rosary.

Celia guessed Mariette could tell she was struggling with all this, because it seemed as though she made an effort to alleviate Celia's concerns. A lock appeared on Mariette's locker, and during their next chemistry lab Mariette made a good show of measuring things properly. *If anything, it's for her own good*, Celia thought. *If other people notice the bizarre things she does, they may not be as timid as I am.*

When the eleventh girl in the sophomore class reached the eve of her birthday later that week, the social microscope was focused on her. She behaved as expected, spending the uneventful day flinching at every surprise and nervously feeling the glands in her throat. The next morning the girl triumphantly appeared, boasting that she'd gotten a paper cut but that couldn't really be enough to qualify for the curse, could it?

"I know you're going to crack on me for saying it, but she's kind of easy, too, isn't she?" Marco said.

"You're not the only one who's noticed," Regine said drily. "Is this whole thing going to ascend to the next order of magnitude of ridiculousness?"

"You mean the curse is only on fifteen-year-old *virgins?*" Brenden said.

Liz burst out laughing. "As if this weren't already the most absurd thing I'd ever heard!"

"I have nothing to add to this conversation," Ivo said, not looking up from his book.

"Well, if we were going to be scientific about this," Marco said slowly, reasoning his way though, "the next sophomore girl . . . with a birthday . . . who's a virgin . . . should have sex and see if she breaks the curse."

"And I've already heard that suggested three times today," Regine said. "Apparently we are living in some kind of tacky eighties horror film."

Liz corrected her. "In the tacky eighties horror films, it was the people who had sex who died and the virgins who survived."

"Who cares? Now every guy in school is going to start propositioning every girl who's about to turn sixteen, figuring if the girls want to avoid the curse, they're going to have to sleep with one of them." Regine rolled her eyes.

"Not every guy," Marco said, smiling at Brenden.

"And, statutory rape, anyone?" Ivo grumbled.

The story played out exactly as Regine had predicted: the next girl on the birthday list endured a week of open propositions and came close to a nervous breakdown. A few days before her curse day, a rumor flew around the school contending she had selected a stud and done the deed. When she made it to her birthday unscathed, the rumor was accepted as truth. Now the curse became topic number one at Suburban, expanding beyond the ranks of the students and into the faculty, and soon enough it made it home to the parents.

"Did you read this?" Celia's mother asked her, the letter from the principal in her hand.

"Yes," Celia said. "I don't know what to tell you."

"Do you feel like you're in any kind of danger?"

"No. Well, not now. My birthday's not for a while." Celia thought her answer was oversimplified, but she couldn't imagine trying to explain everything to her mother, so she left it at that.

"Why do people think having sex . . . Tell me this. Are you thinking of having sex? For any reason?" Her mother sat down across from her.

"Not really. Mom, I've never even kissed a boy."

"Okay. Maybe now wouldn't be the time to start," she said. "At least, not for a reason as ridiculous as this." She tossed the letter on the counter. "Dinner will be ready in ten minutes."

AT THE BEGINNING OF THE next chemistry class Mr. Sumeletso cleared his throat and looked nervously down at his crocodile loafers. "Oh god, is he really going to do this?" Mariette whispered to Celia. "And could he get some new clothes? He wears that plaid shirt and knit tie at least twice a week." Mr. Sumeletso began a halting speech.

"I don't really know how to address this," he started, staring out the window. "But it must be done. I'm sure your parents all have received the letter from Principal Spennicut by now . . . It seems many of you are under the impression there is some kind of curse here at school, on sophomore girls, at least. And many of you girls are considering, erm, losing your virginity as a means to escape whatever curse you think threatens you. Well, as scientists, I think we should apply the same scrutiny to these ideas that we do to our lab experiments."

Kill me now, Mariette wrote in her notebook.

Poor choice of words, Celia scribbled back.

Mr. Sumeletso became more comfortable as he slipped into abstract terminology. "We know that just because there appears to be a correlation between two things—in this case, some injuries and the birthdays of the injured—that in no way guarantees that one has a causal relationship with the other. In the same way, any characteristics—say, being sexually experienced—of the people who have not been injured at the predicted time cannot be assumed to have a causal relationship to their deviation from the predicted outcome."

No really, kill me now.

Okay, I'm with you.

He waded back into the uncomfortable part. "Maybe the most important thing to express to you is that having sex is a very important decision, and certainly not a decision you need to make anytime soon. It is by no means a decision you should make because of peer pressure based on a superstitious rumor. If you have any questions, our school nurse is always available to talk to you, or, if you are more comfortable, any member of the faculty . . ." Mr. Sumeletso trailed off, having found the end of his speech and rushed to it in relief.

"Look at him, praying no one comes to talk to him about sex," Mariette said under her breath. "I want to go ask him an anatomy question, just to watch him squirm."

"They probably told all the teachers with sophomore classes they had to talk about it," Celia said. "I can't imagine he'd have done that voluntarily."

That afternoon in the library no one in the Rosary had much work to do, and soon the dreaded topic found its way into their conversation. "Is it weird no one's doing anything about it?" Brenden asked. "We all count down to the next curse day, but is anyone trying to figure out if it can be stopped?"

"Are you saying we should reopen our curse investigation with our prime subject, Celia's friend Mariette?" Ivo asked.

"No!" Celia, Liz, and Marco said together.

"Because it went so well the first time?" Brenden asked.

"Have you seen her do anything else?" Regine asked Celia. "Anything . . ."

"Witchy?" Marco said mockingly.

"No!" Celia protested. "I must have been seeing things. There is nothing strange about her."

"Here's a better course of inquiry," Liz said. "So, Celia, your birthday is in April, right?" She asked in a low voice, just loudly enough for their table to hear. "If nothing changes between now and then, would you consider losing your virginity in order to escape the curse?"

"Why are you so sure Celia's a virgin?" Brenden whispered at Liz.

"I'm sorry, I was making an assumption." Liz looked at Celia expectantly.

"Can we talk about anything in the world besides my virginity?" Celia hoarsely pleaded.

"Okay, so she's a virgin," Liz whispered, turning back to the others. "I'm not trying to harass her. It just seems like this is going to come up eventually, so why not talk about it now?"

"If we're going to talk about Celia's sex life, we should all be prepared to talk about our own," Brenden whispered. "It's only fair."

"How about we don't talk about anyone's sex life?" Ivo said at nearly full volume, and the other five glared at him. He gave them a look of contempt and returned to his book.

"All right, then," Liz whispered. "I lost my virginity at the beginning of my sophomore year."

"Whoa, are we really doing this?" Marco said.

"You did?" Regine was astonished. "With whom?"

"You don't need to know with whom," Liz whispered. "It was a fling, and in the spirit of full disclosure, I haven't done it since."

"That's sad, Liz," Brenden murmured. "Don't you miss it?"

"Honestly? No. What about you? Is it safe to say you guys are hitting it?" Liz asked, wearing a smile that made it clear she was sure of the answer.

"Yes, it is safe to say that we are having sex," Brenden mumbled.

"Why are you embarrassed?" Marco asked him. He turned to the rest of them. "What do you want to know? Positions? How often? Places we've done it when you guys were there but you didn't realize we were doing it?"

"No, no, too much information!" Regine waved her hand in front of her face.

"What about you, then?" Liz asked Regine, returning the volume to a whisper.

"No, I haven't." Regine tried to be offhand, but she glanced at Ivo. "I'm not sure if I'm ready. When the time is right."

"What did you have in mind?" Marco asked.

"I don't know, nothing earthshattering, but something meaningful," Regine whispered. "Was it meaningful your first time?"

"It was earthshattering, my first time," Marco replied. "But I'm a guy, so I can see how that might be different."

"Congratulations, Brenden," Regine whispered.

"How do you know my first time was with him?" Marco asked, provoking reactions from everyone but Ivo. "It's all right—he knows if he was, and that's all I care about."

"How about you, Ivo?" Brenden asked.

"If divulging my sex life is a requirement for being in this conversation, I'll sit it out, thanks," Ivo said. This time he kept his voice down.

Liz turned back to Celia. "So, if you'll probably lose your virginity at some point during high school anyway, would you consider doing it to avoid a curse?"

"That sounds incredibly romantic," Regine scoffed.

"Except for a vague sentiment from Marco, there was nothing romantic about any of our descriptions of our first time. Well, I guess mine was, in a strange way," Liz said, almost to herself.

"It didn't sound romantic to me," Brenden whispered.

"You weren't there," Liz retorted. She asked Celia, "Is it important for your first time to be romantic? Do you want to be in love?"

"I—I hadn't given it much thought," Celia stammered.

"What do you think?"

"Don't do it just for the sake of doing it," Brenden whispered.

"And don't assume it's going to change your life," Liz added.

"Ouch," Celia said.

"It's definitely different when you care about the person," Marco said.

They all looked at her, and she felt pressured to come up with an answer. "I don't think it's likely I'm going to meet someone, form some kind of romantic relationship with him, and decide to lose my virginity with him in the next five months." Celia looked around, hoping for a tsunami, an airstrike, anything to change the subject.

"It could happen. What about Tomasi?" Liz asked.

"I haven't seen Tomasi since we talked in the bookstore. He may never come back to Diaboliques, for all I know."

"That's too bad," Brenden teased. "Is that a pattern for you? Meet a nice boy, have a nice conversation, boy disappears?"

"No." Celia wrinkled her forehead at him. "Or at least, I hope not."

"So we're back to my original question." Their conversation had grown louder, and Liz dropped her voice again. "If you're not expecting to lose your virginity in the context of some meaningful relationship, would you do it for any other reason? Say, to avoid a curse?"

"I—I . . ." Celia realized she was looking around at them, open-mouthed. She put her hands to her head.

"We've made quite an about-face, haven't we?" Marco chuckled. "Before, we were keeping all boys at ten paces from Celia, and now we're asking her to plan her deflowering like it's a flu shot."

"Promise me we won't talk about this again until April," Celia begged. "Who knows, if these accidents are still happening then, and a whole lot more girls have gotten hurt, maybe I'll feel different."

10

it'll end in tears

FOR EVERY GIRL WHO decided her virginity was not too precious to trade for a worry-free sixteenth birthday, there were four or five other girls who took the risk, and the general outcome, if not the specific result, was always the same. The virgins always suffered: dislocated shoulder, slipped disc, broken nose, torn Achilles tendon, diabetic coma. The titillating suspense gave way to beleaguered dread. The curse remained topic number one at Suburban, though, and the student body continued to check girls off the birthday list. Celia's mother had described to her the stilted parent/teacher conference that attempted to address the issue, but little had been accomplished. The adults only seemed to care whether or not students were having sex.

Nothing had changed for Celia. She still felt the anxiety, but she had no desire to act. When she considered what she might do, she didn't see many realistic options. She guessed there would be no shortage of candidates whose faces she barely recognized presenting themselves to her when the time drew near, but that only added to her sense of dread. If she tried to imagine losing her virginity with someone, the only person she could even remotely consider was Tomasi, but that was pointless, since she had no idea what had happened to him. Celia still hadn't seen him again, either at Diaboliques or at the bookstore. Every day her thoughts found him at least once, and she wondered again what had happened. Every Friday at Diaboliques she looked for the faintest sign he ever had been there, even studying the area of the floor where he had stood, as though his footprints might somehow be visible, but she found nothing. It wouldn't have made a difference. The bottom line was that Celia wasn't ready to consider sex as a real course of action. It was like contemplating being an astronaut.

Regine had something else on her mind. "We have to get ready for Halloween," she said.

"What do we do for Halloween?"

"We defy expectations." Regine smiled over at her. "You remember that orange dress I told you to keep?"

"We're all going to dress . . . normal?"

"I wouldn't call it *normal*. I would call it bright and unexpected. We don't wear costumes. We wear the opposite of what we normally wear. It's the day the rest of the world wears black and puts on too much eyeliner, so we try to balance things out. We still look good, just . . . bright."

"You did this last year?"

"And the year before. It's hilarious. Last year I wore a red, white, and blue blouse and a red skirt. I looked like a cross between the French flag and a flight attendant! I just found a pink floral tapestry jacket that looks like it was made out of a sofa. It's very Molly Ringwald in *Pretty in Pink*. I have to find something to wear with it."

"Do we wear this to Diaboliques, too?"

"No, that's a much bigger deal. Last year Marco made us beautiful masks, like something Marie Antoinette would have worn, and we really dressed up. I can't wait to see what he's come up with for us this year."

THE NIGHT BEFORE HALLOWEEN, traffic at the bookstore was particularly slow. Lippa came out of her office to pass the time. "Still reading about witchcraft?" she asked Celia.

"A little. It all sounds so old-fashioned. Even in the new books, it seems like it's part of another time."

"There's a reason for that. Or at least, *I* think there is. Consider all the different crazy stories people have told for thousands of years—vampires, werewolves, magic, ghosts. At some point it all becomes a bit much, doesn't it? I mean, how is anyone supposed to believe all of it?"

Celia nodded, a little relieved that Lippa's interest in these things seemed to be skeptical. Celia might have had some strange experiences with Mariette recently, but everything was so much easier in the rational world, even if that meant turning a blind eye to certain things.

"But all those fanciful things remind me of that story about the blind men who find an elephant—have you heard it? One of them touches the elephant's trunk and decides the elephant is like a tree branch. Another touches the leg and decides the elephant is like a column. Another touches the tail and describes the elephant as a rope. Each of them is partially right, but none of them understands what the elephant really is, how one animal is all these different things.

"I told you I'm a conspiracy theorist. That's the Troika's thing. So do you want to hear the greatest conspiracy of them all? There may be one explanation for all of the inexplicable things about which humans have told stories for thousands of years."

"What do you mean?"

Lippa looked dramatically around the empty bookstore, as though they might be overheard. "One class of supernatural people with greatly different powers, who do their best to stay unknown to everyone else. Now and then they are revealed, but because they don't all have the same powers, people don't realize they are the same type of being."

"I don't understand."

"Some of them can only use their powers at the full moon, and over time the legends called them werewolves. Others need human blood to activate their powers. They became known as vampires. Others can mix substances and make things happen from a distance. They are called witches." Lippa tapped the book on the desk. "But in reality, they are all the same. The evil ones are the Unkind, and the good ones are the Kind."

"The Unkind?"

"There are legends about books appearing and disappearing that contain information about the Kind and Unkind. The people who claim to have read those books can never prove what they have seen."

"I don't think I understand." Celia stared at Lippa and then looked away, not wanting it to be obvious she thought her boss was crazy. Celia had entertained doubts about a curse at Suburban, about Mariette, but in the space of five minutes Lippa had just grabbed for the brass ring of crazy and fallen completely off the merry-go-round, as far as Celia was concerned.

"There isn't much to understand, really. That's what makes it such a great conspiracy theory!" Lippa's eyes danced with excitement.

"So . . . do you believe it?"

"That's not really the point. When you watch a scary movie, does it matter whether you believe it's true? The point is to suspend disbelief for a little while and go along for the ride."

"Everyone knows about vampires and werewolves. How come I've never heard about the Unkind?"

"They guard their secrets very well and leave us to make up our own stories about them, even if the stories are completely wrong. Halloween is another great example — a holiday grown out of people's misunderstandings of the Unkind. If you'd like, you could join me and my friends tomorrow night. We could tell you more."

"Oh, I'm going to a Halloween party with my friends," Celia said. "But thank you for the invitation. I'll keep it in mind."

"You do. Anytime." Lippa smiled at her and went back to the office. *Oh my god, she is crazy,* Celia thought, but then she remembered Mariette and thought, *What if she isn't?*

ON HALLOWEEN MORNING CELIA put on the orange dress with her mother's coral cardigan, and until Regine arrived she was scared it was a prank and the rest of them would be in some kind of somber costume, ready to laugh at her expense. But Regine was decked out in her pink thrift-store find, and when they got to school they all laughed at the sight of themselves in the parking lot. Marco had made full-length pants in madras patchwork, and Ivo had on a magenta blazer. All day Celia enjoyed the confused looks from her classmates, and she lost count of the number of times she startled herself when she glanced down and saw the bright colors she was wearing.

"I get it. That's funny," Mariette said as they walked to chemistry class. She was wearing brown corduroys and a lumpy green sweater, which Celia took to mean she had not made any special effort to mark the holiday. "It's nice to see you in actual colors. Don't you get tired of all the black and gray?"

"Not really. Do you ever dress up?"

"Not really. I like being comfortable, but I definitely like color." After a moment Mariette asked, "Do you want to go trick-or-treating together tonight?"

"I can't. My friends and I are going to dress up as shipwrecked ghosts and haunt Brenden's front yard for the trick-or-treaters," Celia said. "I think there's even a fog machine involved."

Mariette nodded. "I'll probably go out and get some candy. I'm short enough I can still get away with it. You spend a lot of time with those guys, don't you?"

"They're my best friends," Celia said. "They're the reason I'm surviving this year."

"It's great to have friends like that."

Mariette was unusually quiet during the experiment. Midway through she said, "I have to go to the bathroom. Can you finish up?"

"Sure, we're almost done," Celia said. She watched Mariette grab her bag and hurry up to Mr. Sumeletso, then out the door.

Celia turned back to the experiment, and the room seemed dimmer, as though clouds were moving across the sun. The lab seemed to lose some of its color. Celia felt lazy, and she was tempted to stop working and wait for Mariette to return, but the timing of the experiment was crucial, so she forced herself to continue.

Five minutes later Celia had managed to finish the experiment, but Mariette hadn't returned. Around Celia their classmates slumped over their lab tables, chins in hands, experiments neglected. Celia went up to Mr. Sumeletso's desk. "Do you mind if I go check on Mariette? I think she might be sick." He gave her a concerned nod. Celia went down the hall to the bathroom. She pushed open the door and breathed in humid air.

When Celia turned the corner inside the bathroom, she found Mariette alone in front of the frosted windows at the far end of the rows of sinks and stalls. One of the windows was cranked open, and a charm of hummingbirds hovered around Mariette. Her head was down, and her shoulders trembled.

"Mariette?" Celia walked up to her. Mariette hastily put her hands to her face before she turned around, but her eyes were red and puffy. The hummingbirds darted out the window. "What– Are you okay? What's going on?"

"I'm fine," Mariette said, doing her best to brighten up. She closed the window.

"I told him I thought you were sick."

"No, I just needed a few minutes. Let's go back."

"Mariette." Celia still didn't know what question to ask out loud, so she asked with her eyes, and Mariette understood.

"You've known for a long time, haven't you?" Mariette shouldered her bag, and they stood facing each other by the window.

"Yes."

"There were a bunch of times you wanted to ask me, weren't there?"

"Yeah."

"I would have told you the truth."

"I don't know what the right questions are," Celia said.

"You have . . . powers, don't you?" Mariette nodded. "And there really is a curse, isn't there—or not a curse, but something."

"It's as bad as I told you. Someone is trying to kill one of us girls in order to gain personal powers. I'm pretty sure it's someone here at school, but I can't figure out who. It makes it so hard to protect the other girls. I'm not that strong myself."

"How do you know? What are you?"

"I'll tell you, but I don't want to tell you here," Mariette said. Her voice echoed off the tiles of the big empty bathroom. "We should go back to class." They went out into the hall and headed back to the chemistry lab. Under her breath, Mariette said, "You won't tell anyone?"

"I've never told anyone," Celia said.

"That's not true," Mariette corrected her.

Celia felt her face grow warm. "I only said something once, and I haven't ever again since then."

"Trying to break into my locker." Mariette rolled her eyes.

"Do you have to kill someone to gain power, too?" Celia asked quietly.

"No!" Mariette dropped her voice to a whisper again. "I want nothing of the darkness, only the light. Although I would kill someone if it would stop them from fulfilling this admonition."

"Admonition?"

"What you call the curse. It's really an admonition."

"There are so many things I want to ask you," Celia said outside the classroom door.

"And there are so many things I want to tell you," Mariette said. "Let's hang out this weekend, okay?"

"Okay."

Celia was surprised by how calm she was. In hindsight, her entire friendship with Mariette had led up to this moment. Now she was relieved, excited to learn Mariette's secrets at last, even if they meant coming to terms with more disturbing ideas. Celia thought it must be like having a friend and suspecting she was gay, but never having the guts to ask. It had hung there between them, unspoken by some sort of silent agreement. She wondered if Mariette felt oppressed by her differentness, if she struggled in ways Celia couldn't understand. Now she knew that the curse — or whatever Mariette had called it — was real. It was even worse than everyone else at school believed. For the moment, though, Celia's feelings of protectiveness toward Mariette overshadowed everything else, and her biggest fear was that her mouth would fly open and she would reveal something that would bring scrutiny or even persecution down on Mariette.

Celia's adventures at the beginning of the year had been like the dizzy time in her backyard when she had attempted her first cartwheel. It all had been mildly disorienting, mostly fun, and she had righted herself quickly, proud of herself, in a better place than she had been before. This time was going to be a harder stunt. Celia was on her way heels over head again, and already the dizziness was more severe. She couldn't be sure it would go quite so smoothly, or that the ground would come around when she turned right side up again.

Later, in the library, she pretended to be concerned about an exam in order to stay out of the Rosary's conversation. The shock had set in, and she kept replaying what had happened in the bathroom.

11

dark adapted eye

THAT NIGHT THE DENIZENS of Diaboliques were all out to impress for Halloween. On the first floor the kids were more wildly costumed than ever, and even taller on their thick-soled shoes. Throughout the club there were fortunetellers. On the mezzanine a man sat with tarot cards, and by the main bar a woman read tea leaves. Patrick's room was always a panorama of sophisticated outfits, but even on Halloween the emphasis was not so much on costumes as on characters. Celia saw a priest with a white collar in a black leather suit and a woman in a shroudlike dress with dotted lines on her face, as though a surgeon had marked her for a face-lift. Marco was blown away by a merman in a fishtail gown made of rubber bands.

The girls of the Rosary had gowns and the boys had suits, all sharply tailored in charcoal wool crepe. They had lightened their faces to a deathly pallor, darkened their eye sockets, and draped bits of seaweed and fishing net in their hair and on their shoulders. The merman came up to them to say he wished he had been there to help.

Through the netting that angled across her face Celia

looked for Tomasi, but her hopes weren't high, and her disappointment gradually had dulled over the previous weeks. Midway through the night she went into the hall to wait in line for the bathroom, crossing paths with a woman she'd never noticed before. Celia admired her fiery red hair, which rose from the top of her head in a weightless spiral plume. She flashed a perfect white smile. "You're beautiful," she said to Celia.

"I was going to say the same thing to you," Celia said. The woman wore a china blue dress with a series of buckles up the bodice.

"We're all beautiful here," the woman said. "I'm beautiful. You're beautiful."

"I don't think I'm quite in the same league as the rest of you," Celia said from behind her fishnet veil.

"Of course you are. You must be," the woman said, "or you wouldn't have come here. Shall I read your palm?" she asked. Celia nodded and held out her hand.

"Left hand, always the left hand," the woman said, smoothing Celia's pleated cuff off her palm. "My goodness—so much going on here." The woman traced her fingernails over Celia's skin. They were an inch long, and painted crimson except for the tips, which had the white rim of a French manicure. "So nice to see you're not obsessed with the same old things: health, shape, body weight . . . Well, it doesn't look like you need my help. You're all set." The woman closed Celia's hand and smiled. She studied Celia with a strange intensity.

"What? What kind of reading is that?"

"The truth."

"I thought you were supposed to tell me my future?"

"I could, but you're not ready to hear it." The woman smiled kindly. "You've had enough revelations for this week already, haven't you? Certain things are likely, that's for sure. When the time comes, you'll know what to do, and that's all that matters."

Celia stared at her, feeling that the stranger was toying with her and wondering if she really told fortunes at all. She turned back to the line for the bathroom. Her head felt cloudy, as though she'd been hypnotized rather than had her palm read.

"I love *The Awakening*, too," she heard the woman say, and Celia whirled around, but the fiery red plume was floating away from her. Celia looked after it, not sure she had heard correctly. The woman faded into the crowd until Celia could only see the top of her hair at the end of the hall. Impulsively she rushed after her, tracking the red hair down the stairs and onto the mezzanine, but Celia lost sight of her in the darkness, which was pierced at odd angles by the flashing lights. She had given up and turned to go back upstairs when she caught a glimpse of the mysterious woman, seated on a couch in the shadows against the wall. She looked up unsurprised at Celia and leaned closer to her when Celia perched hesitantly on the edge of the sofa next to her.

Before Celia could speak, the woman brought her lips close to Celia's ear. "I can only tell you this: the moment he can come to you, he will." Then she sat back and looked pleasantly at Celia, who gaped at her, wondering how to have a conversation with someone who only seemed to say half of the words required out loud.

"Where is he?"

"The Leopard is in his room. Wishing he could see you."

"How do you know?"

"How do you know where your hands are when you're not looking at them?" the woman asked, causing Celia to look down at her hands.

"Will he come back here? When will I see him again?"

"If I tell you all the answers, won't that take the fun out of it? The hoping, and the wondering, and the tingly feelings? Patrick is about to play 'Spellbound' and I know you like Siouxsie and the Banshees. It's really time you started dancing."

Celia realized she was staring mutely at the woman. She felt foolish, sitting there next to a stranger, and she moved to get up, then turned back. "So is there such a thing as curses? Or admonitions? I have a friend who—"

"Your friend who touches roses—her greatest strength will be her greatest weakness," the woman said a little wistfully. "She is so excited to share her secrets with you tomorrow. I won't spoil it."

Everything this incredible woman said opened up another box of questions in Celia, but the look on the woman's face made it clear that the interview was over. Celia reluctantly left her and went back upstairs. She rejoined her friends just in time to hear the watery guitar notes that began "Spellbound." Her meeting with the fortuneteller had been so disconcerting, Celia figured dancing couldn't be any stranger. The others smiled happily when she joined them, but during the entire song Celia was preoccupied, sorting through the pieces of her fragmented conversation with the woman on the mezzanine. When it was over, she had no idea whether she had danced well.

THE NOVEMBER AIR WAS CRISP and dry when Mariette sat down facing Celia at the little café across the street from Lippa's store. Celia felt as though it had been much longer than a day since she'd last seen Mariette, and she wondered if it was the difference of location that distorted her sense of time. "I've never seen you outside of school!"

"I know. We both look exactly the same as we do at Suburban, though." Mariette giggled. "Have some." She pulled apart a small cake encrusted with currants and pushed the plate to the center of the table. Celia nodded at the sweet taste.

"Well, there is so much to tell you. I'm just going to jump in," Mariette said, and they settled in for the conversation they both had been anticipating. "I'm a little freaked out to be telling you about these things. I've barely talked to anyone about this. I've been waiting to tell you since the moment we met. I didn't think you knew yet, and I had to wait to be sure. But I'm so excited I found you! Now I have someone to share all this with. We have to keep everything a secret from citizens."

"Citizens?"

"Ordinary people. Well, maybe not ordinary. People without powers."

"What . . . who are you, then?"

"We don't really have a name, really. I guess people just say that we're one of the Kind."

Celia gasped. "The Kind? Really?"

"So you have heard of us?"

"My boss at the bookstore—she told me something about it, but it sounded like some bizarre story, like alchemists."

"She didn't say anything about having powers herself?"

"I don't think so—she and her friends just like to read about spooky things. They think all monsters are really the Unkind, or something."

"Sounds like a nosy citizen. You can't tell her it's true, or any of this."

"Have you always known you were Kind?"

"No. I've only been doing all this for about a year, so there are lots of things I don't completely understand. It's partly knowing, but it's also seeking it out. When I was younger I thought I had ESP, but most kids think that, don't they? And then you find out it's only wishful thinking and you move on. But I had some things happen I couldn't explain. One time I was walking around a hydrangea bush in our yard, and I noticed the flowers on the bush were turning to face me, wherever I stood. I couldn't believe it. I went in and told my parents, but they just thought I was being overimaginative. I guess I *am* overimaginative." Mariette was amused and embarrassed by this self-awareness. "But I knew what I had seen, and I kept going back to the bush. Sometimes the flowers would follow me, and sometimes they wouldn't. I couldn't figure out why.

"That summer we went to visit my grandparents. They asked my dad if he would plant some flowers in the beds around the house, so he went to the greenhouse a few blocks away, and I went along. He picked out some tulips that were orange and yellow, but he wanted eight and there were only six plants there. The florist told him she thought they had more, and went off to another room. Dad wandered around, looking at other plants, but for some reason I decided to follow the florist. I peeked around a partition and saw her at a workbench. She had two pots of dirt.

"As I watched her, she held her hands over the pots, and two plants grew in them—in thirty seconds she grew two full-sized tulip plants! But when the flowers opened, they were pink instead of orange and yellow. She made a tsking noise and then she blew on one of the flowers, and the pink flower gradually turned orange yellow. She did it again and again, until all the flowers on both plants were the right color.

"I sneaked away and went back to my dad, and then the florist found us. She was carrying the two tulip plants she had just grown in the back, and I couldn't tell the difference between those two and the other six.

"The greenhouse was only a few blocks from my grandparents' house, so I went back as soon as I could get away. When I told the woman what I had seen her do, she was alarmed, but then I told her about the hydrangea at my house, and everything changed. 'You must be new!' she said, and asked me to try it with a rhododendron bush she had there. I'll never forget it—she said, 'Rhododendrons are really easy to train,' like they were pets or something. And sure enough, the rhododendron flowers followed me as I walked past, just like the hydrangeas had.

"The woman started to tell me things, but customers kept coming in. I kept sneaking back to the greenhouse that whole visit, until my parents thought I was crazy. I only got the basics from her: I'm one of the Kind. My powers grow stronger if I fulfill my admonitions. I have to keep everything a secret, and I must only use my powers for good. If I use them for bad, even once, I will cross over to the Unkind, and it's really hard to get back. She told me I would learn a lot more on my own just by keeping my eyes open and paying attention, and she was right. My first admonition came to me on the ride home. We were driving through Marietta, and the sign—the one on the edge of town that tells you what city you're entering—didn't say *Marietta, Next Five Exits* or whatever. It said *Mariette, Write This Down*. My parents and my brother didn't notice. I grabbed my diary, and for the next twenty miles, every time we passed a road sign, billboard, anything, a phrase of my admonition was on it. As soon as I finished writing one line down, I would look up and the next line would be coming up on the next sign. And my parents, my brother, never noticed anything."

"That's amazing," Celia said. "What did you have to do?"

"My first one was pretty easy, though the way it was worded, it wasn't clear right away. But my parents were going to give me a choice between going to Suburban for high school or going to a private school, and the admonition told me to choose Suburban. I didn't understand why. Nothing happened last year to make it clear why I was supposed to have chosen Suburban. But this year, I'm starting to think I'm there for a reason."

"To fight the person—one of the Unkind?—who has the evil admonition?"

"Perhaps," Mariette said, more shyly than Celia had expected. "I'm still learning. I have so much to learn. I don't think it ever stops."

"So there isn't a school for the Kind?"

"Not a building or anything like that. This isn't like a profession that you learn. It's your *life*, and *my* life. Each of us develops different powers. It's going on all the time, wherever we are. Once you get started, it's like a machine turns on that runs by itself, and then the world around you becomes your school. You get to see things other people don't see. You receive information from places you never expected. And you try things, when you're ready. It's like the world becomes your chemistry lab, but you have to be careful, because there's no teacher with a fire extinguisher if you blow something up."

"So what's up with chemistry, anyway?"

"I know!" Mariette laughed. "There was no way I could hide it. I have this sense of how things are going to work together. Like when you pour cream into coffee, you look for it to turn a certain shade, and then you know it will taste the way you want it to? I get that from every natural substance. I can tell if two of them are going to work together, or if there's too much of one or the other. I don't know if we all have that instinct, but since I've freed mine up, it's been really useful."

"Hey, we're acing chemistry, so no complaints here." Celia smiled. "And considering the number of kids who failed Mr. S.'s other classes first semester, that's no small feat."

"You seemed to come to terms with my lab skills pretty quickly." Mariette smiled back.

"But the woman in the flower shop—do you know other people? Others of the Kind?"

"Not really," Mariette said. "I go see her when we visit my grandparents, but that's only once or twice a year. She has helped me, and our powers overlap a little, but it's not like she can just teach me to do the things she does. A couple times strangers have given me some sign that they recognize me, but it's been in the middle of a crowd of citizens, so it wasn't like we could talk about anything, really. That's why I was so excited to meet you."

"Me?"

"Don't you see?" Mariette said. "The only reason I'm telling you all this, the only reason I didn't hide all of this from you—the reason you noticed the things I was doing in the first place—is because I think you're one of the Kind, too."

"Me?" Celia stared. "Why do you think I'm one of the Kind?"

"I don't know exactly, but I've heard that as Kind grow stronger, they are able to sense one another, like magnets or something. I don't know if only some Kind can do it, or if they can detect all Kind or only some, but I felt something with you, the first day of school. I can't describe it, but I can sense something in you. I think you're one of the Kind."

"I—I don't have any powers."

"You've never had anything happen that you can't explain?"

Celia tried to come up with something, but she kept returning to the thought that nothing inexplicable ever had happened to her—other than what she had experienced with Mariette. Sure, plenty of her experiences with the Rosary had felt miraculous, but not in the way Mariette meant. Then she remembered the night before.

"Something happened last night that I can't explain, but it wasn't me—it was this woman at Diaboliques. I thought she was a fortuneteller, but she wouldn't tell my fortune. Instead, she told me all these weird things about how the guy I used to see there wished he could see me, and how I was going to meet you today to talk about this."

"That's wild! She's probably Kind. She didn't tell you anything about yourself?"

"No. She said I wasn't ready to hear it, whatever that means."

"Maybe I'm wrong, but it's too late now. You know my secret! I bet something happens very soon, though, and you find out you have powers, too. I think a lot of Kind discover who they are in high school. But I could be wrong about that, too."

"So, what powers do you have?"

"So far, my thing seems to be very much about nature," Mariette said. "I've always been an outdoor person, kind of a tomboy, so it makes sense. Most of what I've learned has to do with plants and natural substances, and physical and chemical changes."

"Like the frost on the window?"

"You did see that. I wasn't sure. Daydreaming is my worst enemy, because I do things without remembering where I am. Yeah, the frost." Mariette tapped her glass on the table between them and ice crystals appeared, quickly melting away.

"And your shadow?"

"My shadow?"

"One day I saw you getting off the bus, and you were getting teased by some kids and your shadow flickered, like you were turning invisible."

"Really? I actually hadn't noticed that. It must mean that I'm getting closer. I really want to be able to turn invisible, but you don't get to pick your powers. Maybe it's coming though, and my shadow is the first thing to go. That would be so cool! I hate the bus. There are three guys who must spend every night thinking of new things to say to me in the morning. They don't know anything about all this, of course. They've just chosen me for their amusement. They don't play fair, and they shout so much I can't hear myself speak to respond. It makes me insane to be around them."

"I could tell you were upset, or stressed. The leaves on the tree above you changed color."

"I have a really strong relationship with plants," Mariette said. There was a half-dead rose in the bud vase on the table. Mariette stroked it with her knuckle and the color flushed back into it, and the sere edges smoothed out. The flower pulled down toward the stem, like a child ducking its chin to its chest when tickled. Celia caught her breath, partly because of what she was seeing, and partly because the fortuneteller at Diaboliques had described Mariette as the one who touches roses.

"So what happens next?"

"Well, nothing, really. I go to school, and I do everything you do. But at the same time I'm studying, trying to improve myself, and hopefully learning to do more things. I'm not trying to be hugely powerful or anything. You have to be a fool not to realize even a little power carries a huge responsibility, and if you screw it up it's going to kick your ass."

"What about the person who's trying to kill a girl in our class, then?"

"There is a dark side," Mariette said. "Some people get started, maybe by the wrong person, or maybe they get started by the right person but then they make bad decisions. And they turn from the Kind to the Unkind. They seek the darkness instead of the light. They try to develop their powers in ways that break things down rather than building them up."

"Can the person who's doing those things at school be stopped?"

"I think I'm supposed to stop it—maybe that's why I was supposed to go to Suburban. But I haven't figured out how yet. Maybe we're supposed to do it together! It's so frustrating, though, because I haven't been able to figure out who it is. If I had more experience, if my powers were more advanced, I think I'd be able to pick the person out blindfolded, but I'm not sensitive enough. And I don't have any experience trying to counteract the actions of someone else. I'm just a beginner, you know?" Mariette grinned. "I'm pretty sure it's someone at school, because all the bad things take place at school or right outside. So it's probably someone there. The best I've been able to do so far is to find this." Mariette pulled her school notebook out of her bag and opened it. Celia eagerly looked onto the page, but even upside down she could see it contained nothing more interesting than chemistry notes.

Then Mariette passed her hand over the paper and the surface changed. The chemistry notes were wiped away, and other text in Mariette's handwriting appeared in their place. "I was so happy when I learned how to do this!" she said. "It's so much less to carry around." She turned the notebook around so Celia could read. "I found an admonition that I think is addressed to the Unkind person behind all this," Mariette said.

"So tell me, what is an admonition? Where do you find them?"

"An admonition is like the instructions for your personal quest. It tells you what you have to do to get to the next place in your journey, and things to be wary of as you go. There are all sorts of admonitions, and they're usually very specific, to one person only. They're hard to understand, and they're even harder to understand if they're not for you. I've seen some admonitions and been sure there wasn't an atom of meaning in them, but of course there must be, to someone. You've never found a twelve-line poem in a strange place?" Celia shook her head. "If you're Kind, your admonition tells you to do good things and rewards you with good powers. If you're Unkind, your admonition tells you to do bad things and rewards you with bad powers. If I'm right, and this is the right admonition, these are the only clues I have to find the person who's causing all the trouble at school."

Celia read:

> *The shortest path to greatest power*
> *Is found the day before the hour*

An innocent girl attains sixteen
Her dying breath does not turn sour

Collect it with your kissing lips
And wait for the next moon's eclipse
Then a new blood, dark and rich
Will flow through your own fingertips

Only beware a different girl
With talent hidden like a pearl
Her hands may render you as dead
And stop your power in this world

"An innocent girl. So that's why nothing happened to the girls who have had sex?"

"That's what it's starting to seem like. Like I said, the meaning isn't always obvious right away."

"So you can vanquish him," Celia said, pointing to the third stanza.

"If it's a boy. Who knows, it could be a girl. I'm pretty sure I have the right admonition, but the clues are so vague."

"Where did you find it?"

"This is going to sound really weird—well, I guess all of this sounds really weird, doesn't it?" Mariette grinned. "I found it in a book. Ever since I found out about all this I've tried anything I can think to learn more about it. I've turned up practically nothing, though. Anyway, a week before school started I went to the public library. I searched for different key words like 'Kind' and 'admonition.' And the computer gave me only one result: a book called *You Are Here*. I had to climb up into this tiny room in the top floor of the library, and when I found the book, it looked like it was a hundred years old, and it wasn't like any book I'd ever seen before. Some of the pages were printed, but there was handwriting on other pages—I wish I had read more of it! There was a chapter with the title 'Suburban,' so of course I looked at that first, and it had three pages. The first page had an admonition that must have been older. It had a line about the dark ages, and I have no idea how it was connected to Suburban. The second page had *my* last admonition, which I hadn't fulfilled yet. And the third page had this one." Mariette pointed to the ominous admonition on the table between them.

"I couldn't believe it. I took the book down to check it out, but they told me it was part of the permanent collection and I couldn't take it home. I should have just sat down and read the rest of it. But I was running out of time, and I figured I would just come back another day and look at it some more. Before I gave it back, I copied the third admonition. I don't know why I decided to do that—the admonition scared me, and I guess I thought if it had to do with Suburban and fifteen-year-old girls maybe I should keep it in mind. You remember how surprised I was when you said something about a curse, back in the first week of school?

"Anyway, a couple days later I went back to the library. But when I climbed up into that room, the book was nowhere to be found. I searched for *You Are Here* in the computer, and there was nothing. I even asked the librarian, and he couldn't find it. He acted like I was playing a joke. It was so strange and confusing, and I was so disappointed, because there was so much more in that book, and I wish I could have seen it all. But I've learned that some pretty unbelievable things lurk around, right there in plain sight, that citizens just don't seem to see. And I think this book was one of them—it was like it had come into existence just for that day, to give me this admonition. I think sometimes things appear at a specific time and place to pass something important along, and then they disappear. I don't know where admonitions really come from. I guess they're like oracles, but that book, it makes me think sometimes admonitions are supposed to be found by people other than the person to whom they're addressed, particularly in situations like this, when someone is supposed to stop them from happening."

"Wow," Celia said.

"There might be a way to track an admonition back to the person to whom it belongs, but I don't know how to do it. And there might be a way to cancel out an admonition so it doesn't work. Maybe not. At first I wasn't sure anything was happening—maybe the person wouldn't try to fulfill the admonition? But when I heard that girl was stung on the first day of school, and then the other girl passed out, I knew someone was trying, and I had to do something. The only thing I've been able to think of is to try to protect a girl when I know it's the day before her birthday, but I'm not doing very well with that, either."

"What do you do?"

"I make a protective serum. I think it works, or at least helps. The injuries probably would be worse if I weren't doing it. They would probably be fatal, and then the person could try to collect the girl's final breath and fulfill the admonition. The serum might work better if I could figure out how to get more of it onto each girl."

"How do you get *any* of it on them?"

"I put it on the lock on her locker at the end of the day before the day it's supposed to happen. I figure everyone has to open her locker first thing in the morning."

"Smart. And now I understand why you were making that chart listing everyone's locker!" Celia laughed.

Mariette laughed, too, in surprise. "You notice everything! See, if you were a citizen, you wouldn't pick up on these things! You have to be one of the Kind!"

Celia shrugged. "Well, no one has died, so you must be doing something right."

"Yes, but there's another possibility. The Unkind who's doing these things might not be very strong, either. This Unkind might be a beginner, like me. If it's someone our age, that's likely. Maybe that person is doing a poor job, and when he or she tries to kill a girl, the spell is weak, so it's only strong enough to hurt her. It's hard to tell if I'm succeeding or if the Unkind is failing."

"According to this, then, you have to kill the person to stop him? Or her?"

"Not necessarily. Admonitions are like oracles—often they don't mean what you think they mean. The way it's worded, it could mean the person doesn't have to be killed but just made to appear dead—maybe just unconscious for a while. If I have to do it, I would definitely prefer that," Mariette said sincerely.

"So you have an admonition?"

"I'm in between," Mariette said. "Every member of the Kind usually has an admonition. They lead us to the next destination on our journey. Once we finish one, we get another one. As one chapter ends, the next one begins," Mariette said. "I fulfilled my last admonition right at the beginning of school, and I've been waiting to receive a new one. Usually it doesn't take this long. I'm starting to wonder if I've been missing it."

"What did you have to do for your last admonition?"

"Is it okay if I don't tell you?" Mariette flushed. "I don't—some admonitions are kind of personal."

"Sure, I understand." Celia turned her attention back to the Unkind admonition in Mariette's notebook. "Can I copy this down? There's so much there, I'd like to look at it again. Maybe I can help you."

"I guess so." Mariette sounded hesitant. "You have to make sure no one else sees it. Promise to keep all of this a secret. It's very important."

"Definitely." Celia pulled out her sketchbook and was turning to a blank page when Mariette stopped her.

"I keep getting glimpses of your drawings, and I'm dying for a better look. Do you mind?"

"Of course not! You've shared so much with me." Celia watched Mariette leaf slowly through the pages. She nodded when Mariette correctly guessed her mother and her father and identified Regine. Then she showed Mariette she was turning to the very last page before she copied the admonition as quickly as she could. "I won't tell anyone about this."

"Not even your friends. No one. Not even the smallest detail." Mariette locked eyes with Celia. "Promise."

"I promise. I swear," Celia said.

"And who knows, maybe you'll get your first admonition soon, and we'll find out *you're* the person to vanquish whoever's hurting girls. Probably the reason I'm not being more successful is that it's up to another Kind to put a stop to it."

"Mariette, you should get help, and not from me—from

someone really powerful. This could be dangerous. This person is trying to kill someone, and if you're trying to stop whoever it is, you could get hurt, or worse. Have you told the florist?"

"No, I haven't. We haven't gone to my grandparents' since school started. I don't think there's much she could do, anyway."

"And there's no one else who's closer?"

"No one I know."

"You should get help. Tell me you'll get help."

"I'll tell the florist. I can probably find the phone number to the greenhouse." Mariette sounded as if she were saying it only to appease Celia.

EVEN THOUGH MARIETTE SEEMED convinced of it, Celia had trouble believing she herself could be one of the Kind. Sure, the list of inexplicable experiences had been growing since school started, but Celia never had been more than a spectator to any of them. Wasn't it far more likely she was a citizen who had glimpsed something that should have stayed hidden, as her boss at the bookstore apparently longed to do? Nonetheless, Celia felt a new devotion to Mariette, one that rivaled her devotion to the Rosary. Two days ago it would have been hard to convince Celia anything could have done that.

That night she sat in her room, trying to feel something. Would it be like a ghost limb she never had known was missing? Would it be a new sense, or new knowledge? She closed her eyes. The seam on her stocking was poking the bottom of her foot. Her calves were sore from the boots she had worn that day. She was hungry for dinner. She had a hangnail on her left index finger. She needed to wash her hair.

I am not one of the Kind. Celia sighed. *Or if I am, I am the dullest, most unpowerful Kind ever.* She got up to work on her dancing.

"TODAY IS THE DAY I'M asking Ivo to the Sadie Hawkins dance," Regine said on Monday morning in the car. "Look at the invitation I made him."

With mixed feelings Celia examined the beautiful collage, then replaced it in the envelope. "I wouldn't have guessed you would want to go to something like the Sadie Hawkins."

"You're right, but I don't get to spend a lot of time alone with Ivo, so I'll take the opportunity," Regine said.

"I know Brenden and Marco are together a lot on the weekends," Celia reflected out loud. "But when we go out as a group, it's always obvious they're a couple. You and Ivo don't seem to act that way."

"Ivo's not like that. He doesn't like to display affection. I can respect that. Maybe it's unusual for people our age not to be so demonstrative with our feelings, but it's kind of a relief, really. Ivo is very subtle when he likes someone. I used to be nervous he liked a girl at Diaboliques, because he talks to her almost every week, but they're just friends, so it's okay."

Celia thought it wasn't her place to help Regine understand how she was mistaken about Ivo, and then she wondered if friends were supposed to try in situations like this. Was she failing Regine somehow by not saying anything? Was today the day Regine's feelings were to be crushed? Celia was nervous on Regine's behalf, but it turned out there was no need. Ivo accepted the invitation, prompting more grumbling from Marco and even comments from Brenden and Liz.

"He does like that girl at Diaboliques—what's her name,

Isadore?" Brenden said. "I think he's going along with this just because he doesn't want the whole disaster of rejecting Regine. He doesn't want the whole group to be affected, so he's just waiting until the year is over."

"I would say that's noble, but it's really just pathetic," Liz said. "When is she going to wake up?"

Celia predicted no one would confront anyone about anything, and then Regine would drag Ivo off to the dance. "I'm so glad neither of us is a girl, or you know Ivo would find a way to guilt us into going to Sadie Hawkins with them," she heard Marco say to Brenden.

"WHY ARE YOU LOOKING AT me like that?" Mariette figured out the answer before she finished asking the question, and she set her pencil down. "You can't stop thinking about it, can you?"

"Are you surprised?" Celia said.

"Think of it this way," Mariette said. "Your drawings are just as amazing and miraculous and completely impossible as any of the things you've seen me do. I'll never understand how you can do that with a pencil."

"My drawings don't do what you can do," Celia said.

"Of course they do. You bring people to life. That's more powerful than anything I can do."

Celia thought for a little. "Still, why do you do all this normal stuff?" She gestured vaguely at the classroom around them. "You could be doing anything else, if you wanted. I mean, couldn't you?"

"Not really. When something is extraordinary it's because all the ordinary things make it extraordinary by comparison. I'm not explaining it well. If it was your birthday every day, after a while it wouldn't be special anymore. It would just be another day. The other three hundred sixty-four ordinary days are what makes your birthday special, right? It's weird, but as awesome as it is to have powers, I really like being 'normal' most of the time, just a high school girl—it helps me appreciate the powers. Does that make any sense?"

"I think so. But I'm still going to stare at you sometimes," Celia said.

"Okay, go right ahead," Mariette said, smiling in a way Celia hadn't seen before.

That night at the bookstore Celia watched Lippa and the rest of the Troika when they came in. The three petite women clustered together as they walked to the back of the store, looking like a benevolent creature in a bundle of astrakhan coats, with three heads and six legs, engrossed in a conversation with herself. Celia wondered what they thought they knew about the Kind and the Unkind. She had no intention of betraying Mariette's trust, but it was like knowing someone who searched for UFOs, and knowing a space alien, and not closing the triangle.

Later, after she had accompanied her friends to the door and unlinked arms with them, Lippa came over to Celia at the counter. "You seem interested in the Troika."

"I was thinking of drawing you," Celia lied.

"I thought perhaps you were still thinking about what I told you before. Stories like that, about the Unkind, are fascinating, aren't they?"

"But do you believe them?"

"You asked me that before. For centuries people have whispered about the Unkind. Most of them have never seen an Unkind in person, despite spending their lives trying. But something about the stories is so compelling, people believe it anyway, without proof. At some point it's not really about be-lief, then. It's something that tells us about ourselves. No mat-ter how rational we are, why is there always a part of us, deep down inside, that believes in monsters?"

"Wouldn't you like to have proof?"

"Like meeting an Unkind, or a Kind? It's just so unlikely. Other people have tried much harder than I have and failed. I think I mentioned stories about mysterious books that appear and disappear, which contain a supernatural history and give messages to the Unkind and the Kind. Having the bookstore, I sometimes wish one of those books would appear here, in the stacks, and I would have a moment to glimpse it myself before it vanished again. That would be proof enough for me."

On her way home Celia pondered the irony of it all. Lippa had told Celia what she thought was a fanciful tale, but it cor-roborated Mariette's story about the Kind and the Unkind. Celia had witnessed things Lippa had given up on ever seeing, but Mariette had sworn her to secrecy, and Celia understood why.

When she got home Celia pulled out her sketchbook to draw the Troika. Her drawing output had dropped consider-ably since the beginning of the year. It wasn't difficult to un-derstand the cause: In previous years she had spent every free moment at school drawing. Now she spent that time with the Rosary or Mariette. In previous years every night had been spent hunched over her sketchbook. Now she worked at the bookstore, or went to Diaboliques, or danced around her bed-room. She still carried her notebook everywhere with her. She would have felt naked without it. But the comfort it gave her was more symbolic now.

12

the art of falling apart

CELIA NOTICED A PALPABLE suspense in the seniors, which grew as December began. First, Ivo got the letter accepting him into the architecture program at his top school, Metropolitan. The next day, Liz found out she was going there, too, as a creative writing major. Finally, Brenden's letter came, accepting him into Metropolitan's interdisciplinary studies program, which he wanted so badly to enter. It was exciting, but there was bleakness to it—it was the first indication that the days of the Rosary were numbered. Metropolitan was a few hundred miles away. When Liz caught the flu, her absence gave them a firsthand experience of what it was like to have someone missing from the group, and no one could ignore the sober truth that lurked behind the seniors' good news about college.

The afternoon after Brenden received his letter, Celia went to meet Marco in the library, but she didn't see him at their usual table. She wandered through the stacks and finally turned a corner in the farthest reaches of the room to find him at a carrel by himself, his head down on his arms. The black rosary beads around his neck between his curls and the aubergine collar of his shirt told her he was trying to reassure himself the Rosary was intact. She put her hand on his shoulder and he looked up, wiping his eyes. "What's wrong?"

"I'm just thinking about him leaving," Marco said softly. "I know it's not for another nine months, but he's going to leave. And I knew he would, but it wasn't real until he got accepted." Marco looked drained. He glanced around to see if anyone else was nearby. "Metropolitan's four hours away, so it's not like I can visit him that easily. He won't be able to come home most weekends."

"I'm sorry," Celia said, largely because she didn't know what else to say.

"I do love him," Marco said. "And he loves me. I know we're young, and maybe I'm foolish for thinking he's the one."

Celia pulled the chair over from the next carrel. "I don't think so," she said. "I think you guys are perfect for each other."

"When he goes to school he's going to meet all these other amazing people. How can I expect him to want to stay with me, even if I get there the next year?"

"You have to ask him that," Celia said.

"I know. I just don't want to bring it up because I know he's excited about getting accepted, and I don't want to be a wet blanket. He deserves to be excited."

"Well, Brenden hasn't said anything to me, but I bet he knows how you're feeling, even if you haven't talked to him about it," Celia said. "He has to be thinking about the same things. I mean, who's to say you couldn't meet someone else while he's gone?"

"I don't *want* to meet anyone else," Marco said. "You know, I stay over at his house almost every weekend. His parents are so cool about us. On the weekends it's almost like we live together. When we all had that ridiculous conversation about sex the other day, I wanted to say you don't have to lose your virginity with someone you love, but when you love somebody, sex becomes something completely different."

"I thought we weren't talking about my virginity until April." Celia was happy to get a chuckle out of Marco. "Listen, you two can figure this out. You're both great guys, and you have a great relationship. I think you should try to enjoy the rest of this year with him, and then figure out what's going to work for you. Just don't let it spoil the time you have left before he goes."

"I know." Marco wiped his eyes again.

"And no hiding from me in the library," Celia said. "We're supposed to be getting our homework done."

Celia's heart went out to Marco. He was always so stylish and self-assured, yet she still could see the dreaming child in him, who gave his love and then depended on those he loved so much it made him fragile. She had decided to make portraits of the Rosary for Christmas presents, and she thought more about him when she was pulling up her mental pictures for his drawing. Marco's joy was close at hand so often. The moments when it strayed, like that afternoon in the library, were shocking. Celia thought of love as a kind of miracle, something beyond her control, to be hoped for but never expected. Most of the relationships she saw at school were not nearly as convincing, but when Marco spoke of love with Brenden, she believed. Maybe love was a miracle, but there it was in front of her. Celia wondered when she might feel it herself.

She thought about each of the members of the Rosary as she worked on their portraits—the way they carried themselves and the way they fit into the group. Celia was better at describing people with her pencil than she was with words, and she worked very hard to capture each of them. She had picked up another copy of *The Awakening* to give Mariette but decided she would make a portrait for her, too.

As close as she had become to Mariette, Celia was even more at a loss to describe that relationship. She felt like a guest in Mariette's world, where fantastic, inexplicable things happened—a world in which she didn't have a place. On the one hand, she wanted to know more, wanted to see more, wanted to share with Mariette the things she had glimpsed. On the other hand, she was scared Mariette would be disappointed when Celia turned out to be merely a citizen who never should have been told any of this. She feared for Mariette, and she feared the terrible thing that was happening at Suburban—a plot that could kill a girl, and perhaps Mariette, if she got in the way of someone with Unkind powers and the desire to use them. How was Celia supposed to make sense of that? And what was she supposed to do, when every option she considered was laughably implausible? Celia focused her energy on the drawings. It was reassuring to do something familiar.

AT HER LOCKER THE NEXT day, Celia was so preoccupied, she didn't notice that someone had approached her until he spoke. "Hi," he said. "Celia, right?"

It was Skip. She had watched Liz watching him so many times, and they had crossed paths over a number of girls on their curse days, but it was a surprise to find him in front of her. "Yes?" Celia looked around, confused. He stood there, at ease in his denim shirt and orange sweater, smelling of cologne, a string of tiny shells around his neck. He was generically good-looking, in the healthy way jocks were, but there was too much gel in his bangs and not enough in the rest of his hair.

"I'm Skip. You're friends with Liz Fourad, aren't you?" He was friendly and completely confident. Celia couldn't imagine being so nonchalant when speaking to a stranger for the first time. She tried to be cool.

"Yes, why?"

"I was just wondering if she's okay. She hasn't been in school for a few days." He looked her straight in the eye and smiled a little, and Celia fought the melting response she knew he was used to getting from girls.

"She has the flu."

"She does? That's too bad. Does she need anyone to get her assignments for her?"

Celia was pleasantly surprised by his question and a little touched by his sentiment, but she couldn't offer him any encouragement. "I think her brother is doing that."

"Sure, of course. Okay, well, thanks for letting me know. I hope she feels better." He hesitated.

"Do you want me to tell her anything?"

"Um, you don't have to," Skip said. "I don't think it'll make much of a difference to her. I'll see you around."

"Okay." Celia watched him go. She turned back to her locker and was trying to make sense of the conversation when Mariette appeared on her other side.

"Do you know him?"

"Who? That guy? No. Well, kind of. Why?"

"His name is Skip, right? He's on the football team."

"Yeah, I know. Why do you care?" Celia had become accustomed to Mariette's knowing unexpected things, but she couldn't guess why Mariette would be interested in Skip.

"I think he might be a suspect," Mariette said, looking down the hall after Skip, who turned a corner and disappeared from view.

"You think he's a suspect? Why?"

"I finally got my new admonition, and it warns against someone who is marked by the number seventeen." Mariette pulled out her notebook. "Here." She wiped the page with her hand and four lines appeared in place of her notes:

> *Beware the one who hides in sight*
> *And seeks the darkness, not the light*
> *Who knows seventeen many ways*
> *And offers wrong disguised as right.*

"Where'd you get your admonition?"

"This one came in a fortune cookie! It was crazy. We went out to dinner, and I took one of the cookies off the little tray at the end, and there were *three* slips of paper in it, with all this tiny writing. I can't understand how it happens. I mean, what if my brother had picked up that cookie?"

"Where's the rest of the admonition?"

"I can't show you that," Mariette said. "But Skip is number seventeen on the football team."

"I didn't know his number. What about the basketball team?"

"No, no one has that number on the basketball team. Or the soccer team. I don't know if he's Unkind, but just be careful around him, okay?"

"It is weird that you would say that. I was going to tell you I've seen him around almost every time a girl has been injured."

"Really?"

"He was there in the parking lot when Elsie got stung, and he was there in the hallway when Tillie passed out. He was there when Lacie had the seizure." Celia hesitated. "But he wasn't in the chem lab when the beaker blew up. Maybe it isn't a pattern. And it's not like I've witnessed *all* the injuries."

"Still, it's very interesting if he's been around for most of them. He might have been close by for the others and you just didn't see him," Mariette said. "I think we have to treat him as our strongest suspect."

"But what do we do? Are we supposed to catch him doing something? How do we prove he's the Unkind?"

"I don't know. We have to think very hard about this. Anything could be a clue." Mariette ran off to her homeroom, and Celia wondered if there was anything she could do, really. Then again, she had seen Mariette do things no one else had noticed. Perhaps if Celia watched Skip she might notice him doing things, too.

ONLY TWO WEEKS REMAINED in the semester, and the next-to-last girl on the birthday list before the holiday recess got scalded when a pipe broke. Celia saw the concern in her friends' eyes—not for the burned girl, but for Celia. The Rosary kept their promise not to bring it up, but the curse had draped its malaise over the whole school, making it both ominous and stagnant, like a room that has been shut up too long.

"Is that what I think it is?" Celia asked Regine in the library.

"The birthday list?" Regine showed it to her. "I'm surprised you don't have a copy."

"It just seems so, I don't know, *callous*."

"Yeah, probably." Regine crossed the scalded girl's name off the list. "Well, this is interesting. You know who's next? Skip's sister, Stella." Regine pointed to the girl's name. "The second-to-last day of school before the break."

"Stella is Skip's sister? I had no idea. She's in my English class."

"She is. Oh, there's Ivo. He's helping me with my Chem Two midterm. I have to get an A on it to get a B for the class, and I never thought I would get a B in a class, much less a C." Regine left Celia with the list and shifted over to the next table, where Ivo was settling in. Celia watched as Regine pulled her chair in close to Ivo's and Ivo eased his chair farther away from her.

Celia returned to the list and found her name, and then Mariette's after that. She returned to Skip's sister's name and got excited.

She waited impatiently for chemistry class, and as soon as Mr. Sumeletso turned the experiment over to them, she told Mariette, "I think I know how we can find out about Skip."

"Really?"

"Did you know Stella Miller is Skip's sister?"

"She is? I never thought about it. Miller is a pretty common last name."

"Well, she is, and her birthday is next week, the next-to-last day of school before the break."

Mariette's eyes opened wider. "If Skip is the Unkind one behind this, he wouldn't try to kill his sister, would he?" Doubt crept into her face. "Do you think she's had sex? If she has, it wouldn't make a difference."

"I don't know. Stella is pretty quiet, and she's not nearly as social or popular as her older brother. I've never heard about her dating anyone at school."

"So it's pretty likely she hasn't lost her virginity, and she's vulnerable to the curse! That means if nothing happens to her, we can be pretty sure it's because Skip spared her."

Now it was Celia's turn to doubt. "Would it be conclusive? We might be wrong. She might have slept with someone out-side of school and no one knows about it. Or she might figure out how to avoid the curse some other way." Celia had regretted drawing the Rosary's attention to Mariette, and she wondered if she should have learned a lesson about making accusations lightly. Or did the possibility of someone's getting killed take precedence over that?

"You're right, but if Skip's our best suspect, we have to pay attention to this, even if it's only circumstantial. Should we try to make friends with her, see if she'll tell us whether she's had sex?"

"That sounds horrible. 'Hi, I know we've never talked be-fore now, but we we're just curious: have you had sex?'" Celia shook her head.

"Yeah. We may have to ask her afterward, though, if she isn't hurt."

THE NEXT DAY ONLY IVO and Liz had lunch at the same time as Celia. With Liz still out with the flu, Celia was uneasy about eating alone with Ivo. She hadn't connected with him very much, and she wanted to ask him why he was suffering Regine's advances but not reciprocating, but that didn't seem like a wise topic. She decided to be optimistic and hope maybe this would be her opportunity to make some inroads with him.

"Are you excited about college?" she asked him at lunch.

"You know, I'm a little freaked out about it," Ivo said. Lately his lunches were composed entirely of raw foods. Celia wasn't sure what had prompted him to adopt the diet. Today he had yellowtail sashimi, pine nuts, cucumber slices, a wedge of mozzarella, a blood orange, and Pellegrino. "Liz wants to be a writer. Brenden wants to be a music critic."

"I thought you wanted to be an architect."

"I don't know. Architecture is kind of a compromise for me. I feel like I'm good at a lot of things, but I'm not sure enough about any of them to say 'This is what I want to do with my life.' I feel like a dilettante," Ivo said.

"Really? That's not my impression of you."

"Well, high school has been easy. I've never had to really work hard—none of us have. Who knows what's happening to Regine in Chem Two. While that's great, it hasn't helped me to focus in on what I'm really good at, what I really want to do. I'm scared I'll go to college and realize I don't want to be an architect and then have no idea what to do instead."

"Well, you still have time," Celia offered. "And there's no harm in changing your mind."

"I'm just not used to not being sure," he said. "I've always known how to get what I wanted out of wherever I've been at the time. Some people are happy just to get through high school and move on to the next thing. I'm proud we've done it our way, on our terms. And when I get to college I'm going to try to do the same thing. The difference is, college is when I'm supposed to make big decisions about who I want to be for the rest of my life. I've never done that. I've always been focused on who I want to be right now. So I don't know if it's going to come so easily. I feel like the thing I have to do, and soon, is figure out what I want to be when I grow up."

"Liz always uses that John Updike quote about imagining your life and then it happens. What do you imagine?"

Ivo was quiet for a moment. The way he looked at her, Celia thought he was trying to decide how much of his confidence she deserved to receive. Then he said, "I want to have a space that's kind of like Diaboliques, but not just a nightclub. I want it to be the kind of place the people from Diaboliques would go for coffee, or dinner, to see an art show or even a performance. It would be like a black box version of Diaboliques, changing over the course of the day. It would be a coffee shop in the morning and then convert into a restaurant for lunch and dinner. Change the tables again and it's a cocktail lounge. Take the tables away and it's a performance space, or a nightclub. But always with the same dark, exotic ambiance, you know? Beautiful furnishings and attention to all the little details. And the best music, all the great music around which we build our lives. I even know what I'd call it." Ivo was caught up in his vision now, and Celia was right there with him. "Darkland: a place for the cognoscenti, anytime of day or night."

"That sounds awesome! So what do you study in college in order to do that?"

"I have no idea." Ivo smiled a little sadly, and in her mind's eye Celia saw the picture he had painted fade away like skywriting. "I almost wonder if you need to go to college for it at all. But I have to go to college, no matter what. I want to be an educated bar owner, not an ignorant one." They laughed at that.

"It's going to be strange not having you guys here next year," Celia said.

"It's going to be strange not being here," he said. "I kind of wish you all could come along with us and we could just keep doing this at college."

"That's nice, but I barely have high school figured out." She smiled.

"You're doing great. I hope you guys keep it up next year, being creative and doing your own thing, whether it's popular or not."

"I hope so, too," Celia said. "But we're not even halfway done with this year. I can't think about next year yet."

For a moment Ivo's façade had come down. Celia was thrilled to have seen a little of the real Ivo behind it, even if he was nervous and conflicted. She wondered if Ivo had told anyone else about Darkland. Celia hoped he hadn't. If he had privileged her with this small piece of himself that no one else had seen, she could believe she truly had made it into his good graces and her place in the Rosary was solid and secure.

"I want an apple. Can I get you anything?" Celia stood up from the table.

"No, thank you. Do you mind if I look at your drawings? I keep glimpsing them upside down, across the table from you, and I've always wanted to have a better look."

"Sure, go right ahead." Celia flushed with satisfaction at Ivo's interest. She waited in line at the lunch counter, believing for the first time that Ivo really considered her a friend. She wasn't sure why she wanted the Rosary's approval so much, but it felt good to have won it.

Oh god, she thought. *I wrote the Unkind admonition in my sketchbook!* She turned and looked across the sea of tables at Ivo. He was bent over her book. He turned a page and she tried to see what was on it, but they were too far apart. *He won't turn all the way to the last page. There are at least a hundred pages of drawings in there, and even if he looks at all of them, when he gets to the blank pages he'll stop.* All the same, she willed the cashier to move faster.

Finally she got her apple and strode briskly back to the table. Ivo looked up from the page open before him — twelve lines of her handwriting plainly visible.

"What is this?" he asked.

"What is what? Oh, that's a poem."

"It's a pretty grisly poem," Ivo said.

"Yeah," Celia said, all plausible ideas about how to change the subject running out of her mind like water through a sieve.

"And it's awfully similar to what's going on around here at school. An innocent girl, the day before she turns sixteen?"

"Well, not really. Nobody's getting killed." She sat down, the apple forgotten.

"Celia, what's going on?"

"What do you mean?"

"Apparently you're taking this curse pretty seriously. Is there something going on that isn't an accident? Are you involved in something I don't know about?"

"No!"

"People don't write random poems like this for fun." Ivo tapped the page.

"I didn't write it!" Celia protested.

"Then where did you get it?"

"I can't tell you!"

"It's okay — I bet I can guess. You've only suspected one of your friends of witchcraft so far this year. Or are there others?" Ivo studied her face, and while Celia couldn't imagine how her expression looked, she was sure it wasn't helping. "Did Mari-ette write this? I don't have a problem with people being pagan or vegan and all that, but a lot of girls have gotten hurt. What is she doing?"

"It's not Mariette—she's trying to stop it!" Celia saw Ivo's eyebrows go up and realized too late that she had revealed far too much. "You can't tell anyone! No one's supposed to know!"

"If you expect me to keep a secret, you're going to have to tell me what the secret is that I'm keeping," Ivo said, his face a mixture of disapproval, curiosity, protectiveness, and envy all at the same time.

"There isn't any way you could just forget about it?" she asked him.

"Not on your life. Not if someone is trying to make this little poem come true." Ivo stabbed his finger onto the admoni-tion.

"It's just, I'm not supposed to tell anyone. Could you please just let me talk to Mariette first? I don't know what I can tell you. It's really up to her."

"You, Mariette, and me—before the break is over. Or else I will tell my parents, and they will tell the school. I'm serious."

"Yes. I'll get her to come. Thank you."

The moment Celia was away from Ivo, she tore the page with the admonition out of the back of her sketchbook. Then she didn't know what to do with the page, so she folded it up and put it in her purse. Until now this secret had been exciting, mysterious, even a little glamorous, and the danger had felt remote. All of a sudden she felt burdened with this knowledge. And she wondered how Mariette would react when Celia con-fessed what had happened with Ivo.

• • •

TWO PERIODS LATER CELIA FOUND Mariette in the hall. "I have to tell you something that you're not going to like."

"What?"

"Ivo found the admonition in my sketchbook."

"Are you kidding? How did he find it?"

"I thought he was looking at the drawings in the front. I didn't think he'd flip all the way to the back! I was only gone for a minute!"

"No one was supposed to see that—I trusted you!"

"I know—I'm so sorry! But I didn't tell him anything else. He promised he wouldn't do anything until I had the chance to talk to you."

"Talk to me? Wait, he knows about *me?*"

"He guessed, because of that time with your locker, and— I didn't tell him anything about you!" Celia felt as if a rodent were gnawing her from the inside. She never had failed someone like this before. It was a new torment she hated immediately. "It would have been okay if he had just thought I had written a twisted poem about the curse, but I said I hadn't written it, and then he accused *you,* and I let it slip that you're trying to stop it."

"This is really bad. I have to talk to him," Mariette said. She was totally focused, serious. "I have to fix this."

"I don't know how to fix it."

"I do. When can I see him?"

"He wants to meet over the break. The three of us."

"As soon as possible."

"I'll find out. I'll call you tonight. Mariette, I'm sorry."

Mariette sighed. "It's okay. I know you didn't do it on purpose. It's just, how well do you know Ivo? Do you know anything about him outside of school? What if he accuses me of something and I get asked a whole bunch of questions I can't answer? Or what if he says something to the person who happens to be the Unkind who's doing all this and I'm exposed? Or what if—and I don't know, but I'm just saying—what if *he's* the Unkind, and I just can't detect him because I'm too new? This could be very dangerous for me."

"I'm sorry."

"And it could be just as dangerous for you, too! The Unkind would know you know something since you have the admonition. And at this point you aren't even able to defend yourself if someone comes after you, because you haven't developed any powers yet. You see why I'm freaking out about this?"

"Yes. I feel horrible!" Celia didn't bother to protest that she really thought she wasn't one of the Kind and never would develop powers.

"We just have to hope Ivo keeps his word and doesn't say anything to anyone until I get to talk to him, or else we're screwed. You have to be careful. Don't go out by yourself unless you absolutely have to, okay? And we need to have that meeting as soon as possible."

"Okay," Celia said meekly.

WHEN CELIA GOT HOME SHE went straight to her room, dug the Unkind admonition out of her purse, and looked for a place to hide it. She pulled an old sketchbook off the shelf and opened it in the middle, intending to shove the admonition in there and close it up again. She stopped short when she saw the page to which she had opened.

It was a sketch she had copied from a perfume ad. A woman in a black dress gazed out of the page, one strap slipping from the arc of her shoulder, her eyes open and wondering, her lips parted as though she had paused in the middle of a thought, her hair weightless around her face like a cloud.

A dark line mustache was scribbled in pen under her delicate nose, and devilish arched eyebrows had been jabbed onto the page over the thin eyebrows Celia had drawn. The memory of a certain day in eighth grade returned to Celia like a baseball hitting her in the chest: an afternoon period during which her sketchbook had gone missing, only to be found later in the cafeteria with dozens of pages vandalized like this one. Celia sat down at her desk as the memory unspooled.

She had come home in tears and was curled on her bed when her father arrived home from work. She had sobbed the story to him and felt his warm hand smooth her frizzy hair and stroke her back through her baggy sweatshirt.

"I'm sorry, honey," he had said gently. "Kids are stupid and cruel sometimes."

"Can't you *do* anything?" she had begged him.

"What do you want me to do?"

"I don't know, complain to the school? Make them stop?"

Her father had sighed, and there was a long moment when Celia waited for him to speak. "Honey, if anyone ever hurts you—physically—I will skip the school and go straight to the police. If anyone ever threatens to hurt you, you can bet I will make sure the school knows about it. And if I thought you were being emotionally torn up by what was going on, I would be spending a lot of time making sure you got the help you needed, with a counselor or someone else.

"But this is what makes being a parent hard: trying to decide when to step in and protect you and when to step back and let you protect yourself. Because growing up includes realizing that some people are stupid and cruel and you have to figure out how to deal with them. Figuring that out makes you a stronger person. Now, if it goes beyond that—if someone is violent, or if the person seems more threatening than just typical middle school stupidity—please tell me. But it sounds like someone is jealous of your talent, and maybe resentful because you don't like the same things they do, and they're trying to get under your skin. Does that sound true?"

Celia took a tissue from the box on her bedside table. "I guess."

"Can I say something else to you? Sometimes I wish you drew a little less. I certainly don't want you to stop, because you're too good and I hope you always use your talent to make beautiful things. But to be a good artist, you need to *live*. And that means spending time in the real world, with real people, doing lots of different things. Which also means occasionally getting hurt and picking yourself up. It's one thing to be a spectator, off in the corner watching, drawing what you see. It's another thing to be an artist, out there in the world, creating things that change the people who see them—things that change the world, even."

"Can a drawing do that?"

"I think it can. I think great art is like a miracle. It shows us things we wouldn't have imagined ourselves. It makes us see the world differently. It makes things we thought were impossible, possible. I wouldn't be surprised if you made art like that one day."

"You think so?"

"I do. Someday you will draw things that will change people, and change the world."

Celia remembered the feeling of his lips on her forehead, his hand helping her off the bed so they could go down to dinner. She put the admonition in the old sketchbook and returned it to the shelf, then went down to see if she could help her mother cook.

THE SECOND-TO-LAST DAY before the break arrived, and it didn't take Celia and Mariette long to learn Stella Miller was out with the flu. "What does that mean?" Mariette said in frustration. "The flu isn't the curse."

"I don't think so." Celia couldn't think of anything intelligent to say. "I guess we have to wait until tomorrow anyway, to see if anything happened to her. Anything that could be the curse, I mean."

"I don't even care, at this point. We have a bigger problem to solve, and that's Ivo."

"I told you, we're meeting on Saturday at the café."

"I know. But you understand how I'm not really going to think about much else until then?"

"Yes. I'll see you in chem." Celia watched Mariette walk away. She looked around the hall and thought, *I'll be so glad to get out of this place for a few weeks . . .*

power, corruption & lies

CELIA STEPPED THROUGH THE snow on her way to
the café on the first day of winter break, thinking she
wouldn't be surprised to find two shadows trailing behind her if she looked over her shoulder. There would be the
usual one, cast by the sun, making a distorted impression of
her on the white lawns as she passed. And there would be a
second one, composed of all the strange secrets that had collected around her, always just out of reach, but never far and
often underfoot. She had hoped to savor the holiday as a time
to relax and forget about school for a little while, but troubling
parts of it had followed her home.

There was the curse, which wasn't really a curse, but a co-
vert attempt by an Unkind to fulfill an admonition. There was
Mariette, whose powers were good—Celia believed that without a doubt—but who *had powers,* strange and fantastic things
Celia had seen with her own eyes. Powers, incidentally, that
Mariette believed Celia would be coming into herself, though
Celia wasn't convinced. There was Skip, who might be the nic-
est guy at Suburban or might be the person who had attempted
to murder a few dozen times during the fall semester. And then
there was Ivo, who had glimpsed something he shouldn't have

and who easily could convene a modern-day witch-hunt if he wanted—or worse. What if it turned out *he* was the Unkind behind all this? And wasn't that the freaky part? A few months ago she never would have considered something like that even possible, much less something to be taken seriously. The cold wind blew, and she shoved her hands in her pockets and pulled her shoulders up beside her neck.

Celia arrived first at the café. She took the same table where she and Mariette had sat on Halloween weekend. A minute later Mariette arrived. "I'm glad you're here early," she said, sitting next to Celia so Ivo would have to sit across from them. "Let me do the talking. Don't say anything."

"I know. This is for you." Celia handed a brightly colored gift bag to Mariette. She hoped it would help to smooth things over.

"For me? Oh, I had no idea we were exchanging gifts! I don't have anything for you!" Mariette was distraught.

"It's okay! It's nothing. Just open it." Celia watched her dig into the tissue paper. First Mariette pulled out the portrait Celia had drawn of her, encased in a frame. Celia had captured Mariette with a smile that filled her entire face, her curls arranged more artfully than Celia ever had seen them in real life. A hummingbird hovered over her shoulder, its wings a blur.

Mariette caught her breath. "This is *not* nothing!" Her eyes grew moist, and Celia was taken aback by the effect her gift had caused. "This is amazing! You are so talented!" Mariette looked up at Celia and her face was radiant, even as a tear escaped down her cheek. "Thank you so much!"

"You're welcome! I really am sorry."

"It's okay. It's going to be fine." Mariette wiped her face with the back of her hand. Then she pulled *The Awakening* from the bag. "Oh, I've been meaning to read this! Thank you! Thank you so much!" Celia was overjoyed to see her friend sunny again, but the next moment Mariette looked across the room and her tone changed. "There's Ivo." Celia turned to see him pushing open the café door. "Like I said, let me do the talking."

They stood up as Ivo approached the table, which felt weird and formal. "I guess you've never actually met. Ivo, this is Mariette; Mariette, this is Ivo." Celia watched the two of them mumble hellos and look each other over curiously. She vowed to not speak again until they'd finished.

"So, we need to talk," Mariette said, sitting down.

"You're right, we do." Ivo pulled out his chair and they settled in.

After a strained silence, Mariette said, "Why don't you ask me what you want to know?"

"Are you, I don't know, a witch?"

"No, I am not a witch. But I do have powers you don't understand."

Celia was surprised Mariette would share something like that so willingly. She had figured Mariette would deliver some kind of plausible excuse in hopes of doing a better job of convincing Ivo there was nothing serious going on. Perhaps a story about a creative writing assignment. But there it was, out in the open. Mariette's eyes were bright. *She must have fantasized about what it would be like to say something so bold to a stranger.* Mariette and Ivo had locked gazes, and it was as though Celia had disappeared and the conversation was between the two of them alone.

"Like what?" Ivo said. "What kind of powers?"

"A lot of my powers have to do with nature, so it's hard

for me to give you a demonstration right here." The bud vases were gone from the tables, so Mariette couldn't repeat her trick from Halloween. And there weren't any glasses handy, so she couldn't create a frost fingerprint. Mariette lifted her hand up between her face and Ivo's and snapped her fingers. For an instant a flame appeared in the space her fingertips left behind. And then it was gone.

Ivo's eyes widened, but he recovered quickly. "That's an old magician's trick."

"Hey, you don't have to believe me if you don't want to," Mariette said airily. "It would be much easier if you didn't believe me. But if you don't, then why are we having this conversation?"

"Are you trying to kill girls on the day before their birthdays?"

"Of course not! Are you insane? And anyway, if I was supposed to kill someone, they'd be dead." Celia thought Mariette's display of bravado didn't strike the right tone. Ivo wasn't sure how to respond. Mariette went on. "I'm trying to stop the person whose poem you read."

"So someone else is trying to kill these girls? Who? Why?"

"You're not going to like this answer: I don't know who it is. But that person is doing it to become more powerful. It's kind of like a sacrifice."

"Are you sure you're not just doing some stupid role-playing game or something? Where people get in over their heads and someone dies because people take something make-believe too far?"

"Actually, that's exactly what I'm doing," Mariette said, sitting back in her chair. "You've figured me out. I am an overly imaginative girl who likes to play mysterious games that mean nothing. Are you satisfied now?"

Ivo smirked at her and shook his head. "Honestly, I don't know if you're serious or not. I do wonder why Celia likes you so much." For the first time Ivo and Mariette acknowledged that Celia still was there. "A bunch of girls have gotten hurt, and it's pretty clear that they've been the kinds of injuries no one could have caused. But if you're getting some kind of twisted satisfaction out of it, or if you're using it as an excuse to hurt someone, I'd say you're a sociopath and someone should know about it."

"Then why don't we go back to the other theory, that I'm actually on the good side. But I still need to convince you of that, so I'll show you something else. Hold out your hand." Mariette extended her own hand over the table, beckoning for Ivo's.

"What are you going to do?"

"C'mon, I'm not going to hurt you," Mariette mocked him.

Ivo hesitated a moment, then offered his hand to Mariette, who took it in hers. She closed her eyes and murmured under her breath. Celia and Ivo watched her intently. When Mariette opened her eyes, he said, "What was that?"

"You didn't feel it? Let me try again." Mariette changed her grip on Ivo's hand, closed her eyes, and moved her lips again. "How about now?"

"No," Ivo said triumphantly. "What am I supposed to feel?"

Mariette looked a little crestfallen and vulnerable for the first time since Ivo had arrived. "Huh. Maybe I'm not doing it right. You know what, I have to go. I'm sorry you don't like me, but at least now you know I'm just a harmless crazy girl. You can do what you like." She gathered her bag and Celia's gifts and got up from her chair.

"Mariette!" Celia got up, too. "Wait!" Mariette was slouching toward the café door. Celia turned to Ivo, who gave her a look that meant he didn't care what she did. "I'll be right back," she said, and went after Mariette, catching her just outside the café door. "Mariette!"

"Stand here so he can't see me." Mariette was grinning mischievously when Celia came around her. Over Mariette's shoulder Celia could see Ivo through the window, still seated at the table. He looked out at Celia and gave her a friendly wave.

"What's going on?"

"It's fine. I fixed it," Mariette said. "Don't stay here. Go back to him."

"What did you try to do? Why didn't it work?"

"Oh, it worked. Have a great Christmas. I'll see you at school."

Celia watched Mariette practically skip down the street. She gave up and went back into the café.

"Who was that?" Ivo said when she returned to the table.

"Who?"

"The girl you were talking to, outside. Who was she?"

"That was Mariette."

"Have you told me about her? Where does she go to school?"

"She goes to Suburban. She's my—" Celia stopped, wondering if she was undoing what Mariette had just done. But Ivo only gave her a blank look for a moment, and then he didn't seem to give Mariette another thought.

"I'm glad we're hanging out," he said. "I feel like we don't really talk much when everyone else is around."

"You're right," Celia said, sitting down, trying not to stare too hard at Ivo while she attempted to divine what Mariette had done to him.

"Like the other day at school. I've never told anyone else about Darkland, not even Brenden. If you haven't said anything to the others, would you mind keeping it our secret? It's kind of a fantasy, and it might sound foolish."

"Your secret's safe with me," Celia said, trying to ignore how completely ridiculous that sounded, considering everything that had happened. *And now Mariette's secret is safe with me again.*

14
∫himmering, warm
and bright

C ELIA WONDERED IF SHE should feel guilty about what
Mariette had done to Ivo, but her relief got the better
of her. She had plenty of other worries, but they could
wait until the break was over. She slept in and worked more
hours at Lippa's to help with the holiday rush. A picturesque
snowfall on Christmas Eve put a lovely touch on the break.
When she left the bookstore that night, Celia took a detour
through the surrounding neighborhood to enjoy the snow. It
felt like its own little village with hedges and detached garages,
slumbering in the white. She stopped in front of a house that
looked like an English cottage, with stucco walls and a roof
that curved under the eaves. Snow had blanketed the roof and
dusted the ivy that climbed the walls, transforming the house
into a gingerbread and powdered sugar confection. Chimneys
rose on either side of the house like ears. Celia tried to imagine
the people inside, until the chill began to seep through her
coat, and she turned toward home.

Christmas morning was quiet, as though muffled by the
cottony snow. Celia was tickled that her mother had found dark
gray paper in which to wrap her gifts, and then overjoyed to receive a framed Mark Rothko print. "Your father liked Rothko,

too. That retrospective at the National Gallery was quite a few years ago," her mother said. "Maybe there'll be another one before long." They hung the print in her bedroom, and Celia was glad she hadn't made any hasty decisions simply to fill up the empty space. She also received a black cashmere turtleneck and a charcoal suede skirt. "I might be crazy for admitting this, but I've grown to like you in black," her mother said, shaking her head. "You look really nice."

"Thanks, Mom." Celia hugged her.

"You know, I was a little concerned at the beginning of school," her mother said. "You made a lot of changes really fast. I wasn't sure how much of it was you and how much was your friends."

"I wondered the same thing," Celia said. "But they're not like that. Each of them is different. They all have their own interests. You should meet the rest of them."

"I'd like to! And they must be a good influence in some ways. You're doing so well in school."

"I guess I am, so far. How are you doing?"

"I'm all right." Her mother smiled. "This Christmas isn't as hard as last year, but it's still hard. I know you miss him, too."

"Yeah, but it's better. The funny thing is, now people think I'm into depressing things, because of how I dress and all that. But I'm not depressed at all. I feel like, even though the sad part never really goes away and I'm never going to stop missing Dad, the rest of my life has come back. I can start to be happy again."

"That's good."

"What are you going to do?" Celia asked her mother. "Do you think you would ever be with someone else?"

"I don't know. Maybe someday."

"Don't wait too long." They hugged each other, sitting on Celia's bed, with the Rothko print looking down on them.

THE BOOKSTORE WAS QUIET on the day after Christmas. Celia absentmindedly updated the bestseller wall, her thoughts on New Year's Day. Ivo and Liz had invited the Rosary to their house for First Night, which Ivo insisted took place not on New Year's Eve but on the evening of New Year's Day. "If we had it on New Year's Eve it would be *Last* Night, not First Night," he'd explained to Celia, as if it were the most obvious thing in the world. She didn't look over immediately when the door opened, but when the customer approached her, she turned to greet him. "Tomasi!"

The look on his face made Celia think he had escaped from somewhere. As many times as she had imagined his gray eyes, she was startled again by their depth. "Hi!" he said. "You probably thought I died."

"No, but I wondered," she said. This time there was no counter between them, and she had an impulse to hug him, but she wasn't brave enough. "Where have you been?"

"I got pneumonia," he said. "Really put a wrench in my plans."

"Oh my god! I'm glad you're better!"

"I wanted to send you a message, but I felt weird asking my mom to do it."

"It's okay. I understand," she said. "It's good to see you."

"How late do you work?"

"I'm here until five."

"Do you want to do something after?" He was very direct, Celia thought, and a little nervous.

"What did you have in mind?"

"We could take a walk, if it's not too cold. There's a park a few blocks away."

"You know this neighborhood?"

"Yeah, I live on the next street over. You know the Tudor house with the wood shingles that curl under the eaves?"

"You live there? That house is beautiful."

"It's all right. Sometimes I wish it were larger. But you're free after?"

"Sure." Celia smiled. He gave a half smile back, and she enjoyed the feeling she had spent a lot of time trying to recapture during the last few months—the warm buzz that flowed through her when his strong features softened even a little. "I'll come back at five."

"You're sure? It won't be two months from now?" She wondered if she was crossing a line, but he chuckled.

"I'm sure. I'll see you at five." Once again he made a quick exit, and Celia wondered if he really would come back. When she turned to find that Lippa had observed the exchange from the end of a row of shelves, she laughed in spite of herself.

"It's been months, and you don't know him any better?" Lippa asked, approaching.

"That's the first time I've seen him since the last time he was here!" Celia said.

"Well, you two are not setting any records, are you?" Lippa teased. She pulled out a pack of gum and offered a piece to Celia. "This is the only thing that keeps me from smoking." Celia accepted, and they folded strips of chewing gum into their mouths.

"I wanted to ask you, you said before—do you really think being old and mysterious is bad?"

"What did I say?" Lippa looked blankly at her.

"'When you are young and mysterious, men write songs about you. When you are old and mysterious, boys throw stones at you.'"

"I said that? Hm." Lippa thought for a moment. "Well, it sounds good. But it's not true. No one has ever thrown stones at me. Has anyone ever written a song about you?"

"Not that I know of," Celia said.

"And we're both rather mysterious, aren't we? So it can't be true at all." Lippa smiled benevolently at her, nudging Celia's elbow. Then she turned to go back to the office.

During the rest of her shift, Celia became nervous about meeting Tomasi. She really didn't know much about him. She wanted to trust her instinct that he was a good guy, and Lippa seemed to approve of him. But he was big and strong, and he had been missing for months, and Regine's cautionary words lingered in her mind. Celia couldn't banish the thought that she would be taking a risk by going somewhere secluded with him.

"It's a little cold for a walk. Do you mind if we just get cider at that place across the street?" she asked when he came back to meet her. He didn't seem crazy about the idea, but her face must have betrayed her hesitation, because he gave in.

When they settled at a table, he looked out the window, and then said, "I'm sorry for disappearing."

"I've never met someone and then had him disappear before," she said. "It was strange. But it sounds like you have a very good excuse." Celia sipped hot cider, and she pulled apart a small cake encrusted with currants, pushing the plate to the center of the table. Tomasi looked at it curiously and then took a small piece.

"That's good. So, how's Diaboliques?"

"It's exactly the same. I think that place is frozen in amber. Not that I mind, because I love it, but it's so consistent. People stand in the same places. They dance to the same songs. When Patrick plays something new, within a few weeks it's like he's been playing it forever. People pounce on it, and memorize it, and it's completely absorbed. Halloween was really beautiful."

"I miss it."

"Well, you should come back," Celia said. "I had gotten used to you being there on the other side of the room, staring."

"Your weird sisters are still being overprotective?"

"They haven't had any reason to be protective since you've been gone, but I think it's time for that to stop anyway. Marco said they were jealous you were paying attention to me."

"Oh really?" Tomasi's eyebrow went up.

They looked at each other until she couldn't stand the silence. "I read *The Awakening*," she said. "Twice. It's amazing. Thank you so much for recommending it. My friends Liz and Regine both read it, too, and I think Ivo might have."

"I'm glad you liked it. It is a completely different perspective on being a woman—so many other women in literature stay within the boundaries that are set for them." It surprised Celia to hear him speak like that. Over the past months she had remembered only his clipped sentences.

"Will you recommend something else? I've read a few other things, but it's so hard to choose. I'm still overwhelmed every time I look through the shelves."

He thought for a moment. "Have you read Henry James yet?"

"No, but we have a lot of him at the store," Celia said. "And my friends love to quote him about being a person on whom nothing is lost."

"Try *The Portrait of a Lady*. I'm thinking of it because it's probably the best female character I've ever read who's been written by a man. So it goes along with the theme, kind of."

"I will get it on Tuesday, when I work again." Once more they looked at each other for a long moment. Celia felt herself grow bolder. She studied his face as though she were preparing to draw it. This time he lost the staring contest and drank from his mug. "So, you must read a lot, then?"

"I wasn't always a reader," he said. "In fact, I used to have a lot of trouble reading. They thought I had a learning disability, but, well, I figured it out, and then I caught up quickly. My mother was a literature major in college, and we have so many books at home. There was a time when I was getting grounded a lot, so I started reading for something to do."

"Grounded?" Celia quickly added, "I don't want to pry."

"My parents are pretty strict, and when I was struggling in school, they thought I was just being lazy." Tomasi sounded resigned about it all.

"Well, if you came out of it having read so many books . . . I should read more."

"Books are my best friends and my worst enemies at the same time," he said a little wistfully.

"Do you have a lot of friends? I mean, people?"

"Not really. Can't you tell?"

"A little. But you don't seem to be shy with me."

"Maybe because you're not shy with me, either," he said, and she got to see his half smile again. "I've been told I can look a little intimidating."

"Where do you go to school?"

"St. Dymphna's. It's a great education, but everything else is kind of a drag."

"What year are you?"

"Junior."

"So you're sixteen?"

"Seventeen. Except in old Father William's class, where we're all twelve." Tomasi grimaced. "How about you?"

"I'm a sophomore at Suburban. I'll be sixteen in April."

"You seem older than that. More mature."

"Well, most of my friends are older."

"Are we friends?"

"I think so," Celia said. "Now that you've reappeared, yes."

She asked him more about having pneumonia, but his answers were vague, and she thought he sounded weary of the whole experience, so she let it go. She imagined him moping around the house, with only the sheets and his school assignments changing, and she thought it must be a relief for him just to be back in the real world. He quizzed her about the Rosary and she was happy to describe them to him.

Too soon it was time for her to head home for dinner. Outside the café Celia tried not to shiver in the winter air. She didn't want her coldness to be the reason they said goodbye and broke this strange, lovely connection. He didn't seem to want to part, either.

"So you'll be at Diaboliques?" she asked.

"I hope so. My folks are still concerned about me going out. They're scared I could relapse or something. It's been a little suffocating. But I certainly hope so. Can I kiss you?"

Celia was caught off guard by his directness. Her feelings quickly sorted themselves, and desire triumphed over her lingering fears. "Yes," she said. She put her hand on his arm when he touched her waist, and she did her best to kiss him back, though she thought he was a little unpracticed himself. But it was electric to her, and strange, and her sense of him as the Leopard returned.

Celia closed her eyes and had a flashback to a park her family had used to go to for cookouts. It was sequestered deep in a forest outside town, at the end of a gravel road that seemed to snake along for miles. In the park, trails through the trees gave way to rocky ridges and bluffs, but in its midst there was a massive power line draped across the terrain. Huge skeletal metal towers held the lines up, with rows of strange ceramic plates on each side where the wires hurdled across them. The trees had been cleared on either side of the lines, leaving a groove that ran through the forest and curved into the landscape. There was so much current in the wires, Celia could hear it humming a hundred feet above her. If she stood quietly she could hear the hum even back in the cookout area. She loved that park and its huge playground made of notched logs, with tire swings and a maze. But it felt a little dangerous, too—she never could forget completely the hum of the power line just beyond the trees. Her family would stay until dusk, when the park ranger started blowing his car horn in the parking lot, and then she would fall asleep in the back seat on the way home, happy and gently exhausted from the day. Tomasi's kiss blended all those feelings together for her, all over again. Celia stepped closer to him, and he slipped his other arm around her back, but then someone was shouting his name and he pulled away.

"That's my dad," he said. He looked rattled, but before they turned away from each other he gave her his warmest smile yet.

The man strode forcefully across the street toward them. "What do you think you're doing? Get home right now!"

Tomasi actually seemed to shrink as his father, who could have been a linebacker, got closer. "Go!"

Tomasi mumbled goodbye to Celia and walked across the street. His father stood guard as he passed, still facing Celia. "I don't care who you are, but he is going to have nothing to do with you anymore!" His words were like a slap across her face, and she stared at him in shock. Then he turned and walked after Tomasi, who was already halfway down the block, and suddenly the enchanted evening was cold and lifeless.

She cried as she walked home, and her tears turned cold on her cheeks until she rubbed them away. The stars were dull in the sky.

CELIA SPENT THE NEXT FEW days putting the finishing touches on the rest of her portraits and mounting them in frames. She couldn't stop thinking about Tomasi and how their date had ended, but like so many things these days, she didn't know what she could do to make it better. Late in the afternoon on New Year's Day, Regine picked her up and they went over to Ivo and Liz's house. "I would say First Night is a tradition for us," Regine told her, "but next year everything will be different, so this may be the last time. I guess they'll probably come home from college for break, but who knows if it'll be the same." Her excitement bubbled over. "You are going to love their parents! They are brilliant and eccentric and so creative. I have fantasized about being adopted into their family."

They were the last to arrive, and Celia finally got to traverse the ivy lawn and go inside the house she saw every morning before school. On the front door a bright brass plate had FOURAD engraved on it.

"I want everything in this house," Regine whispered to her before Liz opened the door. From the moment she stepped inside, Celia could tell the Fourads shared a taste for the erudite and offbeat with their son and daughter. Everything was special, and carefully chosen. The jar next to the phone on the hall table held antique-looking mechanical pencils and fountain pens. The bulbs in the chandelier were the type that mimicked Edison's originals, with oblong glass and glowing looped filaments. Celia admired framed prints in the hall, which she learned were created by people with intriguing names like Rauschenberg, Frankenthaler, and Diebenkorn, and she hoped to have the chance to examine a collection of beautiful old books she noticed as she passed the study.

They assembled in the family room, and Celia was presented to Mr. and Mrs. Fourad, who welcomed her warmly. If Celia had tried to imagine what Ivo and Liz would look like in twenty-five years, she would have guessed something very close to Mr. and Mrs. Fourad. They were darkly stylish and refined, and she could see aspects of Ivo and Liz in both of them. They had a whimsy about them, though, that Celia hadn't found in their son and daughter. "I know your name isn't exactly Cecilia, but do people sing you that Simon and Garfunkel song?" Mr. Fourad asked her.

"I've heard that a couple times." She smiled.

"There's a much better song, by the Motels, and it really is your name," he said. *"Celia, see what you've done, see what you've done to someone . . ."* He sang the line easily, and she thought that she couldn't remember ever having heard her own father sing anything, except to mumble "Happy Birthday" in a crowd.

"I don't know that one." She looked around, and the others didn't seem to know it, either.

They approached the long, low dinner table, around which stood an assortment of upholstered chairs that were all different but somehow matched. Mrs. Fourad took the head, and

Mr. Fourad the foot, and the Rosary filled in the sides. Celia found herself between Brenden and Marco, which pleased her.

"What is this music?" Marco asked. "It's beautiful."

"I'm glad you like it!" Mrs. Fourad beamed. "It's Vivaldi, and it's sung by a countertenor."

"That's a man singing?"

"Yes! I had this same conversation when I heard it the first time. When I was in Paris last August, I heard it in a store."

"A music store?"

"No, a clothing store. Should I tell this story? You have to know it's there. From the outside it looks like a private residence. But if you ring the bell, they buzz you in. You step into this dark hallway, and while your eyes are adjusting, a pleasant, soft-spoken person approaches you and asks you to turn off your cell phone. Can you imagine?" Mrs. Fourad looked around at them amusedly.

"And the whole place is dark?"

"In that hall it is, but you follow the salesperson farther in and it opens up into this raw space, with exposed stone and brick, and ancient rafter beams, and a few skylights way up in the roof, and it looks like it hasn't changed since the French Revolution. But there are racks and racks of the most exquisite clothes. I spent an hour looking at things, and I wound up buying that gorgeous hammered silk blouse I wore on Thanksgiving, you remember?" she asked Liz, who nodded. "At any rate, they were playing this music in the store, and I couldn't believe it was a man singing. They were nice enough to write the name of the recording down for me, and I picked it up first chance I got."

"That doesn't sound anything like any store I've ever been in," Marco said.

"When I got back out on the street, I felt like Alice, fresh back from Wonderland."

"I want to go to Paris," Brenden said.

Mr. Fourad said, "It's so fun to find things like that — things a guidebook wouldn't tell you. Do you remember that door we found on the Aventine Hill in Rome?" He asked his wife, who nodded enthusiastically. "We were on our way to hear these monks sing vespers at St. Anselmo's, and we got there a little early, so we were strolling around the neighborhood, and there are all these high walls outside the private homes. Well, for some reason I decided to look through the keyholes of these huge doors in the walls — they're eight or nine feet tall — to see what was inside."

"You're lucky you didn't get arrested!" Liz said.

"If they didn't want people looking through the keyholes, they wouldn't put them there." Mr. Fourad said it as if it were the most obvious thing in the world, and everyone laughed and protested. "Anyway, there wasn't much to see through most of them, only a glimpse of a house or a car. But I looked through another one and there was this view down a gravel walk, with a row of topiaries on either side, and at the end, framed like a picture, was the dome of St. Peter's! It was like looking into a snow globe. I nearly fell over. And then of course I made her look."

"So you should go to Rome, too." Mrs. Fourad smiled at Brenden.

Celia looked around her friends, feeling almost like an adult, sitting at this table, speaking of art and travel and ideas, and she felt their shared dream of always having new adventures, as long as they lived. If Celia's July self wouldn't have recognized her September self, she would have been completely flummoxed to see herself now, in January. The thought made her smile.

They reminisced about the previous semester, and Celia was grateful no one brought up curses or virginity. But Liz took pleasure in telling her parents about Celia's mysterious admirer. "He was beautiful, and he would stare at her so intently. Then he showed up at the bookstore where she works—he's the one who recommended that awesome book, *The Awakening*. And then he disappeared." It was gratifying to hear someone else describe Tomasi as beautiful. From the beginning Celia had been struck by him, but it was only recently, when she had glimpsed his nervous, softer side, that she really had considered how handsome he was. She wondered again what had happened when he had returned home after their star-crossed date.

Mrs. Fourad said, "Well, as literary as he is, and as laconic, he sounds like quite the Lord Byron: a little mad, bad, and dangerous to know? How very romantic, maybe in a tragic way. What do you think, Celia?"

"That sounds about right." She smiled, thinking there was no point in telling them about her recent encounter with Tomasi. Mrs. Fourad had described it perfectly, without even realizing it.

After dinner they helped clear the table, but Mrs. Fourad shooed them away from trying to wash the dishes. Celia watched everyone wander in different directions. Ivo and Brenden began looking through Mr. Fourad's record collection, and Regine tagged along. Liz asked Marco to look at a blouse she wanted him to tailor. Celia was standing in the family room paging through a book of Edward Steichen's photographs when Mr. Fourad found her. "I don't know what I did with that Motels album. I hate when I lose things in my record collection—it could be anywhere." He smiled helplessly. "If I find it I'll send a copy along with Ivo and Liz for you."

"Thank you." Celia never had felt so comfortable with someone new so quickly before.

"So, Ivo and Liz always talk about your beauty and how well you draw, but they never tell us more banal things. How do you like Suburban?"

"It's good, so far," Celia said. "I didn't really enjoy my first year at the other school. I think Suburban would have been more like that if I hadn't met them."

"They should have invited you over sooner, but I'm glad you're here now."

"Your house is beautiful," Celia told him.

"Thank you! Actually, tell me this." Mr. Fourad glanced at the door and then looked curiously at her. "Will you tell me about Diaboliques? My children have forbidden me to go, but it sounds absolutely brilliant."

"It is!" Celia laughed. "It's like a jewel box with all kinds of secret compartments. You go through all these rooms, and each one is more interesting than the last, until you get to the room where we spend most of our time, and it's amazing. The clothes, the music, everything."

"I wish I could go." Mr. Fourad smiled. "I guess those days are over for me."

"That's a shame. It shouldn't be like that."

"Maybe not, or maybe so. I'm not sure I would go back to high school again just to have the chance to go to Diaboliques." He chuckled. "Some things you have to do at the right time in your life, and I'm just glad all of you are doing it. I have my own memories to cherish." Then Mrs. Fourad was calling him from the other room, and he took his leave.

Celia wandered into the study, where she had seen the old books, but this time her attention was caught by a piece of calligraphy framed on the wall. She read the angular script whose letters intertwined:

Never imagine yourself not to be otherwise than what it might appear to others that what you were or might have been was not otherwise than what you had been would have appeared to them to be otherwise. —*Lewis Carroll*

Celia felt someone beside her and turned to find Liz. "What does it mean?" Celia asked her.

"Be what you would seem to be," Liz told her. "Be yourself." She looked tenderly at Celia for a moment, and then the two of them turned back to reread the quote, standing quietly together. Celia thought if she had an older sister, she'd want her to be Liz.

They gravitated back to the family room again to exchange gifts. Ivo asked Celia to help him retrieve his presents, so she followed him up to his room and had a moment to be awestruck by the black walls, the bare surfaces, the framed photograph of a man leaping from the top of a brick wall, hurtling toward the street below as if it were a void. But the moment he was sure they were alone, Ivo turned to her with a purpose.

"I haven't forgotten, you know," he said.

"Forgotten what?"

"About that poem in your sketchbook."

"Oh, really? I thought—" Celia broke off, unsure what she thought.

"I know something is happening. And you know about it. And I wasn't supposed to find out. And I think you tried to make me forget about it somehow. But I remember."

"What do you remember?" Celia asked.

"I remember the poem has something to do with the curse. I think you're trying to stop it? You did something to me, because every time I try to remember, it's all a fog." He was concentrating, as though he were trying to work out an equation in his head. "You don't want me to know. And I guess there's not much I can do about it. Just tell me: are you in trouble? I mean, are you in danger?"

"No, Ivo, I'm not. I promise you, I'm not. I thought I told you. It was just a scary poem my friend Mariette wrote around Halloween. It's not real. It's just a scary poem."

"Who's Mariette?"

"Mariette? My chemistry lab partner?" Celia saw the blank look on Ivo's face again. "You don't remember meeting her?"

"No, when did we meet?"

"It doesn't matter."

"If you say so." They looked at each other for a long moment. He gave her the same expression she must have given Mariette for weeks before she found out the truth. It was a look that said, *I can't put my finger on it, but something is going on here.*

"A scary poem?" Ivo said finally.

"It's just a scary poem," Celia said. "Let's go back to the party." She picked up two of Ivo's gifts, and he picked up the other three.

The Rosary sat down in the family room with mugs of cranberry tea.

Celia reached for her stack of gifts. "I'll go first, since I'm the newest." She passed them around and waited as they were opened carefully.

"I feel like I'm looking at a photograph," Brenden said,

marveling at his portrait. "A really good photograph." They passed the portraits around.

"They're not just our likenesses—you captured our personalities," Liz said. "You are really talented."

"Well, you were all great subjects, even if you didn't realize it at the time," Celia said, thrilled.

"Were you looking at us when you drew us?" Marco asked.

"No. But I made quite a few sketches of each of you before I was ready to do these."

"You must be as bored in art class as Marco is in home ec." Liz smiled.

"We get to do what we love. It's not that bad." Celia smiled at Marco, who winked at her.

"The senior class is raising money for a mosaic to go in the new computer wing they're going to build this summer. We should have you design it," Liz said.

"That's a great idea," Brenden said.

"I've never done mosaic work," Celia said.

"You wouldn't have to install it. We just have to give a sketch to the mosaic woman."

"I'd love to help with that. Just let me know what you have in mind."

Marco had made each of them black beaded bracelets that resembled short rosaries, with a simple square cross on a short beaded strand. "I know we haven't been wearing rosaries much, but I thought maybe it was because they were a little too long." Immediately the bracelets went on everyone's wrists. Regine had created collage books for all of them, and again, they were passed around for everyone to see. No one was surprised that Brenden had made everyone a compilation CD. "It was so hard keeping these tracks from you." He laughed. "There is some great stuff on there."

Liz gave them each tiny shadow boxes. "What's inside?" Marco asked.

"Well, look and see, but you have to keep it a secret. Everyone's is different."

Celia looked through the hole in her shadow box and found a short poem, lit from behind:

> *One night I shall be awakened*
> *by the horn from the driver*
> *and know before my eyes are fully opened*
> *that the signal is for me.*
>
> *Then I shall descend those stairs,*
> *going out onto the avenue*
> *to ride away in the passenger's seat*
> *without so much as a glance at the driver.*

Celia caught her breath and looked around the room. Everyone had a similar expression. "I can't wait to read your first book," Brenden said to Liz.

"Neither can I!" Liz said, smiling. "If I want to be a novelist I'm going to have to start writing longer things than poems and short stories."

"Well, mine aren't as personal as the rest of yours, but hopefully they symbolize something," Ivo said, handing them identical boxes. They each unwrapped a black metal lantern with a single candle inside. "Let's go for a walk."

They collected their coats and carefully lit the candles, and then they stepped out into the night. The street was quiet, and a brilliant, nearly full moon easily outshone the corner streetlamps. "It really does give a luster of midday to objects below," Brenden murmured.

Lanterns in hand, they walked down to the boulevard and then followed it as it curved through the neighborhood. The lawns rose sharply, lifting the houses above the sidewalks. During the spring and summer a row of trees shaded the sidewalks and street on either side. Now they were lonely coatracks, broken umbrellas spread against the sky. The air was still and warm enough that Celia didn't shiver in her coat, and she was enraptured by the poetry of the surroundings and the procession.

"Is it all right if there's no music? We always have music," Marco said.

"Every once in a while the best soundtrack is silence," Brenden replied, taking Marco's free hand in his.

Celia agreed. They walked farther, in love with the night, the moonlight, the silence, and their solidarity. She linked arms with Regine, thinking this was an ideal moment she would remember—maybe one she even would try to re-create—a moment she never wanted to end.

At the end of the boulevard they reached an empty old mansion surrounded by a small park, bordered by a grove of pines. The evergreens blotted out the streetlights and held the moon back. Now and then a car could be heard shushing along the road beyond the trees. Liz opened a thermos and passed around cups of cranberry tea.

"What shall we toast?" Ivo asked. He looked at Celia.

"To the Rosary, who added me to their string, and knew what I needed before I knew it myself," Celia said.

Regine said, "To the new year, and all it will bring."

Marco said, "To friendships. Each one is unique, but all of them are the same."

Brenden said, "To growing up, but always remembering what it feels like to be a child."

Liz said, "To us, and making the most of every opportunity we have."

Ivo finished: "To right now. Everything that is ahead of us, everything that is behind us—all we really have is right now."

They held up their cups and then drank, and Celia thought she tasted the luminous night air that surrounded them with a thin fog. They might have been standing in a watercolor painting. She imagined the way she might draw the scene: the cluster of the six of them, with lanterns held at various heights, and their dark clothes as different depths of shadow and shade. Around them the looming trees, and above them the glowing moon.

"What are you thinking?" Regine asked her.

"About how I got here, and how I never would have guessed I would be here," Celia said. "I don't think I could have imagined this, but somehow it's happened."

"Sometimes the world stands on its head, just to remind us it can," Liz said. "And we realize what we thought was right side up could just as easily be upside down."

"It's true." Celia held up her lantern, and the rest of them followed her example, so they could look around their circle at each other, smiling quietly.

∫trange time∫

O VERNIGHT BEFORE THE FIRST day of the second semester, a snow squall blew through the area. But the
roads were cleared by morning, so the Rosary's cars
threaded their way to Suburban. As Celia picked her way over
the heavily salted patches of ice in the parking lot with her
friends, she hoped the second half of the year would bring a
fresh start. She didn't know how that could come true. There
was no reason for the curse day accidents, and all the superstitious and cruel things that went along with them, to stop. But
she remembered how alive she had felt on First Night, and it
made her optimistic.

"The ice is bad enough, but all this salt is like walking on
ball bearings," Marco said, slowing down to cross a treacherous
part of the walk. As if on cue, ahead of them a girl threw her
arms in the air as first one foot and then the other slipped out
from under her. She came down on her back, her head cracking
against the icy pavement and snapping sharply up. She lay still
for a moment before she struggled to her knees.

The Rosary stopped, but Celia ran forward and took the
girl's arm. "Are you okay?"

"Why didn't they cancel school?" the girl said. She was

crying a little, but mostly she looked dazed. Celia tried to brush snow and salt off the back of the girl's coat.

"It looked like you hit your head pretty hard," Celia said. The girl's pupils were dilated. "I think you might have a concussion."

"What does that feel like?" the girl said, before turning away and throwing up.

Celia held the girl's arm and looked around. The Rosary had stayed where they were, and it angered Celia. Meanwhile, a boy in an orange cap and scarf was making his way to her. He reached them as the poor girl straightened up.

"I think she has a concussion," Celia told Skip.

"Is your birthday tomorrow?" Skip asked the girl, who nodded. He looked at Celia. "Why do you and I seem to be around all the time when these things happen?" Skip asked, taking the girl's other arm.

I was going to ask you the same thing, Celia thought.

WITH THAT, THE FRESH START promised by the holiday break was swept aside. Once again the school was a morass of anxiety, bizarre speculations about virginity, and predatory propositions. But by midday, new information had traveled through the student body: three sophomore girls had celebrated their sixteenth birthdays over the winter break, and while all of them were admittedly virgins, none of them reportedly had suffered anything on their supposed curse day. "Why didn't anyone notice before that the bad things only happen at school?" Liz asked. "Celia, do us all a favor and stay home on the day before your birthday."

Celia was happy to agree, but Mariette was unconvinced when they discussed it later that afternoon. "This is what I know," she told Celia. "You remember, the admonition says the Unkind has until the lunar eclipse to kill a girl and collect her dying breath, and the next lunar eclipse isn't until the beginning of June. So whoever it is definitely is going to want to succeed before then. So far the girls have been coming to school, but if they start staying away, the Unkind might start going to them and hurting them elsewhere. And that makes it a lot harder for me to protect them, if I'm actually protecting them at all."

"I hadn't thought of that."

"And I still have no idea who the Unkind is. How old is Ivo?"

"Seventeen, I think? His birthday is in the summer. He must be seventeen. You still think the seventeen warning in your admonition is about the Unkind person?"

Mariette nodded. "I know Ivo's your friend, but I can't help wondering about him. I'm sure it's nothing. He would have figured out what I was doing to his memory if he were Unkind."

"Well, you didn't get all of his memory," Celia said. "He forgot you completely, but he still remembers the admonition, so now he just suspects me."

"Oh really?" Mariette was distressed. "That wasn't supposed to happen."

"Was what you did to him an experiment, or did you know what you were doing?"

"Kind of. I was pretty sure . . ." Mariette was quiet for a moment. "What could he do, though? You took the admonition out of your sketchbook. It's just his word against yours."

"Yes," Celia sighed. "He just looks at me strangely."

TOMASI DIDN'T SHOW UP AT Diaboliques on the first Friday in January, and considering the way their date had ended, Celia wasn't really surprised. She never had mentioned her lovely, terrible reunion with him to the others. Her life had divided into separate compartments: she had the Rosary, and Mariette, and her fleeting experiences with Tomasi, and more and more they were becoming mutually exclusive. If anything, the close call with Ivo made it clear they had to remain that way. She never had been in such a situation before. She'd never known any secrets to keep. At Diaboliques that Friday she still looked across the room a few times, trying to will Tomasi into attendance, but for the first time it seemed really futile.

She waited for a song she knew everyone in the Rosary loved. Soon enough, Patrick played "Seventh Dream of Teenage Heaven," and while Celia wanted to dance, instead she told Regine she was going to the bathroom. Regine nodded, hurrying onto the dance floor with the others.

Celia went down to the mezzanine as quickly as she could and stared around in the darkness until she found the red-haired fortuneteller, who looked up at Celia as though she was expected. Celia sat down, but before she could say anything, the woman brought her lips to Celia's ear.

"I will tell you something I rarely tell anyone, but I think you will come to understand it. One of the biggest responsibilities of having secret knowledge about other people is being able to judge when it is right to tell them and when it is better to keep it from them. Maybe they aren't ready to hear it. Maybe they need to find out on their own. Maybe they would misuse the information. Maybe what you know is only part of the story, and it will only confuse them. There are so many possibilities.

"I know you have questions. I know you are prepared to beg me to answer them. But I don't think it's right. Not now."

Celia asked anyway. "Is Tomasi okay?"

The woman looked at her, and Celia couldn't tell if she was irritated or sympathetic. "He is as okay as someone in his position can be. For every time you think of him, he has thought of you twice."

Celia began to ask another question, but the woman gave a barely perceptible shake of her head, and Celia relented.

ON A BLEAK WEDNESDAY CELIA sat at lunch with Regine and Brenden, but all of them were lost in their own thoughts. January seemed to be creeping by, and the cold weather made the spring semester feel like it would last forever. It was a good thing the Rosary had enjoyed First Night together, because now everyone seemed to be preoccupied—with college, with passing Chem II, with the anticipation of a long-distance relationship. Celia couldn't pretend she wasn't preoccupied, too. Even though she didn't expect to see Tomasi at Diaboliques, she was not about to let go of her longing for him. She had had her first kiss, and it had been fantastic, at least until his father had interrupted them. That had changed everything. Now Tomasi was no longer the mysterious guy she might get to know someday. He was *the one*. Celia could not allow him to slip away now as easily as she had that fall. It made her crazy every time she thought about it, which was hourly.

The three of them hadn't spoken for ten minutes when there was an eruption of shouting on the other side of the cafeteria. For a moment Celia couldn't tell what was happening, but soon she made out, "She's choking!" amidst the cries. Brenden and Regine looked in the same direction, their expressions unchanged.

"Why don't you ever try to help?" Celia asked them, exasperated. They stared at her in surprise. Before they could respond, a boy in an orange sweater ran across the cafeteria toward the choking girl. Within a minute Skip had performed the Heimlich maneuver, causing the girl to cough up her food. Then there was more shouting, and Celia gathered that the girl's friends were remonstrating with her for having come to school on the day before her birthday.

"I had an exam!" the girl screamed angrily to the room, storming away from the table, looking humiliated and drained. "I couldn't stay home!"

The noise had drawn teachers out of the lounge in the hall just outside the cafeteria. They lingered, unsure whether they needed to respond.

CELIA STRUGGLED TO STAY AWAY from the Tudor house with wooden shingles, which she now knew was Tomasi's. Each time she went to the bookstore she stopped on Tomasi's corner and looked down the street at the house, knowing it was inevitable — at some point she would walk down there, defy his father's warning, and knock on his door. Something didn't make sense to her. She could understand Tomasi's parents wanting him to be careful as he healed, but his father hadn't shown much in the way of concern. And his wrath had been directed as much at Celia as at Tomasi.

Toward the end of January, having spent three Fridays at Diaboliques aching for him, she surrendered the battle and left her house early for work. She studied Tomasi's house as she approached it for any clue that might help her guess the mystery it contained. But the pair of chimneys, the furry moss on the roof, the flagstones, offered nothing to her. She rang the bell and waited nervously on the front step. A woman in an apron opened the door. "Hello?"

"Hi. My name is Celia. I'm a friend of Tomasi's. Is he home?"

"No, he isn't." The woman pushed the door slightly closed so her body filled the opening. "Who are you?" She looked Celia over, and for the first time in months Celia was self-conscious for dressing entirely in black.

"I—I met him at a club he used to go to on Fridays," Celia stammered. "He recommended some books for me to read."

"What kind of books?"

"Um, *The Awakening,* by Kate Chopin?"

"He recommended that to you?" The woman looked confused for a moment; then her expression hardened again. "Look, I think it's better for you to forget about him. He's not going to that club anymore, and he's not associating with those people anymore. Please leave him alone." The woman's last sentence was more an entreaty than a warning. Her eyes were tired.

"I don't understand," Celia said. "Wasn't he feeling better?"

"Better?"

"From when he had pneumonia?"

"Pneumonia? He didn't have pneumonia." The woman was surprised by the suggestion. "He ran away. So you don't know him very well at all, do you?"

"He ran away?" Now it was Celia's turn to be surprised. She didn't bother to try to hide it.

"Yes." Tomasi's mother paused. "If you really didn't know, maybe I'm taking this out on you when you don't deserve it. Listen, Tomasi's had a really hard time, and we're trying to help him. We're concerned he may have been hanging around with people who were a bad influence on him." The woman's eyes flitted over Celia's outfit again.

"I'm sorry, I had no idea. I had just met him, and then he disappeared, and then I saw him again last week, and then his dad showed up and made him go home."

"That was you." The woman hardened a little again.

"I didn't know he wasn't supposed to be out. We just had cider."

"He wasn't supposed to be. See, our problem is he's sneaked out before and met people we don't know, and we had to stop it. So when he sneaks out and meets you, we're suspicious. We're suspicious of you."

"I'm sorry," Celia said. "I don't know anything about that." She thought for a moment. "I have to go to work. Can I leave you my number? If you decide it's okay for him to call me, I'd really like to talk to him." Celia pulled her sketchbook out of her bag and flipped to an empty page. She scribbled her name and number on the top corner, then tore it off to hand to the woman, who took it.

The woman had glimpsed Celia's drawings. "Are you an artist?" she asked.

Celia started to respond with something modest, the way she always did. *I draw.* Or *I'd like to be.* But then she raised her chin and said, "Yes, I am."

The woman looked at the paper in her hand. "I'll have to see. I can't make any promises."

"I understand. Thank you," Celia said. She turned and walked away, forcing herself not to look back as she wrestled with the conversation. Tomasi had run away? Why? Where had he gone? Was that why his parents would treat him like a prisoner when he came back, or was there more that she didn't know? Her fantasy of a dark green sedan and nights spent watching foreign films was gone. Now she imagined him creeping out of that house in the early morning, carrying everything he owned in a little black case. Where had he gone? What kind of home was that? What could have caused him to do something so extreme? One idea rose to the top: apparently Tomasi had broken out of his own house to see her. She remembered his smile just before his father hauled him away, and she believed that to Tomasi, it must have been worth getting caught. She blinked away tears.

16

twist of shadows

C AN I MAKE YOU a dress?" Marco asked Celia.

"What? I thought you only made men's clothes."

"I do, and normally Ms. Vong lets me do whatever I want, but she's decided we all have to make a dress. The only reason I take that stupid home ec class is because there's nothing else at this school," Marco said, sighing. "Here at distinguished Suburban High you can learn French, music, and *washing*. But I think you have a free period when I have class on Tuesdays, so it would be really easy to do fittings with you. If you want to?"

"Sure, I'd be honored!" Celia said. She wasn't about to pass up the opportunity to see Marco work, and she was sure he would make her something beautiful. He was obsessed with the details of haberdashery, and there was no doubt he was accomplished. His clothes looked made-to-measure. Almost weekly he or Brenden had on some new piece he had made, whether it was a pair of pants or a parka. Marco's prodigious sewing talents far exceeded anything taught in the most advanced home economics class.

Outside the home ec room, Celia had a lovely moment preparing to walk into a new place—for the first time since the art institute, she didn't feel the hair-dryer blast of panic on her back. *It's because Marco's in there,* she told herself. But that didn't change the reality that Celia was going to walk into a strange place and not be completely self-conscious. She smiled and stood up even taller. And when she opened the door, she actually was tickled by the bizarre scenario. In a room chock-a-block with sinks, stoves, ironing boards, and sewing machines, Marco was the only guy among a few dozen girls. He came to her and made a show of kissing her on both cheeks while his classmates regarded her as if she were a minor celebrity.

"Hi! Thanks for coming!" Marco showed her to his work-table.

"Of course! I haven't been here two minutes, and I can tell you are completely out of this class's league," she whispered to him.

"They're all freaked out because they've never made anything more complicated than an apron," he said, wielding a cloth measuring tape confidently as Celia stood in front of him. "I think a buttonhole will be enough to push most of them over the edge."

"Well, I'm excited," Celia said. "What are you thinking of making for me?"

Marco pulled out a sketch. "A sleeveless dress, with a series of pin tucks that form a kind of corset on the bodice, full length, very dramatic, and I'm toying with some kind of stand-up collar. Definitely Diaboliques material," he said. "And you are the perfect model for it. What do you think?"

"It looks beautiful." Celia studied it.

"I don't sketch as well as you do," Marco said.

"What do you mean? I can tell exactly what you have in mind from this drawing. It's a totally different thing," Celia told him. "I draw things that already exist. You draw things that don't exist yet."

"Still, your drawings look like they're alive. And I'll bet you could do it with your eyes closed."

"I never tried," Celia laughed. Marco handed her his pad and a pencil. "You want me to try?" She closed her eyes and thought of his face, letting her hand flow easily over the page, concentrating on her sense of the tip of the pencil against the paper. When she opened her eyes, she was surprised it had worked.

"See, you draw better blind than most people with twenty-twenty vision." Marco shook his head in disbelief. "I will not be drawing any clothes blindfolded, I promise you."

"Did you make Brenden's trench coat?"

"Yeah, that turned out really well. He's my favorite male model." Marco grinned. "If I'm going to be a designer, though, I have to start making clothes for people other than my boyfriend." After a moment, he added, "I want to learn to knit so I can make him sweaters."

"You're so cute," Celia laughed.

"I thought you were going to say queer." He smiled.

"I wouldn't say that!"

"I know you wouldn't. But I kind of like it." Marco examined a seam on her sweater. "It fits, somehow. Everything is queer these days . . ." He reflected for a moment. "Why aren't you dating?" he asked.

"I don't know. Who would I date?"

"Well, that's a good point. Nobody here, that's for sure. You still haven't seen Tomasi?"

"No." She lied without a second thought, and Marco didn't see through her. Who was she becoming?

"I know he's your tall, dark, and handsome nightclub fantasy," Marco said playfully, "but maybe you should consider other candidates, too."

"Maybe. I probably need more experience talking to guys. At some point I guess I'll have to consider someone else," she said.

"At some point you should do a lot more than that." Marco winked at her.

But it wasn't such an obvious course of action in Celia's mind, because Tomasi had earned the privileged spot in her heart—even though she didn't know his last name, even though she was as infatuated with her idea of him as she was with the little she actually knew about him, and even though it was possible he was essentially a prisoner in his own home. *This must be the province of love,* Celia thought: no roads ran straight; no blocks were orthogonal; no bells rang on time. But Tomasi lived there. Just as she had been content to know he was watching her at Diaboliques before they ever spoke, Celia was content to pin her hopes on him now, despite all the uncertainty. The potential was as sweet to her as its realization. She fully believed she would see Tomasi again, and so she was content to wait.

"COLLAPSED LUNG? WHO GETS a collapsed lung in high school?" Brenden asked.

Liz exhaled. "Why did the girl come to school? Was a group project *that* important? We're supposed to be figuring out what we want in this crazy mosaic. Can you focus for a minute?"

Regine said, "Is she, like, a gymnast, or anything?"

"Do they get collapsed lungs?" Brenden asked, ignoring Liz.

"I don't know. I've never been gladder I'm not a sophomore, that's for sure. I'm sorry, Celia."

Celia paged idly through her sketchbook, trying to avoid being lured into the conversation. She still carried her sketchbook out of habit, and would have felt naked without it, but these days she went weeks at a time without drawing. Celia looked through it guiltily, as though it were a beloved relative she'd neglected to visit. She stopped when she reached the page with markings she didn't recognize. The page was missing a top corner—it was the scrap she'd torn out to write her name and phone number on, to give to Tomasi's mother. Next to the torn edge there was a line of faint letters in a hand she didn't recognize.

Brenden was speaking. "At what point do we say, okay, it's crazy, but is there really some kind of curse? I still feel like if something, I don't know, *supernatural* really is going on, don't people call psychics, or exorcists? What are we supposed to do?"

"Have sex with all the sophomore girls?" Marco offered.

Celia looked up and caught Ivo staring at her. Immediately he looked away, and she pulled her sketchbook into her lap to read the faint words she had found there: *Can you see this?*

"Are we even sure that does the trick? I mean, has anyone really looked at this, case by case?"

"You mean, has someone asked each girl if she was a virgin on her birthday? That would be quite an interesting science project."

"I thought people had pretty much concluded there was a connection."

"But has it been proven?"

"To prove it, you'd have to have a set of twins, and have one of them lose her virginity, and see what happened to each of them. And there aren't any twins in the sophomore class."

Below *Can you see this?* Celia wrote, *Yes. Who is this?*

Next to her Brenden continued, unaware. "I'm really sick of talking about girls and their virginity. Why couldn't this be happening to guys, for once? I wish we could put all the guys under a microscope and interrogate them about their sex lives."

"They would all just lie," Regine answered.

"Not if they were going to get a collapsed lung and have everyone find out they were lying."

Celia watched another faint line of writing appear slowly under her own, like lemon juice turning brown while the paper was held over a light bulb. It said, *Tomasi. Sorry.* She drew in her breath and then had to cough so it didn't sound as if she had gasped.

Around her the conversation continued. "Well, that's an interesting question. Why is it only happening to girls? Why isn't it happening to guys? You can't just say it's someone playing pranks on girls, because these injuries—health problems, accidents—couldn't be planned. It's not like someone is sabotaging bathrooms or putting bombs in lockers."

Celia wrote in her sketchbook. *Are you okay?*

"So we're really saying that there's a curse? Is that just crazy?"

"Is it? I don't know how many girls have turned sixteen so far this year, but either something bad has happened, or it's pretty sure they've had sex, or they've been out of school on their curse day. We're way past this being a coincidence, aren't we?"

"But it doesn't matter, because that's the answer," Liz said, exasperated. "If these girls are just smart enough to stay home on the day before their birthdays, this is over, and we never have to talk about it again. It might not explain what's happening, but it works. *The end*."

More writing appeared in Celia's sketchbook. *Yes. I'll tell U. 2night?*

She wrote *Nine o'clock* and closed the book. Her friends on three sides of her hadn't noticed.

In chemistry class she asked Mariette, "Can you write in other people's notebooks?"

"What?"

"Look." Celia pulled out her sketchbook and showed the page to her. "It was like a conversation. One line appeared, and I wrote my answer, and then the next line appeared . . ."

"Are you serious?" Mariette studied the page. "Tomasi?"

"That guy I met at Diaboliques," Celia said. "But then he disappeared for a long time, until I saw him again over winter break, at the bookstore. But I think his parents keep him locked up in his house or something. They don't seem to let him out."

"I can't do that." Mariette pointed at the writing. "But I'm not surprised that it can be done. It's pretty cool. You didn't know he could do it?"

"No, I had no idea," Celia said.

"You realize this pretty much proves he's one of the Kind. You *really* had no idea?" Mariette watched Celia shake her head. "What's he like?"

"He goes to St. Dymphna's. He's kind of big and strong. He loves to read. But I don't think his home life is that great. He's run away before."

"How old is he?"

"He's seventeen, but Mariette, please don't bring up the thing about the number seventeen in your admonition!"

"I have to think about these things!" Mariette protested. "You said his parents won't let him out of the house?"

"Well, I tried to visit, and his mother told me to leave him alone. Oh . . ." Celia replayed that conversation in her mind. "They must have seen something. They must know something about him having powers."

"And they're probably freaked out, and they think you have something to do with it."

"But I don't," Celia said.

"*I* know that. What is it with you, though? You keep finding us! Do you see why I think you must be Kind, too? You have to be careful, Celia."

"What do you mean?"

"I don't want to make you mad, but someone is hurting girls here, and everyone is a suspect, especially if they have power like that. We know Tomasi has powers, but we don't know if he is Kind or Unkind."

"I knew you were going to say that! I thought it was somebody here at school. What happened to Skip as our primary suspect?"

"I can't figure out how to prove it, short of catching him doing something! He could be casting a spell the night before. I've already tried to go to his house, but they have dogs that bark before I get anywhere near. I have no idea anymore. Every guess I've made could be wrong. But how many other people do you know right now who are capable of this?"

"You," Celia said. "How do I know it's not you?"

"Well, I guess you don't," Mariette said, looking wounded.

"If there were a way for me to prove it to you, I would. But if I were doing all of this, why would I be telling you about it? And why wouldn't I have succeeded by now?"

"I don't know." Celia's forehead throbbed. "Even before you told me everything, and I was tempted to suspect you were somehow involved with all these weird things that were happening, I knew it couldn't be you—you're too good a person. And I just don't think Tomasi has anything to do with this, either. He's *not* Unkind. He can't be . . ."

"Give me his address," Mariette said.

"Why?"

"So I can go find out."

"What would you do? You shouldn't go there. If his parents see you there's no telling what they might do to you. His father screamed at me like I was a monster trying to prey on his son."

"They won't see me," Mariette said.

"What would you do to him?"

"Nothing, unless he's Unkind."

"But how would you know? I don't want you to," Celia said.

Mr. Sumeletso stopped by their table. "Is everything okay?"

"We're fine," Mariette said. "We're almost done." She stared at him until he gave up and walked away, and then she turned back to Celia. "Please, you have to trust me. You know I don't want to hurt anyone, but I have to try anything possible to stop this, because no one else can. No one else has any idea what's really happening here. If this guy has the power to write in your sketchbook like that, then I'm sure he's capable of doing plenty of other things, too. And that doesn't mean he's responsible for all of this, but you know I have to find out for sure."

"Promise me you won't do anything unless you're sure. And promise me you'll tell me what happens, whatever it is."

"I promise."

THAT NIGHT CELIA OPENED her sketchbook in her room and watched the clock until it turned nine p.m. At the top of the next blank page she wrote,

Are you there?

His response came in a moment, the letters rising to the surface of the page one at a time:

Hi. Nvr done this bfr.

How do you do it?

Hrd to xpln.

Is it hard? Is that why you're abbreviating?

Yes.

Are you Kind?

U kno abt tht?

Yes. My friend Mariette is Kind, too. Someone is hurting girls at our school, and she's looking for the Unkind who is doing it. You're not Unkind, are you?

Im Kind bt nvr use it.

Why not?

2 mch trbl. & Im nt hrtng any1!

I told her that.

Yr nt frkd out?

By this? No. You ran away?

Ys. Srry I lied.

It's okay. What happened? Your parents?

Ys. They thnk Im evl.

I'm sorry.

Its OK. Gld U gve ppr 2 mom.

Is that how you can do this?

Ys. Beautiful drwngs.

You can see them? Thank you!

Whos hrtng grls?

I don't know—girls at my school are getting hurt the day before their 16th birthday.

Weird. Hw bout U?

My birthday is in April. Mariette says someone's trying to fulfill an admonition for someone to gain power.

Lst pg?

What?

Last page? U tore out?

You can see that, too?

Evrythng in bk. Mrtte snds smrt.

She is, but she thinks it's you!

Its nt.

I believe you.

U got P oa Lady?

I started it. I like it so far.

Srry—hrd wrk. Nd 2 stp.

Okay. Talk to you soon?

Ys. XO

XO

Celia reread their conversation and wished she could see him.

"HE'S NOT THE ONE," MARIETTE said, setting her books down in chemistry.

"What? Who?"

"It's not Tomasi. There's darkness in his house, but it's the citizen kind, and it all comes from his parents. He's a good guy—Kind, not Unkind."

"How did you find him?" Celia hadn't given her the address.

"It wasn't that hard," Mariette said mysteriously. "I wish I could find everyone as easily as I found him."

"So, how did you know?"

Mariette struggled to explain. "It's like asking someone how their sense of smell works. I went to his house, as quiet as an owl, and just standing in his backyard, I could tell."

CELIA NEVER HAD GIVEN MUCH thought to Valentine's Day. This year, though, the storms of February were a good expression of her feelings. She knew she shouldn't expect anything as romantic as a date with Tomasi for Valentine's Day, and while that made her ache a little, the most important thing was that a boy had broken out of his house for the chance to kiss her. That was plenty romantic for Celia. At the bookstore she watched the Troika huddled in the back, but their naïve intrigues didn't interest her. *If they only knew,* she thought.

Every time the front door opened Celia gave in to the silent wish for it to be Tomasi again. She had promised herself she would kiss him right there in the bookstore if he came to her. If there weren't any other customers around. And if Lippa wasn't watching. But she swore to herself she wouldn't pass up the opportunity if it came.

Now she heard the door and played the short film in her mind yet again. She turned from the shelves behind the front desk to greet . . . Mr. Sumeletso.

"Celia? I didn't know you worked here!" He was happy to see her.

"Hi, Mr. Sumeletso! Yes, I work here." He was dressed in jeans and a sweatshirt. Seeing him outside of school was incredibly disorienting.

"I don't make it over to this part of town very often, but I try to stop in whenever I can. The selection is so much better than the big chain stores." He came over to the desk. "It seems like a place that makes you smarter just by spending time in it."

"I've learned a thing or two here." Celia smiled.

"Can I ask you a question, since I've run into you like this?" She nodded. "What do you think of the whole curse thing at school? I've never seen anything like it."

Celia wasn't sure of the best answer to give. "Me neither. I mean, everything that's happened has been a health problem or an accident, but there have been so many incidents . . ."

"A lot of the girls are just staying home on the day before their birthday now, since the bad things only seem to happen at school. Do you think you'll do that?"

"Probably. Mine's not until April, so it's still a few months away."

"I certainly don't want anything to happen to you—or Mariette. You're my star pupils!" His smile was contagious, and she couldn't help returning it. He looked at his watch. "Well, I was stopping in for a book before I go to the dentist." He went to the literature section and returned with a Joseph Conrad novel. Celia rang him up. "It was nice to see you!" he said.

"See you Monday!" Celia replied, and waved as he left. In another moment she was back to wishing Tomasi would be the next person through the door.

· · ·

THE ROSARY SAT IN THE restaurant Ivo had chosen. Once again the truth hung in the air, and they all were careful to look elsewhere and steer the conversation away. Ivo had suggested—begged, really—they all spend Valentine's Day together, never admitting he was trying to avoid spending it alone with Regine.

Celia was sure Brenden and Marco would have preferred to be off by themselves. She tried to guess why Brenden looked like he was ready to burst at the seams. A moment later he reached for Marco's hand and pulled it onto the table. Liz noticed first.

"Is that Brenden's class ring?" She pointed at Marco's hand, and he nodded, his eyes shining.

"I thought Valentine's Day was the right time to ask Marco to wear it," Brenden said. He put his hand over Marco's on the table, and for a moment they seemed to forget that the other four were there.

"You got engaged?" Regine said.

"No, but we are going to try the long-distance relationship next year, so it's a commitment," Brenden said.

"That's really nice! Congratulations, guys!" Liz said.

"Thank you," Marco said. He looked over at Brenden and gave him a kiss.

The wind shook the trees outside. They would be stark and colorless for another month. Celia wished somehow she could have invited Tomasi. She wanted to slip her arms around his shoulders again and feel his arms around her waist. The Rosary were going to Diaboliques later, but she no longer felt a strong connection between the club and Tomasi.

"Is that who I think it is?" Regine asked. The rest of them followed her gaze to see Skip crossing the dining room toward them. "What's he doing here?"

"I don't know, having dinner?" Liz said. Her face shifted from alarm to defensiveness as Skip approached, his eyes on her.

"Hi, Liz."

Liz managed a reply. "Hi. Hi, Skip." Once again Celia wondered why this jock threw Liz off her game in a way no one else did. And Celia couldn't look at him without wondering if Mariette and her suspicions about him were founded.

"It's nice to see you outside of school." Skip looked around the table, allowing them to think he meant all of them, but Celia was sure everyone understood.

"Is that your date?" Liz had found Skip's point of origin. They all looked over at a girl sitting by herself at a table for two on the other side of the room. She folded her arms and tried to look occupied.

"Yeah, I guess I should get back to her. Happy Valentine's Day."

"Is that a strange thing to say when you're out with another girl?" Liz asked.

"Should I have asked you?"

"No! *No.* No." The word seemed to mean something different each time Liz said it.

"Maybe I'll just come by myself next time?" He was backing away.

Liz regained her composure. "That's up to you." She shrugged.

"All right." Skip turned and went back to his date.

"What's the deal with you and that guy?" Regine asked. "I can't tell if you have a hold on him, or if he has a hold on you."

"It's not worth telling," Liz said sharply. "We were friends a long time ago."

"That's kind of hard to imagine," Regine said.

"There's no need to try," Liz said.

"He asked about you," Celia offered. "Before Christmas, when you had the flu. He asked me if you were okay."

Liz turned on her. "What did you tell him?"

"That you had the flu," Celia said. "Nothing else."

"I can't believe he would ask you about me."

"It was kind of sweet, really," Celia said. "He was concerned because you'd been out a few days."

"You should have told me."

"I'm sorry. He said it wouldn't mean that much to you."

"It probably wouldn't have." Liz exhaled. "I'm sorry. Let's just have a nice dinner and then go to Diaboliques. But if Skip is there, too, I will run screaming." They laughed at the idea of both of those possibilities.

17

within the realm
of a dying sun

THE NEXT AFTERNOON CELIA couldn't help herself. She left early for the bookstore and walked directly to Tomasi's. She wouldn't knock on the door—she just wanted to feel as close to him as she could get. She stopped on the sidewalk in front of his house and looked up, wondering if one of the windows was Tomasi's bedroom. A curtain moved, and there he was, looking down at her, one hand pressed against the windowpane. She raised her hand to him, and neither of them moved. She longed to be close enough to see his gray eyes, then wondered if seeing him like this was going to make her feel worse later.

The front door banged open and Tomasi's linebacker father rushed down the walk toward her. "What are you doing here?" he barked.

Celia was mute. It was easy to feel like a bad child under his stern gaze. She hadn't set foot on the property, so she forced herself to stand her ground there on the sidewalk. He stopped two feet from her, and she had to look up to see his face. "I told you to stay away from him!"

"Yes, you did, but you never told me why," Celia heard herself say. Her voice pushed through the nervous catch in her throat and rose to an anger that matched his. "If you're going to accuse me of something, then do it. What have I done wrong? Tell me!"

"I don't need to know who you are to know that you're no good," the man said, seeming a little taken aback that she hadn't retreated. "I will make the decisions about what is best for my family."

"And what is that? Lock him up until he turns eighteen, and then kick him out? You're doing a great job," Celia said. "Have a nice day." She turned and walked away toward the bookstore. She wanted to look back at Tomasi in the window one more time, but then his father would see that she was smiling at her triumph.

"THIS IS BAD," MARIETTE SAID when she found Celia in the hall before school on a Monday in March. "Really bad."

"What?" Celia closed her locker.

"The girl who stayed home on Friday, because her birthday was Saturday? *Electrocuted*. Her family is putting an addition on their house, and there was some kind of live wire touching the metal framing or something."

"Oh my god! Did she die?"

"No. But you know what this means: I was right. If the girls are going to stay away from Suburban, the Unkind one is going to go to them. And I can't do anything to help them. Unless I start going up to girls and saying, 'Hey, take this vial and put this lotion on first thing tomorrow morning, okay?' I don't think that will go over very well."

"You never know," Celia said. "When people are desperate and superstitious, they'll try anything. What do you do now?"

"I don't think I can do anything. But I almost wish the girls would come to school now. I mean, no one's been *electrocuted* here."

THE LIBRARY WAS ALMOST EMPTY when Marco sat down across from Celia. "Hey," he said, setting down his backpack but not opening it.

"Hey." She looked up from her homework.

"This is going to be a really weird conversation," Marco said. "Please just keep in mind the only reason I'm going to say any of this is because I care about you. We all care about you."

"Okay . . ." Celia closed her book.

"I know we promised not to bring it up again until April, but it's March, and your birthday is a few weeks away, and I know you heard about the girl who stayed home for her curse day yesterday." A rotting tree in her backyard had fallen on her, breaking a dozen bones. "So it seems like we're back to the way it was before, and the only girls who are really safe are the ones who've had sex," Marco said.

"Are you going to try to convince me to lose my virginity?" Celia sighed.

Marco wouldn't be deterred. "Yes, I am. But more than that—you shouldn't pick some random guy."

"Well, that's pretty much what I would have to do."

"It should be with someone who cares about you," Marco said. "Brenden and I talked about it, and we both would be willing to—I mean, either one of us would be willing to do this for you, if you want."

"You're offering to have sex with me?"

"I am. Or Brenden is."

"What about Ivo?"

"Ivo is probably just as in need of being deflowered as you

are," Marco said wryly. "Even if he weren't, I don't think he'd be a very good lay."

"Oh, and you would be?" Celia laughed.

"Hell, yeah," Marco said, and puffed up his chest. "I can give you a reference if you need one."

"A girl?"

"No, haven't ever done that. But seriously"—and Celia couldn't help but be touched by his expression—"I would do anything for you, and so would Brenden. Wherever, whenever, however. If it would make you safe."

Celia looked at him for a moment. "You're really sweet."

"Thanks."

"I will consider your offer."

"Who would you pick, Brenden or me?"

"I'm not going to answer that!" Celia rolled her eyes, and they laughed. But the seriousness of the moment returned. "I guess I really have to think about this. I've pretty much been living in denial about the whole thing." They sat for a moment. "What was it like, your first time?"

"For me? Pretty hot, actually. You want the gory details?"

"Well, no, what I meant was, how did it feel? Did you feel any different after you'd done it?"

"Yes. Definitely. Not in the way I thought I would, like *Now I'm an adult* or something. But sex is knowledge, in some way. You know yourself differently. And you know the other person differently, even if it's just for a little while. I'm not doing a very good job of explaining."

"I think I understand what you mean," Celia said.

"So, on one hand, you should want to wait until it's the right time, because it is deep, and it does change you, and you get to know someone in a way you never would otherwise. But on the other hand, if you've already driven the car around the parking lot a few times, you're probably going to do better once you get it out on the street." Marco grinned.

"Ooh, are you using a car metaphor for sex?"

"That's never been done before."

"I look at people sometimes and try to imagine them having sex."

"Really? Dirty girl!"

"I can never really get a clear picture, though."

"You should watch pornography," Marco said in serious voice while his eyes laughed. "It's bizarre, but it definitely clarifies a lot of stuff."

"The things you say!" Celia covered her face with her hands.

"Well, I'll tell you this: I love getting laid on a regular basis." Marco sat back, stretching his arms out to either side.

"Of course you do! You're the horniest creature I know."

"You have no idea." Marco bugged his eyes at her.

"And you don't even have to worry about getting some girl pregnant."

"Cool, isn't it?"

The bell rang and they got up. "Seriously, though," he said. "I meant what I said before, and Brenden does, too. If there's anything we can do for you, you let us know. And no one else has to know about it, not even the other little black beads on our string."

"Thank you." Celia hugged him.

Are you there?
Here I m.
How was your day?
Gd, same. U?

It was fine. I had a nice talk with Marco—he's the shorter one with the curly hair. He's making me a dress. Did you do anything after school?

Home, thts it. Rdng P oa Lady.

Haven't you already read it?

Yes, but yr rdng it.

I like ~~talking~~ writing to you every night. I wish we could talk. I wish it was easier for you.

Me 2.

I still have homework. Talk to you tomorrow?

Dfntly. Gdnt. XO

Good night! XO

"OKAY, IF YOU COULD HAVE one album while you were stranded on a desert island, what would it be?" Brenden asked. "I'd take Cocteau Twins' *The Pink Opaque*."

"That's not an album. It's a compilation," Ivo said.

"Compilations count."

"Oh, this is hard!" Liz thought. "Well, if we can do compilations, I'll go with the Cure's *Staring at the Sea*."

"I'll commit," Ivo said. "Peter Murphy, *Love Hysteria*."

Marco looked surprised. "No one's going with Kate Bush's *Hounds of Love*?"

"Oh, that is a good one," Liz said. "Regine, we know it will be Siouxsie and the Banshees, so which one?"

"I don't care," Regine said, tossing her pencil down. "If you're not going to help me pass Chem Two, you're dead to me."

"You are not failing Chem Two!" Marco said.

"No, but it's killing my grade point average. Seriously, I have never felt so lost in a class in my life."

"I don't understand," Marco said. "You did fine in Chem One. We were in the same class."

"But we didn't have Mr. Sumeletso! There might be a curse on sophomore girls, but I think we need to seriously consider whether Mr. Sumeletso has cursed his chem classes!"

"But Celia's doing fine in his class," Liz said, and Celia had to nod in agreement.

"Yeah, and apparently you have the perfect lab partner," Regine said. "Maybe you have to be a witch to do chemistry well enough to pass his class."

"Are you saying *I'm* a witch?" Celia asked.

"I don't know what I'm saying." Regine picked up her pencil and started another chemistry problem. "Ivo, will you help me?"

"I keep telling you, I barely remember this stuff. And I'm more interested in talking about Celia's secrets," Ivo said.

"What secrets?" Celia hated that she blushed without even knowing what Ivo meant.

"Do you think we don't notice all the little intrigues that follow you wherever you go?" Liz said, though her smile made it clear she was teasing. "You know every time I see Mariette in the hall, she stares at me like you've told her things about us."

"No more than I've told you about her!" Celia protested.

"And I'm pretty sure Tomasi hasn't disappeared as completely as you'd like us to think," Brenden said. "Because every time a guy has tried to talk to you at Diaboliques, you've blown him off. And some of them have been pretty hot."

"That doesn't mean— Okay, fine, I have seen him! Once! He stopped in the bookstore over—"

"Winter break, when you started reading *Portrait of a Lady*? Yeah, we noticed," Brenden said.

"What is going on here?" Celia looked around at them. "Yes, I saw him then! But that's it! His parents never let him out of the house!"

"You love the bad boys, then, do you?" Marco smiled.

"Why didn't you tell us?" Regine asked.

"I didn't know what to say! 'Hey, guys, I saw Tomasi again, but he's probably not going to come back to Diaboliques, and I'm really not sure why.' "

"That is kind of weird. You don't know why?"

"No. It sounds like he doesn't get along with his parents. I think it's been a rough year for him."

"That's too bad. I know you like him," Brenden said sincerely.

"It's okay. It's probably for the best," Celia said, just to try to stop the conversation.

"There's another secret Celia's kept from us," Ivo said. He paused for dramatic effect, and everyone looked from him to her. Celia's stomach sank again. "Who is your mysterious friend who you visit on the mezzanine at Diaboliques?"

"Aha! I knew you were going somewhere besides the bathroom," Liz said. "I could never find you!"

"I knew where you were going. I followed you once," Ivo said. "It's the woman with the fantastic red hair who's always on that couch by the wall." This elicited dramatic *oohs* from everyone. Celia realized her mouth was open and closed it.

"I can do better than that," Marco boasted. "I've talked to her!" More noises from everyone. "I told her I knew you, and I asked her how she knew you."

"What did she say?" Ivo asked.

"She said you thought your life was in danger, and she kept trying to reassure you you'd be fine."

"Do you think your life is in danger?" Brenden asked her.

"I never said that to her!" Celia was puzzled.

"I'd be scared if I were you," Liz said. "I mean, a lot of these girls could have died, if things had gone just a little differently." The table had become quiet now.

"I've never asked her about the curse," Celia said, wondering why the fortuneteller would have told Marco such a thing.

"Maybe you should. She seems to know her stuff. She told me my ring finger looked empty, and that was right before Valentine's Day," Marco said, holding up his hand with Brenden's class ring on it.

"Do you believe people can tell the future?" Celia asked, grasping at anything that might shift the focus to someone else.

"It doesn't matter if you believe in it, does it, if it's true?" Ivo said. He picked up Regine's pencil and held it over the edge of the table. "I don't believe in gravity." He dropped the pencil, and Regine yelled at him to pick it up.

"YOU HAVE A PHONE CALL," her mother said to her. "From a boy."

"Marco or Brenden?"

"I know who they are," her mother said. "I do not, however, know anyone named Tomasi." She watched for Celia's reaction.

"Really?" Celia gasped. "He's a . . . well, he's— Can I tell you about him afterward?"

"Sure," her mother laughed, and handed her the phone.

"I can't believe it!" Celia said into the receiver. "Is this because I'm running out of pages in my sketchbook?"

"Funny," he said. She had missed the sound of his voice. "I don't know what changed. I finished dinner and went up to my room, like I always do, and then my mom knocked on my door and told me I could use the phone if I wanted. We made a deal. If I go to some therapist once a week, they'll start letting me out of their sight now and then."

"How did it get so bad? Why did you run away? I mean, you don't have to tell me if you don't want to. How can you write in my notebook? I'm sorry, that was a lot of questions."

Celia heard him sigh, and she waited. "In eighth grade we had to read this book in school, *The Scarlet Pimpernel.* Except it wasn't the original book, you know, by Orczy. It was some condensed student version, because of course eighth graders aren't going to read that book for real. I was having a lot of trouble with it. On every page there was a jumble of words crowded together, like there were enough words to fill up ten pages. I thought the book was defective or something, but when I showed it to my teacher she didn't see anything wrong. It took me an hour to read one page in the right order.

"The teacher couldn't figure it out. I couldn't read aloud in class, but I knew parts of the story that weren't in the condensed version. It was scary. I spent all this time trying to read everything that was there, and the answers I gave were right, because they came from the real book, but they were wrong, too, because they weren't in the condensed version.

"The teacher told my parents she thought I had a learning disability, and I went to a remedial reading teacher. Fortunately, that teacher was, well, one of the Kind. He figured out immediately I was seeing the words from the real book. I have a different relationship with books. I can only see them as they were really written, not as they've been edited. It's pretty rare, and he told me the only other person he knew about who had this power was a very respected translator of ancient texts—naturally, it would come in handy for that kind of work. Anyway, the remedial teacher explained to me what was happening and how I had to be careful not to let people know about it because they wouldn't understand. And that's how I found out I was one of the Kind.

"But my parents wouldn't let it go. My dad would take books from our shelves and put them in front of me, and some of them I could read just fine, because they were by English authors. But if he picked something translated from a foreign language, I was hopeless, because all the words in the original language were there over the translation. It just freaked him out more and more. My parents are kind of religious, and they tried to make me read the Bible, but you can imagine how crazy that book would look to me, considering how many times that text has changed, and the other languages on the pages."

"Oh my. That must have been bad," Celia said.

"It was really bad. They convinced themselves I was somehow evil, and it got worse and worse from there. They threatened to pack me off to my grandfather's farm. It's out in the middle of nowhere, and Grandpa makes my parents look like softies. He's super religious, and he works from sunup to sundown every day, even though he's in his eighties. It's like the family labor camp."

"So you can only read books that are the original text?"

"Pretty much. It's one of the reasons I like classic literature so much. Or at least, classic English literature."

"And your parents—are they cruel to you?"

"They act so angry, but really I think they're scared. They just changed into different people. They talked to Grandpa, and he decided we had to fast, and we had to pray all the time, and I knew it wouldn't work. I had to get out of there."

"Where did you go?"

"To the reading teacher," Tomasi said. "He was the only person I knew who could understand, and maybe help. And he did. He helped me figure out how to mask the original text so I can see what's on the page."

"How do you do it?"

"Glasses."

"Are you kidding?"

"No. They're not ordinary glasses, let's put it that way."

"That must have helped." Celia tried to imagine Tomasi wearing glasses.

"Yeah, except now I have to read the Bible all the time," Tomasi said. "Good thing it's interesting in most parts. It's definitely an important work of literature. I see its influence everywhere, in so many other books."

"You're not religious?"

"I'd say I'm spiritual. But *religion?*" The word sounded like poison when Tomasi said it. "I try to believe in the goodness of people. Does that count?"

"Of course it does. So, do you have an admonition?"

"Yeah, I've had five, but I've never fulfilled any of them. They keep coming, though. I even got one in a cereal box."

"Why don't you try to fulfill them?"

"Because the power I have has kind of made my life hell. I don't want any more!" He sounded angry, and Celia could understand why.

"My friend Mariette has been working on her powers for a year and a half. I don't know about her parents, but I think she's had a much better time with it than you. Maybe you could talk to her."

"I *have* talked to her. She came over here. She was standing in the backyard, flickering like a lightning bug. I had to pretend to take out the trash just so I could tell her she wasn't invisible and if my dad saw her he'd get his shotgun."

"She didn't tell me that!"

"She seems a little crazy, but nice. I didn't tell her a lot, but I think she understood why I'm not as excited about being Kind as she is. It's different for everyone." They were silent for a moment; then Tomasi said, "It's great, talking to you. Not as nice as if we were together, but it's a lot easier for me than writing in your book."

"How do you do that?"

"That's hard to explain. It's like trying to tell someone how you swallow. The first time I did it . . . Do you ever have dreams where you do things with your body that you can't in real life, like kiss your elbow? It felt like that. It's the first time I've used my power for anything that turned out well."

"So maybe it could be good after all?"

"Maybe. I haven't ruled it out completely. When I get out of the house and away from my folks I might give it a try."

"I love when you write to me, but talking is better. And easier, it sounds like. So can I call you now?"

"For the moment it looks like you can. Anything can change around here, but let's be optimistic."

"I will be."

"HEY, CELIA." CELIA SHUT HER eyes for a moment, then closed her locker door and turned to see who it was this time. She recognized the guy, a junior she barely had given a moment's consideration. Having already endured what was about to happen a dozen times since the beginning of April, it no longer disconcerted her, and she tapped directly into an automatic disdain for him.

"Who are you?"

He was fazed for a moment by her bluntness. "John. I know we really haven't talked that much, but—"

"We've never talked. Ever."

"Hey, I'm trying to be nice," he snapped back at her. "I'm not being a jerk here. I'm just trying to talk to you."

"That's sweet, but I'm not stupid. You think you're the first one to try this?"

"You haven't even heard what I'm going to say," he said.

"Fine. Give it your best shot." She made a point of digging in her bag, pretending to look for something so he'd have to continue without her full attention.

"Listen, I'm not trying to score with you. You're beautiful, and I'd really like to get to know you. I know your birthday is coming up, and you've probably got some things on your mind, but I've been meaning to talk to you for a long time. I mean, who knows, maybe we'd hit it off."

"What makes you think I'm single?"

"I don't know, you're always hanging around with the gay guys?"

Celia looked back up at him in shock. "You know what, this is a big school. I think you should go find somewhere else to be in it."

"Excuse me for trying to help you. You know what could happen. Pardon me for thinking you'd want to explore your options."

"Is that what you're calling this? Exploring my options? Because I call it solicitation."

"So what do you think will happen?" He had given up now. "Maybe you'll get hit by a car? That hasn't happened yet. Or maybe *you'll* get electrocuted, too. That might be good for you, you frigid—"

"Hey!" John went lurching sideways, and Skip took his place in front of Celia. "Don't talk to her like that!" For a moment she thought the two guys were going to fight, but John thought better of it. He retreated down the hallway, calling rude things over his shoulder at both of them. Skip turned to Celia.

"I'm sorry," he said. "I'm so sick of this. I'm sure you are, too."

"You have no idea," she said. "Thank you."

"No problem. Can I say something to you, though?"

"Sure." Celia looked at him curiously. She smelled his cologne and noticed the way his wide neck pushed his shirt collar open, but she no longer regarded him as a simple jock.

"I have no idea what your personal situation is, but if you're even thinking about hooking up with someone—don't, okay? Just be really careful and you'll be fine. Whatever's going on, it's not worth doing something like that."

"I wasn't expecting you to say that," Celia said.

"Well, it's how I feel," Skip said simply. "If you need help, if anyone crosses a line, you let me know, okay?"

"Okay, thanks." Before he could turn away, Celia asked him, "What happened with your sister, Stella?"

"You mean the curse? She was sick, and I guess staying home was enough for her, though I'm not sure that works anymore."

"Were you scared for her?"

"I was concerned. If she hadn't been sick, I don't know what I would have done."

"Why do you think you and I have been around when so many of the injuries have happened?"

"It's not like we've been there for all of them," Skip said. "Why, are you feeling like you're responsible for the curse or something? It's just a coincidence. If someone gets hurt, I try to help. I'll keep an eye out for you."

Celia nodded, smiling in spite of herself. She watched him walk off down the hall.

REGINE STEERED THE CAR through the school parking lot after she and Celia had said goodbye to the rest of the Rosary at the end of the day. "I'm really looking forward to your birthday," she said, "because as soon as you get through it, I can go back to just being annoyed by this whole ridiculous curse thing. As sad as I will be to see this year end, I really hope it puts an end to all the nonsense. Can you imagine if it just kept going through the summer and into next year? The sophomore class would be all boys in no time flat, because no girls would enroll here. Now you don't even have to come to school to get hurt on your curse day. If you stay home it's even worse. It's relentless."

"It's funny how we listen to songs with all these dark themes, but when it happens in real life it's not so glamorous," Celia said.

"What are you saying?" Regine asked.

"I'm saying it's one thing when the tornado is on the cover of an album, and it's another thing when it's coming toward you, ready to rip the roof off your house."

"Of course. Do you think we trivialize that or something?"

"No. I just wonder what the difference is . . . between art and the real world, sometimes."

"I think I prefer art to the real world," Regine said. "Everything should always be mysterious and beautiful and meaningful."

"But what about when it isn't? This afternoon a sophomore girl whose birthday is tomorrow got her chest burned by defibrillator pads in the back of an ambulance on the way to the hospital."

"Then I'm a horrible person, because I'm thankful it's not happening to me," Regine said.

"Is that how you'll feel next week, on the day before my birthday?" Celia asked.

"You're going to be fine." Regine said it sternly, as though that could make it so. "Let's talk about something else. I wish you and Liz were coming to promenade."

"Promenade?"

"Well, that *is* its real name. 'Promenade' sounds so much more elegant than 'prom,' don't you think? Why don't you just let someone take you so you can be there with us? Or you and Liz could go as each other's dates. It'll be the last time we'll get to be the Rosary like that at Suburban."

"Has Ivo asked you yet?"

"No, I think he's planning some kind of surprise to ask me. I'm sure it will be good. I already have my dress. It would just be so much better if all of us were going."

"Can I ask you something? I'm only saying this because you're my best friend." Celia wasn't sure that was true, but she hoped hearing it would make Regine more receptive. "Do you ever wonder if your relationship with Ivo is a little one-sided?

Every time the two of you do something as a couple, it's because it was your idea."

"Ivo's not very good at that. Anyway, I like making the plans."

"I just would hate it if you were disappointed. Have you talked about next year, when he's off at Metropolitan?"

"We're going to try a long-distance relationship, like Brenden and Marco," Regine said, but it sounded like she was making a wish. "Why are you making everything so complicated today? Remember when we used to just listen to CDs and talk about the music?" She turned up the volume on the stereo, and Celia looked out the window.

18
the dreaming

T HE DAYS PASSED BY, and the clock ran down, and Celia's birthday loomed. She knew she was facing a very real danger, and soon it would be her turn in the bull's-eye. Every day she looked at her mother and tried to figure out something she could tell her that wouldn't sound completely crazy. At one point Celia had thought she would make up any excuse, or just beg to stay home. But that week a classmate was hospitalized with third-degree burns — something to do with an electrical short and some gas fumes — when she stayed home for her curse day, so school was looking like the safer, if not entirely safe, place to be.

She didn't accept Marco's offer. Or John's, or anyone else's, explicit or implied. As scared as Celia was, the idea of losing her virginity was such an alien concept, she knew she just wasn't ready. She wished she could feel ready. Her feelings weren't religious, or pure, or chaste; they were messy and incoherent. No matter how she thought about it, having sex now would amount to forcing herself to do something she didn't want to do, and the risk of a curse day injury actually weighed lighter than rushing into sexual experience. All Celia had was blind hope that something would change the situation and take the problem off her hands.

She sat at her desk in her room on the night before her curse day, waiting for nine o'clock, the time for her nightly phone call with Tomasi. She had told him more about Mariette, more about the mysteries they couldn't solve. He asked questions, but it was hard to tell what he thought. Still, talking on the phone was all she could have of him, so she took it.

"So, tomorrow is my curse day," she said after they had talked about school.

"What are you going to do?"

"Be careful, I guess. I'm going to school. At least I'll have Mariette there if something happens."

"I wish I could do something. This is the one time I wish I had powers that could help you."

"It's okay. I understand why you don't want them."

"Do you want to see my admonition?"

"I'd love to! I didn't want to ask. Mariette is very private about hers."

"Yeah, I wouldn't have shown you mine before now . . . but that's because you're in it."

"I am?"

"I think you are. I got it last August, and the moment I saw you, that first night at Diaboliques, I was sure you were the one. That's the reason this is the first time I've tried to fulfill an admonition."

"Wait, so you *are* trying to fulfill your admonition?"

"I was. And then I wasn't, because everything got so bad at home. I want to, but I can't figure out how. You should just read it. Do you have your sketchbook?"

"It's right here."

"I'll write it to you, but I'll have to get off the phone because writing like that takes all my concentration, and then I'll be exhausted. Be careful tomorrow, will you? And call me tomorrow night to let me know you're okay."

"I will." They said good night, and then Celia put down the phone and watched the blank page in her sketchbook. Soon Tomasi's admonition began to unfurl slowly down the page, like ivy creeping across bare soil. She wondered what effort it took him to write this way. Was he gritting his teeth? Was sweat beading his forehead?

> To claim the power that you seek
> Befriend the one you see each week
> Make her rich, no money spent
> And kiss her lips — if not, her cheek
>
> Before the earth eclipses moon
> Your day will darken, though it's noon
> Remember her — to her stay true
> Her hands must draw you close, and soon
>
> Beware the one who knows you not
> But tries to change this story's plot
> Who hopes to kiss her just like you
> And steal the treasure you have sought

Celia remembered her initial fascination with the Unkind admonition with its instruction to kill a girl when Mariette had shared it with her. Seeing Tomasi's rekindled that fascination. Celia studied the stanzas, so specific in some places, so vague in others. Did admonitions ever actually spell out what the power would be? If you misunderstood their instructions, what happened? If you missed the deadline, was there a second chance? Did every admonition include something to be won by a kiss and awarded at the eclipse of the moon? Was there always someone who could thwart your efforts? Or were the two admonitions she'd seen similar by coincidence?

Celia understood why Tomasi thought his admonition described her. For a while they had seen each other once a week. Had he been willing to recommend books because it would enrich her, no money spent? Celia knew now why he had smiled the way he did when his father had caught them: he had kissed her, meeting another requirement of his admonition. His day certainly had darkened after that.

What was left? *Her hands must draw you close, and soon.* Was it up to Celia to fulfill the last requirement, then? The night of their date, had she reached for him? She couldn't remember doing anything like that. She felt the weight of responsibility. What if she didn't see him again before the eclipse of the moon and she unknowingly had squandered her opportunity to help him fulfill his admonition? Celia swore if she had to break into Tomasi's house before June to take him by the hands and pull him close to her, she would do it.

There was the matter of the warning about someone trying to change the plot. Who could that be? A busload of boys — including Marco — had offered to kiss her (among other things) in the past few weeks, but that didn't seem to fit the admonition. Celia couldn't think of anyone else. Having failed to untie that knot, Celia returned to the most important strand. Tomasi must have chosen to share his admonition with her because he hoped she would help him fulfill it. But in doing so, he had revealed something else. All the things that had entranced her about him up until now—the staring, the books, the kiss—were part of a script. Did that mean he was using her? She couldn't accept that. Why, after four other unfulfilled admonitions, would he suddenly want to fulfill this one so badly that he would take all the risks he had, and suffer the consequences, just to lead her on? No, it was much easier to believe that Tomasi was doing all this because he really liked her. Perhaps he even loved her. Celia was prepared to invest everything she had in that theory, because she knew she loved him.

She loved him! It was so simple, but it filled her to overflowing, and she felt the truth creep out of the corners of her eyes and mouth. *She loved him.* It made her smile from the inside out. She had no idea what was supposed to happen next, but it didn't matter. Celia loved Tomasi.

Eventually her head cleared, and the misgivings returned, buzzing around her like gnats. What if he got what he needed from her—if it was just for her to draw him close, how hard could that be?—and then he disappeared again, this time for good? If that was his plan, why would he let her see his admonition? Celia thought of how Regine was deluding herself with Ivo and wondered if she was being just as foolish.

Where had normal, everyday life gone, and how had this bizarre world come to replace it?

Celia stood up from her desk, and a movement on the back lawn outside her window caught her attention. She went over to the glass and looked down. A figure crouched on the grass, and Celia could tell immediately from the wild curls who it was. A book and a flask of water lay on the lawn next to Mariette, and the grass undulated in circles away from her, breaking against the rock garden behind her, as though the lawn were a pond and Mariette had been dropped into the middle.

"She's trying to protect me," Celia said. She suddenly felt exhausted and changed for bed. By the time she had crawled under her duvet she barely could keep her eyes open.

That night she dreamt so vividly, several times she thought she had awakened, only to realize she had moved on to another dream instead. Celia wandered through a city with high walls between the sidewalks and the houses. She bent to look through the keyhole in a door in the wall, and through it she could see the rest of the Rosary walking down a gravel path, away from her. She rang the bell and called out, but when the door opened, she entered a dark hallway. When her eyes adjusted, she was standing outside Tomasi's house in a snowstorm . . .

Celia drove a powerful black car, more luxurious even than any of the cars the Rosary owned. Regine sat in the passenger seat, trying to fill in the lines in a child's coloring book. Strange music played on the car stereo, something threatening and beautiful that Celia hadn't heard before. When Regine asked her what it was, Celia was surprised to find she knew the answer . . .

Celia sat at a huge table by herself in the middle of a cafeteria so large she couldn't see the far side of it. All the other tables were crowded with kids wearing her old clothes. She saw Ivo standing in a doorway, scared to enter the room. She stood up to wave to him but he couldn't see her, and he stayed where he was, trying to light the candle in his lantern . . .

Celia lay naked in a huge bed and felt the smooth sheets against her body. She was aroused, but when she turned she found Brenden and Marco next to her. They were having sex, unaware of her. She reached out to touch the sweat on their bodies, and when she put her fingers to her lips, they tasted of cranberry tea . . .

Celia danced in the middle of the floor at Diaboliques, and she was a foot taller than everyone else. Everyone was dancing to the song that had been playing before in her car. She saw Tomasi and strode across the room to him, feeling herself growing taller, or maybe he was shrinking. When she reached him she picked him up easily and kissed him hungrily. For a moment she was outside her body, and she saw that her eyes were silver and sparkling . . .

Celia stood in the bed of ivy on the Fourads' front lawn. Skip was with her, and Liz was looking down from a second-floor window. Celia turned to Skip and pulled his orange shirt off, then stripped off the rest of his clothes, tossing them into the ivy. Liz wouldn't come out of the house. Celia turned to Skip, who looked down. There in the ivy between them lay a sophomore girl, her eyes closed, her body twisted . . .

Celia led all the girls in her class in a fearsome march through the school. They stormed the halls, carrying burning torches and shouting. Celia ripped locker doors off their hinges, and charms of hummingbirds flew out of each one. The girls herded the boys in front of them, finally trapping them all in the chemistry lab before they set the school on fire . . .

Celia stood onstage in front of the entire student body. Everyone was wearing graduation robes. The students who were virgins wore white robes, and the rest wore red. She looked down and saw that her robe was white, but at the hem a red stain was creeping upward, like a drop of blood diffusing in a glass of milk.

19

should the world
fail to fall apart

WHEN CELIA AWOKE, SHE felt as though she had
been asleep forever, and remnants of her dreams
still clouded her mind. It was fifteen minutes before her alarm was set to ring. She turned it off and sat up in
bed. Something was different. She felt like a different person.
"Who am I?" she asked herself. Then her apprehension about
what harm the day might bring to her pushed all the other
thoughts aside. She got up and went downstairs.

"Happy birthday, sweetie!" her mother sang out when she
entered the kitchen.

"My birthday's tomorrow," Celia said, confused.

"What do you mean? Today's your birthday."

Celia looked at the newspaper on the table and saw that her
mother was right. "What happened to yesterday?" she asked
herself.

"What did you say?"

"Did I go to school yesterday?"

"Of course you did, didn't you? Well, I don't think I saw
you yesterday morning." Her mother stopped stirring her coffee. "Why wouldn't you have gone to school?"

"Did you see me at all yesterday?"

"You know, I don't think I did." Her mother looked confused. "Where did you have dinner?"

"I don't remember," Celia said. "I don't remember yesterday at all."

"Are you sick?" Her mother felt her forehead. "You feel fine." She gave Celia a curious look and went to put the cream away.

What a long sleep I've had, Celia thought in astonishment. Clearly Mariette had done something, but what?

Regine was no help. When Celia asked her in the car if Regine had picked her up the previous day, Regine panicked.

"Oh my god, I completely forgot! How did I forget to pick you up?"

"It's okay," Celia said. Something had happened—something from the secret side of her life, something most people weren't supposed to notice or understand. She had better let it go, lest it turn into another bell she would have to try to unring, as she had tried to do after she had mentioned her suspicions about Mariette to the Rosary, as she had tried to do when Ivo had found the Unkind admonition.

"But that's so weird! You weren't in school, but I didn't realize it until now! How did I not notice? What did you do?" Regine had slowed down so much the car was practically stopped in the middle of the road.

"I don't think I did anything," Celia said, thinking fast. "I wasn't feeling well. I must have slept all day."

"I am completely freaked out. Wait—today's your birthday! Do you think it was the curse?"

"I don't think so. I didn't get hurt. I just skipped the day."

"And nobody noticed you were gone . . ." Regine said. "Celia, I'm so sorry, I don't know what happened."

"It's okay. Maybe it was for the best."

"Well, happy birthday!" Regine returned to business as usual. "You have to wait until we get to school, because we got you one gift from all of us. I can't wait for you to see it!"

In the parking lot the Rosary gathered around Celia to wish her well. She couldn't tell if the rest of them had noticed anything unusual about the day before. They were amusing themselves by singing lyrics from birthday songs. Marco sang "Happy Birthday" by Altered Images, and when Ivo launched into "Unhappy Birthday" by the Smiths, Liz punched him in the arm.

"Isn't this festive? Having your birthday party in the parking lot? Sorry we don't have a great big cake." Brenden laughed. He lifted a gift out of his trunk and presented it to her. When Celia opened it she found an antique box made of dark wood. A pattern of leaves and blossoms was carved on the lid and around the sides.

"This is beautiful!"

"Do you recognize the flowers?" Brenden asked. "The round fruit are pomegranates." He pointed to them. "Which means the flowers are . . ."

"Balaustines!" she laughed. "That's perfect!"

"There's something inside, too," Regine said impatiently. Celia lifted the lid and found a gift certificate to Chris & Cosey's, their favorite clothing store.

"Thank you so much!" She hugged them all. Even Ivo embraced her warmly. "I love it." She carefully wrapped the box back up and put it in Regine's trunk for safekeeping.

They resumed their morning schedule, walking coolly through the parking lot toward school. Ivo fell in beside her, something he had never done before. *Here it comes*, she thought,

He's going to ask me questions I can't answer. But all he said was "Before I forget, I have an idea for the class mosaic to tell you." She leaned her head toward his, the way the Rosary did when they conversed. They walked slowly, deliberately, not looking at the other kids around them, just as they did every other morning.

ONCE SHE MADE IT UPSTAIRS, Celia made a beeline for Mariette. "What did you do?"

"Oh my god!" Mariette hugged her. "You will not believe how badly I screwed up!" She pulled Celia around a corner. "I thought I'd just make you skip the day completely, and you'd be safe! If you were asleep, what could happen to you, right? So I cast a spell to make you sleep through the whole day. But then I had to make it so no one would miss you, or else they'd be concerned you weren't here—or worse, they'd freak out because you wouldn't wake up. So I cast *another* spell to make everyone forget about you for a day."

"I saw you in my backyard," Celia said. "I thought that's what happened."

"Except I made a mistake! When I wrote the spells I used your initials to represent you, and then the spell worked on everyone with the same initials as you! There are a lot of people with your initials," Mariette said, and Celia could see the thrill and the guilt fighting in her friend. It was probably the most spectacular thing Mariette ever had done with her powers, but she'd made a mess of it. "There must have been two dozen people out of school yesterday—everyone with the initials C.B.—and no one noticed!"

"Really?"

"It was crazy. Two teachers were out, and of course no one

covered their classes, so it was chaos, because people would show up for a class, but then they couldn't remember who was teaching it, so they'd leave. All day I had to bite my tongue and just wait for it to be over."

"It sounds crazy."

"It was hysterical, kind of. That's what I get for trying stuff I probably shouldn't be doing," Mariette said. "But it was the best thing I could think of. Anyway, you're safe! You're sixteen! Happy birthday!"

"You are crazy," Celia laughed, and hugged her again. Mariette gave her a peck on the cheek, and they went off to their classes.

Celia wasn't out from under the true curse, however: the scrutiny of her peers. No one questioned where she had been the day before, but once it was established she was unharmed, her sexual status came into sharp focus. Celia found herself cornered on a few occasions, and she used some of the rudest words she'd ever spoken while defending her privacy. The student body was polarized for a time. Because no one at school was claiming to have scored with her, some were sure she must not have had sex. Others figured because of her exotic style and her affiliation with a clique that held itself apart from the rest of the student body, she easily could have had sex with someone unknown at Suburban. The most optimistic among them speculated that the curse finally was broken, either through Celia's actions or by coincidence. Two days later, those optimists were proven wrong when the next sophomore girl due for a birthday broke a rib in gym class.

Near the end of April, Mariette said to Celia, "I was so focused on getting you through your day, I forgot the damn Unkind would just keep trying. There's no way I can try that spell again and just knock each girl out for a day. It was complete chaos."

"Still, you should do it yourself, on the day before your birthday," Celia told her. "Cast a spell to make everyone forget you, and then stay home."

"Oh, I'll be fine. I don't consider myself to be in the same category as the rest of you."

"You're not a fifteen-year-old virgin about to turn sixteen?"

"Yes, but I'm not a *citizen*."

"Does that mean you've finally accepted I am just a citizen and not one of the Kind?"

"No . . ." Mariette's face betrayed her inner conflict. "You could be Kind but still defenseless against the Unkind because you haven't developed any powers yet. In which case, I still did the right thing.

"Enough about that! I want to go for ice cream sundaes for my birthday."

Celia laughed. "Sure! Why don't you come over to my house first? You can even come inside this time!" Celia wanted to tame Mariette's hair and maybe put a little makeup on her. And if Celia could talk her into letting go of a few of her most unfortunate sweaters, she would consider it a complete victory.

"That'll be great! See you later." Mariette headed off to her homeroom.

CELIA MADE HER WAY to the home ec room for a dress fitting. Marco's classmates seemed to have been expecting her, and they smiled shyly. Celia was amazed to find that Marco's dress for her looked nearly complete.

"Oh no," he said dismissively. "The lining isn't done, and none of the hem."

"Still, it looks fantastic! You're the only person who could make a thimble look elegant," she said as he waved his hand at her, the metal flashing on his index finger.

"It's turning out really well." He smiled.

She went to put it on. "It's going to be a little long," he said to her through the changing-cubicle door. "Stand on your toes like you're wearing heels."

When she came out and saw herself in the mirror, Celia was taken aback. It was as if the secret world of Diaboliques that she shared with Marco and the Rosary had collided head-on with the world of Suburban. Within a moment thirty girls had gathered around to admire the narrow black crushed velvet gown, which widened into a small fishtail in the back. Marco went about the fitting without giving them a second look, and Celia began to feel hot with all the eyes on her. It was one thing to play the part of a foreign dignitary visiting this room, but it was another thing entirely to be scrutinized like this. This was closer to the first time she had walked into her homeroom in September. She was trapped, and with Marco fussing around her ankles she certainly couldn't run anywhere now. The impulse to fill in the unspoken disparaging comments still lurked deep in her.

"It looks amazing on her," one of the girls said.

"She's so pretty," another said.

Ms. Vong herded the others back to their machines, and Marco stood up from adjusting the hem. "I told you you're gorgeous," he said, his eyes glowing, "the first day I met you." He was proud of the effect they had achieved.

"I didn't believe you." Celia smiled.

One of the girls had lingered near them, and when Celia noticed her the girl took a few steps closer. Celia dropped down from her toes, and still she was six inches taller than the girl, who said, "I'm sorry—I just wanted to ask you . . ." Celia nodded, using a finger to flip her long, smooth hair behind her shoulder. "My sixteenth birthday is next week, and I'm scared. Do you know what I should do?" Her eyes betrayed the terror the rest of her face tried to control.

Marco looked curiously at Celia, and she thought hard. "I think you should come to school," she told the girl finally. "And when you get here, make sure the first thing you do is to go to your locker."

"Go to my locker? You stayed home, didn't you?"

"I did, but . . . I think you'll be safer here," Celia said. "I'm sorry, I don't really know what to tell you. I just think you'll be safer at school." She could tell the girl wasn't happy with the advice. "I—I'm sorry. I don't know any more than everyone else."

The girl gave her a nod and a shrug that said, *Okay, I'm not convinced, but it was worth a shot,* and she returned to her worktable.

"Why did she think I would know something?"

"Well, you beat the curse. Didn't you? Or did you . . ."

"No, I didn't. I don't know what happened. Am I supposed to feel guilty for not having something bad happen to me?"

"No, but I can see why it would be confusing for her. Let me finish your hem."

with sympathy

T HE MORNING OF THE day before Mariette's birthday, Celia stood by her while she crammed things into her locker.

"Are you sure you should be here?"

"I'm sure," Mariette said. "I might not be very good at protecting other people, but I definitely know how to fortify myself." She pulled a chain around her neck out from under her shirt and showed Celia an amulet that hung from it. "It would take a lot more than anything I've ever seen here to hurt me today. And besides, the Unkind needs to get someone innocent, and I don't qualify."

"Because you're Kind?"

"Yes," Mariette said defiantly. "And because I'm the 'different girl' in that admonition."

"I'm still scared," Celia said.

"That's very sweet of you. But I'll be fine. And then we can go for sundaes to start my birthday festivities!"

"I'll see you in chem," Celia sighed.

All morning she heard Mariette's name on the lips of people who normally wouldn't have given her a second thought. Celia was infuriated by the mean things some of them had to say. How Mariette's virginity could be taken for granted. How no one had bothered to proposition her. How stupid she was for tempting fate by coming to school, and all the grisly things people speculated would happen to her when the curse claimed her.

Celia finally confronted a group of them. "When has she ever done anything to you? So she's not the most popular person in school. Are you really wishing harm on her? What kind of sick people are you?"

"Why don't you go put some more of that black shit around your eyes?" a boy taunted her.

Celia turned to him. "Is that the best you can come up with?" For once, she was happy to be four inches taller than a boy.

"Whatever—you'll just go cry to your senior friends," he sneered.

"No, I won't." Celia shoved him. It wouldn't have been serious, but the boy tripped on the cuff of his baggy pants and went down, just as Mr. Sumeletso turned the corner and came upon them.

"Celia! What are you doing?" He seemed more shocked than angry. "You'd better come with me." He helped the boy up and made sure he was okay, then escorted Celia to the assistant principal's office.

The assistant principal wasn't there, so while they waited in the outer office, Mr. Sumeletso attempted to address the situation himself. "What happened back there? I know you wouldn't do something like that without provocation."

"They were talking about Mariette. Tomorrow's her birthday, so that whole stupid curse thing is supposed to happen to her today. They were saying all these mean things about how they hope she gets hurt."

"It's very nice of you to stick up for Mariette. You're a good friend," he said. "Mariette's a strong girl. I've seen her deflect some pretty mean things other students have said to her. I wish teenagers were kinder to each other, and especially to Mariette, considering how nice she is to everyone. Hopefully there will come a time later in life when those students will realize being true to yourself is one of the most important things you can do." He thought for a moment. "I'll tell you what—I don't think there's any need to concern the assistant principal with this. But you are very lucky you didn't hurt that guy. We won't say 'Off with her head' this time."

"Thank you very much. I'm sorry." They went back out into the hall.

"I hope Mariette survives the *curse*." Mr. Sumeletso made quotes in the air with his fingers when he said "curse." "She volunteered to help me inventory all the swim team equipment during last period today. I've been putting it off since last semester, and I really could use the help."

"I'm sure she'll be there," Celia replied. As she walked back to class, she decided she really liked Mr. Sumeletso. He had earned her respect as one of her best teachers, demanding but fair. Most of the student body disagreed, and the rest of his classes absolutely dreaded him, but Celia was inclined to blame the students, not the teacher.

CELIA SAT IN HER LAST class, idly sketching in the margins of her notebook. She almost had banished the nervous feeling that had been fluttering in her all day. Soon school would be over, and as Mariette had predicted with the utmost confidence, nothing had happened to her. The number of potential targets was shrinking fast now, and Celia braced herself for even grislier injuries during the last month of school as the Unkind became more desperate. She wondered if at some point whoever it was would give up on the supernatural route and just attack a girl in person. It was riskier, but for the Unkind it might be a last resort. If the culprit decided to attack a girl in person, it was just a matter of luring a victim to an isolated place, and there was no shortage of those at Suburban.

Celia felt a new fear rise in her. The pool was an isolated place — what if Mr. Sumeletso was Unkind? No, she thought, there was no way that mild man could do anything of the sort. She remembered the kind way he had spoken about Mariette that morning. But suddenly she wasn't so sure. She thought back to the day he had made his uncomfortable speech exhorting girls not to lose their virginity based on a superstition. No other teacher had done that. Had Mr. Sumeletso's real reason for urging girls not to have sex been his desire to keep his list of potential victims as long as possible?

Celia couldn't sit there any longer. Grabbing her things, she went up to the teacher and stammered that she was going to be sick; then she rushed out of the room before the confused man could respond. All the way through the halls, down the stairs, across the lobby, past the gym, and toward the pool, she told herself, *I'm silly. It can't be Mr. S. I'm just being crazy.* She practically ran down the last hallway to the pool.

When Celia pushed open the door to the swimming complex, the humid, chlorinated air hit her like a warm blanket. She hurried out from the shadow of the stadium seats to the edge of the pool.

No one was there. A jumble of board floats were scattered at the far side of the pool deck. More sailed lightly in a small fleet on the undulating water. Overhead the gymnasium lights flickered and turned shades of purple and green, as if they were still warming up.

"Mariette?" she called. No one answered.

Then the pool erupted. Mr. Sumeletso broke the surface, struggling with something, and it was a moment before Celia saw the body in the crook of his arm, red hair slicked across her blue-gray forehead and cheeks. Mariette's mouth gaped open, but her eyes were closed. The teacher reached the side of the pool and hauled himself out, dragging Mariette after him.

Celia screamed and dropped her books. Across the pool Mr. Sumeletso's head jerked up. "Celia! She fell in! Get help!" He turned back to Mariette, cradling her head in the crook of his arm. He bent over Mariette and pressed his lips to hers. Their darkened clothes clung to their bodies, and the water puddled around them. He was pinching her nose, and his cheeks puffed in and out as he tried to force his breath into her lungs, but all Celia saw was a kiss.

Celia ran out of the pool and back down the hall, and she started yelling before she had reached the lobby. Several people rushed out of the main office in alarm, and she begged them to call an ambulance, gasping that Mariette had fallen into the pool and she couldn't swim. Then she ran back to the pool, followed by the adults.

Nothing had changed. Mr. Sumeletso looked defeated, and it was hard to believe anything could help Mariette now. Celia collapsed in a heap next to her, wiping strands of wet hair off Mariette's face, shaking and crying. Soon enough the EMTs arrived and continued the CPR Mr. Sumeletso had attempted.

Eventually they lifted her body onto a stretcher. Celia pushed forward before they took her away and carefully unclasped the amulet from Mariette's neck. And then Mariette was gone.

SCHOOL WAS CANCELED THE NEXT day. Celia sat on her bed and looked out the window onto the back lawn where Mariette had knelt a few weeks before. She thought there should be some fairy ring around the place where Mariette had been, perhaps an empty halo of mushrooms, sprung up as silent witnesses to her visit. Celia already had known what it was like to lose someone precious to her, to lose someone at too young an age. She had felt this pit open up inside her before, and she knew better than to try to cover it over. There was nothing to be done.

The same thoughts lurked in that pit as the ones that had risen up to torment her when her father died — dark thoughts that made her shrink inside her own skin. Most days Celia could forget how in one hundred years almost no evidence of her life would remain. In a thousand years not even the records of her life would remain. It had taken her months to wrest herself away from the thoughts in this pit. Now they rushed back to her. If there was any privilege to youth, it was the ability to believe she would live forever, but already Celia knew better. Her father's death had cured her of that beautiful, naïve idea. Now she was doubly cured.

Celia focused on what she believed for sure: The Unkind admonition belonged to Mr. Sumeletso. He had hidden in plain sight all year. He was the source of the curse, and he had killed Mariette. Celia's anguish over Mariette was sharp and persistent, but it was crowded by this sudden, horrifying clarity about Mr. Sumeletso. That man had lured Mariette down to the pool under the pretense of doing inventory. He had waited for his opportunity and then pushed her into the pool. He'd jumped in—he probably hadn't even known she couldn't swim—and held her under, fighting her, overwhelming her. When he was sure she was dead, he had pulled her out. And Celia had watched him kiss her, collecting her last breath by pretending to administer mouth-to-mouth resuscitation in accordance with his admonition. It was the perfect crime. If Celia accused him, no one would believe her—what could she say that wouldn't make her sound crazy? Now all Mr. Sumeletso had to do was to wait for the eclipse of the moon in a few short weeks and whatever Unkind powers he had earned would come to him. Celia shuddered, wondering what he would be capable of doing then. She wondered what powers he already possessed.

Celia's anger gave way to fear. She reasoned Mr. Sumeletso probably didn't know about a few crucial things. If he had known Mariette was Kind, and the ways she had impeded his Unkind plans, he would have taken steps a long time ago to stop her from meddling. Celia guessed he didn't know that Mariette had found his admonition, just as Mariette hadn't been able to trace it to him. And if that was true, there was no way he could have known Mariette had shared everything with Celia. When she'd found him with Mariette by the pool, fortunately Celia had been so shocked she had done nothing to reveal all these secrets she knew. He had no reason to doubt that she took his account of the "accident" at face value.

But Celia couldn't be sure. What power might Mr. Sumeletso have—or have soon—to discover how much she knew? And even if he didn't find her out, how could she seek revenge for what he had done to Mariette? Who could help her? Her mind ran in all directions. There was only one person she could tell who wouldn't have her committed. Tomasi would understand, but he was even less experienced than Mariette. What if Celia got him hurt, or worse, by asking him to take on an Unkind much stronger than he? There was some florist in a garden center by Mariette's grandparents. Celia never had met Mariette's parents, so what would they think if she called them and asked for their help tracking the florist down? There was the fortuneteller at Diaboliques. Celia would have to convince her to give a straight answer to a question, though, something the woman never had done. Perhaps the teacher who had helped Tomasi? There had to be someone who could stop Mr. Sumeletso, keep him from gaining more power and harming anyone else.

In the meantime, to keep herself safe, she had to hope Mr. Sumeletso didn't suspect her of anything, and she had to be supremely careful to not betray herself. Her life very likely depended on it. She didn't want to imagine what he might do to her if he suspected she knew the truth about him. Celia had to summon back the quiet, withdrawn girl she had been less than a year ago, and when she returned to Mr. Sumeletso's classroom she must do everything she could to fade into the blackboard, the lab table, anything.

She wasn't hungry, so she sat on her bed, looking at the studies she had made of Mariette during the winter, in preparation for drawing the portrait she had given her. Eventually, she flipped back to the next blank page, wondering if it would be painful or therapeutic to draw her again. But words from Tomasi were appearing there.

What hppnd 2 Mariette?

She picked up a pencil and wrote back. *How did you hear? Are you at school?*

Ys. I cld feel it. Ystrdy?

She drowned in the pool at school. I should have stopped her from going; I knew she couldn't swim.

Im so srry.

Thank you. I think I'm still in shock.

Celia couldn't stop thinking of all the parts of this story she was leaving out. She wanted to tell Tomasi everything, but she was scared of what he might do, and what trouble that would cause with his parents. No matter what, she decided if she did tell him, it wouldn't be this way, when it was so difficult for him to communicate.

Fnrl?

It's tomorrow at St. Francis. Are you thinking of going?

Im gng 2 ask. Myb Ill C U thr.

THAT NIGHT CELIA'S MOTHER found her on the couch in the living room when she returned home from the parents' meeting at Suburban. Celia had been there for hours, *The Portrait of a Lady* on her lap, but again and again her thoughts had drifted. She had imagined her mother in the school auditorium at night, and then the empty halls, and next she thought of Mariette. As much as she wanted to deny that Mariette was gone, the memory of her face—dripping and gray, her lips apart, her hair clinging to her skin—made it real, made it final.

Her mother sank down next to her and sighed. "That was probably the strangest meeting I have ever attended."

"What happened?" Celia set the book aside.

"Well, they let parents talk for a while, and everybody said the same thing: how could something like that happen, and what steps were going to be taken to make sure it never happened again, and how were they supposed to feel safe sending their children to Suburban when all these accidents kept happening, and now a poor girl had died. Finally the superintendent got up and told us about some comprehensive safety review they're doing, and how the pool would be locked and students could only enter the pool area with adult supervision. And I just thought, that wouldn't have saved Mariette. The only reason she was there was to help the teacher."

"I don't even know why she said she'd help him. But she was so nice, she'd help anybody."

"They've suspended him for the rest of the year," her mother said. "It doesn't sound like charges will be filed, since it was an accident. Some parents were pretty upset about that. But they're going to have a review, and he probably will be fired."

He's gone, Celia said to herself. It felt as if a stifling scarf had been pulled away from her face and neck. Things still were awful. Mariette never would come back, and Mr. Sumeletso wouldn't be prosecuted for her murder—no one was going to accuse him of anything more than negligence. But at least there was a good chance now that Celia never would see him again, and he never would find out that Celia knew the truth about him. It was cold comfort, but she felt the relief like a breeze. She breathed in, and it felt as though the air completely filled her lungs for the first time in two days. And then the dull ache in her chest flared up. It was the same ache, the familiar one, the sad hand she shook every day.

"I know you liked him. You're doing so well in chemistry,"

her mother was saying. Celia stared at the far wall. "But it's the right thing. He was responsible for her safety."

The scarflike fear had distracted her from this other, much older discomfort. Now Celia remembered the last time the scars on her heart had ached this hard. It had been on the first day of school, riding in a mock funeral procession, telling herself it wasn't the same, it didn't mean anything. She wondered what it would be like this time, taking the ride for real again, walking into another church, seeing another coffin. The ache burst the scars on her heart now and welled up until she couldn't hold it back.

"Oh, honey, you miss her." Celia's mother put her arm around her and smoothed her hair away from her face as she cried.

"I miss *him*," Celia gasped. "I miss her, too, but not as much as I miss him."

"Of course." Celia heard her mother's voice break. "Of course you do. I miss him, too." They sat for a while, arms around each other.

Celia remembered the quote Regine had tossed out on their first drive together. "I hate that saying—'In the midst of life, we are in death,'" she said when her breath finally grew regular. "It makes life and death sound like rooms, or tasks. Life and death are too big to fit in the same sentence."

"I wish you could have been older, before . . . You shouldn't have to think about death when you're young."

"I'm not going to think about death." Celia sat up, wiping her eyes and looking at her mother. "I want to think about life."

"You should." Her mother studied Celia's face. "Sometimes that's easier said than done, though."

"It is more complicated than that, isn't it."

"There are some questions that just don't have answers. But you know that."

Celia nodded.

Later Regine called. "Are you okay?"

"I'm still in shock," Celia said.

"We'd like to go with you to the funeral, if that's all right with you."

"You don't have to do that. You guys never really even met her."

"I know. But we'd like to be there for you," Regine said. "Now I wish we had gotten to know her. Anyway, people know you were closest to her, so it might be good to have us around as a buffer."

IN THE MORNING CELIA LOOKED through her closet. Almost everything in her wardrobe now could be worn in a funeral outfit, she thought wryly. Mariette hadn't owned a single piece of black clothing, though, so it didn't seem fitting to wear it now. Finally Celia put on the orange floral dress she had last worn at Halloween. She brushed her hair and lined her eyes, trying not to think about how she had planned to brush Mariette's hair and make up her face just days before. Sitting there at her desk in front of her mirror, she felt her throat tighten and the tears push out. "Oh, there's no use," she scolded herself. "Just stop, right now!" But she couldn't follow her own advice. After a minute she wiped her eyes and started her makeup over again.

Regine picked her up and they made the rounds, adding the beads to the Rosary before they headed to the church. "The first day of school, I thought we were in a funeral procession," Celia told her.

"Yeah," Regine said in a low voice.

"I never thought we really would be going to one."

"Me neither. Is this in poor taste? We don't have to take three cars."

"No, it's fine. This is what we do. This is who we are." Celia let her thoughts wander, and in a minute Regine asked her why she had laughed quietly. "I was thinking about the mix Brenden could make: This Mortal Coil, Christian Death, Death in June, Southern Death Cult. And think of the songs: 'Ashes to Ashes,' 'Dead Souls' . . .'"

"Celia, he wouldn't do that."

"I know. What does it mean that so much of the music we like is so gloomy? We're not gloomy people. Not at all."

Regine considered for a moment. "The way I understand it—the way it makes sense to me—is we see the value of looking around in the ugliness to find something beautiful. We look around in the darkness for the flicker of light. But maybe that's wishful thinking. Maybe we're just looking for ways to be different."

"No. It kind of sounds like Mariette," Celia said.

When they entered the church, Celia looked around, but she wasn't sure what she was expecting to see. She was worried Mr. Sumeletso might come, but she told herself he wouldn't be welcome. Celia wasn't surprised there weren't a lot of kids from Suburban in attendance. Most of the student council had come, and Brenden introduced them to Celia. She could tell they were uncomfortable, but she shook their hands and accepted their condolences.

Despite the poor showing from school, a number of other people of all ages were there. Some looked like high school students, though they weren't from Suburban. Others could have been Mariette's grandparents. Celia wondered if Mariette had a large family, but most of the people kept to themselves and didn't speak to anyone else. It reminded Celia of the way people distributed themselves at Diaboliques: mourners were ranged throughout the church, dressed a little unusually, not speaking much, looking mysterious and thoughtful.

"Wow, Mariette knew a lot of people," Brenden said as they took seats.

"Hey, is that Tomasi?" Liz asked. Celia followed her gaze and found Tomasi on the far side of the nave. He was looking at her already, and when they made eye contact, he raised his hand. Celia raised her hand back to him.

"Did you know he knew Mariette?" Liz asked.

"It's kind of a long story."

Throughout the ceremony, Celia couldn't take her eyes from the casket, thinking the same thoughts she had thought over and over at her father's funeral: *She's not in there. Not really. She's not in there . . .* After it was over, she went over to pay her respects to Mariette's parents and little brother. The Hansens were a short couple, plainly dressed, and she could see Mariette in both of them. The boy was grade-school age. He looked scared and tired, and Celia could remember those feelings when she had stood in his place. "I'm Celia. I went to school with Mariette."

"Oh, Celia!" Mariette's mother's face brightened, and she hugged Celia tightly. "She spoke about you all the time. Thank you for coming."

"I'm so sorry," Celia said.

"Thank you. I know you meant the world to Mariette. Thank you for being such a good friend to her." Mrs. Hansen

looked a little glazed, and Celia would have understood completely if she had taken a pill in an attempt to keep her composure.

"I always felt like she gave me more than I could give her in
return."

"That's Mariette." Her mother dabbed the corners of her
eyes. "Tell me, are most of these people here from Suburban?
Are they teachers?"

"Actually, no. The principal is here, and that's her homeroom teacher. The student council is here, and a couple of my
friends, but I think that's all," Celia told her. She was pretty
sure she knew who the other strangers were, and she hoped
Mrs. Hansen wouldn't grow too curious.

"I just figured they were from school. Is it rude to ask them
how they knew Mariette?"

"I don't know, but if they're here, I'm sure it's because Mariette meant something special to them," Celia said, and she
meant it sincerely, even if Mrs. Hansen couldn't understand.
She wondered what those people would say if Mrs. Hansen
asked them.

"That's very nice to hear. You know, I was straightening up
her room, and I found a note addressed to you on her desk. I'll
be sure to get it to you."

"Thank you. If I can be of any help, with school, or anything . . ."

"I'll let you know."

Celia turned to make her way back to her friends, but she
saw Tomasi waiting to speak to her, so she went over to him.
He was in his uniform of black shirt and trousers. His face was
soft with concern.

"I can't believe this happened," he said. "I'm so sorry, Celia." He reached to hug her a little hesitantly, and she slipped inside his arms and enjoyed the comfort of his embrace. For a moment her idea of him blended with who he really was.

"Do you know all these people?"

"No. I think more experienced Kind can feel when another Kind dies. It must be like the way they—we—can recognize each other. I don't really understand it. But everyone mourns when something like this happens."

"They're all Kind, right? None of them are Unkind?"

"I don't know them, but of course they're Kind. I've never met an Unkind—at least, not that I know of—but I assume the difference would be obvious. Maybe I'm wrong about that."

"Mariette was sure she was safe. She'd made some kind of charm."

"She was almost as new as I am. The night we met she told me some of the things she was doing, and I don't know if half of it had any effect at all. She must have felt like she was supposed to face it on her own. Maybe I wouldn't have asked for help, either. But she should have."

"That wasn't really her style," Celia said. "She was the most independent person I've ever met. Are you going to get in trouble for being here?"

"No, that's calmed down a little," Tomasi said. "Just a little."

"So, you kissed me . . ." Celia began, searching his face.

"Because I like you," he said. "You're wondering if it's for other reasons. I'm sure my admonition is about you. But I wouldn't have kissed you if I didn't really like you. You know"—he put his hands gently on her arms—"none of this matters, really. One day I curse the world for mixing me up in all this. The next day I feel like I understand, and I try to make peace with it. But I've never embraced it and tried to live up to my calling. Maybe I should. One thing I know for sure: there is no honor in deception and manipulation, and nothing good can come from them."

"What power would you gain?"

"I have no idea. You don't find out until it happens. It's all a matter of faith."

"Wow."

The Rosary were watching the two of them intently. "Your friends are waiting. I'm glad I got to see you," Tomasi said.

"So what happens? With you and me?" she asked.

"Honestly, that's up to you," he said.

"I want to see you."

"I want to see you, too. Hopefully things will continue to calm down at home, and then I'll be able to." He half smiled at her. He was a different person from the brooding creature who had stared so intensely at her all those months ago at Diaboliques. He turned to walk away, but she caught his hand and drew him back to her. Celia put her arms around his shoulders and hugged him again. She could tell he was surprised, but his arms encircled her waist.

"I'm so sorry about Mariette," she said in his ear. "You might not have gotten to know her well, but she was one of your Kind. I don't want anything to happen to you."

"It won't," he murmured. "I'm glad I got to see you."

When Celia returned to the Rosary, Regine asked, "What haven't you told us?"

"Forget that, go straight to the juicy details," Marco said.

"He lives close to the bookstore," Celia said. "He stopped going to Diaboliques because he caught pneumonia, and he's only been better for a little while." She chose the lie because there was no way she could tell them anything approaching the truth. They watched as Tomasi exited a side door of the church.

"No, the *juicy* details," Marco said.

"What do you mean?"

"I could see the chemistry between you two from fifty feet away!"

"Oh, don't talk about chemistry now," Celia said.

god's own medicine

O N THE NEXT DAY, back in school Celia quickly grew tired of questions from people with whom she'd never spoken before. "If you're so interested, if she was so important to you, why weren't you at the funeral?" she snapped. People started to steer clear of her, and she wound up feeling isolated in a way that reminded her of her life a year before, when she had wanted desperately to be left alone and then felt so lonely whenever she got her wish. Celia knew the way to walk that meant *Stay away*. Before, she had used it in an attempt to be invisible, and then she had learned to use it to reinforce her mystique and that of the Rosary. Now she dared the people around her to get in her way. She had anger to burn.

She arrived at the chemistry lab, where a pear-shaped woman with a chopstick in her hair studied the class list. Celia's relief to see the replacement teacher was small compared to the tinderbox of emotions she associated with the lab room. The traces of evil Mr. Sumeletso left behind were chased around the room by her joyful memories of Mariette. Lost in thought, Celia was startled when the new teacher called her name. Celia went up to the desk.

"I see Mariette was your lab partner," the woman said. "How are you?"

"I don't know," Celia said plainly.

The teacher smiled kindly, pityingly. "The two of you have the highest averages, so don't worry about this class. I don't see how you can get anything less than an A."

"Thank you."

"Maybe you could tell me, since your grades are so good. Do you have any idea why this class has been doing so much better than Mr. Sumeletso's other sections? I've looked through his grade books, and it's like night and day. Not everyone in here is doing as well as you, but they're all doing well enough. In the other Chemistry One section, and in Chemistry Two, it's a miracle if half the students are passing. I had a line to the back of the room of people asking for extra credit. I can't figure it out."

"I don't know. I always thought he was tough but not impossible," Celia said honestly. She was sure it had something to do with the secret truth about Mr. Sumeletso, but there was nothing she could say to this woman.

"Here's another strange question, then: have the lights always flickered in this room? It's been driving me crazy all morning." Celia followed the teacher's gaze up to the fluorescent bulbs, which took turns faintly shifting in intensity. Dark rings traveled up and down their lengths, and now and then one of them blinked.

"I don't think so. I never noticed."

"I'll have to call the janitor," the teacher sighed. "Would you like to join one of the other lab groups?"

"Actually, I think I'd rather work by myself," Celia said. "But thank you."

And she was happy to find she was able to do quite well on her own. She knew Mariette would have been proud of her, even if she did have to measure everything carefully and the experiment took her the full period. Celia's attention was divided, though. In that room Mr. Sumeletso never left her thoughts. He had been so unassuming, so mild, it was easy to understand how she and Mariette never had suspected him, and she was bitterly unsurprised that no one would think to accuse him of anything worse than negligence. She hated him, from his knit tie down to his crocodile loafers, and even though she didn't fear him as much, now that he was gone, it made her insanely angry that the strongest punishment he was likely to receive for killing Mariette was losing his job.

Celia was in agony about it, but she couldn't think of anything to do. She had learned and kept a good many secrets this year, but she didn't want to keep the things she knew about Mr. Sumeletso to herself. The list of people in whom she might confide shortened, though, every time she thought of how one of them would react. Her mother, Regine, Marco, anyone in the Rosary. *I think Mr. Sumeletso drowned Mariette on purpose* . . . She might as well just say, *I've taken leave of reality, and please listen to this insane story* . . .

She still wanted to tell Tomasi, but every time she entertained that thought she remembered Tomasi cowering away from his father, and the way his mother kept the door almost closed, as though she were containing some kind of animal that might try to run between her legs. Celia imagined all the time he must have spent locked in his room while they sat downstairs, weaving their own guilty superstitious ideas about what kind of demonic child they had brought into the world.

And she thought of Mariette, cold and lifeless at the side of the pool. For all the miraculous things Celia had seen Mariette and Tomasi do, they were kids, just like she was. If she told Tomasi what she knew about Mr. Sumeletso and he did something foolish, he would get hurt, or worse. It might not even be at the hands of Mr. Sumeletso. Celia was sure Tomasi's parents were more than willing to take drastic measures to control the son they feared because they didn't understand him.

She preferred to hope that with Mr. Sumeletso gone from Suburban, all the danger was gone, too. It might have been altruistic, or selfish, or downright foolish, but it was the decision she made. Celia found small comfort in the idea that at least no other girls would be hurt for the rest of the year. Soon enough school would be over, and then she would pray for the news that Mr. Sumeletso wouldn't be returning to Suburban in the fall.

Liz showed Celia the obituary before she published it in the school paper.

Mariette Ann Hansen died on May 1, the day before her sixteenth birthday. She was a sophomore who had distinguished herself as a scholar and a free spirit. She was well known at Suburban for her strawberry blond hair and her exceptional kindness. Mariette was particularly gifted in science. Her chemistry partner remembers her conducting experiments as easily as if she were baking a cake.

No one ever expects to confront the death of someone as young as Mariette. No one ever should have to. We need our school to be a place where we can learn and grow, safe from the dangers and concerns of the world outside. It is a tragedy that her death could have been prevented simply if it had been better known that she couldn't swim, and this terrible accident casts a shadow on our new swim facility in its very first year.

Our responsibility to one another as a community—students, faculty and administration—is to look out for one another, even at the most innocuous times, so nothing like this accident ever happens again.

Mariette is survived by her parents, Ron and Justine Hansen, and her brother, Steven. Funeral services were held this past Wednesday. The family suggests that charitable donations be made to the botanical garden in Mariette's name.

THE FOLLOWING WEEK ANOTHER sophomore girl chose to stay home on the day before her birthday, but Celia knew the curse really was over this time. The requirements of the Unkind admonition had been met, and all that remained was to wait for the lunar eclipse. In their ignorance, however, the student body was reminded of Mariette again, and new rumors percolated. The flickering lights in the chemistry lab, which the janitor had been unable to fix, were attributed to Mariette's ghost. Some students refused to get into the pool, claiming they had seen Mariette's body at the bottom. Somehow in death Mariette had transmogrified from a left-of-center curiosity into a creeping monster. Once again Celia found herself saying rude things to strangers who had grown bolder as more time had passed. One afternoon Brenden pulled her away from a trio of junior girls, and she found herself sobbing in his arms.

"She wasn't just some weirdo who was killed by a curse!" Celia cried. "She was a beautiful person, and if any of these people had actually gotten to know her they would have seen that, and they wouldn't be asking me if she died because nobody wanted *to have sex with her!*" She spit the last words down the hall at the retreating girls.

"That is really tasteless. I'm so sorry." Brenden hugged her close. "C'mon, let's go to the library."

"I have to go to class." Celia dug in her bag for a tissue.

"So do I. Let's go to the library."

They found a table in the back and sat down. "I keep forgetting how hard this has been for you," Brenden said. "Even at the funeral you were so composed. If I lost a friend like you have, I would be a mess."

"I don't know. I just hate how I feel now, doubting all the time, fearing all the time." Celia realized Brenden couldn't understand what she meant. She thought of all the magical nights she'd had—the visits to Diaboliques, her first kiss with Tomasi, First Night—and all the promise they represented. But since Mariette's death the nights had been lonely, blackened oceans for her, filled with apprehension and loss. "It shouldn't be like this. She shouldn't be gone."

"Tell me something about her."

"About Mariette?" Celia thought of Mariette running happily down the hall on her way to class. "One of the reasons I wound up liking her is she was just as fearless as you guys. You know? You do what you want, wear what you want, listen to what you want, and if people don't understand, screw them. She was the same way. Girls would tease her about her clothes or her hair, and she'd just look at them as if to say, *At least I don't look like you*."

"I remember we judged her the same way," Brenden said.

"I'm sure you guys would have been nice to each other, but she was just into different stuff. I didn't even know about a lot of it."

"You're a much stronger person now than you were when this year started."

"You think so?"

"Sure. You never would have ripped into those girls like that," Brenden said.

"Probably not. Today I was ready to kick them down the stairs." Celia remembered pushing the boy down in the hall before and wondered where she had picked up this violent impulse.

"The first day of school I could tell you were a little overwhelmed by all the foolish things we like to do. But you were even more grateful to have a group to belong to, so you put up with all of it."

"I really do love it, though. All the things you've shown me, all our interests, our secrets."

"And we're lucky you do. But back then, we were protection for you. You don't need us for that anymore. In fact, I wouldn't be surprised if when we look back on this year, we relied more on you than you did on us."

"I don't know about that."

"I think so. I've been thinking about this a lot lately. Ivo and I have been friends so long, and he's always been the leader. He wants to be roommates next year at college, but I almost wonder if I should say no. Maybe I should try being my own leader. Anyway, I think no matter what happens here next year, whether you and Regine and Marco decide to continue with the things we've done or not, you're going to be fine making your own decisions and choosing your own course."

"I'll bet we keep on with the foolish things." Celia smiled.

"You know we'd be happy if you did."

22

kiss me, kiss me, kiss me

THE WOMAN AT THE counter was nice. Celia had helped her a few times before, and she was a good customer. She bought novels by French authors like Zola and Hugo by the handful, and she always complimented Celia on her style. But Celia couldn't wait for her to finally sign her charge slip, collect her things, and leave, because Tomasi was standing behind her, waiting patiently.

"Hi!" she said finally when the woman had left.

"Hi!" He stepped forward to take the customer's place at the counter. His mouth barely moved, but Tomasi's eyes were all Celia needed to see to know how he felt, and right now they danced. "I can't stay long. Mom needed milk, so this is a test. I have to be back soon."

"That's okay. I don't want you to get in trouble." This time Celia came around from behind the counter to be closer to him. They stood, each with one hand on the counter, facing each other, just enjoying being near each other again. Once again Celia felt the invisible current between them. *I am such a girl,* she thought blissfully. "So, how are you?"

"Good. I mean, not great, but better than usual, so that's something. I get to buy milk."

"So, at the funeral, I drew you close . . ."

"I thought that's what you were doing."

"Does it mean your admonition is fulfilled?"

"I don't know. I hope so. From everything I've heard about admonitions, they're rarely obvious. There could be something completely different I should have done, a different interpretation of any of those words. But it would be nice if you've done it. I would like it a lot if you were the one to fulfill my admonition and give me new powers. I just have to wait until the lunar eclipse and see if anything happens. Then we'll know for sure."

Knowing that this moment was going to be fleeting, as all her moments with Tomasi seemed to be, Celia was not about to squander it. "There's something I've always meant to ask you, ever since you wrote to me in my sketchbook."

"What is it?"

"Why did you—how do I say it . . . show me who you were—Kind—by using your power, writing in my sketchbook?"

"Well, you didn't freak out about it."

"But how did you know I wouldn't?"

Tomasi made sure no one was near. "A couple reasons, I guess." He took her hand, and she looked down at her delicate fingers in his grasp while he went on. "To start, you know the little power I have has caused me more trouble than it's worth, so far. Who cares if you can read old texts, if it makes your parents think you're possessed? This was the first time I could use my power to do something that felt good. So I guess part of me didn't really care." She looked up and saw the corners of his mouth lifting again in a half smile.

"I'm glad you did, but you know it's dangerous if regular people—citizens—find out. I mean, your parents . . ."

"Definitely. And maybe I was foolish to tell you. But the other part of it is, I don't think you're a citizen."

"Mariette said the same thing! She was sure I was Kind, too. Why do you think that? I've never done anything powerful. I've never received an admonition."

"I know, but see, the Kind can sense each other. At least, as you get stronger, you can sense when someone else is Kind or Unkind. I don't know how it works, and I can't really do it myself, because I've never taken it seriously before now. But sometimes I think I can tell—it's like someone kind of glows from the inside. Or I'll feel something, almost like the way a magnet reacts when you hold it close to another one. Or I'll hear it, like there was a noise in the background that I hadn't noticed, but near one person it goes silent. I'm pretty sure that when I feel something like that, I'm sensing another member of the Kind."

"And you feel that around me?"

"The first night I saw you at Diaboliques, it was like . . . You know how dark that room is, right? And how loud the music is? The moment you were there it was like everything was slightly out of focus, except you. When you moved, I could see where you'd been for a second, like you were leaving a faint trail in the air, light gray. That's why I couldn't stop staring at you. Well, and you're beautiful."

"Wow." Celia slid her free hand back and forth across the surface, wondering if Tomasi was seeing something in the air around her.

"So when I wrote to you, I didn't feel like I was taking a risk. Because I don't think you're a citizen. I think you're Kind, too."

"But I can't—I mean, wouldn't things be happening to me?

Wouldn't I discover I could *do* something, that I have some kind of power?"

"I don't know. I'm still learning about all this. I just know what I can feel when I'm around you. And you don't feel like anyone else."

"Well, I feel that way around you, too." Celia smiled.

"I wish I didn't have to go." Tomasi stroked the back of her hand with his finger.

"Don't get in trouble. It's not worth it."

"I think you're worth it," he mumbled, suddenly shy. "I'll call you later?"

"Okay," she said. He hesitated, then leaned in to kiss her. His mouth lingered against hers, and it was heaven, and then he squeezed her hand and walked away. She watched him on his way out the door and then waved to him when he looked in the window as he walked by. Celia turned to see if Lippa had been spying on them again, but no one was there.

WHEN CELIA GOT HOME there was a letter from Mrs. Hansen, who had enclosed Mariette's note addressed to Celia. She unsealed the envelope and read Mariette's familiar script.

Dear Celia,

> *I don't know why I am writing a last will and testament, or whatever this is properly called. Nothing is going to happen to me, and I don't really have any possessions that should be distributed to anyone. But I suppose there is a tiny chance something <u>could</u> happen to me, and if it does, there are some things I'd really want you to know.*

First of all, I love you. You are beautiful and smart and such a good person, and I love you. It's so amazing to write that! I would have told you, but I knew there wasn't any point. I understand you won't ever feel the same way toward me. Don't worry about it. Being close to you is enough for me. Protecting you is enough for me.

Second, Tomasi loves you, too. Or he will, if you let him. And I think you will love him, too, so I hope you will be happy with him. I never told you how I met him when I went to his house. Apparently I still haven't figured out how to turn invisible! We had a nice talk, mostly about you, of course! You can trust him, and I think you can help him, so pay close attention to his admonition. Speaking of admonitions, you have helped me in a way you couldn't know. This is mine:

*Strength and power come to you
Like night flowers or morning dew
If you protect the one you love
And keep her safely, tell her true*

*If she puts you to paper soon
Before the earth crosses the moon
The course is fixed toward your goal
To light your way, like sun at noon*

*Beware the one who hides in sight
And seeks the darkness, not the light
Who knows seventeen many ways
And offers wrong disguised as right.*

When you gave me my portrait at Christmas it was all I could do to keep from kissing you, because of course you had fulfilled my admonition by putting me to paper! I wish all my admonitions were so enjoyable (and that they all involved you)! You see now why I was sure you are one of the Kind? A citizen wouldn't be able to fulfill an admonition like you have—at least, I can't imagine it.

And I might as well tell you about the admonition I fulfilled at the beginning of the year—the one I said was too personal. It was to find you at Suburban and become your friend. I suppose you won't be surprised to learn that now!

If you have this letter, though, it's because I didn't make it to the lunar eclipse and never gained the power you helped me to earn. But I cherish my portrait for so many reasons, regardless. And I figured "tell her true" didn't just make it okay for me to reveal who I am to you—it was something I __had__ to do. Maybe I was supposed to have told you about my feelings for you, instead of my other secrets. Who knows . . .

Something terrible must have happened to me, as unlikely as I think that is. Probably the one of whom I was to beware got to me. I have spent hours every day puzzling over this, and I don't think I've ever come close to figuring it out. I'm so sorry for being suspicious of everyone (unless it turns out one of them is the Unkind)! All I can say is, I was grasping at anything that might make sense. Who knows, maybe it really is someone who is seventeen and I haven't found out who. Or maybe it's something else entirely.

If I am gone, I don't want you to pursue this, though. Please don't. It will only put you in danger, and I won't have it. There are so many things I wish I understood better, and I can't give you any proof, but I have a deep feeling there is more than one person behind this darkness. If only I were more experienced! I would have been capable of so much more, and things would have turned out so differently.

What I really want to say is, please be careful. I would ask you to turn your back on everything I've told you and eventually this whole crazy secret world will close up, like a wall that used to have a door in it. But I don't think you can. I think you have a place in this strange world. And you have Tomasi, so I can't imagine it another way. Just be happy, please? And remember me as a devoted friend. The one who loved you more than you could ever know.

XOXO
Mariette

Celia wiped her eyes and put down the letter. She remembered the day she met Mariette, a bundle of perpetual motion, like the hummingbird they had seen outside the window. Mariette never had spent a moment waiting for her life to start. She simply had lived it, following anything that excited her in whatever direction it led.

The number seventeen was perhaps the last mystery to solve, but now, with everything she knew, Celia untangled that knot easily. Mariette even had rattled it off on the bus to the field trip back in September. Seventeen was the atomic number of chlorine, and chlorine was such an obvious marker for a high school chemistry teacher who was also the swim coach! Celia cursed the admonitions, cursed whatever gods were responsible for writing them. She didn't care if she was calling their wrath down on her.

Mariette had been in love with her. She could see it now. She understood why Mariette had been crying that day in the bathroom, and what her kiss on Celia's cheek on her birthday had meant. Celia folded the letter and put it back into the envelope. On her dresser next to Liz's poetry box sat the carved wooden box the Rosary had given her for her birthday. It already contained the amulet and chain she had taken from around Mariette's neck. She opened the box and put the letter inside.

Celia went through her old sketchbook to find the single page she had hidden there last fall. She reread what she now knew was Mr. Sumeletso's admonition, wondering if any of it would make more sense this time. But the words still swam around on the page, offering her fragments she understood and plenty that was still unclear. She tucked it back into the sketchbook she carried with her, thinking it didn't make a difference now. And she had a feeling she would look at it again in the days to come.

CELIA WAS LATE COMING DOWN to the lobby after school, and she didn't find any of the Rosary there. She made her way out to the parking lot and found the five of them over by their cars. They didn't seem to be looking for her. Regine stood in front of Ivo, her body angled at him like a knife, and he was motionless, arms folded, looking away from her. The others stood by, watching uncomfortably.

As Celia approached, Regine was shouting. "I knew I

wasn't being paranoid. I mean, it's only two weeks un-til *prom*"—Regine spit out the short word Celia knew she hated—"and you still haven't asked me? I thought, how long is he planning on waiting? But no, you weren't going to ask me anyway!" Other students stared, and this time the Rosary looked around nervously, but Regine looked only at Ivo.

"What do you want me to say?" Ivo asked her.

"Why don't you like me?" Regine was crying, but her rage trumped her despair, and her body stayed on the offensive.

"How am I supposed to answer that? You know I like you as a friend. You are so important to me—"

"Of course we're friends! Except I'm the idiot who's been fooling herself for *years* while the rest of you"—Regine whirled around to accuse the rest of them—"watched and snickered!"

Liz spoke up. "What did you want us to do? If I had said, 'Regine, I don't think Ivo likes you that way,' what would you have done? I bet you would have lashed out at me the same way you're lashing out at him now!"

"I can't believe this!" Regine ran to her car, yanked open the door, and got in. The rest of them stepped out of the way as she backed out and drove off. Before she was even out of the parking lot, Regine's car was going faster than Celia had ever seen it, though that wasn't saying very much.

"Oh my god," Celia said. The others looked at her, and she said helplessly, "She didn't even put on her driving gloves."

"Well, I think we all saw that coming," Brenden said. "I feel horrible for her."

"So she asked you why you hadn't asked her to prom?" Liz asked Ivo. Ivo nodded. "And what did you say?"

"That I'd asked Isadore from Diaboliques," he said.

"You asked *her?*"

"I want to go with her! Why shouldn't I ask her?"

"Of course, but don't you see how that's a double whammy for Regine?" Liz remonstrated with him.

"What are we going to do?" Brenden asked.

"I don't know," Ivo said, rubbing his forehead. "This is my fault. I tried my best to avoid this all year, and it didn't work."

"We wondered why you kept going along with it," Brenden said.

"I didn't want to hurt her feelings! And I didn't want to mess up what we have, all of us. I didn't know what else to do. I guess that didn't turn out so well."

They stood there for a little, each pondering the situation. Finally Brenden said, "Come on, Celia, we'll give you a ride home. There's no point in standing around here."

Celia got into the back seat of Brenden's car and they drove away at the usual speed. Celia felt a little guilty. This was such a normal high school thing, and after all the decidedly un-high-school-like things that had happened to Celia, it was a relief, in some crazy way, to be thinking about things as silly and unthreatening as crushes and prom. The guys in the front seat had stayed quiet. Eventually Marco said, "Wow. Regine was really pissed. What's going to happen?"

"Well, if nothing changes, it's going to be very chilly between them, and I don't see it getting warmer before school's over," Brenden said.

"They'll avoid each other, and we'll get stuck choosing sides whether we like it or not," Marco said. "It's going to be miserable."

"So we have to find a way to change it," Celia said. Compared with her problems about which the Rosary knew nothing, this had to be completely manageable somehow.

"Do you have any ideas?" Brenden's eyes found her in the rearview mirror.

"Maybe." Celia hoped what she wanted to say would sort itself out as she spoke. "When I met all of you at the beginning of the year, it was clear you all are very devoted to each other—maybe too devoted. Think about it. If you guys weren't together, could you imagine dating someone outside the Rosary? Liz can't. Am I wrong, or has she kept Skip at bay all this time because of her devotion to you—to us? It's great for the group, but maybe it's a little too insulated sometimes.

"When Regine realized she liked Ivo, she must have thought it made sense. You guys are a couple, so why shouldn't she and Ivo be one, too? Of course it's not that simple, but at least she could see it as a possibility. I'm sure she thought how perfect it would be.

"Now we know that's not going to happen, so what's left? Your devotion to the Rosary. Regine leaves her house forty minutes earlier than she has to every morning so we can make the rounds and arrive at school together. When my curfew was earlier than the rest of yours, we all left Diaboliques together, even though you could have stayed hours later. Because you have to go to the school dances, Brenden, we all go with you to keep you company. When my friend died, you all came to be with me at the funeral. That's how it's been, all year.

"What is going to help us through this situation? The fact that our devotion to each other trumps everything else, including unrequited love."

"That's great, but what does it mean for this situation, now? What is Ivo supposed to do?" Brenden asked.

"I don't know how strongly he feels about taking Isadore to prom, but I would say the only thing that could replace Regine's desire to go to prom with Ivo would be her desire to go to prom with all of us."

"We all go together." Marco considered the idea.

"I think that's the only alternative Regine could accept. She won't get Ivo, but she gets to have us all."

"That's very wise," Marco said. "It makes a lot of sense."

"So we have to convince Ivo to have his date with Isadore on another night, and then convince Regine we all want to go together and that that's more important than any of us having individual dates," Brenden said.

"You can make it up to me afterward." Marco smiled at him.

"I will." Brenden patted his knee. "Celia, I think we have to try it. If I talk to Ivo, will you talk to Regine?"

"Sure," she said. "I'd be happy to."

At her house, Brenden and Marco got out and hugged her. "It's a good thing Regine found you," Brenden said.

"See you tomorrow!" Celia kissed them both on the cheek.

After dinner Brenden called Celia to tell her he had convinced Ivo to go along with her idea. Celia dialed Regine, and some time later it was settled. Marco immediately went to work to coordinate their outfits.

Being able to make something better—to resolve something, even if it was as foolish as plans for prom—helped Celia feel like her grasp on reality was restored. Mariette was gone, and nothing would change that. But so was Mr. Sumeletso, which meant that school was just *school* again. She could feel happy and sad about the same things as everyone else. Life was returning to normal, at least a little bit. Celia spent a moment hoping she would attend a prom with Tomasi. It was a lovely thought, a lovely feeling, and then she set it aside for next year.

23

big night music

CELIA STOOD IN FRONT of her mirror in Marco's finished gown. Her mother had helped her put her hair up in a twist. She pulled on elbow-length gloves and stepped into her heels. When she looked out the window on her way downstairs, she was surprised to see all three black cars pull up in front of her house.

"We thought it was appropriate to reverse the order," Brenden said when she opened the door.

"You all look amazing!" Celia welcomed them in.

Marco had a white lily corsage for her that matched the other girls' and the boutonnières on the guys' lapels. They arranged themselves in a tableau in her living room, and Celia's mother took pictures. Then they went out to the cars and did it again. Mrs. Balaustine whispered to Celia, "I wish your dad could have seen you tonight."

"Me too!" Celia hugged her.

In the car, Regine said, "Thank you so much for helping me get through this."

"It's the least I could do," Celia said. "And I'm glad we're doing this together, anyway. I know we still have the summer before the others go off to college, but this may be the last opportunity we have to do something as special as this."

"It's going to be really tacky," Regine giggled.

"What do you mean? It's going to be awesome," Celia countered with a smile.

They pulled into the parking lot of the country club, and Celia remembered the first day, standing in the school parking lot with these strangers, wondering what was going to happen next. Now she knew how to walk deliberately, as they did, with the pride and indifference that was the trademark of the Rosary. The moon overhead was a slender crescent. It would be full, and eclipsed, in a matter of weeks. Around them, girls in confectionery-colored dresses and boys in ill-fitting tuxedos rustled by, and she wondered how they would remember this night. The Rosary made their way to the entrance and a man in livery opened the door for them. "Where's Rufus when you need him?" Brenden asked. He raised his voice and said, "Twinkle, twinkle!" to which they all replied, "Release the bats!"

The ballroom was darker and more elegant than Celia had expected. It wasn't nearly as beautiful as Diaboliques, but she judged it a decent fit for the Rosary. They took a table and looked around at the rest of the students, who slouched in their chairs and played with their napkins. *It's just an overdressed high school cafeteria*, Celia thought, and the Rosary soon turned back to their table.

"I'm glad we're here," Regine said. "And I'm sorry again for freaking out."

"Don't worry about it," Brenden said. "I think we're all glad it turned out this way."

"Good," Liz said. "What did you bring for the DJ, Brenden?"

"'Nemesis' by Shriekback," he said. "A song about the apocalypse seemed fitting."

"We should be so lucky." Liz smiled.

After dinner the Rosary idly watched the dancing, arranged around their table like a royal court sitting for a portrait. Soon Skip made his way toward them. Celia admired him for still wearing all the pieces of his tuxedo, since most of the guys had shed jackets, ties, and cummerbunds by then. It was the first time she ever had seen him not wearing something orange.

"Well, it wouldn't be a night out without a visit from Skip," Ivo said.

"Shut up," Liz retorted.

Skip stopped in front of them. "Hey, everybody," he said.

"Hi." Celia gave him a smile. She didn't care if she was deviating from the Rosary's code of detachment. Now that she knew for sure that Skip was nothing more than a goodhearted citizen, it felt good to be kind to him.

He smiled at Celia but quickly returned to his purpose. "Hi, Liz."

"Hi, Skip. Where's your date?"

"I didn't bring one. Remember last time? We decided I should come alone to the next one."

"We did?"

"Well, *I* did. Would you like to dance?"

"Not to this song," Liz said.

"C'mon, Liz, give him a break. He's really putting himself out there," Marco said.

"Stay out of this! If everybody minded their own business, the world would go around a great deal faster than it does!"

"What's to stay out of? All I know is he's been really nice to you, and you've been really cold to him, but you look at him every chance you get. Why don't you tell me what it is I'm supposed to stay out of?"

"Screw you guys." Liz got up and walked off, her black full skirt cutting a swath through the candy-colored dresses.

"Should I go after her?" Skip asked.

"Why don't you stay here," Marco said. "She has to come back eventually, and maybe you can explain some things to us in the meantime."

"Sit down." Celia patted the seat next to her that Liz had vacated. Skip looked after Liz for a moment, then sat down. "See, if we didn't know any better, we'd say Liz likes you. We even wonder if you guys have some history together."

"We do—back in first year," Skip said. He paused between each sentence, as if he were trying to decide how to tell the story. "We went out for a while, and I thought it was going well. Then she broke it off. I got over it, because I didn't have much of a choice, but I still care about her, and I wish we had at least stayed friends."

"Did you know about this?" Brenden asked Ivo.

"Of course I did," Ivo said.

"So what happened, then?"

Ivo looked at Brenden as though the answer were obvious. "We were starting to get into alternative things. We were starting to do the things we do now. And Liz couldn't imagine having a boyfriend who looked like this." Ivo gestured at Skip.

"Seriously? Are you kidding? That's the most ridiculous thing I've ever heard," Marco said.

"It's not that simple, and you know it," Ivo rebuked him. "Anyway, I'm not saying it was right. I'm just telling you what happened."

"But she's never dated anyone else, has she?" Brenden asked. "And clearly she still has feelings for you," he said to Skip.

"And I like her, too. I mean, we're going to graduate in a week and go off to college, so it's not like I'm trying to get back together with her. I've just been thinking back over high school, and it feels like we've never really made peace with everything that happened."

"What can we do?" Celia asked.

"There's nothing to do," Ivo said. "This isn't some after-school special on TV. Liz makes her own choices, and that's all."

"But if she's really avoiding Skip because of some Capulet and Montague, upstairs-downstairs thing, couldn't we at least let her know that it doesn't matter to us?" Marco asked.

Celia got up. "I'm going to see where she is." She headed off in the direction Liz had gone. Outside the ballroom the dimly lit hall that led to a side entrance was empty, but on a hunch she went down it and pushed though the double doors that opened onto a small side lobby. Liz sat there on the floor, her back to the wall, knees to her chest, her clutch at her side. The aroma of pine trees and the sound of the breeze drifted in through the open outer door.

"Liz, come back," Celia said.

"Is Skip still there?"

"He is—he's a really nice guy."

"You've been talking to him?"

"We all have. He just wants to have one last memory with you before school's over."

"Did he say that?"

"He didn't have to. It's obvious. And it's really romantic. He came to prom alone, and he's hanging out with us, and I'm sure he's taken a lot of ridicule from his friends already." Celia thought for a moment. "You lost your virginity with him, didn't you?"

"Yes," Liz sighed.

"So, what happened?"

"It was a mistake."

"How?"

"I wasn't ready. I mean, I wanted to, but when it was over, I wished I hadn't done it, you know?"

"I think so."

"When I think about it now, it's so hard to sort it all out. I didn't know what I wanted, but I regretted doing it. Ivo was starting with these dark things we do now, and I jumped in. I used it as a way to get away from Skip."

"Did Skip pressure you?"

"No, he never did. He was such a good guy. He still is. I remember he told me he didn't care if we didn't have sex again. He practically begged me to keep going out with him. But I . . . You don't always do things for the right reasons, you know? You don't always think about how what you're doing affects someone else." Liz looked at the ceiling. "He gave up, eventually. And after a while I thought it was all behind me. But something about senior year . . . it made me think back on everything, and the truth is, I was a jerk to Skip. I have been for years, just because it made it easier for me to justify the way I'd made a mess of it." Liz paused. "I wonder what might have happened."

"I think Skip might be wondering the same thing," Celia said. "I can understand why he needs closure with you."

"And I probably need it with him, too." Liz sighed.

"Come back." Celia held out her hands to Liz. "Talk to him. It'll be good for both of you."

Liz allowed Celia to pull her up from the floor and lead her back to the hall. Skip was still there, and he stood up as they came over. "I'm sorry," she said to him.

"It's okay."

"I guess we should talk." Liz's face had relaxed, but she had trouble looking directly at him.

Skip turned to the table. "We'll be back. Thanks, guys." The two of them headed off. Skip put his hand on the small of Liz's back, and Celia was happy Liz didn't brush it away.

"There's more to that story. I'm sure of it," Regine said. "Does anyone else feel like something's been going on right under our noses and we just haven't noticed it?"

"I don't know," Celia said. "Sometimes things really are exactly how they look."

The dance was in full swing, and the Rosary observed it stoically from their seats. Celia kept looking for Liz, but it was ten minutes before she returned. She looked drained, and Celia wondered if she had been crying. "Are you okay?"

"Yeah, I am." Liz was sincere. "But I don't want to talk about it, okay?"

"Sure." Celia put her arm around her, and Liz turned and hugged her for a moment. Celia had acquired yet another secret to keep, this one about Liz. Of all the revelations Celia had experienced in the last months, this secret ranked rather low on her list.

Brenden got up. "Well, I guess it's time for me to talk to the DJ."

When "Nemesis" started with a crash, the Rosary made their way onto the floor, and the rest of the students ceded it to them with barely any display of confusion. Celia thought they even might have been expecting it. The six of them danced in the middle of the floor while everyone else stood in the dimness on either side. Her friends' faces were cool, but Celia saw the joy in their eyes, more than she had ever seen it at Diaboliques. Celia remembered standing off to the side, those first times she had been there with them, watching and admiring the other five. Now she was fully a member of the group. The rosary bracelets on their wrists were proof, but she knew it much more deeply than that.

Celia was elated. This moment of solidarity with her friends felt like the ultimate proof that her life was returning to normal. She might have lost a beautiful, secretly powerful friend. She might have to content herself with fleeting moments with a beautiful, secretly powerful boy. But these were her friends, too — the ones who had no preternatural powers, no deadly secrets, only their love for darkly beautiful things and their fierce devotion to one another.

When the song began to fade, the six of them smiled, sharing their final triumph together. The rest of the students began to applaud, and Celia looked around in surprise. Her friends seemed just as taken aback. "Maybe we weren't as intimidating as we thought," Liz said as they returned to their table.

"Do you need any more proof we have been a central part of this school?" Ivo replied.

"I think we've made our mark," Brenden agreed. "It makes it even more bittersweet that this is almost the end."

As the night wore on, the Rosary enjoyed themselves more than they would have admitted, even giving in and dancing to popular songs they would have scorned at any other time. Celia slow danced with Marco, and then Brenden, and then adored them as they danced with each other. Ivo danced with Regine, and Liz even danced with Skip. Later, when another slow song came on, Ivo came over to Celia. "We should dance," he said.

"To this song?" She smiled, taking his hand.

In the middle of the dance floor, he said, "I've been meaning to tell you something for two months."

"Really?"

"There's something I've never been able to figure out. It was right before your birthday. The day before—no, it must have been two days before—I was at home and I had an idea for the class mosaic. So I put a note in my knapsack, to make sure I remembered the next day." Celia felt a flush on the back of her neck. "I got to school the next morning, and I found the note. *Tell Celia about idea* was all it said. But I had no idea who Celia was. All day I looked at that note, but I couldn't figure out who it meant. It was the strangest thing. I left the note in my bag, because I didn't know what else to do with it.

"The next morning, your birthday, I found the note again when I was getting ready for school, and I knew who you were. And you remember, I told you my idea in the parking lot, after we gave you your present."

"I remember," Celia said. She was breathless, waiting to hear what he would say next. Just a moment ago she had been caught up in the quintessential high school dance. Of course nothing could be that simple.

"When I found that poem in your sketchbook, maybe I overreacted. I mean, Edgar Allan Poe never did all those things he wrote, so why should I think you would? It bothered me for a long time, but eventually I decided it was none of my business and let it go. But when the thing with the note happened, well, I couldn't get over it. Things like that just don't happen. People don't just fade away for a day and then come back. Plus, it was your curse day, and that didn't seem like a coincidence. It was like you disappeared for a reason. If you had just stayed home from school one day . . . but to stay home from everybody's memory is something completely different." He looked at her, and she met his gaze as sweat dripped down her back under her dress.

"I think something has been going on, maybe this whole year. I don't expect you to tell me anything. I value my own privacy, so I respect yours." Ivo thought for a moment. "At the beginning, before we took the Rosary as our name, we called ourselves 'the Suburban cognoscenti.' We like to learn and share things the rest of these people don't know, whether it's music or art or culture. But I'm starting to think if anyone belongs to a real Suburban cognoscenti, it's you. What's the singular of *cognoscenti*? *Cognoscente*?" Ivo smiled at his confusion, and Celia hoped it meant he was moving on to a lighter subject. He grew serious again.

"I'm just going to ask you this: will you take care of the others—Marco and Regine—next year? If I've learned anything this year, it's that anything can happen, even things we never would have guessed. If next year there's a curse on seniors or something . . ."

"Ivo," Celia said. "You're right. Anything can happen. And I would do anything I could for Marco and Regine, for any of you. But if you think I have some kind of power or some-thing—I don't."

"I don't believe you," Ivo said, not harshly, but with a quiet resolve that made it clear he wasn't going to be swayed. "I don't think everything can be explained, and so I won't ask you to explain. You can say whatever you want, and I understand why you wouldn't want to tell me something like this. I'm just ask-ing you to look out for them."

"Okay," Celia said, choosing the path of least resistance.

"Thank you."

They danced in silence for a while, and then Celia said, "How long have you been dating Isadore?"

"Two years."

At the end of the night Liz began to look under chairs. "Has anyone seen my purse?" She carefully knelt and lifted the tablecloth to check underneath. "I know I had it at dinner."

Celia remembered all of a sudden. "I know where it is!" She left them, crossing the empty dance floor and going out the door to the side hall, back to the side lobby where she had found Liz and coaxed her back to the dance. Celia was sure they had left Liz's clutch on the floor there, and she thought it unlikely someone else would have come across it. The sconces were still dim, and it didn't seem as if anyone else would have used this hallway all night. She pushed through the inner doors to the side lobby. One of the outer doors was still open, and the night air coming in through it had grown cooler. Sure enough, the clutch was there by the wall. Celia stooped to pick it up.

She was startled when the lobby door banged closed. "It must be windy," she said to herself, and turned to go back.

He was standing there, ten feet away from her. Celia had no idea how he had gotten in without her noticing. Celia let out a shriek, but Mr. Sumeletso regarded her with the same benevolent expression he'd worn all year at school.

"Hi, Celia. Did I startle you? You look beautiful. Did you have a good time?"

"What are you doing here?"

"I had volunteered to be a chaperon for the dance. I'm kind of disappointed I didn't get to be a part of it. But I also wanted to see you. I have something to return to you." His voice was pleasant and mild, and after weeks of imagining him as nothing but a murderer, it confused Celia. He held up a copy of *The Awakening*. She stared at the book, but neither of them moved from where they stood on opposite sides of the lobby. "It was Mariette's. I know you gave it to her because of the inscription you wrote in the front."

"Where did you get that?"

"I had to take it away from her. It was so hard to come down on Mariette. She was so nice, and it wasn't like she was struggling in my class. But she never paid attention." Mr. Sumeletso laughed quietly, and he really looked like he was having a nice memory of Mariette. "It was the day before your birthday, when you were out, and she was reading it in class—not even trying to hide it. I told her I would give it back to her at the end of the year, but I guess that's not going to happen now.

"I never got to tell you how proud I was of you. I'm glad I got to teach you, and Mariette, too. You make it easy to enjoy teaching. There are a lot of things I won't miss about Suburban, but I do miss students like you."

Celia didn't believe he had come looking for her at prom to compliment her on her grades. She waited for his real purpose to become clear. No matter how harmless he acted, she was sure something worse was coming. But he kept up with the small talk. "You know, you don't seem like the rest of the students."

"Really? How?" Her mind kept racing away. *He might have no idea. Don't give yourself away,* she begged herself.

"Well, you dress differently. You carry yourself differently. You're interested in different things," he said offhandedly. "And that's good. Too many people are content to do what everyone else is doing, and they never learn to make their own way."

"I guess so." *What do you want?*

"But I think you're different in other ways, too. Less obvious ways." He was charming and curious. "When things started happening to your classmates this year—the injuries, the accidents—it was very unsettling, and I was surprised people weren't even more upset. I mean, things like that don't happen over and over, do they?"

Celia felt like she had to respond. "It didn't really make sense."

"Now, not everyone got hurt. Apparently, the girls who lost their virginity didn't. It seems like such a ridiculous reason to do something so momentous, but it worked for the girls who did, so I suppose it was defensible, somehow."

Celia just stared at him.

"And you—you just vanished from the planet for a day when it was your turn. Where did you go?"

"I just stayed home," Celia said.

"Okay . . ." He didn't sound convinced. "This is what I really want to know, then. On the day Mariette drowned, why did you come down to the pool, in the middle of a period? Surely you had to cut class to do it, and you're not the type to do that. You knew Mariette and I would be there, because I had told you that morning, but why would you come looking for us?"

"I—I was concerned. I knew she couldn't swim, and I thought maybe—maybe I should remind her to wear a life jacket, or something—" Celia caught her breath as Mr. Sumeletso took a step toward her. But his face still was mild.

"Of course. You are a good friend. But you also knew it was Mariette's day for the 'curse.'" Again he made quotations with his fingers in the air. "Who would have guessed, way back on the first day of school, when that girl got stung in the parking lot? But why was Mariette's curse day different? I mean, Mariette died because she fell in the pool and she couldn't swim. But if it was because of a curse that caused girls to get hurt, why wasn't Mariette just injured, like everyone else? Why did she have to *die?*"

"Because none of the other girls had," Celia said, and immediately she felt her throat close up, as if to choke the words off and keep them from passing out of her mouth. But it was too late.

"Yes!" He pointed the paperback in his hand at her as if she'd answered a chemistry question correctly. "If that first girl had died from her allergic reaction, no one else would have been injured. Your friend Mariette would be alive today. This whole year would have been radically different. I wasn't sure you realized that. I mean, why would you even think such a thing? In all the time the school talked about a curse, no one ever said anything about someone dying. But now you've confirmed you knew the curse wasn't about girls getting hurt, that it was really about someone dying. That makes me a lot surer of my theory. And that is this: *you* are the reason all those other girls didn't die!" He frowned like a thunderstorm, and suddenly he was menacing, even though he was still six feet away from her. Celia flinched. "With the first few girls, I wasn't doing a very good job with the spells, so I could understand when they didn't turn out the way I wanted. But I got better! I was sure I had it figured out, yet somehow the girls didn't die! Someone was protecting them."

Celia's legs were stone. She could stand up just barely, but she couldn't move.

"For a while I thought it must be another teacher," he continued. "But none of them have any powers. Then I thought it must be someone very new, like I was, because I couldn't sense her power. It was someone who knew just enough to get in my way, but nothing more. And I might have gone the whole year without ever figuring it out—until you showed up at the pool that day. You had saved the other girls, and you had saved yourself. The year was almost over. But Mariette, being the free spirit that she was, decided she was invincible, and you couldn't convince her to stay home. Am I right?"

"No, I couldn't," Celia whispered. She was holding Liz's clutch so tightly she could feel the lipstick and phone inside through the fabric.

"I'm right. And so this is the last part of my theory: You didn't know it was I, just like I didn't know it was you, but you figured it out that afternoon. Maybe you remembered the stupid speech I gave months before about not having sex, or maybe you finally found a way to identify me. And you came down to the pool, knowing I was going to take one of my last opportunities, with my bare hands, to make sure things finally turned out the way I wanted them to." He glowered at her, pleased with his deductions. "And you were too late. You surprised me, but the hard work was over before you arrived, so it didn't matter. There was no reason why you wouldn't just accept my version of the story. It wasn't until later that I realized you knew what had really happened. You knew, and you were playing along to keep your own secret." He waved his hand and the bulbs in the chandelier over their heads sputtered to life and then kept blinking.

"I couldn't be sure. After all, you are such a timid thing, or at least, you were for most of the year. I had a hard time believing it could be you. But now I know your secret. Just like you know mine. All that's left is to figure out what we're going to do about it."

"But I'm not the one—it was Mariette! Mariette was the Kind!" Celia protested. The rapidly blinking lights made pinging noises and she was terrified they would explode and shards of glass would pour down on her.

He looked at her blankly for a moment. "Mariette was? That would be . . . No, of course you would say that! There's no way to prove it. But even if you're right, that doesn't change the fact that you know far too much. It doesn't change anything." Mr. Sumeletso rose up to hover a few inches off the floor. Celia heard a little scream escape her mouth.

"Obviously you are a liability to me, and so you will have to die, too." He looked with satisfaction at her widened eyes. "What did you think I was going to say? *Enjoy the summer, and good luck next year?* No. You may not be able to convince anyone what really happened in the pool, but surely you will find people who can help you, if you haven't already. You really should have done something by now. You could have come for me before I came for you. Not anymore." Mr. Sumeletso waved his hand and the lobby plunged into darkness.

Celia screamed. She felt the air rushing around her, growing colder and colder until it felt as if she were in a blizzard. Her skin prickled as if she were being attacked by thousands of slivers of ice. She raised her hands, trying to ward off whatever was coming at her in the darkness.

The cold wind died down, and the lights came back on, at first so dim Celia could see only shadows around her. But they slowly regained their brightness, and she could see Mr. Sumeletso in the same spot in front of her, his feet on the floor, looking winded. Mariette's book had fallen by his feet.

"You are stronger than I thought," he said. "Not Kind? Of course you are. No matter. The power I will gain for killing Mariette will make me much stronger. The lunar eclipse is coming. I bet you knew that, too, didn't you? And I'll be able to find you wherever you go."

His face was gruesome, but Celia glimpsed insecurity there. The cracks in his façade closed as he issued his threat. "Soon it won't matter where you are. It won't matter what you do. I'll be able to get to you no matter how far away you run. So say goodbye to your gloomy friends. Your time is almost up!" He snapped his fingers and the chandelier flashed brightly, then faded back to a steady dimness. The outer lobby doors banged open, and he rose off the floor again and floated out into the night. The inner doors slammed apart, and Celia ran as fast as she could in her heels.

She fled down the dim hall and veered into a bathroom and then into a stall, sinking down onto the seat, hyperventilating at the horror of what she had just experienced. *Why didn't he kill me? What did I do?* She opened Liz's clutch and took out the cell phone.

"Hello?" It had felt like an hour before Tomasi came to the phone, but Celia was relieved he was there and his mother had allowed him to take the call.

"Tomasi? It's Celia."

"Hi! Are you at prom? What's wrong?"

"It's my chemistry teacher! He killed Mariette. He thinks I'm the one who's been protecting girls all year! I knew he was the one, but I thought he didn't know I knew and so I was safe, but he figured it out, except he thinks *I* was the one protecting the girls, instead of Mariette! And he told me he's going to kill me after the eclipse!" Celia tried to keep herself from crying.

"Wait, wait. You knew it was your chemistry teacher? Why didn't you tell me?"

"Because I didn't want to make things worse for you with your parents!" Celia thought she heard the line click, but Tomasi answered her.

"Well, I'm glad you told me. There are people who can help us."

"What can they do?"

"I don't know, but I'll find out. Tell me what happened."

"Liz had left her purse in a side lobby where no one else went, and I went to get it, and he cornered me. He has this power to make the lights go on and off, and he was levitating—" There was a gasp on the phone, and Celia stopped. "Was that you?"

"No," he said. "Who was that?"

This time Celia was sure she heard the click of a phone hang up. "Are you there?"

"Yes, I'm here—" Tomasi was interrupted by voices in the background. "What are you doing? Were you listening?" he asked angrily, and Celia knew he wasn't speaking to her. She heard his parents' voices, and the sounds of a scuffle. Then the phone went dead. She tried calling back several times, but the line was busy. Finally she put the phone back in Liz's purse.

Celia looked around. She was alone, in a strange bathroom

in an unfamiliar place. There was nothing, no one to whom she could turn for even a fleeting sense of security. "You have to get it together," Celia said to herself. "You have to go back to the others and pretend nothing happened. You have no choice." She pulled herself up, tried to make her face presentable in the mirror, and then returned to the ballroom.

Almost everyone was gone. "Where have you been?" Marco said as they gathered around her. "Are you okay?"

"I—I got locked out. Your purse was in that side lobby," Celia said, handing it back to Liz. "But someone must have locked the inside doors, because I couldn't get back in. I had to walk around the building." *The lies roll off my tongue so easily now.*

"You look like you've seen a ghost," Brenden said.

"No, no ghost. Someone startled me. That's all."

"All right, let's go home." Ivo took Celia's arm and they went out to their cars. Celia was relieved Regine was tired. They barely spoke on the drive home, and Celia was free to focus her will on her heart, which still beat so fast she might have been running down a dark hallway with Mr. Sumeletso chasing her.

the *sky's* gone out

THE NEXT DAY CELIA arrived at the bookstore with one thought that had expanded to force out all the others. She took her place at the front desk and waited for the Troika to break up. Finally they walked out of the office, and Lippa said goodbye to her friends before she turned to Celia. "My dear, you don't look at all like yourself today. What is wrong? Wasn't your prom last night? Did you not have a good time?"

Celia had hoped she wouldn't break down, but she was crying before she could speak. "I need your help!"

"Oh my goodness! With what? Tell me." There were no customers, and Lippa led Celia to a pair of wingback chairs in an alcove and sat down with her.

"When you told me about the Kind and the Unkind, I didn't believe you. I thought you were crazy."

"You and almost everyone else," Lippa said pleasantly, confused.

"But you're right. My friend Mariette was one of the Kind."

"Your friend who died?" Immediately Lippa grew serious.

Celia nodded. "Everyone thinks she drowned by accident, but our teacher killed her—he's one of the Unkind. And last night he told me he was going to kill me when his power gets stronger from the admonition he fulfilled by killing her!"

Lippa stared at her. "Your friend was one of the Kind, and your teacher is one of the Unkind?"

"I didn't believe you before, but it's true! I've seen their admonitions, and I've seen them use their powers! You have to tell me what to do! He's going to kill me!"

"Celia, calm down." Lippa took her hand. "You have to pull yourself together." She waited while Celia worked to slow her breathing and wipe her eyes.

"My boyfriend, Tomasi—you remember when he came to see me here—he's one of the Kind, too, but he hasn't developed his powers. I asked him for help, but his parents think he's evil because they found out about him and they don't understand, and now I'm pretty sure they've sent him to his grandfather's because he isn't responding when I write to him. He can write in my notebook from wherever he is, so something must have happened. My teacher actually tried to kill me last night, but he said my power was stronger than he realized, and I don't even know how to use it! I wouldn't have asked you, because you said you've only heard stories, but I don't have anyone else to ask. Do you know anyone? Do you know anything I can do?"

"*You're* one of the Kind, too?" Lippa's voice was calm and careful.

"I don't know—Mariette thought I was, and Tomasi does, too, but I didn't think so. But last night my teacher didn't kill me, and he said it was because of my power, so I don't know. Maybe I am?"

"Celia, I know you lost your friend, and it's been a terrible time for you. But I think you've become a little susceptible to the stories I've told you."

"You don't believe me?"

Lippa spoke slowly, trying to make Celia hear it the way it had sounded to her. "You think you, and everyone around you, are one of the Kind or the Unkind . . . When someone dies, we all grieve differently, but many people are tempted to latch onto anything, no matter how fanciful, to help them deal with the loss."

"You don't believe me," Celia said again. It felt as if the ceiling had dropped a foot or two closer to their heads.

"It's not about what I believe," Lippa said sadly. "What you've told me, it doesn't sound like something I should believe or not believe. It sounds like someone who has been under a lot of stress these past months, and who has seized onto a conspiracy theory I told her about, in a desperate attempt to make sense of why bad things happen."

"I thought— You said . . ."

"I shouldn't have. If I had known it would plant seeds in you that would grow into these ideas that everyone around you was part of a crazy supernatural world, I never would have said anything. I never would have invited you to join the Troika." Lippa patted her hand. "Do I believe the Unkind and the Kind might exist? Yes. But your friends, your teacher, you—this is not the same thing. You know that. I'm sorry."

Celia nodded again. She had pinned her hopes on Lippa, and now she felt even more alone. The death threat was drawing closer to her moment by moment, and as an added bonus, now her boss thought she had lost her mind.

· · ·

CELIA FELT LIKE A SLEEPWALKER during the last week of school. She turned in final exams and couldn't remember a thing she had written. She passed books back in and stared into space until someone called her name or everyone got up to leave. Gradually her locker emptied out, becoming hollow and unrecognizable, like she felt. She wandered the halls between periods, preoccupied and unseeing. After two mornings of asking what was bothering Celia, Regine had given up. The rest of the Rosary seemed to think she was taking her turn to be moody, not an unwelcome trait for their collective persona at Suburban. Part of Celia wished they would press her more, but the other part was scared to be asked, because she didn't know what she could say.

For so long, her life had felt so full. She'd had an amazing group of brilliant friends who were constantly showing her new things. Now they were a distracted cluster of kids on the verge of splintering in several directions.

Before, she'd had the attention of a beautiful guy who would break out of his own house if necessary, just to see her. Now she assumed he had been shipped off to his grandfather's farm for some kind of puritanical remediation. No one ever answered the phone at his house. Every night she opened her notebook, hoping to find something new from him, but it held only the words she'd written before: *Are you there? Are you there?*

Before, she'd had a lovely friend whose exuberance for life could overpower the gloom of an entire classroom. Now she had a letter and a necklace, and a second funeral in her young life. Before, she had been a sophomore whose life seemed to grow broader every day. Now she had been promised death by an Unkind who had killed her friend, a man who was only waiting for an eclipse to deliver the power he needed to do it.

To Celia, being in shock felt like being zipped inside a sleeping bag—she sensed the real world out there somewhere, but it couldn't reach her. Her mind spun continuously in the middle of these thoughts, but her body felt nothing.

She paused on the stairwell to look out at the Rothko trees, flush with new leaves so green they seemed to grow larger as she watched them. Off to one side a recently deposited construction trailer was occupied by the people who would spearhead construction of the new wing as soon as the students were out of the way. In the fall there would be yet another ridge in the school's backbone. If she lived to see next year, she might be asked to draw it all over again for the school newspaper. It all seemed so pointless.

She went to her last chemistry class, where they spent the time cleaning the lab before the summer break. The lights still flickered overhead. Everyone believed it to be a reminder of Mariette, but Celia knew it was the remnants of Mr. Sumeletso's Unkind energy lingering in the room. She looked out the window, hoping to see a hummingbird, but found blank sky instead. Once this final period was over, Celia might never come in here again.

When she got home from the last day of school, Celia felt stifled. The freedom from homework only meant that another evening stretched out before her, with nothing to distract her from her fate. She changed out of her school clothes and pulled out the only pair of jeans Regine had allowed her to keep and her father's sweatshirt with gray stains on it from when she had painted her room. She crept downstairs and went to the garage to pull out a bicycle she hadn't ridden in years. Celia wobbled down the driveway and eventually found her balance halfway down the block. Her knees came up too close to the handlebars, but she kept pumping, trekking several miles across town to a place she hadn't been in almost a year.

The parking lot of the high school where she'd spent her first year was deserted. The flag hung limp, and the shadow of the pole lengthened in the evening sun. Celia wondered if she was being foolish, coming here alone when Mr. Sumeletso had promised to erase her at a time and place when the murder couldn't be traced to him. But what difference did it make if he killed her now or in another twenty-four hours?

Her old high school was a massive cube pierced at regular intervals with windows and doors—the exact opposite of the sprawling complex that was Suburban. She dropped her bike and walked toward the building, but she stopped before she got there. A faint breeze rose and played in her hair, and she felt the coolness of the approaching nightfall. She used to dread coming to this place, but now those days seemed so much simpler. She had leapt from this cauldron of misery with such relief, and for a long time she had been sure she was in a better place—for a while all the risks she had taken had paid off, more richly than she ever would have guessed. But now she found herself in the fire, looking back up at the cauldron and wondering if it had been so bad after all.

The darkness loomed, and no one was going to come out of it holding a lantern to show her the way and make sure she got home safely. Her shoulders quivered as the evening air seeped through her sweatshirt. The chill finally forced her to take up the little bicycle and pedal back home. Her mother met her with concerned reproval and a plate of food. She was on her way out. Celia tried to eat and then went upstairs to prepare for Diaboliques.

Hours later, Regine looked over at her in the car. "Won't

you tell me what's wrong? You've been somewhere else since promenade."

"I miss Mariette." It was the only thing Celia could think of to say.

"Oh, of course. I wondered about that. You didn't seem to mourn as much as I expected. I guess you're still dealing with it?"

"Yeah," Celia murmured, looking out the window.

At Diaboliques Rufus still called her Paperwhite out of affection. She tried to find some solace in her favorite place. Other regulars nodded to her now, and sometimes she even spoke with them. Ivo chatted with Isadore while Regine stood indifferently just a few feet away from them. Celia felt Marco at her side. "Did he ever go on a date with her?" he asked.

"I think so."

"She is pretty. I could see them as a couple."

"I can, too."

"Who knows, if he had gotten up the nerve to ask her out a few years back, maybe they could have been."

Celia still knew how to be the quiet one, but what did these foolish secrets matter? She was too agitated to wait for the others to dance before she left the room. As she walked away she wondered if any of them would follow her, but she didn't really care.

Down on the mezzanine she found the woman with the fiery red plume of hair. Once again the woman looked as though she had been expecting her. Her perfect white smile beamed up at Celia, and she patted the cushion on the sofa. Celia sat down.

"It's been a little while. Let me see," the woman said, and Celia willingly offered her hand. The tips of the woman's nails moved lightly across her skin. It was so dark, Celia was sure the woman couldn't possibly see anything on her hand.

"There's been some deepening, but it's all here." The woman closed Celia's hand inside her own and looked up at her.

"I need help!" Celia said. "I don't know what to do!"

"See, that's not true," the woman said easily. "You don't need help, and you will know what to do when the time comes. Really." She looked at Celia with compassion. "I told you before you would be fine, and nothing has changed."

"But my teacher is one of the Unkind! He killed my friend who was one of the Kind, and he's going to kill me!"

None of that surprised the fortuneteller. "No, he is going to *try* to kill you."

"But what's going to stop him from *actually* killing me?"

"*You* are."

"You can't tell me what to do? Please, please, you have to help me!"

"No, I can't. And, my dear, no one else can, either. The Leopard's parents have taken him to his grandfather's farm. I can tell you this." The woman paused a moment to consider her words. "The thing that makes you who you really are is what gives you your power."

"I have power?" Celia asked her.

"Of course you do," the woman laughed. "How could you think otherwise?"

"Is that why he didn't kill me? How did I stop him?"

"No, you didn't stop him. The stupid man isn't powerful enough to do what he tried to do, with his darkness and cold. He is a coward, after all. He only uses his bare hands as a last resort, you remember. But he is correct that his Unkind power is going to increase greatly, and then things will be very different."

"Do I have an admonition?"

"What do you mean by that? Are you asking me if there are things you must do in order to become the person you want to be? Absolutely. But that is true of everyone. Every black bead on your chain has told you their admonitions this year."

"They have?"

"Think back. At some point this year every one of them has told you something they know they have to do in order to become the person they want to be. If we are wise, we give ourselves admonitions our whole lives and do our best to fulfill them."

"But the Kind—their admonitions are different."

"Only because they come from a different place."

"So what is *mine?* How am I supposed to stop him?"

"You will know what to do when the time comes." The fortuneteller patted Celia's hand and released it. "Go back to your friends. Patrick is going to play 'Second Skin' by the Chameleons, and I know you love that song."

Celia couldn't understand how this woman could send her away with the feeling she had learned something, when her answers never seemed to match up with Celia's questions. Celia was tempted to hate her for not sharing every scrap of knowledge that might help Celia to save herself. She looked at the woman one last time, wondering if she would ever see her again, and then got up. At the bottom of the stairs she turned to look back, but in the sweep and flash of the lights she couldn't see where they had been sitting. Back upstairs she joined her friends on the dance floor, and sure enough, as the song faded, she heard the slender keyboard notes that began "Second Skin." Then the drums came, and the guitar, and while she knew the lyrics by heart, it was as though she was hearing them for the first time.

> *I realize a miracle is due*
> *I dedicate this melody to you*
> *But is this the stuff dreams are made of?*
> *No wonder I feel like I'm floating on air*
> *Everywhere*
> *Oh, it feels like I'm everywhere*
> *Like when you fail to make the connection, you*
>   *know how vital it is*
> *Or when something slips through your fingers you*
>   *know how precious it is*
> *And you reach the point where you know*
> *It's only your second skin*
> *Someone's banging on my door . . .*

Celia cried a little as she danced, and she raised her eyes to the ceiling. At that moment, she felt so connected to the world around her, she might have been in a church. No mysteries were solved—they loomed on every side. But she felt more alive than she ever had before. For the rest of the evening the remnants of that moment trailed around her like a fog. Her mind was far away, chasing in all directions to find Tomasi, rushing down endless hallways in hopes of reaching Mariette in time, turning to see who was pursuing her in the darkness, clutching the armrest in the passenger seat of a car as the world flew by outside the window.

Everyone told her she was strong, stronger than before, and

Celia wanted to believe them. But she knew the weakness hidden within her. She could welcome it back whenever she wanted, and now seemed like an excellent time. For each thing she had gained, it seemed she had lost something. In one moment the haze cleared, and Celia thought with incredible clarity, *I am going to die.*

Eventually it was time to go. Regine was sensitive to Celia's mood. In the car, she put on music and stayed quiet. The whole way home, Celia tried to be hopeful. Her flame-haired advisor had assured her she could solve this problem, meet this threat on her own. Celia couldn't fathom how, but she wanted desperately to rediscover her faith in herself. If she was going to survive, that had to come first.

In her gray room Celia sat on the edge of her bed and felt the despair weighing her down like a lead overcoat. When she cleared away everything else—Mariette, Tomasi, the Rosary—she could see a straight line down the center of a very straight road. In less than twenty-four hours the moon would be eclipsed. Mr. Sumeletso would receive the Unkind power he had earned by killing Mariette and sucking away her dying breath. And his first priority, he had promised Celia, was to wipe away the only person who knew what he had done. He would destroy her in whatever way he could.

If he became as strong as he seemed to expect, and everything truly was different, as the fortuneteller said it would be, then he probably was going to be able to kill her without touching her, as he preferred. Celia felt herself withering away like a tree in a punishing drought, with no idea how to save herself, nowhere to turn. She imagined doctors telling her mother they couldn't diagnose her and there was nothing they could do.

Or maybe she would be extinguished like a candle flame,

gone in a single gust, her eyes instantly turned to glass. He would send a deadly spider, or an eighteen-wheeler, or just an aneurysm, and it would be over in an instant.

He wouldn't let her off that easily. He would torture her first, she feared. Her skin would turn to boils and flake away. Her bones would yaw and snap inside her body, stabbing her from the inside. Her tongue would swell up, slowly clogging her mouth and then her throat until she suffocated. Celia wept with fear.

It was four in the morning. She ran a bath and sank into it. *The fortuneteller would have told me something very different if I were going to die, wouldn't she? She wouldn't have patted my hand and told me I didn't need help and I would know what to do. Why am I placing so much faith in a woman whose name I don't even know? What other option do I have?*

She had added more hot water to the bath three times, and a feeble light was peeking through the trees before Celia finally got out and dried off. She studied the wrinkles on her fingertips and then examined her face in the mirror. Her hair clung in strings to her skin, and she imagined this was how she would look if she drowned. She ran her fingers through her hair to get it off her face. "What do I have to do to live?" she asked her reflection, but her voice sounded hollow and weary.

I will know what to do when the time comes. That's what the woman said. Celia didn't know what to do, so did that mean the time hadn't come? She hated how she had used this strategy of being passive so many times. In the drawing class last summer, when Regine had walked up to her and taken charge. In the parking lot at the beginning of the year, when she had stood there like a calf, waiting to be led into school. At Diaboliques, when she had waited for Tomasi to come to her. In

April, when it had been her turn to face the curse. She hadn't known what to do, so she had done nothing. But this time Mariette wouldn't come to kneel on her back lawn and cast a spell to keep her safe. Tomasi was gone. Finally her mind grew as exhausted as her body, and Celia slept. She didn't have to get up until it was time to get ready for the graduation ceremony in the afternoon.

25

black celebration

C ELIA SAT WITH REGINE and Marco in the auditorium, waiting for their friends to march in. The stage looked like a meeting of the United Nations, with the faculty seated in departments, a number of flags arranged behind them. Celia could feel the clock ticking down to the eclipse, and she held her anger in check, knowing it was a desperate sword that would do nothing to protect her. When she had awakened in the early afternoon she hoped a plan would be waiting for her, but she felt no closer to understanding what she was supposed to do or how she was to escape the fate Mr. Sumeletso had promised her. At last the ceremony began, and they all stood and focused on the seniors in their caps and gowns.

"It's strange how they all look the same," Marco said. "We try so hard to be distinct, and look, Brenden couldn't even do his hair." Brenden saw them and waved as he passed, his face a little unfamiliar under his mortarboard. "We're going to visit Metropolitan in July. I can't wait to see where he'll be." Celia tried to listen to Marco, but she didn't really care.

Once everyone was in place, Principal Spennicut stepped to the microphone. Celia was tempted to tune him out, but he spoke briefly about the tragedy the school had experienced that semester and asked for a moment of silence to honor the student they had lost. Celia looked at the floor, feeling Marco's hand on her back, and her rage approached a boil again. Her mind unspooled the year, from Mariette's funeral to the crazy things she had done to protect Celia, to the way she had cried over her gift, to Halloween, when she finally had shared her secret, to the inexplicable things Celia had witnessed, to that day in chemistry lab when she had laid eyes on Mariette for the first time. Celia had been so excited about the person she was becoming, about the people they all were becoming, but Mariette's death was like a bucket of water over all those lovely hopes.

Celia was jolted back to the present by the voice of the principal, who had moved on to the news of the new wing that would be built over the summer. He told the assembly about the money the graduating seniors had raised for a mosaic in the hallway of the new wing, commemorating their class. "I am happy to share with you now this artist's rendering of their mosaic!" Principal Spennicut exclaimed, and an image of the drawing Celia had produced under Liz and Brenden's direction was projected onto the screen at the back of the stage. The audience applauded, and Regine and Marco poked her, telling her how good it looked. She smiled for them, but when she looked up at her lines projected on the screen, she barely recognized her own work.

IT'S NICE MY BODY WILL stand *and sit, and smile sometimes and talk a little, without me having to tell it what to do,* Celia thought as she wandered around the Fourads' home during the graduation party. *Because I don't know what to tell it now.* At a few points she thought her self actually might have left her body and she could look down on the room from somewhere up by the ceiling. She wondered if her father had felt this way, when he knew he was going to die. She wondered if there was some place where she might see him. She knew she should be taking this opportunity to say meaningful things to her friends, who were all so happy around her. If she was going to die, shouldn't she make the most of the time she had left? But she had no idea what she possibly could say.

"You're so quiet," Regine said when she found her in the study, rereading the Lewis Carroll quote on the wall.

"I know. I'm sorry," Celia said. She looked over at Regine and realized too late her eyes were filling with tears.

"Celia!" Regine put her arms around her and stroked her hair. "Last night you were upset, too! You've been a shadow of yourself for a week! Is it Mariette? Is it the end of the year? It's like the life has drained out of you."

"I don't know." Celia looked at the ceiling, searching her mind for something she could say. "I just feel like it's all over."

"I know," Regine said, and Celia was soothed by her voice. "I guess, in a way, it is. It won't ever be the same. It makes me sad, too, when I think about it. But we have to carry on. Next year we'll have to figure out how things are going to be. We have to stick together. And we will. We'll be okay."

"What if we're not?" Celia asked. "What if we don't make it?"

"Why wouldn't we? And especially you? You're the reason we're all still together, don't you realize? If it weren't for you, we wouldn't be here now. You know it's true."

"You guys would have been fine," Celia said weakly.

"Maybe, maybe not. But the way it happened, the way it

really happened . . ." Regine was silent for a moment. "I wish I were as strong as you are."

"But I'm not! I'm not strong at all!" Celia caught a sob in her throat.

"Yes you are! You may not feel like it, but I know better. I might have believed you when we met. But now there's no doubt in my mind." Regine pulled back and looked at her. "You look exhausted. Let's go. It's getting late, and it's not like we won't be together again soon. We have the whole summer to go to Diaboliques before anyone goes anywhere."

Regine steered her gently through the party. Celia hugged each of her friends, ignoring their looks of concern, not saying anything when Regine told them Celia was tired and emotional about the end of the year. Finally they made it outside, where dusk was creeping up behind the trees. "It's kind of chilly." Regine shivered. "It feels like it could storm, but there isn't a cloud in the sky."

Celia settled into the front seat of Regine's car, and impulsively she turned and pulled the gray cashmere blanket from the back seat, spreading it over her lap. Regine watched her and said, "I don't think anyone has ever used that before."

"I've always wanted to," Celia said. She looked out the window, where the sky ranged from orange to purple to indigo above her.

On the post above their car, the streetlamp blinked on and then flickered, struggling to wake up. It reminded Celia of the fluorescent lights that had sputtered and pinged in the chemistry lab and the chandelier in the lobby at the country club, where Mr. Sumeletso had made his threatening intentions clear. She closed her eyes for a moment and listened for the music from the car stereo. It was a song she liked, but something about it was stale now. She'd heard it too many times. Celia opened her eyes again and stared out the window.

Regine drove at her usual stately pace down the street. As they passed under the next light post, the oval lamp flickered on like an alien eye lurching to life above them. Farther down the street the lights remained dark. Celia waited for the next post, and as they passed under it, the lamp sputtered and lit up. "He's coming," she said under her breath.

"What did you say?" Regine asked her.

"Drive faster," Celia said.

"What?"

"Drive faster!" Celia pleaded with her. Outside the window the next streetlight blinked on ominously over them. "I need to get home."

"Okay." Regine sped up to the actual speed limit, and still each streetlight came awake just as they passed underneath it. Panic filled Celia like a cat in a burlap sack, thrashing around inside her as it heard the sound of the rushing river coming closer. She fought to keep her fear from escaping up her throat and past her lips.

The daylight was almost gone, and when Regine turned a corner the full moon swung into view out the front window, impossibly large, pale, and alone. On this street, too, the lights stayed dark until their car approached; then they blinked and flickered to life. Celia thought she could hear them pinging overhead, as if a large white moth were struggling to get out of each glass. Why didn't Regine notice? Regine had lapsed back into her customary slow speed, and Celia was in agony counting down the blocks, lifting her eyes to each new Unkind sentry quivering like a dying firefly above the car.

Celia opened the door before the car had completely stopped at her front walk. "Are you going to be okay?" Regine asked.

"I don't know." Celia got out and pushed the door closed before Regine could say anything else. Once again there were just two girls as she and Regine stared at each other through the glass. Inside the car the first girl looked scared and hurt. She gave Celia a searching look. Reflected in the window, Celia could see only the silhouette of the second girl. The chilly wind pushed by her, and the trees creaked overhead. Regine got out.

She implored Celia across the black roof of the car. "Why won't you tell me what's happening?" The wind pushed her bob into the corner of her mouth.

"When we met in that class last summer, why did you choose me? Why did you bring me into the Rosary?" Celia asked.

"Because . . . because I could tell. You were right for us, even if you didn't know it."

"*How* could you tell?"

"Well, I wasn't wrong, was I?" A tear escaped Regine's eye. "Are we still right for you?"

"Of course you are! I'm sorry. I'm just . . . There's something I have to do alone. I'm sorry."

Finally Regine drove away. Up and down the street in both directions the streetlamps shone, but they took turns switching on and off, threatening her like giants rattling their sabers. The cold breeze lifted her hair above her head. Celia looked in every direction, but she saw no one. Overhead, the full moon was large and orange, and the earth's shadow had begun to slice into one side.

And then everything was calm. The wind died. The street-lamps shone evenly. There was no sound, no movement. On the eclipsed edge of the moon a bloody red tinge was seeping across the orange face, like the first leak of death after a guillotine has fallen. Celia turned and ran into her house.

Her mother was waiting for her. "How was graduation?"

"It was fine. It was long." Celia tried to escape to her room, but her mother stopped her.

"Wait—how about the party?"

"It was nice." She hated shutting her mother out, but if she tried to explain anything at all, it would only get worse.

"Are you in a hurry?"

"Kind of. I need to go upstairs." Celia had no idea what she was going to do, but she needed to escape her mother's small talk.

"Well, are you hungry? There are some leftovers in the fridge."

"I'm not hungry."

"Can we talk later? I haven't caught up with you in a while."

"Can we talk tomorrow?"

"Okay. Is everything all right?"

"I think so. I'm not sure. I think so." Celia tried not to run up the stairs, but halfway up she lost the battle and sprinted the rest of the way.

In her room she sank onto her bed, but she didn't feel any safer than when she had been standing on her front walk. Four walls, a locked front door, her mother—none of that was going to make any difference. Celia looked around helplessly.

Nothing happened. *What is he waiting for?* she thought in anguish. *I know he's close by. He must be waiting to get stronger.*

She thought about dying. Celia knew all the versions of

the story: a bright light, her life flashing before her eyes, the stranger who would appear to escort her to the other side. Now Celia guessed it would be different from all those things. There was going to be terror, and then there was going to be nothing—infinite nothing, deeper and darker and colder than the deepest space in the universe, so absolute it would instantly drive her insane, except by then it wouldn't matter. Celia wondered what she was supposed to do with these final minutes. She reached for her sketchbook.

She paged through the pictures she had drawn of her father and her mother. She found the sketches she had made of Liz and Ivo, of Marco and Brenden, of Regine, and of Mariette. She looked for a picture of Tomasi, but she never had drawn him, and her heart grew heavy with regret. *I don't really love him*, she tried to convince herself. *It will be so much easier to lose him if I don't love him.* If she believed that, she could stick to a depressing but neat equation that balanced the two people she loved in the world: she was going to leave her mother behind and be with her father again.

But Celia's heart rose up in protest. A beautiful possibility pounded in her chest, and she knew its name as surely as she knew her own. *Tomasi.* She cursed the province of love. No roads ran straight, but it made no difference because she was being driven away, and she couldn't bear to leave. No bells rang on time, but what did time matter, anyway, now that it was running out? It only made Celia wish she never had found that province at all, yet she knew she didn't mean it. All she wanted was to see Tomasi again, even if it was for the last time. There were pages and pages of their conversations in the sketchbook, but his face . . . How was it she never had drawn him?

"I am such a fool," Celia said, reaching for a pencil. She

glanced out her window, where the earth's shadow continued to creep across the bloodied moon. On a blank page she roughed in Tomasi's eyes, his nose, lips, and the square set of his jaw. She drew confidently, even though her memory depended on so many shy glances she had stolen, so many moments she literally had dared herself to look at him. She teased out the scruff of hair on his head and set his ears against each side. All the while the luster of blood orange moonlight gradually drained away from the front lawn. It would be another hour before the eclipse was total. She shaded in the planes of Tomasi's neck, the way it widened to meet his shoulders. It was comforting somehow, even if she never would see him again. Celia's eyes welled up—what cruel world would put all these beautiful people in front of her, only to snatch them away again?

By the light of her bedside lamp, Celia thought she saw her drawing stir on the page. She blinked, rubbed the tears out of her eyes, and looked carefully again. In her drawing, the lines of Tomasi's lips moved. Next to his face, letters appeared, much more ornate than his own handwriting, and forming words much faster than when he had written to her before.

Looks great. Can I come over?

Celia stared. *Now?* she jotted next to his message. *Aren't you at your grandfather's?*

Immediately a shadow filled the page and then stretched out across her bedspread. A silhouette rose up the wall, and Celia recognized Tomasi's broad shoulders, forearms beneath sleeves rolled to his elbow, legs slightly apart. The shadow darkened to black and then turned around, and Tomasi was there, standing in front of her, looking as surprised as she was.

"I've never done that before," he said, looking around curiously.

"How did you do that?" There in her bedroom it felt as though she had allowed an exotic, possibly mythical creature in from the wild, and now she was about to discover how tame it was after all.

"I think that's the power you just gave me." He gave her a half smile, but it faded when he saw her expression. "I'm so sorry about that phone call, when you were at prom. My parents completely freaked out. They gave me five minutes to pack, and they didn't even tell me where we were going, but I knew. Grandpa's asleep at the farm right now," he said bitterly.

"Why didn't you write back before?"

"He locked up all the books! I looked everywhere, but he knows everything that happened, and he decided not to take any chances, I guess. I just convinced him to give me a freaking Bible tonight! We have to get help—the eclipse has started, and your teacher is going to be after you."

"I think it's too late," she said.

"Why didn't you tell me before?" His voice was harsh, but she knew it was because he was confused.

"I didn't want you to do anything that would get you hurt!" Celia cried. "Mariette *died!* If something happened to you and it was my fault—" She began to sob, and felt Tomasi sit next to her and take her in his arms.

"It's okay. But we have to do something now. At least we know who we're up against."

"What can we do?"

"I don't know." Tomasi concentrated, but he stayed silent, and she could tell that ideas were not coming to him.

"How did you travel through the book?"

"I don't know. I had tucked the paper from your sketchbook in the Bible, and I was sitting there reading, hoping you would write to me, and suddenly it was like I was a skydiver looking through the open door of a plane. I could see you out there in the sky, and I just . . . jumped. I don't know how to explain it. But it was because you drew me. You *drew me close*."

"Like your admonition said," Celia said. "I didn't realize . . ."

"I know! I thought you were right, and you had fulfilled the admonition when you pulled me back to you at the funeral. But apparently it was literal. You had to *draw* me. And it worked, just in time. You *do* have power!"

"None of my drawings ever has done *that* before," Celia protested. "I think I just gave you *your* power. What is *my* power?" In her mind she heard the fortuneteller laughing pleasantly at her.

"I don't know," Tomasi said, taking her hand in his. They looked down at her slender fingers among his. "Nothing has happened with your drawings before?"

"No, nothing."

"Well, we have to get help," Tomasi said. "We have to find my old teacher, the Kind who helped me before. He'll know what to do."

"How do we do that?"

"Maybe I can take you through the book," Tomasi said.

"Can you do that? How do you know where we'll end up?"

"I don't, but I can't think of anything else. At least you won't be here for him to find you." Tomasi stood up from the bed and pulled her to her feet, but Celia nearly fell.

"My feet are asleep," she said, feeling the needling numbness from both her ankles down.

"Shake them," Tomasi said impatiently.

Celia couldn't get her feet to move. She tried frantically to get the blood flowing, but the numbness was creeping into her calves instead. "It's getting worse!" She looked up at Tomasi and screamed when she saw Mr. Sumeletso hovering outside her window behind him.

Tomasi turned and saw him there, too. He was ten feet away from the house, standing still, as though he were on an invisible platform, with a calm, malevolent look on his face. Behind him, the moon was thinning into a bloody sickle.

"Who is that? Is he floating?" Tomasi stared.

"It's Mr. Sumeletso! What can we do?" Celia gasped. She sank back onto the bed, no longer able to support herself because she barely could feel anything below her knees. Her feet were like lead weights on the end of her legs.

"I don't know!" Tomasi balled his fists and pressed them against his temples. "I don't know!"

There was a knock on the door. "Celia, are you okay? Was that you?" her mother asked from outside.

"I'm fine!" Celia called desperately. She looked at Tomasi, who was wide-eyed. *You have to go!* she mouthed at him, pointing at her sketchbook, which lay open next to her. He silently protested. "Go back! I don't want him to get you, too!" she whispered to him.

Outside her door, Celia's mother said, "Was that you a minute ago? It sounded like you screamed."

"I stubbed my toe!" Celia called. She watched Tomasi turn back to the wall and darken into a shadow. He sank down the wall and across her bedspread to her sketchbook, shrinking into the page.

Her mother opened the door and looked in on Celia, who lay against the pillows on her bed, her thighs cold and numb. "You're all right?"

"I'm okay," Celia said, and she almost laughed at how pointless her lie was. "I'm tired. I'm going to go to sleep." She felt her vision start to close in. Around the edges her sight was blurry and dark.

"Okay. Hey, do you want to take another art class this summer? I thought maybe you'd like to try a painting class this time." Her mother pointed at the Rothko print on the wall.

"Sure," Celia said helplessly. She glanced out the window. The Unkind man hadn't moved. Just beyond the light from the room, his eyes were fixed on her.

"Maybe Regine would like to take it with you," her mother suggested.

"I'll ask her." Celia felt the coldness creeping up to her hips. She touched her knee, and it felt like it was frozen solid.

"Okay, well, let me know soon. I think the deadline to register is coming up. Good night, dear." Her mother smiled at her and pulled the door closed.

Celia turned to look out again at Mr. Sumeletso, who had floated closer to her window. She was calmer than she had been since the graduation ceremony. Everything had been cleared away. "I will know what to do when the time comes," she said in a low voice. He raised an eyebrow but didn't speak. It was as if he knew that no matter what she said, Celia didn't have a clue.

She looked helplessly at the sketchbook on her lap. On the open page her drawing of Tomasi's face was alive. He looked up at her imploringly. She touched his lips with her finger and then flipped through the book, unsure what she was looking for. She couldn't feel anything below her stomach.

From the back of her sketchbook the loose page with Mr.

Sumeletso's admonition peeked out. She pulled it out to look at it for what felt like the hundredth time. She could see only directly in front of her now. Celia squinted at the admonition. "It has to be here," she tried to convince herself, and the last stanza floated up to her eyes.

> *Only beware a different girl*
> *With talent hidden like a pearl*
> *Her hands may render you as dead*
> *And stop your power in this world*

"What did the principal call my drawing this afternoon? An artist's rendering?" Celia thought aloud. "My drawing gave Tomasi his power. Maybe it can take yours away." She kept her eyes away from the window and reached for her pencil again.

"Your eyes are a little too close together," she said breathlessly as she drew the teacher's eyes closed. "And your nose is a little crooked." The chill was in her chest now, and she was having trouble breathing. She barely could see what her pencil was doing; She was drawing in the dark. "Your lips are thin, but your jaw is square. Your hair is wavy."

Celia looked up when she heard a noise at the window. Her vision cleared for a moment and she could see Mr. Sumeletso raising the window from outside. He floated through it, watching her, but his face looked frozen. His expression matched the one she had just drawn. She held the book up to hide the page from him. The man didn't seem to be able to move his neck. His body floated up to the ceiling and turned prostrate so he could look down at her. His arms stretched out toward her. Celia hurriedly started to draw his upper body.

"Here are your hands folded on your chest. Are you sleeping? No, no one sleeps with their hands folded like that." As Celia roughed in the man's arms, overhead Mr. Sumeletso's arms flew up and together, sticking to his chest in the position she had drawn. Celia struggled to raise her head to look up. In the tunnel of vision she had left, she saw his legs kicking frantically. Her eyes on the ceiling, Celia drew without looking at her pad. She quickly outlined his body, and when she reached his feet the man became still like a corpse, pinned to the ceiling.

She fought to recover her sight, but she could see only directly in front of her. "Why are you still here?" she said in desperation to the man who hung lifeless in the air above her. In frustration she tore the page from her sketchbook and crumpled it up. The man's body jerked as though he were being stung by a swarm of bees. Celia threw the crumpled drawing out the open window and Mr. Sumeletso was sucked after it. She heard him yell in pain, and then he was gone from view. Outside there was a crunching sound as his body hit the ground.

She still couldn't move most of her body. Celia worked to fill her lungs with air, and gradually the feeling returned to her chest. Her vision began to fill out again. Celia flipped back to the page where her drawing of Tomasi waited with an anguished expression.

What's happening? said the letters next to his face. Celia caught her breath when she saw the graphite tears on his cheeks. She touched the drawing and wiped them away. *Come back*, she wrote.

Immediately his shadow filled the page and spread across the wall. In a moment he was kneeling next to the bed, then springing up to look out the window, and then returning to her side. "Where is he?"

"I think he's in the rock garden," Celia said, trying to lift her legs as the blood slowly returned to them.

Tomasi went back to the window and looked down. "He is! He's not moving."

"In a minute I'm going to have to go get Mom to call the police," Celia said. "As soon as I can walk again."

"What happened? What did you do?" He sat down and helped her massage her feet and calves. "You're freezing!"

"I drew him. I rendered him as dead, like his admonition said. I always thought Mariette was the different girl who could stop him. But since my drawing of you gave you your powers, it made me think Mariette was wrong. That maybe I was the one."

"That's amazing!" Tomasi kissed her and wiped his cheeks with his hand. "I didn't want to leave you. I didn't know what to do."

"It's okay. I had to do it myself," Celia said. "I was the only one who could do it."

"I know, but I still wish I could have done something. That I could have gotten more powerful people to help you."

Celia eased herself up and swung her legs around to put her feet on the floor. "You know what you can do? Just hold me for a minute. I'm still cold."

He moved closer and wrapped his arms around her, pressing his chest against her back. "Say something. Are you okay?"

"I think so." She felt his warmth around her like an electric blanket. "I'm getting better."

"I thought it was over," he said, pressing his forehead into her shoulder.

"Me too," she said. Celia reached up to stroke the nape of his neck.

"What did it feel like?" he asked.

"What?"

"Killing him?"

Celia started. "I didn't kill him!"

"You didn't?" Tomasi got up, and this time she was able to stand and walk to the window with him. Down below, Mr. Sumeletso sprawled on the rocks, his legs and arms askew. His eyes were open. When his mouth heaved like a fish out of water, Celia jumped. She closed the window and ran for the door.

"Where are you going?"

"I have to go down there. He can't hurt me now." She stopped Tomasi with an outstretched arm. "You can't come—what if my mother catches you?"

"At least get her to go with you, then," Tomasi pleaded. "Please be careful."

She called to her mother as she ran downstairs. When she stepped out the back door the electric charge in the air that had haunted her on the way home was gone. Celia looked up and found a sliver of bone white moon emerging from the eclipse like a bleached sand dollar.

Mr. Sumeletso lay still. When she stood over him his fearful expression looked like a child's. "I . . . can't . . . feel my body," he gasped.

"I felt that way a few minutes ago," Celia said. "But you knew that."

She heard her mother come out the door, calling her name and then shrieking when she saw the body. "What happened? Who is that?"

"I saw him in the tree outside my window, and then he fell," Celia told her, wondering if her voice was too calm, if she was supposed to be hysterical in this situation. "I think he's hurt pretty badly."

"I'll call an ambulance!" Her mother dashed back to the door.

"And the police!" Celia called after her. In her bedroom window Tomasi was visible, watching her. She waved him away from the glass, and he obeyed. Then Celia turned back to Mr. Sumeletso on the ground. She studied him curiously, trying to find the connection between the Unkind predator and the helpless, cowardly man.

"I'm sorry," he whispered up at her.

"You should be. You thought you were going to float away from here and be long gone before anyone found me. But now I'm going to tell everyone you drowned Mariette, and I have a feeling they might believe me. You might wish you were dead after all."

"You could do it," he said. "Right here, before the ambulance comes."

"No. I'm not like you. I can be happy knowing you will suffer, but I am not a murderer. I will never hurt someone else for my own gain."

Celia heard a siren in the distance, then a rustle in the trees at the back edge of the yard. She looked up and saw a figure rise from the bushes and pass up through the branches. It stopped just as it emerged from the leaves at the top of a tree, its torso visible, legs still obscured. In the light from the house Celia couldn't tell if the figure was a man or a woman. Some kind of wrap or shawl draped over what might have been a suit, and long wisps of hair rose from the face like tendrils of smoke. For a moment Celia was sure the figure was looking down at her, and she felt its gaze like a cobweb across her face. Then it shot up into the sky like a rocket, disappearing into the night, black on black. "Who was that?"

"Someone terrible," the man on the ground said softly. "Someone far more powerful than you and I."

Celia stared down at him. "Tell me!"

"You don't terrify me nearly as much as —" Mr. Sumeletso gasped as veins of lightning spread across the sky, washing out everything around them for a split second, like a flashbulb at close range. His mouth snapped shut as if it were spring-loaded.

When Celia realized he was not going to speak again, she said, "I'm new to all this, and there's a lot I don't understand. But I promise you I will use everything I learn to keep you, and whoever that was, from ever harming anyone else."

She turned when she heard her mother approaching behind her. "What were you saying to him?" she asked.

"That he got what he deserved," Celia answered. "Creep."

the moon and
the melodies

ONLY NINE MONTHS AGO, she had entered the upstairs room at Diaboliques as a nervous guest, sure
the beautiful people who had bothered to look at her
could tell immediately she didn't belong. The dark, stylized
play had gone on around her, and she had watched, feeling
hope rise up in her like a flood. That first night could have
been a lifetime ago.

Now she was tall and elegant and mysterious, standing with
her friends to the side of the dance floor. Tomasi stood with
her, and the Rosary were arranged around the two of them in
a darkly beautiful pose. Marco had been speaking with Tomasi
while holding hands with Brenden. Regine was at Celia's elbow, with Liz next to her and Ivo not far off. Celia thought
she might be glowing with the satisfaction of having them all
together in this perfect place. At the first notes of "Stranger" by
Clan of Xymox, the rest of the Rosary stepped onto the dance
floor, and Tomasi looked at Celia to see if she would follow.

She brought her lips close to his ear. "I want you to meet
someone." He nodded, and when she took his hand in hers he
squeezed it twice. Even though they had known who Tomasi

was for almost a year, the Rosary were just getting to know him now, and even from the dance floor they still watched her with him. She loved them for it.

Celia led Tomasi out of Patrick's room. On the landing the man with metal spikes protruding from his face waved to her, and she waved back. She took Tomasi down the stairs to the mezzanine. At the bottom she paused, peering into the shadows.

"Where are we going?" he asked.

"I hope she's here," Celia said, as much to herself as to him. Then she caught sight of the plume of red hair in its familiar place on the couch under the stairs and drew Tomasi along with her.

"You look particularly lovely tonight," the fortuneteller said when Celia perched on the cushion next to her. Tomasi hesitated over them, and the woman patted the cushion on the other side of her. He stared down at her, and Celia saw the red-haired fortuneteller through his eyes—so regal, so self-possessed. Tomasi carefully took the seat she had offered. She turned back to Celia, and they bent their heads together as they had before. "Perhaps it is this lovely new accessory you are carrying."

"I wanted you to meet him," Celia said.

The woman turned to him. "Hello, Tomasi. I'm Cassandra. It's nice to meet you." He clumsily let her manicured hand take his and mumbled hello. Keeping his hand in hers, Cassandra bent her head toward him, and he dutifully leaned in to hear her words, looking past her at Celia as he did. His eyes widened for a moment; then he nodded and sat back. Cassandra exchanged a look with him and he stood up, his hands covering his lap, and carefully leaned over to kiss Celia's cheek.

"I'll see you upstairs," he said, and moved off in the shadows toward the stairs.

"What did you tell him?" Celia asked Cassandra.

"Something he needed to know. But there is something you need to know, too." Cassandra took Celia's hands, and Celia felt the tips of her fingernails grazing her palms. "Isn't there anything you want to ask me?"

"Will you give me an answer if I do?" Celia asked, and Cassandra's amused eyes said *Touché*. She nodded.

The invitation opened a kaleidoscope of questions in Celia's mind. She tried to sort through them and choose the most important one. Cassandra waited patiently, and Celia cleared her head.

"Why haven't I received an admonition?" she asked finally, and Cassandra's smile told her she had chosen well. Then her face became serious.

"Because you are not one of the Kind."

"Oh . . . okay." Celia wasn't sure what to say. Part of her was relieved. She had witnessed Mariette and Tomasi do amazing things, but they had paid high prices for their gifts. Celia had spent the year staking her claim as someone who cultivated her legitimate strangeness, who was different because she was being true to herself, not just for the sake of being different. But given the choice, she would have been happy to stick with a legitimate strangeness that brought no admonitions, no special powers, no lonely roads beyond the ones every teenager has to travel.

And yet she had seen what her drawing had done to Mr. Sumeletso. And hadn't her sketch of Tomasi given him his new powers? If Mariette had lived, Celia's drawing would have bestowed power upon her, too—how exactly did these things happen, then? Surely Regine couldn't have accomplished the same things with her collages? And what about the things Tomasi had said about the trails she left in the air that he could see, and how he was convinced she wasn't a citizen? Something didn't make sense. "But before, you said I had power."

"Don't worry!" Cassandra said lightly. "Just because you aren't one of the Kind doesn't mean you are a mere citizen. None of this would have happened if you were."

"What am I, then?"

Cassandra smiled proudly. "You are an Ambassador, like I am. Only an Ambassador could have discerned your friend's true nature when she was hiding it, and only an Ambassador could have bestowed the gifts you gave to her—and to that handsome thing I just met. And it was because you are an Ambassador that you were able to defend yourself against that crocodile. He didn't know what you are, but it's why he felt as threatened by you as he did. Mariette was too new to know what you are, either. But I knew the moment I first touched your palm. You are an Ambassador. I had to wait to tell you. You had to do all these things to earn your place." Cassandra had tears in her eyes. "We are a rare breed, you and I, rarer even than Tomasi and his kind. I have only known one other Ambassador in my life. Sometime I will tell you about Caesar. He is long gone now. But we Ambassadors play a very important role. We connect the Kind to the rest of the world."

"We do?"

"The Kind really are like rare and exotic mythical creatures. It's easy to forget, because they are also high school girls. And young men about whom we have deliciously impure thoughts." Cassandra smiled. "But underneath, they are foreigners who struggle to speak without an accent. I am not telling you this to make you fearful of them. Tomasi will never harm you. The Unkind crocodile teacher was another matter, but he is someone who had a choice, and who chose wrong. And now he is a quadriplegic who has been stripped of his powers, thanks to you. But forget the Unkind for now. The Kind will be some of the loveliest people you ever meet. And sometimes these lovely people need the help of someone who can guide them a little, get them through the rough spots, and preserve their secrets."

"I think I understand," Celia said.

"My dear, you don't understand at all." Cassandra looked pleasantly at her. "You've only had a taste. The time is coming soon when you will meet a brand-new member of the Kind—someone who is so new he hasn't fully realized it yet. He will emerge from the Ebentwine and you will be his Ambassador as he grows into his new life. It will be very rewarding, but it will make a serious impression on you. The Kind always do."

"What did you say? Ebentwine?"

"I still can't tell you everything!" Cassandra laughed, and once again Celia was amused with her despite herself. "Don't be frustrated with me. You still must learn much on your own. And there are plenty of things I don't know. I can't see that dark figure that flew up into the sky any more clearly than you."

"Mr. Sumeletso—the teacher—was terrified of it, whatever it was."

"And it remains to be seen whether we should be terrified, too. I am sure it is powerful, since I can sense almost nothing of it."

"Will you help me?"

"I will do whatever I can. But you will find that just like a political ambassador to another country, you will do most of your work alone, a unique individual surrounded by powerful people. Your role is to make small but crucial contributions to other people's lives, which will enable them to do far more incredible things. In a way, isn't that what we all do for the people we love?" Cassandra smiled at Celia like her mother. "I've never spoken so directly to you before, but it was time for you to hear all this."

"Could I have saved Mariette?" Celia asked her.

"That is a question for which there is no answer," Cassandra said. "Yes, you could have saved her. But no, you couldn't have saved her. You must know, nothing has changed: sometimes we suffer, and if we think back we see how we could have suffered less. There is nothing to be done about it now. If the crocodile or your friend had been stronger, they would have recognized the other instantly, on the first day, and everything would have been completely different."

"But shouldn't we have known? Half the kids in his other classes were failing until the substitute teacher came. Was that because he was Unkind?" Cassandra nodded. "But why didn't it happen to our class?"

"Mariette's Kind energy counteracted his Unkind energy. She balanced things out so his malaise couldn't affect your class. She didn't realize it was happening, and if he did, he thought it was coming from you," Cassandra explained. "You'll think back on all of it, and you'll make sense of some of it. Other things always will be a mystery. Just don't let it make you serious all the time. I can tell you have had enough of death for a while. It is time for you to live."

"That is the best thing you've ever told me," Celia said. "I never even knew your name before," she added, laughing in amazement.

"Now you do. I've kept you long enough. Go dance with that handsome man-child."

They kissed cheeks and Celia stood up from the couch. She picked her way across the mezzanine to the stairs, smiling in the dark. At the foot of the stairs a tall man stepped out from the shadow, startling her.

"I thought you went upstairs!"

"I was waiting for you," Tomasi said.

"What did you think of Cassandra?"

"She scares me a little," he said sheepishly. "I felt like a young boy."

"What did she tell you?"

"That I should be good to you," he said. He kissed her there, and then he took her hand and they returned to Patrick's room. She went ahead of him, but halfway there, his tug on her hand stopped her, and she turned back to look down at him from the next step up.

"I just wanted to ask you . . ." He searched for words. "Are you happy? Being here, with me? I mean, is there anything I can do, I should be doing?" He looked up, his silver gray eyes sparkling.

"I am happy," she said. "I feel strange saying that, considering all that's happened. But I am. I'm happier than I've ever been since my father died. It's really up to us if we're happy or unhappy, isn't it? But you make me very happy." She put her palm against his cheek. "You do." He hugged her around her waist, and she put her arms around his neck when he laid his head against her chest. She ran her fingers over the soft short hairs on the back of his head, and then she took his hand again and they returned to Patrick's room. When they took their place at the edge of the dance floor he kept his hand on the small of her back.

In Regine's car on the way home at the end of the night, Celia still was ruminating on the things Cassandra had told her, and Tomasi seemed equally distracted. She suspected Cassandra had charged him with something more significant than being good to her. But his hand held hers again, soft against the cashmere blanket between them, and she figured if she was supposed to know, it would be revealed to her in good time.

When she stopped the car in front of Celia's house, Regine turned to the two of them behind her. "All right, Tomasi, I can drop you off at your house if you want."

"Thank you, but I can walk from here," he told her.

"I get it—you want to say goodbye properly, without a chauffeur watching you in the rearview mirror. Well, have a good night!" She smiled, and they got out of the car.

They lingered on Celia's front walk, waiting for Regine to drive away. "Can you tell if she's awake?" she asked him.

"She's awake." He pointed to the front window, where the television glowed through the curtains.

"Okay, I'll go in and distract her, but wait for me, okay?" She kissed him and then opened the door. They slipped quietly inside, and Celia went into the living room and sat down on the couch by her mother, knowing Tomasi was creeping up the stairs and into her room. "I'm surprised you're still up."

"I haven't seen this movie in ages," her mother said dreamily. "So romantic. They look so young."

"Is it over soon?" Celia watched her mother nod, and she kissed her cheek and said good night.

Up in her room she found Tomasi looking out the window. "If my neighbors see you . . ." she teased, and he turned to her.

"Would they say something?"

"No one can see. I don't think anyone could get through that thicket of trees and bushes behind our yard." She smiled. "I'm glad you came." They sat down on the bed and she leaned against him, enjoying the feel of his hand on her hair. The next minute of silence was the most exquisite minute she could remember. She felt her life coursing through her, telling her anything was possible. "I'm really glad you're not completely trapped at the farm."

"As long as Grandpa lets me keep the Bible," Tomasi said, "and he doesn't work me so hard I'm too exhausted to travel through the book and visit you after he's gone to bed. But it's a really good thing, since I think I'm going to be stuck there for the summer."

"I'm sorry."

"It's okay. It'll be good exercise," he said.

"That's putting a positive spin on it," she said sadly.

"I've discovered other new powers," he said, raising his head to look around the room. "*The Awakening*— it's in that wooden box on your dresser, isn't it? And *The Portrait of a Lady*, too?"

"Yeah." Celia nodded. "My keepsakes of you."

"And a letter . . . from Mariette?" He saw her nod again. "I wish I could have gotten to know her better. That night when she came to my house, it was a little tense at first. Once I convinced her I wasn't the bad guy, all she wanted to talk about was you."

His attention shifted from the box on her dresser to the mirror, where the photograph of her old, pink room still hung. More recently Celia had added a photograph her mother had taken of the Rosary before they had gone to prom. The six of them were arranged in front of one of the sleek black cars. "You look like you're in a movie, or a magazine."

"That's the way the Rosary like it."

"The Rosary?"

"How have I never told you our name? We're a set of small, shiny black beads who string along together, finding beauty the rest of the world has overlooked."

"Is that your motto?"

"I don't know. Regine said it once, and it made sense."

"You guys always look so elegant."

"That was prom. They're all amazing people, so intelligent, and talented, and cultured. I've learned so much from them."

Tomasi took her hand and studied it as if it were a piece of coral he had found on the beach. "I was scared you wouldn't like me. I'm not very good at talking, and saying the right things, and being polite."

"I don't know what the right things are anyway," Celia said. "There might be right and wrong, but most of the time life is somewhere in between."

"That sounds true," he said.

They were quiet for a moment. "Do you think about having sex with me?" she asked him, and felt her cheeks flush. She had lost count of the number of times she had blushed in front of Tomasi, but this time she had the new sensation of enjoying her embarrassment.

He stared at her. "Is that a trick question?"

"I didn't mean it to be. I've spent months thinking about having sex, talking about having sex, even turning down offers to have sex, because of that whole stupid curse thing. Right before my birthday, I wondered if I should do it. It didn't seem unreasonable, considering everything that was happening. But you were the only person I would have asked, and I didn't know where you were."

"How do you feel about it now?"

Celia thought for a moment. "When I first saw you standing on the other side of the dance floor, you scared me a little. It was like an electric current running through me, just knowing you were looking. Even when we had cider, that night when your dad caught us, I was still nervous around you. That's why I didn't want to go to the park."

"I figured that. I wouldn't do anything to hurt you. I wouldn't." His gray eyes looked like watercolors.

"I know. Now every time I see you, I still feel like there's an electric current running through me, but it's not fear. It's strong, and maybe it's a little dangerous, but I'm not afraid of it. Being close to you doesn't feel like getting electrocuted. It's more like being recharged."

As if to illustrate, Tomasi lightly touched his fingertip to the inside of her wrist and slid it lightly to the crook of her elbow. The tingle continued up her arm and shivered in her back. A spark returned to his eyes. "That sounds like a good feeling."

"So, do you?"

"Of course I do." He grinned, embarrassed, too. "I can't believe you're asking me this."

"Everything that's happened—it's made me realize things can change at any time. I don't want to wait for my life to happen. I don't have that kind of time." Celia looked plainly at him.

"I like that," he said. "But I don't think it's wise for you to jump on me right now. Your mother is still awake."

"How do you know?"

"She went up to her room, and she's reading a book, something about Ophelia. I can feel the pages turning."

"Oh."

"Can I come back tomorrow night?" Tomasi raised her hand and pressed his lips to her palm and then the inside of her wrist.

"Please do," she said.

"Okay." He kissed her and started to get up.

"Don't you want to stay?"

"Of course I want to stay!" he groaned. "But if Grandpa finds me missing from my room, or if your mom walks in on you again . . ."

"You're right," Celia sighed.

"But I do. In the worst way." He held his lips to hers for a long moment, then stood up and looked down at her.

"Write me when you get back, so I know you're safe," she said.

"Sure." Tomasi turned toward the wall, first darkening into a shadow and then sliding back into her sketchbook before appearing as a face on the page. He blew her a final, two-dimensional kiss.

I'm back. You're beautiful. Good night.

Good night. Celia got up with her sketchbook and laid it on her desk, still open to Tomasi's page.

In the bathroom she washed her face and brushed her hair, and then she regarded herself in the mirror. "I am an Ambassador. I am tired." She brushed her teeth and went back to her room.

She curled up on her bed. Outside her window the moon was a tranquil white, the white of chalk and of bones that have been bleached by ocean water. There was a song she wanted to hear, so she got up again and thumbed through her CDs. As she shed her clothes and crawled into bed, a soft, strange song wafted through the room, like a transmission from the Arctic Circle. Against a quiet, steady drumbeat, the Sisters of Mercy sang quietly about what it felt like to be one of the chosen, one of the few to be sure, and about snow coming down like a curtain outside a car window. She closed her eyes and wondered what the summer would bring.

A
S BRENDEN SAYS, "Everything is better with the right soundtrack." Each of the chapter titles in this book is the name of a real album, an example of the dark alternative music Celia discovers as her story is told. I encourage you to seek these treasures out, along with the other music, literature, and art scattered throughout this story. Nothing would please me more than for you to love these works even half as much as I do.

acknowledgments

To Zoe Shacham, who made me into a published author and then broke my heart! You were my dream come true as an agent, and I am so happy we found each other. I wish you the best, and I will be forever grateful for all you did to make this dream a reality.

To everyone else at Nancy Yost Literary Agency, especially Nancy Yost and Adrienne Rosado, who shepherded this project through to completion—it has been such a pleasure getting to know you, and I am so appreciative of all your efforts on my behalf.

To Margaret Raymo—thank you so much for taking this first-time author to the dance! You and the brilliant team at Houghton Mifflin Harcourt have coaxed a better novel out of me than I knew I had, and dressed it up so beautifully, I barely can believe it's mine. This has been a fantastic experience, even when you were gently pointing out that there are not, in fact, seven weeks in October . . .

To all the musicians, authors, artists, and designers to whom I pay tribute in this book: You've enriched my life and inspired me to be my own creative person. I only hope I am introducing you to many others who will find you just as transformative and inspiring.

To my own Rosary, a now lengthy string of beautiful friendships from high school and beyond, which have sustained and expanded me—thank you for sharing my love of darkly beautiful things; your spirit and style are on every page of this book. You number too many to list here, but there are a few beads I must count:

To Alli Cooke, from the latest decade, who was Celia's first champion and an invaluable reviewer of this manuscript every time I dared to ask—all of the thanks!

To Lisa Schieler Blackman, from the high school decade, who knows perhaps better than anyone how autobiographical this novel is, in a fun-house mirror sort of way—this book is just the latest in a shoebox's worth of mix tapes, as far as we're concerned.

To Mr. Gates, from his own decade, who lives and breathes his aesthetic more deeply than I could ever hope to, and who has figured out how to make me look passably human in photographs—I want to see the world the way you do.

And to Andrea Gangloff Klores, from all the decades, who has watched my creative impulse thrash about in so many directions for more years than either of us will admit, and who elevates friendship to an art form all its own—may we never come down to earth again!

Finally, to my parents, who have never wavered in their support for me, and who I believe answer my phone calls with the unspoken, loving question "What have you done now?"—I hope you know how much you mean to me.

credits

Love Is a Stranger
Words and Music by Annie Lennox and David Stewart
Copyright © 1983 by Logo Songs Ltd. and Astwood Music Ltd.
All Rights in the United States and Canada Administered by Universal
Music—Careers
International Copyright Secured All Rights Reserved
Reprinted by permission of Hal Leonard Corporation

A Forest
Words and Music by Robert Smith, Laurence Tolhurst, Simon Gallup, and
Matthieu Hartley
Copyright © 1981 by Fiction Songs Ltd.
All Rights for the world Administered by Universal Music Publishing MGB
Ltd.
All Rights for the U.S. Administered by Universal Music—MGB Songs.
International Copyright Secured All Rights Reserved
Reprinted by permission of Hal Leonard Corporation

Second Skin
Words and Music by David Fielding, Mark Burgess, Reginald Smithies, and
John Lever
© 1983 EMI VIRGIN MUSIC LTD.
All Rights in the United States and Canada Controlled and Administered by
EMI VIRGIN SONGS, INC.
All Rights Reserved International Copyright Secured Used by Permission
Reprinted by permission of Hal Leonard Corporation

coming in fall 2013

PULL DOWN THE NIGHT
BOOK TWO IN THE SUBURBAN STRANGE SERIES

Another year at Suburban High School, and another stranger arrives—Kind or Unkind remains to be seen. Every corner of the school conceals a secret, and every answer poses another question:

If you found a hidden clearing behind your house with the power to transport you across town, would you use it?

If you were given a ghostly note with the place and time to catch your boyfriend cheating on you, would you go?

If you received an admonition instructing you to do the one thing you'd sworn never to do, would you reconsider?

Who is Bruno Perilunas, and will he and Celia find the answers fast enough to survive the year at Suburban? Death has been promised, but everything can change with the stroke of a pen, the discovery of a book, or a step on a secret staircase.